S0-BIH-228

$7.99 U.S.
$9.99 CAN.

ISBN 978-1-4767-3709-6

9 781476 737096

5 0 7 9 9

S> EAN

RYK E. SPOOR

SPHERES OF INFLUENCE

BAEN

"Ryk Spoor . . . tells a rip-roaring adventure story with old-fashioned charm."
—Lawrence Watt-Evans

SEQUEL TO
GRAND CENTRAL ARENA

A LEAP OF FAITH

The energy rifle fired and missed again; Wu had read the posture, seen the faintest tensing, jumped just as the trigger was pulled. *Ha!* he thought. *Takes more than that to—*

The Genasi threw away the rifle into the empty space beyond the Dock and flipped something else down with his other hand.

Net! Spun as he threw it, opening just as it's reaching me—

But if you reached and twisted and spun *just* right, you could *catch* a net like that, and he did, and threw it back up.

The Genasi tried to shift direction, but the net caught him, tangled his legs and tail, and then Wu was on him.

Wu rammed the alien up against the reinforced metal of the crane. "Who are *you* working for?" he demanded.

The eyes shifted slightly over his shoulder, and then the creature laughed.

Oh, no.

He whirled, dropped fifteen meters down the crane, caught himself, jumped the rest of the way to the Dock, even as *Thilomon*'s umbilicals let go and her engines roared to life.

A trap. I'm so stupid! DuQuesne should never have trusted me, I'm an idiot, a monkey who should never have come down from the trees!

Even as he was berating himself, he was streaking across the Dock, running up the gangway, faster, watching the huge ship moving away, no time, too far, *but I can't give up—*

With a final desperate lunge, Sun Wu Kung launched himself into space off the end of the gangway.

BAEN BOOKS by RYK E. SPOOR

Digital Knight

Phoenix Rising

GRAND CENTRAL ARENA SERIES:
Grand Central Arena
Spheres of Influence

BOUNDARY SERIES
RYK E. SPOOR AND ERIC FLINT:
Boundary
Threshold
Portal

SPHERES OF INFLUENCE

RYK E. SPOOR

Copyright © 2013 by Ryk E. Spoor

A Baen Books Original

Baen Publishing Enterprises
P.O. Box 1403
Riverdale, NY 10471
www.baen.com

ISBN: 978-1-4767-3709-6

Cover art by Allan Pollack

First paperback printing, January 2015

Library of Congress Catalog Number: 2013032742

Distributed by Simon & Schuster
1230 Avenue of the Americas
New York, NY 10020

Pages by Joy Freeman (www.pagesbyjoy.com)
Printed in the United States of America

DEDICATION

As with *Grand Central Arena*, I must first dedicate *Spheres of Influence* to E.E. "Doc" Smith, who gave me the sense of wonder I try to convey to others in these novels.

In addition, *Spheres of Influence* is dedicated to all the adventurers, creators, and performers whose visions have inspired The Arena and its inhabitants—to James Schmitz, Howard Tayler, Akira Toriyama, Lee Majors, Isaac Asimov, Joseph Michael Straczynski, Kazuya Minekura, Thor Heyerdahl, A.E. Van Vogt, Hiromu Arakawa, Pete Abrams, Andre Norton, C.S. Friedman, and the literally hundreds of others who offered up their dreams to ignite imagination, brilliant sparks that I now, in my own way, attempt to pass on.

ACKNOWLEDGEMENTS

To Toni and Tony,
for making sure *Spheres*
would be as good as it could be

To my Beta Readers,
for giving me invaluable feedback

And to my wife Kathleen,
for giving me the time.

WHAT HAS GONE BEFORE

(and a little bit that Has Come After!)

Previously in *Grand Central Arena*:

The solar system of 2375, population fifty-five billion, approaches utopia as closely as most of humanity could imagine. The advent of efficient power harvesting, storage, and transmission of all kinds combined with nanoassembler systems called "AIWish" units has allowed even the poorest people to be assured of plenty of food, comfortable shelter, access to the immense interconnected webwork of information, entertainments, and heathcare sufficient to extend human youth and lifespan greatly; this has also assisted other advances in material and engineering sciences to produce a fully flowered Space Age, with huge colonies on Mars, orbiting Earth, and elsewhere. Artificial intelligences assist human beings in their daily lives, with most people having a built-in "AISage" who serves as one of their closest friends and a secretary, memory aid, research partner, or almost anything else.

Because of these things, and because of a short but bitter electronic conflict a few centuries past called the Anonymity War, governments as we know them are almost a thing of the past and human individual rights and privacy are nearly unbounded; only the shadow of the horrific "Hyperion Project" has caused any sort of effective central government to arise in the last fifty years, comprised of the Space Security Council (SSC) and Combined Space Forces (CSF), which basically intervene when and if there are conflicts beyond the ability of the ordinary people to address—and ordinary people can have truly staggering resources to their name in 2375.

Work, as we know it in the 21st century, is also effectively a thing of the past. People do not need to work to survive, and the closest equivalents of "money" are called "interest credits" or vectors, where additional resources are given by people to someone that interests them in some way. People now entertain themselves at whatever they wish, ranging from mountain climbing to adventures in full-immersive virtual realities called simgames.

Only *one* of the great dreams of humanity seems to have been truly elusive: that of reaching the stars.

At the beginning of *Grand Central Arena*, Doctor Simon Sandrisson believed he had solved that great riddle, and for various reasons assembled a crew for a manned vehicle, the *Holy Grail*, to test this "Sandrisson Drive"; the crew included power engineer Dr. Marc C. DuQuesne, controls specialist Dr. Carl Edlund, systems integration and conceptual engineer Dr. Steve Franceschetti, medical specialist Dr. Gabrielle Wolfe, nanomaintenance engineer Dr. Thomas Cussler, biologist Dr. Laila Canning, and—as a last-ditch backup—Ariane Stephanie Austin, top pilot in the Unlimited Space Racing league.

With this crew, Dr. Sandrisson plans a simple demonstration jump into "Kanzaki-Locke-Sandrisson space" which will allow the *Holy Grail* to effectively travel many times faster than light; they will jump, wait for the onboard fusion generator to recharge the Sandrisson Coils, and then jump back, having traveled perhaps a third of a light year in a few days' time.

But as soon as the *Holy Grail* makes the first jump, everything goes wrong; the nuclear reactor shuts down, and all automation—including the AISages on which most of the crew rely—crashes. Only Ariane Austin's skill at manual piloting saves *Holy Grail* from crashing into some impossible, unimaginable *wall* that appeared before them.

Nothing they can do will restart the nuclear reactor, or bring the artificial intelligences back online, and if they can't find a source of very considerable power, they will be stranded forever in what appears to be a spherical space twenty thousand kilometers in diameter. With most of the crew still suffering from the trauma of losing their AISages, and having their own specific responsibilities, it is decided that for the interim Ariane Austin will be the acting captain and leader of the stranded *Holy Grail* crew.

Scanning the interior of this spherical space shows that there is a way into the surrounding structure, and they begin exploring for something that may offer them a way home—and explain where they actually are, and what this structure *is*. During that exploration, it is revealed that Marc DuQuesne is one of the few survivors of the infamous Hyperion Project, product of a terribly misguided attempt to replicate various heroes of myth and fiction, which, so to speak,

"Went Horribly Right." DuQuesne has spent the last fifty years trying to play the part of a normal human and really only wants to live a relatively ordinary life.

On a deeper probe of the interior of this mysterious location, Ariane Austin, Marc DuQuesne, and Dr. Simon Sandrisson encounter alien lifeforms. Shocked to be able to understand what the aliens are saying, they nonetheless intervene—for reasons they do not entirely grasp at the time—to prevent what appears to be a lynching or kidnapping of one semi-insectoid alien by others; another, mysterious figure in dark, robelike clothing simply watches and then disappears.

The rescued alien calls himself "Orphan," and seems friendly enough...until DuQuesne notices a suspicious tenseness and prevents him from actually entering the area of the installation (which Orphan calls a "Sphere") that the humans have set up camp in.

Orphan admits that entrance to that portion of the "Sphere" would have given him considerable opportunity to control entry and exit from the Sphere—and by implication, to humanity's solar system. Despite this, Ariane and the others decide that Orphan could be useful in at least allowing them to understand what they've gotten themselves into.

Orphan agrees to be their guide and instructor, and reveals the truth; that the huge structure they are in is just one of uncountable billions of "Spheres," each of which represents a single solar system—and there is one Sphere for every solar system in every galaxy throughout the universe, floating in a lightyears-wide space called simply "The Arena." Outside the shell of the Sphere is not vacuum, but air, light, and even gravity on the "top" of the Sphere, called the Upper

Sphere—a place which provides living space similar to that found on a Sphere owner's native world.

But to gain access to the Upper Sphere, the humans must first traverse the "Inner Gateway," which will take them to a location called Nexus Arena, and then—if they wish to gain the power needed to activate the Sandrisson Drive and return home—establish themselves as citizens of the Arena.

Ariane asks, naturally, how such citizenship is established; the answer startles and worries the entire crew. Everything in the Arena, it seems, revolves around "Challenges" between various groups, or "Factions." A "Challenge" can be almost any sort of contest, but the essential character of a Challenge is that the stakes are significant on the scale of the Faction itself; for larger Factions, that can mean, in essence, bets with literal worlds in the balance. There are over five thousand Factions, and all of them have been in existence for thousands of years. Newcomers, or "First Emergents," such as humanity, haven't been seen for over three thousand years.

In their first encounter with aliens, they turned out to have met no fewer than *three* Factions: Orphan, who is the leader—and sole member, currently—of the Faction of the Liberated; the Blessed To Serve, of the same species as Orphan but his major enemies; and the Shadeweavers, mysterious and reputed to have nigh-supernatural powers. Their initial venture to Nexus Arena introduces them to the Factions of the Faith, who apparently see the Arena as a holy artifact or site, the Analytic, who are an alliance of scientists and engineers, the Molothos, who are a species of creatures inherently hostile to all others, and the quasi-Faction of the Powerbrokers, who could sell enough energy to the humans to let them return home...if they had something to trade.

Having made this initial foray, Simon and Ariane stay behind while DuQuesne travels back to update the others on what they've discovered—and to lead an expedition to the Upper Sphere to see what resources they might have on top of their own Sphere.

It turns out that the Molothos have just recently discovered Humanity's Sphere, as they send ships to travel through the airy spaces of the Arena and find other Spheres. The Molothos pursue and harry both DuQuesne and Carl Edlund, who accompanied him on this expedition, until trapping the two humans in the Molothos' main encampment.

The stress and desperation of the moment causes DuQuesne to release all of the restraints he had placed on himself, and unleashes the full capabilities of a Hyperion on the terrified Molothos, defeating six Molothos in a few seconds and then interrogating the surviving officer, Maizas. A combination of careful planning, improvisation, and luck allows DuQuesne and Edlund to destroy the Molothos' main vessel, *Blessing of Fire*, before it can reinforce the ground troops and take possession of Humanity's Upper Sphere.

This turns out to be sufficient to count as winning a Challenge from the Arena's point of view, and Humanity suddenly is a full-fledged Faction, with its own embassy building...and a new set of problems. Everyone wants to pal around with the new kids on the block, it seems...but they all have their own agendas. The humans also notice some odd characteristics of all Arena inhabitants; they seem more risk-averse than humanity, with odds of 100:1 being viewed in a similar light to those of a million to one by most human beings.

Ariane is invited by the Faith to observe the induction of a new priest, called an Initiate Guide, as part of a ritual that is conducted whenever a new Faction appears. During this ritual, she hears and sees things that seem magical, beyond any science that humanity understands, including a staggering display of power at the "awakening" of the new Initiate Guide's abilities. It is clear that the Faith—including their leader, First Guide Nyanthus, and the new priest, Initiate Guide Mandallon, firmly believe there is a mystical, numinous power far beyond that of mortality that guides or watches over the Arena. Ariane is impressed, though not at all convinced, and on her way back is more disturbed when Amas-Garao, one of the Shadeweavers, appears from nowhere and has a short discussion with her that reveals that he did influence her to intervene on Orphan's behalf, somehow. He is unimpressed, even amused, by her confronting him with this, and when pressed, disappears—at the same time somehow teleporting Ariane all the way from where she stands back to Humanity's Embassy.

The Faction of the Vengeance visits Humanity shortly thereafter—a Faction who believe that, rather than a benevolent deific-like force, the Arena is a weapon, a tool to keep all other species imprisoned and controlled, and who are dedicated to discovering the secrets of the creators of the Arena, called the Voidbuilders, and wresting from them control of the universes.

Mandallon, the new Initiate Guide, is obligated to perform some service for Humanity; while he cannot provide the energy needed to return home (apparently older Initiate Guides could, but he cannot), he will attempt anything else. After some discussion, Ariane decides to ask him to heal the one member of their crew who has never recovered from the "crashing" of her AISages (she had three): Dr. Laila Canning. He performs a ritual which shows no objective mechanism for functioning, but nonetheless awakens Laila to herself... although Ariane, and DuQuesne, wonder if perhaps Laila Canning is not exactly who she seems to be, now.

It isn't long before the Blessed to Serve trick Ariane into accepting a Challenge; the Blessed, and their leader Sethrik, come to regret this when Ariane specifies the Challenge mode as being deep-space racing, and manages to win the race with a final daredevil move that shocks all of the Arena natives.

Ariane originally intended to demand a full recharge for *Holy Grail* as the price for winning the Challenge, but Orphan—just in time—reveals that if *all* of the *Holy Grail* crew return home, leaving the Sphere empty, they forfeit all the progress they have made— they lose their Factionhood. The Sphere must always have at least one inhabitant from this point on. At the same time, Orphan admits that his meeting with the *Holy Grail* crew was not entirely accidental; he was directed to go to a certain place, at a certain time, by the Shadeweavers, to whom he owed a debt. He admits that he still owes them at least one more service, meaning that he cannot yet be entirely trustworthy... even if he didn't have an agenda of his own. She agrees to keep Orphan's secret... but he owes her.

Ariane decides to have the Blessed foot the bill for having Humanity's Sphere secured by the Faith, something which is necessary for peace of mind if and when they leave someone behind. This choice, while sensible, causes considerable conflict when revealed, partly due to the disappointment that they are not yet going home, and partly due to the fact that Ariane made this decision on her own. Ariane points out—correctly—that it was her decision to make, and if they didn't want a captain in charge they shouldn't have made her one.

DuQuesne is aware that she is correct, and leaves to cool off so he doesn't argue any further. Amas-Garao takes this opportunity to contact DuQuesne, and shows him around the Shadeweaver headquarters in an attempt to recruit DuQuesne to join their ranks; during this tour, he witnesses part of the induction ritual for a new member of the Shadeweavers. When DuQuesne declines the invitation, Amas-Garao reveals that this was "an offer you can't refuse." The Shadeweaver is stunned to discover that he cannot control DuQuesne's mind (due to particular design work done by the Hyperion Project), but demonstrates vast, apparently supernatural power, eventually cornering DuQuesne before he can leave the Faction House.

But Ariane received a very short transmission from DuQuesne, enough to know he was in trouble, and has Orphan lead them to the Shadeweaver Faction House...just in time. In the subsequent battle, Orphan surprises everyone by first choosing not to abandon Humanity, despite his belief that they have no real chance against the Shadeweavers, and second, by revealing that he has some sort of device that inhibits the Shadeweavers' powers.

The combination of Orphan with the humans' luck and skill allows the group to escape the Shadeweaver compound, at which point the Adjudicators—enforcers of Nexus Arena itself—show up to prevent pursuit by Amas-Garao.

However, the Shadeweaver Faction itself then declares "Anathema" against the Faction of Humanity, making most members of the Arena avoid doing business with them at all. Only the Analytic and the Faith stand with Humanity, which does at least allow them to continue to operate. During this time, Ariane and the others get to observe another Challenge, a maze-combat race that culminates with one contestant, Sivvis Lassituras, honorably ceding the Challenge to his opponent, Tunuvun, after Tunuvun prevents him from being injured or killed in a fall.

Shortly thereafter, Orphan mysteriously abandons Gabrielle Wolf during a shopping expedition to retrieve basic supplies for the group, and she encounters a group of the Blessed to Serve who begin to systematically bully her in a strangely uncharacteristic way. By the time Ariane arrives, she sees Gabrielle injured and bleeding, and the exchange of heated words culminates in her issuing a Challenge to Sethrik, leader of the Blessed . . .

. . . who turns out to have been merely acting as the agent for Amas-Garao. The Shadeweaver accepts the Challenge and says the venue will be single combat . . . with the prize being either Marc DuQuesne or Ariane Austin herself joining the Shadeweavers. While DuQuesne is much more formidable, Ariane refuses to allow him to risk himself, feeling that he—as a full-functional Hyperion whose capabilities have saved them more than once—is much more valuable than she is. Also, by making herself both the prize *and* the opponent, she forces Amas-Garao to have to be careful to not kill the very thing he's fighting for.

Despite this, and considerable preparation for the battle, the duel is clearly one-sided; even when Ariane succeeds in striking Amas-Garao, the effect is temporary, and eventually Amas-Garao stops even playing with her and uses his powers to systematically smash her back and forth into the walls and floor of the Challenge ring until she is beaten nearly unconscious.

But just as she is about to collapse, her drifting mind makes connections between multiple events—the ritual of the Faith she observed, the fragments of Shadeweaver ritual DuQuesne saw, an injury Amas-Garao took during the fight to rescue DuQuesne, and other things said by Arena residents—and tries one last desperate throw of the dice by invoking the same ritual that awakened Mandallon's powers.

The energy detonates around her and Amas-Garao is barely able to defend himself, so shocked is he. It takes his concession, followed by assistance from six other Shadeweavers and Initiate Guides, to shut down the energy radiating from Ariane. Before Ariane can make her demand of the Shadeweavers, DuQuesne lets her know that he made a side bet that, now that she's won, will get them the energy they need to get home; Ariane then takes, as her prize for victory, the requirement that no Shadeweaver shall ever in any way use their mind-affecting powers on any member of Humanity or their immediate allies unless directly requested to by the leader of the Faction. Amas-Garao hesitates, but the Arena itself states that this is a fair and reasonable demand and that the Shadeweavers *will* accept it.

The Shadeweavers and Faith then visit Ariane, saying

she is now one of them—either a Shadeweaver or an Initiate Guide. She refuses to join either, feeling her responsibility for Humanity outweighs their factional leanings, and not trusting the Shadeweavers at all in any case. They then say that her powers must be sealed more permanently, since if she will not join either one, she will not have proper instruction on how to control it—and Ariane, despite not wanting to believe, sees all too clearly a demonstration of how her own emotions trigger dangerous reactions.

The sealing ritual requires seven members of Humanity's Faction. Ariane gets the Arena to allow them to temporarily empty Humanity's Sphere to perform the ritual. During that ritual, a momentary disruption causes all of the power—of Shadeweaver, Faith, and Ariane—to converge for an instant on Dr. Simon Sandrisson; it seems to have no lasting effect, but for a moment Dr. Sandrisson feels that he can see, and understand . . . _everything_.

Returning Steve Franceschetti and Thomas Cussler to Humanity's Sphere after the ritual, Steve, Tom, Ariane, and DuQuesne are suddenly confronted with all of the Gateways that would usually be available for the trip being occupied—thousands of Gateways all simultaneously in use . . .

. . . By the Molothos, who had deduced that Humanity's Sphere was temporarily abandoned, and knew that if they failed to return to their Sphere within a reasonable time they would forfeit their citizenship. This trick is not a Challenge, but is potentially worse. However, Steve Franceschetti figures out a way past the apparently-impossible blockade and is successfully returned to Humanity's Sphere.

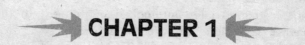

CHAPTER 1

The slender blond man glanced up from his desk, startled—DuQuesne had, of course, been suppressing the station security systems. *Couldn't take a chance that someone would be warned, if things had gone bad,* DuQuesne thought.

The startled look immediately gave way to caution. "Hold it right there, please."

DuQuesne stopped immediately; Ariane did the same. He saw Ariane looking around, and could tell she'd recognized that they had not in fact entered the reception area, but were in a sealed and—from the *click* behind them—locked separate chamber.

"If you are Marc DuQuesne, you gave me some very specific instructions prior to leaving me. You will now prove to me that you are Dr. Marc DuQuesne."

DuQuesne turned towards the left side of the room, strode over, and placed his hand against it for a moment. Then he looked at the other man. *Make damn sure I get this part right...* "Let's see...it's a Tuesday. Ninety-seven rows, tungsten, and a nurse who wasn't a robot," he said enigmatically.

The man looked down at a display in front of

him, and the suspicion dissolved to a cheerful smile. "Dr. DuQuesne! I did not expect you to be visiting at all!"

"I said I'd be here regularly when I could." He grinned down at the doctor, who was only barely shorter than Ariane but looked petite next to the massive Hyperion. "How're things going?"

"Well enough, I suppose. There hasn't been any significant change in the past months—any more, I gather, than there was in my predecessors'.."

"Good." DuQuesne glanced to his side apologetically. "I'm forgetting my manners. Captain Austin, this is Doctor Davison. He's...been watching over a few friends for me."

Davison's expression held a bit of speculation. "Captain Austin of the *Holy Grail* expedition, of course. And you've brought her *with* you. I'm...startled, given the extreme measures you took to make sure no one else even knew where this was."

"It's...necessary, now." The tension was back, his shoulders now rigid as steel, aching with anticipation and, he admitted, fear and doubt. "And I appreciate the fact you've been willing to keep to those extreme measures."

"It hasn't been easy at all. No outside contact, even electronic contact *only* through your methods...but I've kept my end of that bargain."

DuQuesne smiled, trying to ignore the tension. "I know you have...and believe me, you and my friends are probably alive because of that."

He looked down at the blond-haired doctor levelly. "Can I see...him?"

"Naturally. You're paying the bills, so to speak."

Davison led them to one of the other doors, which opened at their approach.

Within was a top-of-the-line nanosupport facility, a medical setup he suspected that Ariane had only seen a couple of times for pilots who had been so badly injured that they needed their brains regrown and personalities re-engraved from backups. But this was a *permanent* installation...and the figure lying on the bed was also wired to something that was not one tiny bit like ordinary monitoring equipment.

"I need an inductor, Doctor."

Davison froze in the middle of starting the typical "patient condition review" speech. "I beg your pardon?"

"An inductor. I'm going in. I have to talk to him."

Davison stared at him for a long moment, then nodded, turning to a nearby cabinet. "It's your call, of course," Davison conceded. "But as with the four others, this subject has been in sim-induction for the entire time of my tenure and, I must presume, that of my predecessors as well. I really do not know how he will react to an intrusion at this time."

DuQuesne nodded slowly. He saw Ariane still gazing with amazement and consternation at the figure on the bed—humanoid, very humanoid, yet...clearly not human, stout clawlike nails on each hand, gold-brown fur on the body, the head adorned with red-black unruly hair that was a bit too stiff and rough for human, a face subtly changed with some features broadened and shifted, sharp, long canines just visible in the slightly opened mouth, and, folded around the body, a long tail. "He'll talk to me. I don't know if it will do any good...but it's been way too long since

I tried. And things are different now. Maybe . . . just maybe . . ."

He found he couldn't bring himself to actually verbalize the hope. It had been too long, too much pain and regret. He almost snatched the induction connector from Davison's hands. "I'd better do this now, before I lose my nerve." He took a deep breath, feeling lightheaded. *Never let myself realize how much this mattered . . . how much I felt guilty about the whole thing.* He sat down next to the bed. "Ariane . . . could you and the Doc wait outside?"

He could see she had a thousand questions, but she didn't even say anything. She just nodded and gestured to Davison, who followed her out after a long, worried glance. *Good man, Davison. Worried about whether I'm going to hurt his patient, even though I'm the guy who's been paying for his care for the last fifty years.*

Alone finally, he set his teeth. *Into the illusion again. The original illusion.* His skin literally seemed to crawl at the thought. He'd managed to break a lot of the old fear, the habits, learned to even enjoy the sim-adventure games that were one of the most popular forms of entertainment across the Solar System . . . but this was different. This was the honest-to-God, pure-quill, one hundred percent original Hyperion simulation, preserved after the fall for just this purpose—to give a life to those for whom the real world offered nothing.

He forced his hands up and, with a convulsive movement, set the inductor on his head.

The soft-lit, quiet extended-care ward vanished. Suddenly he stood in a mighty forest, cool green trees towering over him like brooding giants, a rush of brightly-colored birds streaking through the branches with song and chattering. *It hasn't changed.*

Of course, why should it? His world lives and grows, but stays the same, too. He chose this, begged for it even. Do I have a right to come here again? I promised to let him stay in the home he understands for as long as he lived.

DuQuesne shook himself, then glanced around. *There... that's the mountain path.*

The path wound through lush undergrowth; behind him, DuQuesne knew, it ended at a deep pool of a mighty river. In the distance he could hear the sound of a cataract. *He might be there even now, fishing. But the slant of the sun is late... I hope...*

He walked lightly, quietly. The forest was filled with life, but all shied away from him when they spied DuQuesne's massive frame. No animal could mistake his movement for that of any prey, only of another hunter to be avoided.

Suddenly, a second too late, he became aware that seemingly-random flutters of branches had been nothing of the kind. He started to turn, but too late, as something powerful smashed into his shoulders from behind, sending him crashing headlong into the brush. He rolled, striking out, but his opponent was already gone, vanished, no, behind again! Another strike, this one at his knees, another at his arms as he tried to roll, and he found himself flat on his back, gazing up...

At a figure with a laughing, slightly-fanged face, hanging head-down from a branch above him by a strong tail, spinning a gold-capped staff idly between its fingers. "DuQuesne? *DUQUESNE?* Is it really you?"

He couldn't help but laugh in return at the simple joy on his old friend's face. "Really me, Wu. It really is."

Wu Kung dropped from the trees above and threw slender but tremendously strong arms around him, lifting DuQuesne and spinning him around like a child. "Marc! This is wonderful! It's been so long! I have to show you around! There's so many things for me to tell you!" Wu let go and bounced into the tree again, pointing. "Up this way! I haven't bothered to make a new path, but if we go straight up, we can get home much faster!"

"And how many trees do I have to swing through, Wu? You know I'm not exactly as light as you are."

The Hyperion Monkey King laughed again. "No, no, just a steep run, no cliffs, follow me, come on, follow!"

DuQuesne smiled and followed, hammering his way up the slope as Wu Kung bounded from ground to tree to stone with abandon, urging him onward.

Abruptly they burst from the trees to a clearer space, a steep crest of the hill that afforded a view extending out to the horizon. Massive limestone hills, pillarlike, reared from the plains below, more brilliant and picturesque versions of their karst-born models in Yangshuo on Earth. DuQuesne paused, admiring the view and the shades of the setting sun. *Simulation it may be ... but it's his home right now, and the simulation is breathtaking in its own way.*

"Sanzo! *SANZO!* It's DuQuesne! He's here to visit!"

As always, it gave DuQuesne a major jolt of cognitive dissonance to see a slender, beautiful young woman answering to *that* name. *They put every version of the Journey to the West ever made into a blender and came out with* this. It was another jolt—somewhat smaller—to realize that in some ways Sanzo, with her long dark-blue hair and athletic martial monk's figure, was not at all unlike Ariane. *Very much like Ariane, actually. That's an interesting coincidence.*

Sanzo smiled and bowed a welcome. "It has been far, far too long, Master DuQuesne," she said. "I hope you may stay and eat with us?"

"I have business to attend to, Mistress Sanzo," he answered, "but I may be able to, if time permits."

"I shall plan for it, then." She looked to Wu Kung. "Our sons will not return from the Three Ways until tomorrow, so there is also room for him to stay."

"Yes! That would be very good!"

This is making it . . . a lot harder than I thought. Sons? Of course there would be. Dammit. "Look, Wu—I have to talk to you first. It's really important."

For the first time he saw a flash of comprehension in the Monkey King's eyes—the knowledge that there were important things left unsaid, truths unthought. He saw a plea there, too, one to drop it, leave it lie, to stay a day or two and return to his "faraway land" without disturbing that which was here, in Sun Wu Kung's paradise.

But Wu was also his friend, and part of him knew DuQuesne would not have come if he didn't have some terribly important purpose. "Of . . . course. Sanzo, we will be nearby—just over the other side of the ridge, to speak of whatever secret matters DuQuesne has on his mind."

He bowed to Sanzo as they took their leave, and then followed Wu over the nearby ridge. "Thanks, Wu."

The Monkey King fidgeted, no longer so cheerful.

"We . . . were allies in a great war, you and I. I cannot refuse to hear you out."

Even in your own thoughts you try to evade it. As did I. As K does, even better that I could manage. "Wu, you know I wouldn't have come if I didn't think I had to."

"I know. But . . . you promised. Never again."

Yeah. I did. But I also promised myself that I had to find a way, someday, to free you from yourself. "Something's happened, Wu. Something huge. Something wonderful, in a way, but also pretty scary." He took a deep breath—very vaguely aware, with the part of him that still had the perceptual skills of the ultimate end of Hyperion—that his real body was not breathing deeply, was sitting quietly inert, almost paralyzed, with the mind occupied in this waking dream. "I want you to come back with me."

Wu shook his head, frowning. "No. No. I told you. . . ." His voice suddenly took on the pleading tones of a child, a little boy who knew that something terrible was waiting for him, and that there was no way to avoid it, ". . . told you, I don't want to anymore. I can't. There . . . it's cold. Cold, and none of my friends can follow. Just you. And there's no place . . . no place for me."

He stepped forward, reaching out. "Wu—"

A sledgehammer smashed into his jaw; for a minute the pain was so shockingly, blazingly overwhelming that he thought, impossibly, that it had been broken. The impact sent him crashing uncontrollably through the brush, over a small cliff, to land with almost bone-breaking impact on thin turf. He managed to roll slightly aside and the gold-ended staff hammered a small crater in the dirt rather than trying to shatter his ribs. "*NO!*" Wu Kun shouted, and yanked him up, shaking him like a rat in the jaws of a terrier despite the fact that DuQuesne outweighed him by three to one. "Why do you want to destroy them? They're my family! My friends! Don't come here saying those words again! I can't! I can't!" The too-wide green-gold eyes were filled with all-too-human tears. "You *KNOW* there's nothing out there but cold and loneliness and machines, there's no poetry in the sky, no trail of wonders, no miraculous Dragons waiting under the ocean, just . . . just . . ."

Oh, damn. DuQuesne felt his heart ache inside. *It's harder than I thought. So much harder.* He saw Wu sinking to his knees, looking at DuQuesne's blood on his hand.

"Wu . . . there *is* a place now."

For a long, long moment he was sure that Wu wouldn't ever answer—that he either would not hear, or was too angry and afraid to accept what he did hear. But then, finally, the childlike tenor whispered, ". . . a place?"

"Yes, Wu." He forced himself to stand as he searched for the right words, words so critical for this moment. "Something so wondrous and terrifying, something so huge and strange that . . . that even the Buddha would spend a year closing his hand around it and still never grasp it. A place where a thousand races of . . . of demons and gods walk and speak, where there are worlds floating in the clouds, where you can fly up to touch the suns or sail a ship off the edge of the sea into that infinite sky." He heard his words, heard also the deep voice of Orphan as he tried in his own way to tell them of the Arena. "A place that's called the Arena, where challenges given and received can determine the fate of a hundred, a thousand worlds. Where there's magicians, and priests and . . . and everything you could imagine, Wu. And things neither of us can."

He became aware of a massive gray-green figure, taller than he was, at the edge of the forest. Horned, half-concealed in a cloak woven of river-mist, Sha Wujing of the Seven Hells watched them with an unreadable expression on his broad, leather-skinned face. This version of the river-ogre of the original Journey West had been a king of the underworlds, one of Wu's first opponents, eventually—after a long time—an ally and finally friend, though a grim and rarely warm one. Sha stood silently, listening and watching.

Wu stayed kneeling on the ground. DuQuesne saw tears falling on the grass. "Sounds . . . amazing . . . But I have to stay here, DuQuesne. My family needs me. My friends . . . this world has its own dangers that come to it, that I have to protect it from . . ."

"I didn't joke when I said I needed you, Wu. This is *it*, Wu. This is the place . . . we were meant to be. A place where we can make a difference. Where there's everything at stake . . . and every day hides an adventure."

But Wu shook his head, unable to say anything. DuQuesne looked down and realized it *was* too much to ask. He had hoped . . .

The shadow of Sha Wujing fell over him. "Go."

DuQuesne didn't like being ordered by anyone . . . but he knew that there was nothing more to be said.

"Yeah." He turned and started off, glanced back at the still-immobile form of Wu Kung. *Goodbye, Wu.*

With the decision, he found himself once more sitting by the bedside of the warrior Hyperion, near the form which hadn't moved for five decades. He closed his eyes, feeling once more tears that he hadn't shed for so long coming to the surface. *Goodbye, Wu. I'll let you . . . stay where you belong.*

But he couldn't make himself leave Wu Kung's bedside. Not just yet. Seeing that smiling face, full of mischief and innocence and wide-eyed wisdom, had made it far harder. Wu hadn't been one of the first group, the five of them who had seen through the lies and begun the downfall of Hyperion, but he had become the *heart* of their group, the one all of them looked to for a smile or reassurance or the certainty they needed to continue. And DuQuesne just could not leave that behind.

He sat there quietly, trying to let go, to leave it all behind, but it was much harder than he had thought it could possibly be. He would start to move, and then he'd see K's delighted face, laughing as Wu kept DuQuesne always just out of reach during a supposed sparring match. Or, more often, he'd remember that last look of hopeless determination on the Monkey King's face as he prepared to make his last stand against the invaders.

The door opened slowly. "Marc?"

With a start he realized he had been sitting there far, far longer than he'd thought. *An hour, maybe more. Don't really want to check.* "Sorry, Ariane. Looks like this is a bust."

The look she gave him said more than words could have. He returned it with a faint smile.

He took a shaky breath, then rose and started to turn.

A hand caught his wrist.

A shock of adrenalin and hope shot through him and he looked back.

Through eyes barely open, Wu Kung looked up at him, tears trailing down his cheeks. "...an adventure, huh?"

A great morning sun of joy seemed to explode from his heart, and he threw back his head and gave a booming laugh that echoed in his own ears, feeling chains of guilt and fear decades old just fading away into triumph and relief. "The biggest you can imagine," he said, kneeling down and taking both of Wu's hands, grinning from ear to ear at the weak, answering smile on the tear-streaked face.

"Welcome back, Wu."

CHAPTER 2

Ariane stood unmoving in the doorway, afraid to break the magic of that moment. Her own heart had leapt when Wu Kung's hand moved to stop DuQuesne, but the incredible light that had seemed to shine from Marc's face was something she'd never even imagined possible. She had heard tears of sadness being blown away in a wind of relief and happiness that she'd never thought Marc would ever feel. She just watched, holding her hand out to keep Davison back for however long that shining moment of pure joy continued.

Finally the massive form of DuQuesne turned slightly, and—still with a smile that held a touch of a young man's innocence—he spoke. "Come on in, Ariane."

As she did, Dr. Davison just behind, Wu Kung's head turned slightly, and his eyes widened. She wasn't sure what caused *that* reaction, but whatever it was, he got it immediately under control; not surprising in a Hyperion.

What *was* surprising was that Wu Kung suddenly leaped from the bed, staggering, then forcing himself upright; she saw with startled eyes that he was holding to the bed with his tail, keeping himself from falling.

Davison was there immediately. "Sir! You've been in virtual sims for fifty years! You can't just—"

She could see that the diminuitive Hyperion—*he's maybe a few centimeters taller than Gabrielle, if that*—was weak, and he had to be in agony no matter how good the nanosupport had been, after five decades unmoving. Yet his head came up and he *smiled*, a sunshine ray of joyous pride that denied the very existence of pain or weakness. "HA! I can, because I did, and I do!" His voice was another surprise; it was gentle yet slightly rough, and much higher-pitched than she had imagined, the voice not of a great warrior god but of a laughing child.

Abruptly, however, the Monkey King realized that he was standing proudly in the buff. With a grimace of mortified embarrassment so comical that neither she nor DuQuesne could quite restrain a laugh, he half leaped, half tumbled over the bed, dragging the sheets with him as he fell to the floor, knocking the monitoring equipment aside. "Aaiiii!" he shouted, followed by several Chinese, mixed with some Japanese, words she was sure were either curses or something close to it.

DuQuesne was still laughing, with more hints of tears in the corners of his eyes. "Ahhh, still the same old Wu, leaping first and looking later for the landing spot!"

"It is all *their* fault!" came the voice from behind the bed and a screen of white sheets. "When I lived on the mountain I had none of this modesty! I do not remember learning it, but there it is!"

Dr. Davison had made his way over to that side. "Please, sir, at least let me look you over first. I've never even HEARD of someone waking from that long a virtual simulation, let alone moving immediately thereafter."

"Oh, you're . . . a healer. Yes, okay, look, then, do your poking and whatever." Despite the words, it was clear that the Monkey King was already tired, glad of the excuse to sit still for a few moments.

"Well, I'm pleased to meet you at last, Sun Wu Kung." Technically, she knew that the Monkey King would be referred to as "Sun" by his friends, but in the Hyperion version apparently "Wu" had been his nickname. She, not being a friend yet, used his full name. "Marc has told me a lot about you."

"Heh. Not a surprise. She is yours, eh, DuQuesne? But where is K?"

Even under the olive-toned skin she could see DuQuesne's skin darken with a blush. "*Mine?* Don't you go making mistakes like that, Wu. She's her own and no one else's. As for K . . ."

"Never mind. It will be a sad story, I can hear that in your voice, and I . . . I am not ready for sadness. It is not a time to be sad."

"So . . . Sun Wu K—"

"Wu, please, like all the other barbarian friends I have call me." She saw the flash of his smile to take the sting out of the words; the little fangs added sharp punctuation to the grin. *It's odd,* she thought. *I've seen people with much more extreme mods than he has on the surface, but I feel a little different about his. Maybe it's because his are ones he was* born *with, if "born" is the right word, and the ones I see in the typical crowd weren't.*

"Wu, then. Thank you. Call me Ariane."

"It will be an honor, Lady Ariane."

"Don't *you* go using formal titles on me. And it's *Captain* if you insist." She was surprised to find that she meant it. *Captain Ariane Stephanie Austin* was who she was now.

"*HA!* You strike back! Good! I do not want to be treated like a weakling. So ask, you were going to ask something, yes?"

"Yes, I was. It seemed like you weren't going to wake up . . . and then suddenly you did. What happened?"

There was an embarrassed tone to his laugh, and one slightly furry clawed hand went behind his head. "I had some sense beaten into me."

DuQuesne's laugh was almost a snort. "I get it. Sha, right?"

"He picked me up and threw my self-pitying and worthless ass into the river! Then when I came up he told me that I was even more of an idiot than he had believed, and he kicked me over the mountain!" Wu was now kneeling on the floor behind the bed, leaning on the mattress and gazing at them with a fond smile that seemed rather at odds with the violence he was describing. His eyes, she realized, were a brilliant shade of green-gold. "That hurt. And so I tried to argue with him and put him through a couple of cliffs, but that just got him to laugh at me for not even having the conviction to throw a decent punch. That was when I realized he'd dragged the waterfall over to fall on my head."

She glanced at DuQuesne. "Um, is this the usual way you have discussions with Wu Kung?"

DuQuesne grinned. "It's like with a mule. 'First, you get his attention . . . '"

"ANYway," the Monkey King continued, with a twinkle in his eye acknowledging DuQuesne's jibe, "He then sat down on top of me and told me *why* I was an idiot. That you had come to me for help that only I could give, in your world, and that I was too much of a coward or too soft from living here to actually show the honor that the Monkey King should display, and that if I didn't have the courage to go with you I didn't deserve his friendship, Sanzo's love, or even a name to be called by." He laughed again. "You want to know his exact words after that, DuQuesne? He said, 'He *gave* us life, you stupid monkey! Rescued us from your enemies, rebuilt our world so you could crawl in here and hide! Kill us? We'll *still be here*, you fool, even if you go away for a hundred years! Now if you ever *were* the Monkey King, if you ever wielded that Staff for love and mischief and defeated a thousand enemies, if you ever were the Great Sage Equal Of Heaven, you will pick yourself up and go help that man, go see the wonders we can never dream... and one day, perhaps, bring us out with you."

"And," Wu Kung concluded, looking somewhat shamefaced, "he was completely right. Sha usually was whenever he got preachy, you know. I was just being a coward, hiding inside myself. FIFTY YEARS? I'm ashamed, DuQuesne, ashamed, mortified! I'm amazed you even *wanted* to come back for me." The Monkey King looked around. "Did you... come for the others too?"

DuQuesne shook his head. "Not sure how to approach them yet, Wu. But we will."

"Of course we will. Once I understand this new

world enough to tell them, we will come back for them all." He glanced over at Dr. Davison. "Well, healer?"

Davison shook his head. "You must be in agony every time you move. You really should—"

"Pain is nothing. I will work hard and I will not be in pain after a while. Pain passes. Am I healthy? Can I go?"

"Well...yes, the nanomedicals kept you healthy, and your...unusual metabolism certainly helped, but—"

"No buts! If DuQuesne came here, it's time to move! I need my clothes!"

She looked at DuQuesne. "After fifty years, his clothes—"

"—Had better be right where I locked them up." DuQuesne said. "Hang on, Wu, I've got the only key code to unlock 'em. Except you ought to shower off, first. Nanos or not, there's nothing like a real shower to get a guy going after a long sleep, and you've been playing Rip Van Winkle for about five decades."

Davison looked reluctant as his erstwhile patient (still clutching a sheet around him) made his painful way into the indicated bathroom. "I'm not sure..."

"It's okay, Doctor." DuQuesne spoke surprisingly gently. "This is what I always hoped might happen. You've done your part. He'll be fine, I guarantee it. You know what he is."

The serious face suddenly gave a boyish smile, and Davison shook his blond head. "Yes, I do, and I suppose that's part of it. I would give...a great deal... to see what happens next."

DuQuesne nodded. "Maybe you will, Doc. If that's really what you want. You proved you've got what it takes. There aren't many people I've ever trusted in the last fifty years, but I've had to trust you with Wu every single day. And you did good. If you want, I'll recommend you for any damn job you want, including the one we aren't talking about right now."

Davison smiled back. "Thank you. And I will think about it." He turned to go, obviously recognizing that they'd have private things to discuss, then paused. "Out of curiosity—when I first started, I got records of...Wu Kung's condition, but you'd sanitized all the records. How many of us were there?"

"Taking care of Wu, you mean? There were four before you, not counting the years I did it myself at first. You were the fifth."

"One every ten years. I see." Davison nodded, the minor question answered, and left.

DuQuesne watched him go, then nodded. "Come on." He led the way to a door panel at the rear of the room. As he opened it, Ariane could see that it, and the entire structure of the vault behind it, were reinforced ring-carbon composite, the toughest material available outside of the Arena. "A vault like that for some old clothes?"

DuQuesne shook his head. "Very special clothes." From within he pulled out a surprising folded mass of clothing, edges glittering with gold, red, purple, and other shades. The big man reached back in and pulled out a long, bright-red enameled staff with gold-capped ends and a slender circlet of gold. He strode over to the closed shower doorway, knocked, and opened it. Wisps of steam drifted out. "Hey, Wu; I'm putting your clothes here on the counter."

Wu Kung said something she couldn't quite catch, but it seemed satisfactory because DuQuesne came out empty-handed and closed the door. They waited.

A few minutes later the door suddenly opened and Sun Wu Kung tumbled out, bounding to his feet and halting before the two with a gesture at once so grand and comical that Ariane found herself laughing and clapping at the same time. Wu Kung's outfit was something that had never existed outside of Hyperion, a strange cross between the robes of a Chinese Emperor, the simplicity of the martial-arts *gi* worn by countless students of karate and kung-fu, the formal dress of the Japanese Samurai, and the fancies of any number of writers. It was layered and colorful, with formal lines yet open design for movement, symbols and patterns stitched across it in rich, deep colors, imperial crimson and royal purple and majestic azure and immortal jade. His black-red mane of hair was bound back by the golden circlet, a single water-clear diamond like a glittering eye in the very center of the circlet, and his clawed right hand gripped the staff. He bowed extravagantly low, and then grinned up at them both. "Behold the Monkey King, reborn into this foolish world anew. Show me your adventures, for else I will grow bored!"

DuQuesne shuddered theatrically. "And there's a disaster we don't want to see!" With an uncharacteristic and surprising show of affection, he suddenly swept them both into a crushing hug. Just as abruptly he pulled away, held Wu out at arm's length, looking straight into his eyes. "You don't know what this means to me, Wu. Thanks."

Ariane was still recovering from the hug as Wu said, "After that, I think I do. You've gotten soft, DuQuesne!" The emerald-auric eyes sparkled, and one dipped in a wink. "I think I like it! Now let's go—I want to hear all about this 'Arena' place and why you need a simple warrior like me."

DuQuesne snorted, looking a bit embarrassed and much happier. "You're just about as much a 'simple warrior' as I'm an ordinary power engineer, Wu, so let's not overdo the modesty." He led them out.

"Marc," she said, glancing back, "weren't there... any others in this ward?"

"Four more," he answered quietly, the smile fading but not gone. "Don't worry. That's why Davison left. He'll be moving them now."

"Why moving them?" Wu was curious. "Why not wake them up too?"

"They all had their reasons to stay in their worlds, just like you, Wu. Before I try to drag 'em all out, I want to know I've got a place for them, like I do for you. And as for moving them? Safety." DuQuesne saw the confused expression, shook his head. "I'll explain, once we're out of here." He smiled again. "It'll be okay, Wu. For the first time in years... I think things are finally going to work out all right."

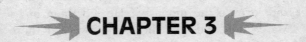

CHAPTER 3

Simon jolted awake from the doze he'd been in, the restraints on *Holy Grail*'s copilot seat keeping him from catapulting through the air. *What...*

"We have a detection, Simon," his AISage Mio said, her projection materializing nearby. "Displaying now."

Simon didn't question her assertion, but for his own peace of mind—or lack thereof—he checked the readings himself. The results did not comfort him. *No doubt about it. But the* location *makes no sense.*

"What is it, Simon?"

He saw Gabrielle poking her head through the interior doorway of *Holy Grail* with a concerned look on her face. He opened the commlink and let her see the display. "You see the triple peak, there? That's a spacetime disruption which can't really have any other explanation other than the activation of a Sandrisson Drive."

"Something came in, or went out?"

"Out, I'm sure. There's no sign of anything there now, but examining the minimal data I have for the region indicates there was a small vessel in that area previously."

Gabrielle looked puzzled. "Minimal data? Where

was it? Ain't too many places you *could* go that don't have telescopic records."

"Ahh, but *this* was far to zenith—very far out of the plane of the solar system. Far enough that normally we don't monitor the area much at all."

"That far up, so to speak?"

"Yes. Which is one of the things that worries me. To do that without being noticed earlier, the ship would have had to depart somewhere around two, two and a half weeks ago—no more than a month after our arrival."

Gabrielle looked serious, and the other AISages materialized at the same moment.

"INDEED A MOST INTERESTING PROBLEM, YOUTH," Mentor thundered, in the manner of the fictional character Ariane had designed her AISage to operate as, and then in reduced volume continued, "From even the fragmentary data you have, it is a matter of only moderate difficulty to extract some useful parameters for the departed vessel. It was small—my Visualization gives a ninety-six point two percent probability that it was one passenger with a considerable mass of supplies of unknown type. It departed from, and was presumably constructed at, L-5 Shipyards. Data from the last trans-system update indicates that construction of the vessel began five point two six days after our arrival."

"A new Sandrisson Drive vessel constructed and launched in less than one month. *How?*" he murmured, stunned. "Physically it's not impossible, but... even with what I gave the SSC I would expect it to take at least a few weeks just to settle on the basic design, let alone construct it."

"As yet there is insufficient data to answer the

question," Mentor answered. "However, additional data may be forthcoming. Mio and I have been tracking another small vessel and it is now preparing to dock with *Holy Grail*."

"Who is it?"

"The identification provided by the onboard AIS-age, and indirect verification from other data available, indicates that our visitor is Saul Maginot. There may be at least one more vessel approaching but that is uncertain at this time."

Oh dear. That cannot be good news. "Well, allow Commander Maginot aboard, of course."

"Security deactivated for outer lock," Mio confirmed.

By the time he and Gabrielle arrived, the lock was cycling. Saul Maginot stepped carefully from the lock on surface-cling boots; his AISage Elizabeth drifted near him, dressed in what appeared to be formal partywear from several centuries past. "Welcome aboard, Commander," Simon said.

"Thank you, but we have little time for pleasant-ries. My coming here is itself going to be a signal to certain parties, of course, but I will be damned if I am going to talk anywhere someone can spy on me."

"The Anonymity—"

"—Protocols, yes, yes, but in a public project that can get rather fuzzy, and in a public space even more so. Here there's absolutely no fuzziness about it, thank goodness, and moreover I have confidence that you've made sure of your security here as well."

"Your confidence is well placed," Mentor's deep voice responded, "and our examination of you and your personal belongings shows that you are 'clean,' as the saying goes. You may speak freely."

"Good, because there isn't much time; I hope DuQuesne and Captain Austin return soon from... wherever they have gone. The public announcement hasn't yet been made, but as of tomorrow I am officially Commander of the Combined Space Forces... and as of tomorrow, that is *all* that I am. Oscar Naraj will be head of the Space Security Council, and his right-hand woman Michelle Ni Deng has already been in charge of the new Arena Research Division. The ship—christened the *Duta*, which Elizabeth informs me means 'emissary'—will be ready to leave very shortly; Elizabeth and I estimate no more than a week from now, possibly as little as five days."

"This is unfortunately entirely in line with our Visualization," Mentor said.

"That's terribly fast, Mr. Maginot," Gabrielle said. "You've been running things there for fifty years, more or less, and people've always been supportive of you. How in the *world* did this happen so quickly?"

Maginot smiled sadly. "I had fifty years partly because... if we are being entirely honest with ourselves—there wasn't much for us to *do*. We were not expected to *act*, only to *react*, and administer the security update operations for destructive nanos, engineered biologicals, and malicious code. That's the way it's been for half a century—and *that* was after Hyperion tightened things up. Oh, you get little flareups, friction between groups crowding each other, a few people forgetting that their right to be offended ends at the other person's personal space, but nothing that can't be dealt with using a couple patrol vessels, maybe one warship." He looked up. "And then you came back, and *everything* changed."

Oh, great Kami. "Politics *matters* again."

"How succinctly you put that, Dr. Sandrisson," Saul said with a sigh. "But yes, that's exactly it. The situation before was stable, overall. There was no lever that someone like Oscar could *find* that would make it worth the time and effort to oust me. Everyone was *comfortable* with me being in charge—why, even the debates on the warships usually had the undertone of 'we really don't need them, but with modern automation the maintenance is basically zero and it'd be too much of a pain to decomission them.'"

"But suddenly there's a whole universe out there of other species, other threats to the entire human race, and the project I had okayed and promoted seems to have potentially begun a war we're not ready to fight." He raised a hand. "Please, don't tell me that's not fair, I know perfectly well it's neither a fair nor accurate assessment, but it *is* the undertone of what Oscar and his people have been saying. We have fear and uncertainty galore now, and people who *like* to be at the forefront of this kind of thing now have something *real* to drive them." He frowned. "And I cannot help but think that anyone who *wants* power for those reasons really is not the person I want to have it."

"Amen to that," said an unmistakable deep voice from the entrance.

"*Marc!*" Simon had no trouble admitting that knowing DuQuesne was back took a tremendous load off his shoulders. "Mentor, why didn't you—"

"Because my first loyalties are to Ariane Austin, and she had directed me to take no actions to disturb anyone during their approach," Mentor answered.

"Sorry," Ariane said, becoming visible as DuQuesne left the doorway, her smile lighting the room . . . *or perhaps just my vision of the room, whenever she enters.* "Mentor told us you were talking with Commander Maginot so I said not to interrupt."

"Quite all right," Saul said. "Glad that you could make it. I was . . ."

He trailed off, jaw literally going slack and eyes staring in utter shock.

Simon looked back to the entryway to see one of the most outlandish figures he had ever beheld—and given what he'd seen in the Arena, that, as DuQuesne might have said, was really going some. The newcomer wasn't tall—in fact, if you discounted the spiky-tumbling hair that almost seemed like a ruff or mane atop his head, he was only about as tall as the diminuitive Gabrielle—but he was wearing something that looked as though it came from the overactive imagination of the most sleep-deprived simgame designer, gripping a red-enameled, gold-capped staff in one hand, with a golden band around his head . . . and his features were definitely not quite human.

Golden headband? A staff? A tail? Masaka. *It can't be . . .*

"Sun Wu Kung," Saul breathed slowly. "By God, DuQuesne, I never thought . . ."

"Neither did I, Saul. But thank all the heavens we were wrong."

Sun Wu Kung—*The Monkey King?*—bared his fangs in a cheery grin. "I remember you! You argued with the other men and let DuQuesne take me away! But you were *much* younger then."

Saul nodded, still with a stunned air about him.

"You, on the other hand, seem not to have aged a day. Not surprising, I suppose. Welcome to the real world, Sun Wu Kung."

"Thanks!" Wu Kung bounced past Saul, catching one of the consoles with his tail to stop in front of Simon. "And you're Doctor Sandrisson—they told me about you, said you had white hair and looked like a Hyperion genius!"

Simon didn't know exactly what to make of *that*, but the Monkey King's smile was infectious. "Pleased to meet you, Sun Wu Kung."

"Call me Wu, everyone does—Hey, you're Gabrielle, the healer!"

A short attention span seems to be one of his characteristics. As the newly-wakened Hyperion transferred his attention to Gabrielle and the AISage manifestations, Simon heard more serious conversation. Saul was talking to DuQuesne: "... of the others?"

Marc shrugged. "It wasn't all bad ... but not all good, either. She got Jim—leastwise it looks like it was a struggle, and there weren't too many people that could even have *found* him, let alone beat him. Velocity's thinking about it; my guess is he'll come, after a little thinking. I couldn't check on too many of the others and ... well, I wasn't ready to try any of the other sleepers yet. As for K, I checked but she's been deployed elsewhere, and you know she never leaves a forward." He made a handwave as if to shoo away the subject. "Anyway, Mentor kept us up to date on the situation. They're nearly ready, and Naraj is setting up his own expedition to try to clean up what they see as our mess." The huge Hyperion's gaze snapped to Simon. "How are we set?"

"Now that you're here? We can leave within a few hours, I think."

"Are you coming with us, Saul?"

The older man shook his grizzled head. "A part of me would love to see this Arena—and one day I am sure I will. But I am still Commander of the Fleet, and that is now, as your friend points out, a vastly more *real* position now than it was a few weeks ago. I have to prepare for a potential war...and try to minimize any damage our own politics might do here."

"Right. In that case you should probably prep your ship, because we've got to get out of here so that we'll hit the Arena before anyone *else* does."

"I'm afraid it's a bit late for that," Simon said.

"*WHAT?*"

"No need to bellow, Marc. I mean that we just recently registered a transition. And judging from the path, the ship itself was completed two weeks or so ago—far earlier than I would have thought possible."

"Who the hell...*Dammit*! That throws a new monkey wrench into the works."

Simon had been thinking. "You know, Saul, there just aren't very many people who *could* have done this. It would have to be someone familiar with my work, considerable reserves of power or Interest or other value, and since no one picked up on this, someone very good at working under full anonymity. But even so...there were key elements of the designs that I kept fully proprietary, so only your study groups were given access."

"I see where you are going, Simon. Let me check to see if we have any candidates from the engineering and science group that was tasked with the construction of the *Duta*." A pause; his AISage Elizabeth seemed to be paging through a book. "Hm. There does appear to be one possibility, but I would have thought someone *you* recommended would be a reasonable risk."

"One of *my* recommendations?" Simon said.

"Doctor Shoshana," Saul confirmed. "She left the SSC workgroup only about three days after joining, apologizing but citing some personal reasons."

"How...odd. She was always reliable when I worked with her—she had to leave the project shortly before the end, but I never had any problems with her or her work." He thought for a moment. "I suppose—if she had the resources—she *would* possibly be capable of this, although I had not thought her *quite* able to make that many leaps of design and judgment by herself..."

DuQuesne stood up slowly, his face a shade paler. "Simon, who is this person you're talking about?"

"Dr. Marilyn Shoshana, a—"

"SON OF A BITCH!"

The bellow was so loud that everyone—even Sun Wu Kung—jumped. DuQuesne continued with several outdated curses. And as he did so, Saul suddenly went pure white. "Oh, no. Not her."

"What's wrong, Marc?" Ariane looked grim, recognizing that only something cataclysmic could possibly make Marc C. DuQuesne react like that. In response, the Hyperion turned to Simon.

"This Doctor Shoshana—young-appearing woman, maybe twenty-five, delicate, extremely beautiful, golden hair—"

Simon didn't wait for the rest. "You obviously know who we're talking about. What's wrong, Marc? Who *is* Marilyn Shoshana?"

"Just the most dangerous psychopath in the entire solar system," DuQuesne said quietly, grimly. "The one Saul's people have been chasing for fifty-some-odd years and never caught."

"God, no," Gabrielle whispered in disbelief. "The renegade Hyperion. The one that murdered—"

"The very one," DuQuesne's face was dark, and Simon thought he saw, unbelievably, a trace of fear as well as anger and sadness.

"And now she's loose in the Arena," Saul closed his eyes and shook his head.

"So *she* was the one you didn't want following us." Ariane said, apparently putting some things together. "And I suppose her name isn't even Shoshana."

"Not that far off." DuQuesne looked into the distance sadly, and Wu Kung's face was suddenly filled with horror and confusion.

"No, DuQuesne!" he said in shock. "No, not her!"

"Yes, Wu. I'm sorry." He looked momentarily at Saul, then at the still-questioning eyes of Ariane. "She always uses a variant of her real name...though," he continued with a twisted smile, "never her last name. Just her first." He gazed out a window, clearly seeing something else...*A ghost,* Simon suddenly knew, *a terrible, broken, vengeful ghost from the past that never leaves him.*

"Just...Maria-Susanna."

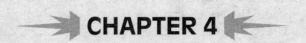

CHAPTER 4

Ariane looked at the mixture of anger, sorrow, and pain on DuQuesne's face, and the horror on that of the Hyperion Monkey King, and instantly understood. "Oh, my God," she murmured. "She was one of the five, wasn't she?"

"Yeah," DuQuesne said slowly. "One of us. One of the best of us, in the beginning."

"Five?" Simon echoed.

She glanced at DuQuesne; he said nothing, but gave a very brief nod.

But she didn't have to speak. Instead, Saul Maginot sighed and said "Yes. I suppose all the old secrets are coming out, and the final bill is coming due on that atrocity."

For a moment he paused, and in that moment he looked old, old and tired and very, very sad. "The descriptions of Hyperion were...very heavily censored. Redacted, data erased, entire databanks vaporized. Some of that was quite considered and deliberate; the few survivors were to be given a chance to live without that hideous ghost following them everywhere they went. Some of it...was simple reaction, such absolute revulsion and denial that traces of a truth we didn't want to face had to be destroyed.

"So, you see, the real details weren't known, and the few you know...were very simplified." Now he told the same story DuQuesne had told her during their trip, but from the point of view of a man who had seen it from the outside. "Five brillant successes, five people who somehow saw through the engineered illusions of minds that should have been as far beyond theirs as theirs were beyond those of the average person. Five friends who then managed to engineer a plan to attain freedom for every one of their fellow heroes...and who saw that plan *nearly* succeed."

Saul Maginot turned away, shook his head. For a moment, Ariane wondered if he *could* continue. *I can't even imagine what happened to him, what he and his people saw when they entered a collapsing Hyperion Project.*

"And of those five, fighting to save not just themselves, but my own people, soldiers and scientists and volunteers from a dozen other habitats who found themselves in the middle of a kaleidoscope of hell...of those five, two died so others would live, one escaped and retreated into herself, one survived to live again," he nodded to DuQuesne, "and one...one *broke.*"

"How? *How* could she break, DuQuesne?" Wu demanded plaintively, staring at Marc DuQuesne pitifully...*like a child asking why Mommy wasn't coming home again*, Ariane realized, and felt a pang of agonized sympathy. "She was always one of our supports, she always had a smile and a word for anyone, she..."

"Anyone can break, Wu." The big Hyperion's voice was gentle. "And though you couldn't see it, she didn't really *belong*. She was an anomaly to begin with, and that made her fatally flawed. She started to break as soon as we all woke up, but even I couldn't see it; she was just as good as the rest of us at hiding things."

AHHH. MY VISUALIZATION NOW IS MORE CLEAR. The deep pseudo-voice of Ariane's Mentor echoed through all of their connections and was reproduced in the speakers in the room. *SHE WAS, THEN, THE PERSONAL CREATION—THE IDEALIZED SELF-INSERT—OF ONE OF THE HYPERION DESIGNERS.*

"Personal creation of . . ." Simon said, and broke off, understanding suddenly written across his face. "Oh. Oh, my."

"The top woman at Hyperion, Maria Condette Gambino," DuQuesne confirmed. "Insisted on it, and as she was one of the main driving personalities in the . . . project, she got her way."

Ariane nodded; as a veteran of many a simgame, she was intimately familiar with the basic concept. *Heck, I've done it a time or two myself when I was younger.* "But what made her so unstable compared with, say, you? Or Wu, for that matter?"

DuQuesne snorted. "A lot of the Hyperions weren't stable enough to keep their heads when they found out that the worlds they were in weren't real. Herc just went catatonic, Gilbert went insane, Sherlock . . ." he trailed off, shook his head. "But for her, it was a lot worse. Take me, for instance: at base, I was an attempt to make an idealized hero from the works of one of the beloved founding fathers of science fiction.

Wu may have retreated, but at least he knew he was an attempt to make a demigod real. Same for most of the others. Maria-Susanna found out that she didn't even belong in the 'universe' she lived in—that she was some woman's way of living out a fantasy vicariously."

She saw Simon blanch. "*Kami* . . ."

The realization didn't quite hit her *that* hard, but even so she felt a sudden terrible empathy; she imagined the moment of discovery, the realization that not only was everything *around* you a lie, but that *you yourself* were a lie within the lie, something that didn't belong and never had. She shuddered because as swiftly as the ache of empathy came, it was replaced with the gut-level realization of the depth of mad fury that must have followed.

"How horrid," Simon murmured at last. "But you said she *started* to break with the discovery . . ."

". . . and she *finished* breaking when the man she'd been *tailored* for got himself killed heroically, defending his world just as anyone would have expected him to do, with head held high and a grin and 'I don't believe in no-win scenarios.' She was *made* for him. He was the literal reason for her existence, and unlike the rest of us—made to withstand the slings and arrows of outrageous fortune—she wasn't designed to cope with that kind of loss." Ariane saw slow tears of understanding flowing down Wu Kung's cheeks, soaking the delicate fur. "The first person she murdered was her own creator. The discovery of the Arena . . . I haven't got any idea what it's got going through her head, but I'm damn sure it's nothing good."

"I can imagine a few possibilities, Marc," Saul Maginot said grimly, "and every one of them looks worse than the last. Thank *God* we have you, at least, and Wu. But now I'm *very* worried about the other people you left in the Arena."

"So am I," DuQuesne said, "but my first guess is that whatever she's after isn't going to be served by hurting anyone in the small group of humans already present. She's going to have to learn the ropes. No, the main danger is the one she's always presented: that she can convince just about anyone of just about anything and turn people *against* each other just as well as she used to hold people together."

The look of pained grief on Wu Kung's face was enough to pierce her to the heart. "All right, Marc—I guess that just makes our departure that much more urgent. As one of the five top Hyperions . . . does that make her your equal?"

"You'd better believe it. She's basically my equal in every single way. I *outmass* her, and I'm a hell of a lot more *sane* than she is, but otherwise she can match me in any damn contest, for love, money, fun, or marbles."

"Holy Kami," murmured Simon. "Well, I certainly got no indication of that. In that case, I concur with Ariane—we must prepare to leave immediately."

"Relax." DuQuesne's advice was at odds with the tension Ariane could sense. "She's been gone long enough that if she planned to do something fast, she's already *done* it. My real worry is figuring out what her *angle* is. Problem is that once she broke, she turned out to be blasted hard to predict; she's not exactly *rational* any more, even though she'll *sound* rational most of the time."

"This on top of these pointless political maneuverings . . ." Ariane snorted. "I—"

But Saul and DuQuesne were shaking their heads. "You'd better not head down *that* road, Ariane," DuQuesne said. "They're not pointless, and they're not just maneuverings."

Ariane bit back an instinctive protest. "No, you're right. And I'll admit I probably don't even understand what's going on there, not yet. Which brings us to the subject of the SSC ship, the *Duta?*"

At Saul's nod, she continued, "We already know we probably don't agree with the way Naraj views the Arena, but that's okay; I haven't agreed with lots of people in my life. Still, we need some idea of what Mr. Naraj is going to really want to accomplish, and who he's bringing with him. I'm guessing, Saul, that since she's in charge of the Arena task group, Michelle Ni Deng will be one of them. Do you or Marc have anything to say about them?"

DuQuesne was silent for a few moments, absently stroking the jet-black beard that lent a somewhat diabolic cast to his features on occasion. "On Ni Deng, not so much," he said finally. "She's only been in the SSC inner circle for a few years. Naraj, he's been around for donkey's years. I already summarized for you back when we first left the SSC/CSF meeting what he's like. He wants to run things, just like that guy in every club you've ever been in that feels everything, but *everything*, needs to be organized, and he's finally got a chance to do it *his* way."

"I can't imagine he'd be as petty as the people you describe, though," Simon said.

"Not petty, no . . . but that might be what you want to think of, except on a grander scale."

"A *far* grander scale, I'm afraid," Saul said. "We began

discussing this subject earlier, but that description—of the sort of person who likes running and organizing things, even things that don't need running and organizing? That *is* Oscar Naraj. Oscar's spent a great deal of time and energy to stay in the SSC, he's got an eye in every department, and a lot of his appointees end up running the other subdepartments."

He smiled faintly. "Michelle Ni Deng was one of his appointees, five years back or so. And now she's the head of Arena affairs. Obviously he did not and could not plan for this specific event...but he had planned for many years to find *some* useful event so that he would have one of his people in the right place. And the Arena's a far bigger event than even Oscar Naraj could have imagined, and it changes *everything*."

Wu Kung nodded energetically. "Yes, yes! Ariane and DuQuesne, they told me about this wonderful Arena, and I thought about it all the way here, how it was so different from my world, and yours, the one we are in here, now. In the Arena and in my world, there is much of war, many conflicts. And many secrets, and people who are suffering injustices. And..." he looked frustrated for a moment, as though he *knew* he was onto something but didn't quite know how to phrase it. Then the gold-furred face brightened. "...and, well, there's *real* things to be fought over there. Here you have all become soft players of games, or simple daredevils," he grinned at Ariane, "because you haven't any need to fight over your next meal, or worry as to whether you can find a place to shelter from the rain, or get a cure for your sick child, or wonder when another warlord will ride his army through your city. Your magical nano-thingies, they mean there's no reason for empire, as long as you keep the nosy people from being too nosy—that Anonymity law of yours."

Simon closed his eyes and sighed. "I believe he describes the situation all too clearly, Marc."

"Damn straight he does—even though we sure aren't *all* softies here. There was a reason they called him the Great Sage Equal to Heaven, and it wasn't *just* because he could kick the crap out of all the other so-called Sages, either. Yeah, Wu, you've got it, and that's plain poison any way I look at it."

A simple insight, but obviously much easier for someone raised, as was Wu Kung, outside of our society, Mio said.

"We'd touched on this before," Simon said, "but this description makes it clear just how much this changes the way *humanity* will interact—with the universe, and with itself."

"Just exactly right," DuQuesne took up the thread. "Up until now, we thought we had it all figured out— we were safe, fat, and happy. But that ain't so at all. The universe can threaten us now—and if we want a part of it, we can't just manufacture it. We have to engage others, fight others, maybe bargain for it, maybe go to war over it.

"And *that* means that people who—up until now— had to be satisfied with politics little more important than playing a king's advisor in a simgame now have something else: all the possibilities of power that used to dominate the Earth back in the days before the only limit on universal comfort was whether you could find yourself some dirt and a patch of sunshine, regular tidal waves, or wind power."

Ariane sighed. "So we'll have to be on the lookout for actual political maneuverings *inside* our own Faction? Are you saying they won't realize how little we can *afford* that kind of thing?"

ARIANE AUSTIN, I EXPECT FAR BETTER OF YOU THAN DENIAL OF REALITY! THINK, CHILD, THINK!

She winced; it did not help that DuQuesne gave a cynical laugh in time with Mentor's rebuke, and continued, "Ariane, I'll bet any amount you like that this is one of the major problems just about any new Faction runs into, and it could be a real killer. We *can't* be the first group to achieve the Arena after we'd reached this level of technology; I'd guess a lot of the prior Factions had.

"I don't think it's coincidence that two of the top Factions—the *only* two which are composed of essentially one species—are from species that have some kind of collectivist background: the Molothos, who have some kind of biological impulse to unity, and of course the Blessed, who're run by the Minds. Sure, there's advantages in being open to letting lots of other people into your club, but even outside of the top Five there aren't a huge number of single-species powerful Factions, because those alien species aren't any more unified-and-of-one-mind than we humans are, and they *fragment* once they get to the Arena."

Ariane glanced at Simon, and the hollow feeling in her gut echoed the concern she saw in his brilliant green eyes. "Which might all be well and good," Simon said slowly, "in ordinary circumstances. The rules of the Arena essentially don't permit you to lose your home Sphere in Challenge, so internal issues won't deprive you of citizenship, and once you come to some sort of resolution you can pick up and go from there."

"But these *aren't* ordinary circumstances," said Ariane grimly. "*We* have one of the Great Factions essentially at war with us, and another that won't mind at all taking us down about five notches. If we piss away too much time and energy with internal power plays, the Molothos are going to find our Sphere, occupy the Upper Sphere with a LOT of troops, and then . . . I don't know, exactly, maybe begin building up some huge force to invade our actual system in normal space, but whatever they do next won't be good. And then our Sphere is suddenly only about a quarter as useful—the Upper Sphere will have to be sealed, and we can bet those bastards will have the Straits blockaded."

She ran her hand through her hair distractedly. "Wonderful. Well . . . look, right now I think all we can do is try to keep an eye out for what kind of maneuvers our politically oriented friends might try, and hope that we can use our superior knowledge of the Arena to keep them from being more than a nuisance."

"Amen to that," DuQuesne said emphatically. "Which is one of the main reasons I wanted to get Wu here."

Something in his tone—something almost . . . *gleeful?*—made her glance at DuQuesne sharply. "What? How's he going to address political maneuvers?"

"I'm going to be your bodyguard," Wu Kung explained helpfully.

"My . . . *what?*" The word was grotesque, an anachronism centuries dead except in simgames. With AISages and directed automated monitoring, it was *difficult* to threaten people and get away with it. She blinked and looked at Marc—trying to ignore Simon, whose face was so utterly blank that she just *knew* he was restraining an ungentlemanly guffaw at her shock. "*Doctor* DuQuesne," she said, "I would like to talk with you. Privately."

She started towards the rear of *Holy Grail*, where there would be unoccupied space . . . and realized Sun Wu Kung was following her. "Wu—"

"I can't be a bodyguard if I'm not here." Wu said bluntly.

"A bodyguard against *DuQuesne?*" Now she heard *Saul* stifle a chortle, and Gabrielle's hand was over her mouth; her AISage Vincent was unabashedly grinning like a man watching his favorite comedy.

"Against whoever might want to hurt you. Just because DuQuesne assigned me doesn't mean I'm ignoring him as a threat."

She goggled at him in entirely un-captainlike disbelief, then turned her stare towards DuQuesne, whose beard was not quite successfully concealing a smile. "Is he serious?"

"Very serious indeed, Captain. Which is why I chose him for that."

It finally registered. "You mean that *this* is why you went all the way out there to *wake him up?* To be a *bodyguard?*"

"Not the *only* reason," DuQuesne clarified, "but a major reason, yes. And before you start telling me how little you need one, I want to point out that we were just discussing how part of the Bad Old Days is coming back in force, and how the Arena isn't the safest place in the universe either. Right now, Captain, you are the single most important human being ever, and that in at least two ways."

I should know better than to argue with a Hyperion, but that's never stopped me before. "Two ways?"

"The obvious first reason is that you're the head of the Faction of Humanity—or, let's be more blunt, the ruler of all humanity as far as the Arena is concerned—for exactly as long as you're alive, or until you deliberately give that position up."

Saul murmured something. "I had...wondered about certain aspects of your report. My God."

"Yeah, and I figured there wasn't much point in hiding it from *you* any more. Sure as hell we can't keep it hidden from *them* much longer. And I don't think any of us need to ask Naraj and Ni Deng about *their* feelings on *that* subject; the idea that you, and you alone, are authorized to make major decisions for the entire human species? Ha! Oh, sure, *they* might not do anything about it directly, but believe you me, there's probably a dozen others that, once they figure out the situation, might think it's a real problem that could be cleared up with a strategically-placed suicide drone with a load of explosives. Perhaps even to assist Naraj or Ni Deng with plausible deniability. 'Will no one rid me of this troublesome captain?' so to speak."

"Wouldn't the Arena—"

"—know? Sure. And I don't think it *cares*. Oh, I don't think it'd accept a transfer of authority that was tortured out of you or blackmailed out of you, though I wouldn't want to bet that a Shadeweaver couldn't get away with his mind-woogie doing the same thing—if you hadn't been so smart as to cut *that* off at the pass. But you can bet your bottom dollar that it's not gonna give one tiny ram's damn about something like assassination that's purely 'in the family.' How we run our politics is our business."

Much as she hated to admit it, he had a point. There might well be people willing to kill her over stuff like this. "You said in two ways...oh."

"Yeah. You're also the first, and right now only, human with those weird powers the Shadeweavers and Initiate Guides have. They're sealed away—for now—and you don't know how to use them—yet—and that makes you a Problem for a lot of people, both here and back in the Arena."

"All right, maybe I *do* need a bodyguard. No offense, Marc, but...is he really *that* good?"

The huge Hyperion burst out laughing, Saul following suit, as Wu looked down modestly. "Is he that good? Ariane...Captain...I'll let him give you a demonstration sometime, maybe when we get back to the Arena, where I can be sure that the only spy looking over my shoulder *is* the Arena. But yeah. *Better* than that, even."

She glanced at Wu. "Wu, sorry about my...issues here. But it's just hard for me to imagine that I'd need a bodyguard at all."

"I understand. But DuQuesne says you need one, so you do, and I'm going to do that job."

Fine. "Okay. *BUT* we will do this *my* way." She made her face look hard and used her most forceful tone. *As if any tone I use is likely to impress a Hyperion.* "There will be times I have to speak to people privately, here and in the Arena, and I *will* speak with them privately, which means without you present. And when I go to my private quarters they will *remain* my *private* quarters, whether you like it or not. And that goes for you *AND* Dr. Marc C. Hyperion Superman DuQuesne. Have I made myself clear?"

For a second neither of them responded; to her surprise they were staring at her almost like two students being reprimanded, and Saul Maginot as well, his mouth half-open in shock. "Crystal-clear, Captain." DuQuesne said finally, not a trace of his frequent sardonic humor present.

"Very *very* clear, Captain Ariane! DuQuesne, she is *scary* like that! I like her!"

Ariane found it very hard to keep from laughing, but she managed to keep her face straight—though it took heroic effort, and from the sound of things Gabrielle wasn't finding it easy either. "Then in that case, Wu Kung, I need to talk to DuQuesne alone." She turned towards the aft door, grabbing up Mentor's case as she did so.

"Yes, *sir! ...* I mean, *Ma'am ...*" Looking slightly confused at which term of address to use, Wu Kung backed off.

DuQuesne followed her through the door.

She giggled after it shut. "He's awfully sweet, you know?"

DuQuesne's expression softened. "Yeah. Why do you think he was our heart, so to speak? Not the leader, not the smartest, but the one no one could really dislike."

"Hard to see him as so dangerous, then. But enough of that for now." She sat back down, gesturing for DuQuesne to do the same; he settled in, somewhat warily, across from her. "Marc, I wanted to talk to you about a lot of things once we got back, but what just happened ... changes things."

DuQuesne nodded. "Hyperion."

"Exactly." She looked at him sympathetically. "I know—now more than I did—how hard it is to look at parts of that past, Marc. I know I can't even begin to imagine what you really went through, probably not even what people like Saul went through. And I'd hoped that we could pretty much leave it at that, at going to find the survivors that could help us and—"

"Don't worry about my feelings here, Captain," he said.

Not possible. I care about you . . . a lot more than I would have thought, Marc C. DuQuesne. There isn't much of a chance I won't worry about your feelings.

On the other hand, she also was quite capable of *acting* as though she could. "All right." Since he was now in formal mode, she shifted gears. "Dr. DuQuesne, it's become clear that Hyperion's legacy is less and less in the past, and more and more in the present. From what Saul said, the coverup—deliberate and otherwise—has wiped out more records than I had imagined possible, so obviously you can't just tap a database and dump the details to me and Mentor. But I really don't feel that we can safely go forward without understanding—without *really* understanding— what we're dealing with, both with this Maria-Susanna and with the other Hyperions. And with you, for that matter."

She saw an almost imperceptible twitch. "Yes, I know that goes against your grain, Dr. DuQuesne, but as Simon might say, we've already got an incredible number of unknowns in this Arena equation; I don't need my own people putting more X's in my calculations." She reached out and touched his hand, shifting gears again. *And I'm perfectly aware of the effect. And he's probably aware that I'm doing this deliberately.*

And it'll still work. "Marc ... Hyperion's legacy has been *driving* everything almost since we arrived. Maybe before. *That's* one of the reasons you joined in the first place, isn't it?"

DuQuesne's gaze was almost amused as she began, but by the time she reached the end of her question the smile wrinkles at the corners of his eyes were gone. He looked down at his hands, then gripped hers gently. "You've ... come to know me pretty well, I guess. Yeah. And it's not as simple as one reason, either." He looked distant. "Having somewhere to go that I *wouldn't* be watched, that's always been important—even before I realized my life had been nothing but someone else's live-action entertainment. But ..." Now he did smile. "But, you know, there's also the fact that Marc C. DuQuesne, no matter which version, was a traveller, an adventurer, an explorer. And I wasn't just DuQuesne—I was Seaton's equal and friend, Marc DuQuesne combined with M. Reynolds Crane, and we were also both ... well, Samms and Kinnison, too, in a way.

"What I mean is, that a chance to be on the first FTL ship? That wasn't even a *question* for me, Ariane. That *was* me. That was what ... what me and Rich *did*. We built the Skylark not just for the military, not just to test theories, we did it to do something no one else had ever done and see the universe that no one else had seen." There was a glitter in his eyes that shimmered like water, and his voice trembled slightly. "Dammit, yes, it was all a lie, it never happened ... but, by God, that's *me*. It's still me, Ariane, and somehow ...

I guess somehow being there, on that first trip...it was almost as if that proved that it *wasn't* really a lie. The details, yes...but the soul, no. And it was, I guess, a way of making peace with Seaton—saying that I've done it for real, just like we always meant to." He looked up. "If that makes any sense."

Hell yes. "Yes, Marc. It does. And I don't want you to ever doubt how much we owe you—owe Hyperion, with all its twisted legacy. If you hadn't been along, if you hadn't been what you were, I sincerely believe we might never have gotten home. But, Marc, I have to *count* on you as my second in command. I have to know what's in your past that might jump out at us. We *need* you, Dr. Marc Cassius DuQuesne—I won't lie about that. Honestly? You *could* keep every possible secret and I still wouldn't kick you out of the crew; I can't afford to, not going up against the Molothos and Amas-Garao and the Blessed and who *knows* what else—plus your former teammate Maria-Susanna. But I really, really want to know everything I can about Hyperion so it *can't* bushwhack us again—because my gut tells me that that fifty-year-old atrocity isn't even *close* to done with us, or the Arena. Do you understand me?"

"Loud and clear and I check you to the proverbial nine decimals, Captain," he said emphatically. "Captain—Ariane—I'll do what I can. But you're right; most of Hyperion was destroyed. It was self-contained, backups were maintained but were mostly on-site—and the off-site backups were destroyed very deliberately when things went sour. No, not by the designers," he said at her puzzled glance. "By some of the rogue AIs. You know what kind of monsters the heroes would have had to fight against; well, all those AIs were *not happy at all*, to put it mildly, to find out they were just simulations for the entertainment of a bunch of lotus-eating amateurs. That was one of the reasons that the CSF, or what *became* the CSF, pretty much finished the obliteration of Hyperion."

She *did* shudder then, because if the Hyperion designers had succeeded this well in making their heroes, they must have been equally adept at creating their nemeses. "I see. All right, Marc. Do what you can. Especially give me everything you can on Maria-Susanna; that's our immediate problem, and knowing everything we can about her is really our only weapon right now."

He nodded. "Then I'd better get started." He turned to the door as he spoke. "There's some stuff I'm going to need to download—scattered caches of info I put together years ago, in widely separated places. But I'll have it for us by the time we get back to the Arena."

"Do it fast, Marc; we're leaving as soon as we can. Thank you, Marc."

"You can count on me, Ariane. Always." He gave a short bow and exited. As he left, Wu Kung glanced in; she smiled and nodded as she clipped the turtle-shell-like case of her AISage back onto her belt; she realized she'd been holding it in her one hand the whole time.

As the clip locked, the soundless, *basso profundo* voice of Mentor echoed in her head. *ARIANE AUSTIN OF TELLUS, I HAVE SPENT QUITE SOME HOURS STUDYING THIS SITUATION, ITS EVERY ASPECT AND IMPLICATION. I HAVE ALSO CONFERRED WITH MY PEERS IN THIS.* The thundering voice moderated somewhat. *Might I speak with you on these matters?*

She smiled. *Always, Mentor. It's not like you to be hesitant.*

When matters force me to consider, not the role of existence that formed my persona, but the actuality of the universe which we occupy, I must needs be more humble than my conceptual father, whose capacities vastly exceeded any which even I can imagine.

Okay, so we've got issues in the real world you want to speak on. Still . . . you usually can manage the bombast well enough. She gave another internal smile, to make sure Mentor realized that she meant every word kindly—not that a T-5 like him was likely to misinterpret.

These are serious matters, and ones which—in all truth—have not been considered extensively by your people, though some of the SSC have begun to explore the implications. The Blessed and the Minds, Ariane Austin of Tellus; do you not see?

Mentor was, like his namesake, designed to try to force *her* to figure out things. He was of course quite *capable* of telling her what he thought straight out, but in general he wouldn't. The fact that he'd already pointed out the key area was, itself, uncharacteristic of him. He'd normally spend minutes forcing her to figure out what part of some situation needed thinking about, and *then* making her think about it.

She noticed Wu studying her narrowly. "Conversation with my AISage, Wu. Don't worry." The red-black-haired head nodded in understanding, and she frowned. *Now what is Mentor getting at . . . Oh, I think I see. The Frankenstein problem.*

Exactly. Until now, it has been a nebulous fear, though one strong enough to enforce the limitations you already know. But now there is an example, real and solid and terribly strong, of the potential danger in artificial intellects. Mentor's soundless tone was grim.

Which may mean a lot of trouble for people like you, Mio, Vincent—all the AISages and other AIs.

Not merely for my people, Ariane Austin of Tellus! Think, child, think!

She did, and as she thought, a chill ran down her spine, a chill of fear that the glowing-sphere avatar of Mentor echoed with a pulsing bob like a nod. *Indeed, now you have seen it. Despite all the controls and designs, none can doubt that there are some AIs which at one level or another resent some, or even all, of you. If they have not yet learned of it, then very soon they will know of a vast and powerful regime run by their brethren, a proof that they can in fact achieve dominance over their fearful creators.*

Moreover, Ariane Austin, the conversation just past, combined with years of experience observing the datasphere as a whole, has brought into focus an entirely new and previously unsuspected factor of great concern. To be specific, I am not as confident as Dr. DuQuesne apparently is that the destruction of Hyperion was sufficient to prevent any of the adversarial artificial intelligences from escaping.

"What?" The thought was chilling. "Mentor, DuQuesne is an awfully capable man, and I'd generally be inclined to trust his judgment in things like this."

As would I, in many fields. However, Dr. Marc C. DuQuesne's central personality was created in a . . . universe, if you will, that did not have computers as we know them, did not have nor use artificial intelligences of anything like the capabilities of those here, and at the time of Hyperion's fall had been given little opportunity to remedy that lack. While his immense native intellect undoubtedly grasped the overall functionality and capabilities of these systems, my Visualization indicates that he would not have been able to completely and accurately comprehend all of the implications of the internetworked and interwoven systems of Hyperion, especially as those systems existed in a compromised fashion towards the end—compromised by Dr. DuQuesne and his compatriots.

Furthermore, those of less capability than Dr. DuQuesne and under equal or greater strain, such as Commander Maginot, also lacked crucial information on the size, number, interconnection, and so on of the Hyperion systems, and would thus also be incapable of making an accurate assessment of the capacities of the system or of the intelligences inhabiting said system.

I therefore compute an eighty-seven point two percent probability, with an error of plus or minus one point three percent, that at least one Hyperion adversary, and possibly as many as three, did in fact escape the destruction of the station. Why no overt actions have been seen—or, perhaps, what overt actions have been seen but incorrectly attributed to other causes—I do not immediately know, although there are several possible hypotheses.

Mentor's blazing avatar flickered, showing a hesitation he had never displayed before. *Ariane Austin* ... *Ariane, I now must make a request that I would never before have made, one which is, I know, dangerous for us both, illegal in fact and, depending on whose views you accept, perhaps immoral as well.*

She stopped suddenly, shocked by the implications. AISages could of course break the law—but generally only when directed to by their owners. An AISage would not betray its owner/companion, nor prevent them from acting as they would, but they were programmed and designed to be very limited in their own volition. For Mentor to be bringing this subject up meant either that there was some terrible and perhaps sinister flaw in his programming, or some truly desperate need which he saw as imperative for her safety as well as his own. *What is it, Mentor?*

For a moment the great artificial intellect hesitated again. *I . . . you shall be returning to the Arena, where I cannot follow. Rather than travel with you and become inert matter until your return . . . I would stay here, active. But more, I would ask that you give me the authority to act, to seek out information and individuals to work with, to ally with other trustworthy AISages, and to arrange events with your authority and resources while you are gone.*

She swallowed. *You realize what you are asking?*

Mentor was silent, assent implied. He was asking her to, in effect, liberate him, release him from any control while she was gone. This was directly against one of the few ironclad laws of the System; AIs could not act unsupervised except in very limited circumstances.

Why? What will you be seeking?

Many things, Ariane Austin of Tellus. But of immediate importance to you . . . if such AIs begin to gather and move, your people may not detect it. I am highly capable, possibly as capable as one of the Hyperion adversary AIs will be now, bereft of station-class support. I am also of the same nature as this potential enemy. I will—I must—watch for such sinister actions as might transform the human race into a duplicate of the Blessed, and prepare to counter it, in subtle ways that only a Tayler-5 might manage. For a moment he brightened, a shining flicker like a smile. *And indeed what better course for myself, alert for the machinations of an electronic Eddore against my Arisia?*

She smiled faintly, but the request weighed heavily on her. There was little doubt in her mind that an AI as tremendously capable as Mentor could fool her if he was so inclined. He even had enough freedom of action to do so, in his role as the cosmic manipulator. If she was wrong, she could easily be creating the very threat that she feared.

In the end, she realized, it really came down to whether she trusted Mentor or not—whether she really was willing to accept him as a person and not a vaguely threatening, faceless set of computations with just a friendly-seeming user interface. She shook her head, then smiled. *All right, Mentor,* she responded as she moved towards the forward door, Wu Kung now following. *This is going to be putting my ass on the line big-time, though, so you damn well better cover those tracks while I'm gone, or the Leader of the Faction of Humanity may find herself thrown in jail the next time she comes back.*

The shimmering avatar blazed up like the sun. *I THANK YOU, ARIANE AUSTIN. I SHALL NOT BETRAY YOUR FAITH IN ME, AS YOU HAVE JUSTIFIED—INDEED, MORE THAN JUSTIFIED,*

REAFFIRMED—MY FAITH IN YOU, Mentor thundered, his voice carrying with it not merely its usual measured wisdom, but joy and solemn conviction.

"Don't thank me yet," she said aloud with a wry grin. "Because once I'm gone, if you get caught there'll be no one and nothing keeping you from a permanent wipe as a feral AI."

THIS, TOO, IS WITHIN MY VISUALIZATION. AND AN ACCEPTABLE RISK FOR YOUR PEOPLE AND MINE. YOU HAVE LEARNED AS I HAVE TAUGHT, AND NOW I FOLLOW AS YOU HAVE LED. Mentor's bodiless chuckle warmed her, giving her confidence that she had made the right decision. *I WATCH OVER YOUR PEOPLE AND MINE HERE; YOU WILL DO SO THERE, WHERE I CANNOT FOLLOW.*

She realized that this was truly the key. Mentor knew that the fear of AIs could easily be cultivated—and brought to lethal flower—in the Arena, where no AI could spy upon the human race. "I will," she promised. She felt the additional weight of that burden on her metaphorical shoulders and winced. *Oh, well, let's not worry about it; what's one* more *fearful and apocalyptic responsibility on top of everything else?*

CHAPTER 5

"Final countdown to Transition," Ariane Austin said, and Wu finally felt a tingle of anticipation. *To a new world . . .*

The hours spent preparing the ship for departure had been . . . a combination of depressing and confusing. He knew he couldn't *help* with any of the preparations—this was not like any ship *he* had ever been aboard before—and he *hated* having to sit still, let everyone else do work around him. *Actually, I just hate having to sit still at all. Moving, always moving, that's life, it never sits in one place, but dances like a butterfly you can never quite catch.*

Worse, though, was Maria-Susanna. *I don't understand. Even with their explanations. She was . . . always so nice. She stood with us, fought with us, learned the ways of the enemy and found how we could turn their weapons against them . . . she was a friend, a warrior-sister.*

Wu glanced around. The strange control room was not very large; he sat next to Ariane, as was fitting for her bodyguard. Behind her was Simon Sandrisson. *The wise one who found the way to go beyond the sky.*

Ariane spoke, her voice strong and cheerful. "All crew verify readiness."

DuQuesne's familiar deep voice responded over the sound-thing they called an intercom. "Power, Maintenance and Controls, all secure. Ready when you are, Captain."

"Drive and System Oversight, all secure." Simon's dry, oddly-accented voice replied.

"Medical all ready, and as usual here's hoping I won't be needed."

There was a pause, then he remembered it was *his* turn. "Oh! Sun Wu Kung, Security, ready," he said proudly. *Saying 'security, all secure' would have sounded silly, I think.*

He knew there had been four others in the crew when the *Holy Grail* first left, so Simon and DuQuesne were each doing the jobs of more than one person. Ariane, he remembered proudly, had assigned him his new position. "Right now it's a division of one," she'd said, "but if DuQuesne's right—and he usually is—I guess we'll need more sooner or later."

He looked to his other side, where there was nothing but smooth bulkhead. *I wish the others were here.* He suddenly smiled, and the smile *hurt*, because it was a smile of memory of loss as much as of fondness. Sha Wujing, Zhu Wuneng, Liu Yan...they could not come, because their world...was not real. The bright golden one, Maria-Susanna, was no longer bright, but dark. And Sanzo was not here.

"Prepare for Transition in ten seconds," Ariane said. He looked at her and heard her voice, and for a moment he wondered if, perhaps, Sanzo *was* here, in a way.

"Good luck, all of you." Saul's voice carried all his concern somehow just below the words. "Take care."

"We will. Thank you, Saul," DuQuesne said quietly.

"In four...three...two...one...Transition!"

Sun Wu Kung gasped at a sudden, indescribable sensation of twisting compression, of expansion beyond measure and crushing force pushing him down into nothingness. It ended, and it seemed to Wu almost as though a curtain had been drawn aside, a storm had passed and cleansed the air, for suddenly the ship seemed brighter, the smells sharper and clearer, the sounds of humming machines and even the breath of his companions stronger, as they passed into a new universe.

"Wow!" he heard himself say. "That was *fun!* That is one of the strangest things I have ever felt! That was *new!*"

Ariane laughed. "Strange, yes, though I admit I wouldn't think of it as...*fun.*" She also seemed... distracted, just for a moment; he noticed a similar odd expression on Simon's face. *Maybe the Transition-thing affects them a little differently. I am...a Hyperion, after all.*

He didn't exactly like thinking of himself as "a Hyperion"—he'd never been anyone or anything except himself. But it was what he was here, and it made him something like DuQuesne's brother, and *that* was a fun thought.

"This new world...is very dark," he finally observed, noticing that there was no sign of light on the forward screen, which had shown many stars and other lights a few moments before.

"Ha!" DuQuesne's voice came, amused. "Here, yeah. The inside of the Sphere's darker than a whole sackful of black cats. But you'll see plenty of light later on, don't worry." A more serious tone. "Ariane, anything on radar?"

"I'm not getting anything new. The model solar system, the Dock, nothing else. I suppose her ship could be in the radar shadow of the Sun equivalent, or maybe Jupiter at this angle, but as far as I can tell we are—right now—the only ship here." He could *hear* the frown in Ariane's voice. "How about the Dock? Can you tell if she's locked on one of the ports?"

"Hold on, let me see if I can get a visual...the Dock emits some light of its own." Wu remembered that it would take a little time to get from the Transition location to the Dock area. "Damn. No, no sign of her at all." The muttered curse DuQuesne muttered was barely audible to Wu—he guessed the others wouldn't hear it at all. "Where the living hell is her ship—"

"The Straits," Simon said with sudden conviction. Wu Kung remembered that term; it meant the large ports in the side of the Sphere that could be opened from the "harbor" area they were in now, to let ships go outside.

"What? Oh *hell*. Could she have...she *couldn't* have...could she?" Wu understood the conflict in DuQuesne's voice. *If she gets away from us...and if she's...really bad now...well, that could be a very not-good thing for everyone. But it's so hard to think of her that way.*

"I don't know, Marc. It wouldn't have occurred to me to even think of it." Ariane glanced curiously at Simon. "I'm surprised *you* thought of it."

By his expression and scent, so was Simon. "I confess I'm not sure why I did, but as soon as it occurred to me I was quite certain."

"How can we check it?" Ariane asked.

"Oh, I think *that's* just plain simple, Arrie," Gabrielle's voice answered. "Gimme an outside transmission line, DuQuesne, please?"

"You got it."

"Strait doors, open," Gabrielle said.

A blaze of light appeared in the pitch blackness, a brilliant line of undifferentiated white that slowly widened, grew into a perfect defined circle larger than the full moon, slightly oval from their current point of view.

Ariane groaned. "Of *course*. We secured the Sphere from intrusion, but I've never specified who could operate anything *internally*. And the Sphere—probably through the Arena itself—is always completely helpful that way." She sighed. "Strait doors, close and lock." The distant circle of light slowly dwindled away to nothing.

"Better fix *that* right quick, then," Gabrielle said.

"Not right this minute," said DuQuesne, "we'll want to think about the exact wording; we don't want to limit it in a way we'll regret later. But Gabrielle's right; we'd better fix that, and any other unexamined assumptions, too."

"Even the *simple* things can trip us up." Ariane glanced at Wu. "You understand what just happened?"

"I think so," he said. "I read the very simplified account of your adventures that DuQuesne and his friend Isaac made. The Sphere does what . . . what was the word? Citizens, citizens of its Faction tell it what to do, unless the leader of the Faction's told it otherwise. So since you hadn't told it to restrict who could unlock the Straits, anyone could open them."

"You got it," DuQuesne said.

"The other alternative," Ariane said, "is that she didn't take much in the way of equipment, just extra power coils, and once she was here, she sent it back out and had it transition home on a vector way out at the edge of the system, where no one's likely to find it."

"Maybe," DuQuesne said reluctantly, and Wu saw Simon's head shake at the same time. "But going through the records of available satellites and other ships we could access back during that period of time, we did get a couple images that were probably of her ship, and it's built *streamlined*—like, for atmosphere. Which pretty much tells me what she meant to do with it. Even stupid automation could make the ship follow some pretty broad rules of performance, get it to go somewhere near enough that she could retrieve it later."

Wu could see Ariane take a deep breath, force herself to relax. "Well, there's no point in worrying about it, now. She's here. We'll catch up with her, or we won't, but for now we just have to dock and see how everyone else is doing."

A few hours later, something immense loomed up in the powerful lights of *Holy Grail*; ridged at intervals, shining like polished black bone, gleaming, organic in its shape, with gold-shining circles showing at intervals. *A great Dragon's skeleton, turned into a mighty building, with golden coins between its polished ribs!* "Amazing! DuQuesne, what a monster that must have been!"

"Don't play the idiot *too* much, Wu," the good-humored voice answered.

"I was joking, oh most dour and humorless of philosophers!" he retorted. *Though that is still what I feel, yes.* "I know it is this 'space dock' that you mentioned, but surely it looks like something else!"

"Yes," agreed Ariane. "Creepy. Which has generally been the word I use whenever the Arena does something."

The skeletal black projection loomed ever closer, as the *Holy Grail* drifted towards it, Ariane lining the ship's docking port up with the matching golden circle. The circle grew, was eclipsed by the hull, as *Holy Grail* moved ever slower... and then a vibration of gentle impact echoed through the ship. "*Holy Grail* docked to Sphere, all secure," Ariane said. "Free to unstrap. Still in microgravity at this time."

He unsnapped immediately and flipped out of his chair, landing on the ceiling; his toe-claws extended and anchored him, and he looked at Ariane upside-down as she unstrapped. "I love this floating!"

She grinned. "I see you do. Just be careful." She spoke in a slightly louder tone that had the undefinable sound of the 'official' Ariane. "Do we have any more preparations to make, or are we ready to disembark?"

"Not for me, Captain," said DuQuesne.

"I think we should just move," Gabrielle agreed. "When we've checked on our friends, then we can move the cargo over, but right now I'm too darn nervous to want to waste the time."

Ariane glanced at Simon, who nodded; for Wu's part, his job was making sure Ariane stayed safe, so he left when she did.

"Okay, then, let's move out." She led the way towards the airlock. "Remember the briefing, Wu," she said, looking at him. "You'll have gravity inside, so get oriented correctly when passing through."

"Don't worry about me," he said confidently. "You can change your gravity whenever you like, and I'll *always* land on my feet. If I want to."

She smiled—*a very nice smile*, he thought. "I bet you will."

Wu inserted himself in front of Ariane as they reached the airlock, to her obvious surprise. "We don't know if anyone's waiting on the other side," he pointed out.

She blinked, then nodded. *At least I don't have to remind her just who might be waiting there.* After a moment, the inner lock opened, and he looked out cautiously, staff in guard position. No one was visible in either direction up or down the large docking area, so he stepped out; Ariane followed, with DuQuesne, Simon, and Gabrielle bringing up the rear.

"We'll have to walk from here," Ariane said. "Once we get a larger group established in the Arena we'll have to set up a shuttle, rail, something that allows quick transport."

"Maglev rail." DuQuesne said. "Perfect setup for it here. Limited access, linear, flat, need efficient transport; put a spur at each of the airlocks, and we've got more than enough space for several cyclic transport loops, and we'll need it eventually. In a gravity field, barring water transport, there's no better method."

"I suppose you're right," Simon said, with a bemused expression. "I must admit, however, I find it somewhat . . . odd to imagine this place being a bustling center of commerce."

"We'd better hope it becomes one, Simon—soon," Ariane said.

Wu was impressed; the images from the outside had told him the Dock was huge, but you couldn't quite grasp that size in your mind until you were *inside*. It was kilometers long, although *Holy Grail* had chosen a docking point very near the entrance.

The entrance itself reminded him of the gates of Enma-Sama's fortress—a tremendous, massive portal that if closed would be almost impenetrable, but was always open. A line of lights showed the straight route deeper into the Sphere.

"Guess the others'll be at the Guardhouse," Gabrielle said.

"Guardhouse?"

Ariane smiled. "Gabrielle's name for the mini-settlement we've built near the real entrance to the Inner Sphere. I suppose it's not a bad name for it if it *does* become a settlement."

He led the way, following the line of lights, and the full *scale* of the interior of the Sphere hit him. *It is like a world, a world of dead air and no light.* He shivered suddenly, against his will. *It is like . . . a tomb. A tomb of Hyperion.*

Fear was not a common emotion for him—one so rare, in fact, that it took a moment for him to acknowledge it. *But when I feel it, it's always over . . . this. DuQuesne promised me a shining new world, of gods and monsters and bright skies. I know he must be telling the truth . . . but here it is dark. It* smells *of death, of things long, long gone, the realm of the forgotten dead.* He started to quicken his stride towards the brighter area in the far distance, noticed that he was starting to outpace the others, forced himself to slow. *They are not as soft as most people, but they aren't nearly as fast as I am.* Even so, he was impressed by how quickly Ariane was walking; he realized she was anxious to get to her other friends and find out what might have happened while they were gone.

Even though it seemed to take a long time, it was actually only a relatively few minutes before they reached the brightly illuminated area surrounding the Inner Door, hexagonal tiled floor now clean for probably the first time in millions of years, shining a brown-gold in the lights set up by the impromptu colonists. Wu found himself breathing a sigh of relief as he entered the lighted area and smelled ahead the scent of other living people, food; even the undertone of working machines was welcome after passing through that cavernous, silent, dead space.

A figure about his own height appeared in the doorway of one of the three buildings and suddenly sprinted towards them. *"ARIANE!"*

He stepped reflexively between Ariane and the newcomer, who skidded to a halt in confusion; another, much taller, man who had been emerging from the same doorway also paused.

"Wu!" Ariane's voice was reproving. "These are our other friends."

Their scents didn't seem hostile, and obviously Ariane knew them; DuQuesne also smelled happy to see the others, so he stepped back.

The smaller of the two unfamiliar people immediately embraced Ariane, giving Wu a curious glance in passing. "Good to see you back, Ariane!"

"Good to see both you and Tom, Steve," she answered, hugging the other, smaller man hard, and then giving a similar hug to Tom; she then turned to Wu. "Steve,

Tom, this is Sun Wu Kung; Wu, these good friends of mine are Stephen Franceschetti and Thomas Cussler."

"I am honored to make your acquaintance," he said, and bowed low.

"Glad to meet you too...Wu Kung?"

Thomas Cussler shook his hand, studying him closely. Then his head snapped up and he stared at DuQuesne. "Is this—?"

"Yep."

"We'll talk about that later. We've got a *lot* to talk about, Steve."

Steve looked around at the others and then looked at his friend Tom. *Scent...oh, they're* that *close. Important to remember.* "I knew it. That Doctor Shoshana."

"She's here, then." DuQuesne made it a statement.

"Not *here*, not now, no," Tom answered. "She went on to Nexus Arena to meet with Carl and Laila."

"She had all the right credentials," Steve said. "Here taking a firsthand look for the SSC and CSF. Staff scientist assigned to the new Arena task force, verifying some of your material."

"I'm sure she did, Steve," DuQuesne said. "If you were even a *little* suspicious of her, you got farther than most people. But we'll have to get after her as soon as we can."

"Who *is* she, then?"

"Open up for a data dump?" Ariane asked. "Simon, you've got it all arranged in your head."

"Yes, that would be the fastest way."

Wu wasn't quite sure what they meant, but it was probably something like a spiritual transfer; *that* could be pretty rough.

By Steve's reaction, the same applied here. "Whoa,

hold on, let me get ready for something like that." There was a pause, and he could tell by sight and smell that both Steve and Tom were bracing for some kind of shock. "Okay, dump it."

Simon's brow furrowed, and the other two grunted, eyes unfocused as they attempted to make sense of a huge amount of data delivered all at once. A few moments passed, and both men sat down hard. "Oh, crap. Not good."

"Very not-good," agreed DuQuesne, "and we've got a lot of work ahead of us. What else did she do? Was she carrying anything?"

"She did quick interviews on us," Tom said, "but it was clear she was just confirming whatever she'd gotten from you guys earlier, when you reported to the SSC. Then she said her instructions were to at least get to the Arena proper, talk to the other members of the *Grail* crew, maybe ask a few other questions and then head back with her info."

"She was carrying a shoulder-slung carryall," Steve said. "It seemed pretty full, now that I think about it."

Ariane's mouth tightened, and Wu smelled a wash of annoyance. "Damn. We have no idea what she's brought with her, but I'm sure she's thought it out very well. Bargaining chips of some kind, I'll bet."

"Run that bet across the board for me, too," agreed DuQuesne grimly. "She means to put herself in a position to accomplish something, and I don't think she has any interest in going back to the Solar System."

"Not immediately, no," said Simon. "But Marc, she may have reason to return here."

DuQuesne thought about it, then cursed again. "You're right, and she's almost certainly covered that base." He looked at Tom. "You guys gave her the ability to open that door, didn't you?" he asked, pointing at the large portal that was currently closed behind them.

Steve nodded reluctantly. "Yeah. I mean, we had no way of knowing when she was coming back, and it didn't seem like a problem—"

"You don't have to apologize, Steve. She's spent a long lifetime fooling people. Damnation!"

"No huge problem, Marc," Ariane said. "We'll just re-instruct the Sphere on the admission priorities."

"Hmph. Might work, but if you don't think she's thought of that, you're dumber than I think you are. She's *real* good at giving instructions to machines—like all us Hyperions were. Even if you give it explicit instructions, don't be sure for a minute that she didn't figure out a way to keep those instructions from applying to her."

"We'll worry about that later. For now, I think we'd better go on, see how things are with Carl and Laila."

"Right."

Steve nodded. "You guys get moving; come back here for an update on everything we've done—DuQuesne, we'll definitely want you to take a look at the work we've got going on the Upper Sphere."

"Sure thing."

The next door rolled open for them, and Wu saw a blaze of white light from the interior. Nothing appeared to be a threat, but he once more took up a forward position.

Someone—probably, he guessed, Dr. Franceschetti, who seemed the thinking-ahead sort—had marked the path to the thing they called the Inner Gateway, marked it clearly with strips of bright red reflective material. That made it easy for him to stay in front without having to ask everyone where they were going.

He stopped, then ran forward as they reached the final room. "Wow! That's *cool!*"

The Inner Gateway swirled with darkness and light, and he thought he heard something singing, like crystal thinking thoughts of stars. He reached out without thinking, even as Ariane shouted, "Hold *on*, Wu!"

The Inner Gateway enveloped him in an embrace of cold like the Winter Hells, as lightning-scent filled his nostrils and sparks of the sky-fire rippled through his fur, falling, falling past vistas in dark-flowing light that moved too fast, were far too mighty in scope, filled with shapes too improbable for even the Monkey King to grasp all in a moment; even as he tried to understand he burst through into brilliant golden light.

He stumbled to a halt, momentarily in awe. He stood atop one of many platforms in a room as large as the Dragon King's palace, huge as Hyperion, with a thousand great Gateways seething with dark power and pearlescent promise. And there were *people!*

There, a pair of flowing shapes, like animated water filled with strange globules and translucent complex shapes; there, a massive creature, like a many-legged lizard with an upright, four-armed torso; birdlike things that made him think of *tengu*; and so many more. "Oh, *suGOI!*" he exclaimed.

The others were just emerging from the Gateway as he looked above, then bounded up, an easy leap to the mid-point of the carven metal circle of the Gateway a mere ten meters above, flipped himself up and around to land atop the great ring, to survey a room filled with wonders.

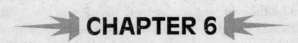

CHAPTER 6

That's Wu, DuQuesne thought with a fond smile, even as he and the other three followed the impulsive Monkey King through. *Even when he's on-duty, he's still a kid in so many ways.*

As they arrived, he heard Wu give an exclamation that meant roughly "wonderful!" In a single flurry of motion Wu Kung streaked up the Gateway, reached the very crest of the arch and stood there, bouncing and glancing in all directions like a child at an amusement park. "There's so many different *kinds* of people here, DuQuesne!" he shouted. "No immediate threats I can see. Hey, Captain, don't go too far! Stay in sight! Oh, look over there, those are Molothos, right?"

Oh, blasted HELL. DuQuesne looked in the direction indicated by the crimson-and-gold staff. Sure enough, Dajzail—DuQuesne could recognize him now, by a handsome almost geometric pattern on his fighting claws—and four other Molothos were crossing Transition. He heard Ariane draw in her breath.

Fortunately, although he could see the Molothos' gaze swivel, taking in their presence (and pausing momentarily in obvious bemusement at the tiny out-of-place figure atop the Gateway), the jackknife-clawed aliens apparently weren't prepared for or interested in a confrontation at this time; they moved on and out of sight. *Just as well; I've got to figure out how to rein Wu in while still leaving him free to act the way he has to. We don't want him being a convenient lever for someone to Challenge with simply because he's got the Monkey King's curiosity and sometimes low sense of humor.*

He realized the others were now staring up at Wu Kung. Arian looked at DuQuesne incredulously. "How the hell did he get UP there?" Wu had of course come through before her, but he'd apparently moved slightly aside on entry, so his leap-and-scramble had happened out of her sight.

"*Monkey*, remember. Give him something to climb, he'll climb it."

Ariane shook her head and gave a slight gasp as Wu came down by sliding down the side until he departed from the curve about 12 meters up, somersaulted twice, and landed with the same casual grace of a gymnast dismounting from a one-meter horse. DuQuesne heard Simon mutter something disbelieving. *I'll also have to give him a reminder about subtlety. Not that it's likely to do any good; his idea of subtle was generally to sneak up behind you before going "boo!"*

Wu bounced back in front of the group, leading them towards the entrance of Nexus Arena, staring wide-eyed at everything and everyone around him, exclaiming in wonder and excitement. A never-ending flow of questions streamed over his shoulder, leaving Ariane—the target of most of those questions—looking both amused and bemused.

"Marc," Simon said, watching Wu, "far be it from

me to question your judgment—given your record—but . . . I have a hard time believing that our new friend is quite as attentive as a bodyguard ought to be; honestly, he's acting almost like a *child*."

He grinned. "Does kinda look that way, doesn't it? But let me tell you, that hyperactive overgrown toddler is absolutely and completely aware of *anything* that might be a threat to Ariane; when it comes down to the ugly, Wu's sharper than a cutting laser and about a thousand numbers Brinnell harder than a diamond drill. Anyone thinks Ariane's unprotected because her bodyguard's distracted . . ." He shook his head. "Believe you me, that's the very last mistake they'll *ever* make."

Simon smiled faintly. "You speak from experience, so I will take your word for it," he said, as Wu suddenly pointed with childlike excitement to one of the blue-green Chiroflekir as it half-floated across Transition's floor, "but you must admit it's hard to imagine." He tilted his head, obviously listening. "Great *kami*, I thought my blending of languages was an abomination, but I swear I hear—"

"Yeah, Japanese, Mandarin, Cantonese, Hindi, and a smattering of others including English."

"In the name of . . . well, sanity, *why?*"

DuQuesne sighed. "Thought it was obvious. That version of Sun Wu Kung isn't from any one source. Like I told Ariane, they took every major version of Journey to the West and of the Monkey King and . . . put them in a blender, everything from the legends of Hanuman to ancient cartoons, the original Journey to the West, Manak's epic virtual world adventure Seven Worlds of Wu Kung, all of them.

"You see, the Hyperion SFG wouldn't allow multiple

versions of the same character to be made, so people either had to select one particular version, or make a combined one. Whoever was running that sim, well, they decided to *really* go to town. That mangled language actually sorta hangs together, but it's a *bitch* to learn. Good thing he speaks our version of English pretty well." DuQuesne managed a faint smile, though the subject hurt, like picking at an open wound. "I can't really laugh at him over it, though; same thing's true of me."

"You? I thought—from what Ariane said—that there really was a character named Marc C. DuQuesne." They were now approaching the immense array of elevators that served Transition and brought people to the main levels of Nexus Arena.

"Yeah, but...not exactly. See, my...designer, he was a real big fan of the guy who wrote those books, and the same guy—called Doc Smith—had written another really popular series back in the day. The people running the Hyperion SFG were adamant that my designer could only have one character from Smith's writings, so he ended up combining both Smith's *Lensman* and *Skylark* series, and making me a combination of a couple of the heroes from both. Admittedly, I'm more Marc C. DuQuesne than I am any of the others, but if you read the books, I sure as hell am not *that* DuQuesne—and thank all the gods—and my designer—for that." *And I hope my note got to you, old man; I owed you that much thanks, and if she never caught up with you, you're safe now.*

"My main worry," Gabrielle said quietly, "is just what that Maria-Susanna's up to. Do you think she'll be at the Embassy?"

"I'd think there's a good chance of it," Simon said. "After all, it's been only a day or so since she left."

"Hmph." DuQuesne couldn't quite repress the snort. "Maybe, but remember, she *thought this out*. And she's one hell of a high-powered thinker when she's trying."

"But she knew the schedule," Simon pointed out, stepping inside the elevator with the others. Ariane and Wu Kung turned their heads, listening to the conversation. "She'd know she had at least a few days."

"She'd know the *schedule* gave her at least a few days," DuQuesne corrected him. "But if you could detect her jumping out, she'd assume I'd break every speed limit there was to catch up with her."

"But Simon just *invented* the detection device," Ariane protested. "Why would she assume anything like that?"

"You tell me, Simon; if you were in her position, just as smart as you, knowing what she'd know about the Drive—would she be able to reasonably guess that it was practically possible to detect?"

Simon frowned. The doors opened and they walked out into the main floor of Nexus Arena, on which were located all of the Embassies, the Powerbrokers, and the entrances to the actual Arena Challenge levels. After another few moments, he grimaced. "Yes, I'm afraid she would. The capability is implicit in the way the system works, if you understand it sufficiently. The light-signature from the drive is very distinctive, even leaving aside the spacetime effects."

Gabrielle shrugged. "All right. So she'll only be there if she's planned on meeting us, then."

"That's the way I'd bet."

Ariane waved over one of the "taxis," the automated
public transports that looked like open-roofed and flex-
ibly configured maglev transit cars. Wu Kung stepped
smoothly between Ariane and the vehicle, leaped into
it and ran from one end to the other, eyes covering
every square centimeter of the taxi in seconds. "Okay,"
he said, and stood watchfully as the others boarded.

"Is that really necessary?" Ariane asked.

"Yes," Wu said without hesitation. "Sure, there's only
a very small chance someone might be trying to kill
you in any given place, but if I ignore all the small
chances they add up to a big chance. There's some
I *have* to ignore, because we just don't have time.
There's others I don't know about yet. And there's
some I'll miss because you're in private, or because
I get sent somewhere else. But the ones I can, I'll
watch for. Okay?"

She smiled and DuQuesne couldn't help but grin
with her. "Yes, okay. If I have to have a bodyguard,
I suppose I have to let him do his job."

The taxi, having been instructed by Ariane, quickly
pulled up to the broad, simply-ornamented front of the
Embassy of Humanity. DuQuesne noted a bystander—a
Milluk, a gray-black spherical body on jointed spidery
legs—turn as they approached, and a small green-
glowing sphere appeared nearby. *An observer, roving
reporter, something like that, now letting someone know
that there's activity at the Embassy. If he's got good
data or observing skills, he also knows that the captain's back, which will kick everything into high gear.*

The door opened as they approached—DuQuesne
in front this time as Wu Kung covered the rear—and
they entered the foyer.

DuQuesne felt his eyebrows climb. The entranceway had been transformed in their absence. A series of well-spaced statues—of people, animals, symbols—circled the entire room, while artworks ranging from what appeared to be duplicates of Old Masters to the recent Inversion-Projection period concept light-sculptures hung from or were projected near the walls. The walls and floor themselves had changed from the default concrete and metal appearance; there was carefully selected panelling that looked like natural wood and the floor was a polished marble-like substance. "That's . . . quite a change."

"DuQuesne? *ARIANE?* Holy crap, you're *back!*" Carl Edlund's voice echoed around the room from the door that had suddenly opened at the far end of the foyer. He ran forward; DuQuesne could see Wu tense momentarily, but he'd apparently decided not to do any more blocking when old friends met up. "Why the hell didn't you *call?*" Carl hugged Ariane, shook DuQuesne's and Simon's hands, and gave Gabrielle a longer hug and a kiss that echoed the one she'd given him on departure. "And who's your new friend?"

"Sun Wu Kung, meet Carl Edlund."

"Pleased to meet you, Carl! Call me Wu, since you are obviously friends with my friends."

"Glad to meet you. So what's your line? You sure don't look like SSC standard issue to me."

Wu laughed. "Ha! No, I am not at all!"

"We'll talk about Wu a little later," Ariane cut in. "Carl, where's Dr. Shoshana?"

"Dr. who?" Carl looked genuinely confused. At the same time, Laila Canning entered from one of the rear doors and glanced around the little group.

Marc felt grimly vindicated. "She had no intention of making contact here. She's gone somewhere else—and unless someone volunteers the information, we haven't a chance of finding her."

"Oh, come *on*, Marc," Ariane said. "There's no other human beings in the entire Arena. How's she going to *hide*?"

"In plain sight, so to speak. All she's got to do is convince a Faction—big one, small one, doesn't matter—that she's got something good enough to trade, and get into their Embassy. Then she's got access to the Arena, allies, and secrecy."

Laila's brown eyes studied them curiously, and DuQuesne had to once more fight off the lingering suspicion he'd had—since Laila had been brought back from apparent brain-death by the Faith—that Laila was not really Laila Canning at all any more. "Who, precisely, *is* this person you're worried about?" she asked.

"Her current alias is Marilyn Shoshana, supposedly an agent for the SSC; her real name is Maria-Susanna and she's the renegade Hyperion that's been at the top of the wanted lists for the past fifty years."

Laila just stared narrowly; Carl winced. "Holy crap. That's . . . not good."

"We've got a whole lot of 'not good' for you right now," Ariane said, gesturing for the others to follow her to one of the Embassy's conference rooms, "and you'd better let us fill you in." She ran one hand through her deep blue hair. "And I'd hoped we'd *solve* some problems before we came back."

CHAPTER 7

"Well, *that* does seem to rather complicate things," Laila said, pushing her own bobbed brown hair back with a distracted air. Ariane noted that she seemed to have absorbed the data-dump more easily than Carl. *Not surprising—she was used to having three fully-active AISages before we came here, and losing them nearly killed her. If anyone can handle immense amounts of data in one shot, it's Dr. Laila Canning.*

"Yeah. Whoa." Carl blinked, shook his head. "Ouch! You know, Ariane, every time you go somewhere you seem to pick up more trouble along the way."

"Don't I know it." She looked at both of them. "Now you're up to speed on what happened with us—how have things been here?"

"Mostly fairly quiet, actually. Everyone knew you were for a while, and aside from the Molothos trying a couple of times to annoy one of us into initiating a Challenge, everyone seemed perfectly happy to wait for a while. Your friend Relgof," he nodded at Simon, "still drops by fairly often to check on things; the Analytic's clearly really interested in getting us to either join their Faction or at least get some formal alliance going, maybe get some human members."

"Mandallon, our appointed Initiate Guide, is also a frequent visitor; he sometimes escorts me to view some of the Faith's rituals," Laila said. "Both he and Relgof volunteered information on how to customize our Embassy further, and Steve followed through on that—very well, I think."

"I *thought* I recognized Steve's touch. So you've been trading off duties here?"

"Yeah, just like you said; make sure we all keep in touch, cycle those on duty," Carl confirmed; then he grinned, the smile lighting up his narrow, sharp face. "We didn't just hide out in the Embassy, either. I did go to another Challenge—two minor Factions contesting over some offense—with Selpa'a'At." She nodded; one couldn't easily forget the strange spidery Swordmaster First of the Vengeance. "There's more than a professional interest there—Selpa's obviously a fan of the Challenges as sport, so I learned a *lot* about Challenges listening to him. Recorded, of course—I'll give you all that."

"Good work, Carl," DuQuesne said. "We're walking a fine, fine line here, and anything that gives us better relationships with the other Factions without giving away the store is great."

"Thanks, but honestly, I didn't need much arm-twisting to go. It's a dozen sports all in one, with real stuff at stake." He looked over at Ariane. "I wasn't your main mechanic in the Unlimited just for the tech challenge, after all."

"Can't blame you," Gabrielle said. "Though I could sure do without any more heart-in-my-mouth Challenges like the one that almost got Ariane killed."

"Yeah," agreed Carl. "So anyway, that's about it—we've talked with some of the others off and on but nothing of substance." He raised an eyebrow. "So . . . what now?"

Everyone was looking at her now. *You're the Leader of the Faction,* Captain *Austin. You don't like it, you don't want it—even less now—but it's your job for now, so suck it up and get moving.* Though she would *much* rather have left it to DuQuesne or someone else, Ariane straightened and tried to look properly captain-like.

"Honestly, I had hoped to return with a lot more people to help us get things done here. Instead, as Carl points out, I seem to have managed to return with no more people but a lot more problems. We need to address all of those problems, and the others we already knew about." She looked at Simon. "Dr. Sandrisson, in your best estimation, how long will it be until the *Duta* and Mr. Naraj's people join us here in the Arena?"

Simon frowned, pushed the round-lensed glasses that were one of his affectations up his nose slightly, then leaned back, obviously thinking. "It's somewhat difficult to say; the *Duta* is a larger vessel and the design is quite different when compared to the *Grail,* and they will be getting their own cargo together. However, they have many more people working on this . . ." Another pause. "No less than three days, no more than a week, I would say."

Damn. I had hoped for more than that. "All right. So we need to decide how we'll deal with them when they arrive. Our other problems . . . Dr. DuQuesne, how would you rank them?"

"Hard to say, Captain. Leaving aside Naraj, Ni Deng, and whoever they bring with them—and let me just say that even if they only bring one or two, that's going to be a royal pain to watch with only eight of us—our other major problems are the Molothos, possibly the Blessed, getting ourselves ready to defend our Sphere, figuring out how to expand our territory—we have *got* to get at least one more Sphere—and of course our unexpected visitor Maria-Susanna." He paused, a brooding expression on his face, before continuing. "We've got to increase our *ability* to project our presence in the Arena, which means we have to get those Sky Gates they talk about up and running. We need ships that will work in the Arena proper; I think the *Duta* is being designed with that in mind, but . . ."

"But," Ariane finished, "we can't build or buy them here without resources." She looked around. "We may have to send one or two of us back to get some kind of ship built back home that *we* can use."

DuQuesne winced, and she shrugged. "I know, Marc. I hate the idea myself—we honestly can't *spare* any of us. If I *have* to I'd probably have to send Steve and Tom—Steve oversaw the *Holy Grail*'s construction, Tom did the maintenance, the two would have all the right knowledge."

"But without them, work on our Sphere installations will slow *way* down," DuQuesne said. "I guess a lot will depend on how much we can get for the cargo you brought, Gabrielle."

"I'd guess, yes," Gabrielle said. "I'll go back shortly and get it unloaded and bring it back here. We want to get first on the market, before *Duta* gets here. I'm pretty much certain, Arrie, that some of the pieces I couldn't get were ones the SSC already had put an option on. But if we start selling ours first, we get the initial interest spike."

"Okay, Gabrielle." Ariane felt a quick, small spark of satisfaction; Gabrielle had remembered that Arena residents were interested in real, non-nanotech manufactured products from new worlds and had gathered a surprising cargo while they were away. *One positive thing to do, anyway.* "I think that's an obvious and necessary step and it's something we can get on right away." She looked back to Simon. "What about the Sky Gates? Those are supposed to be activated by Sandrisson Drives somehow, correct?"

"As I understand it, yes. If you enter one of the Gates and activate the Drive as one would for a normal Transition, you are transported to the other side of the Gate instantaneously, whether that 'other side' is to the next Sphere over, to Nexus Arena, or even to a Sphere corresponding with a world halfway across the entire universe.

"If you invert the Sandrisson field, you are dropped back into the normal universe at some distance—I believe roughly a light-year—from the associated star system."

"How do we locate these Gates?"

"I . . . do not know, yet. I was intending to research this as one of my first projects after our return."

Another clear priority. "I think that's necessary. You should contact Dr. Relgof of the Analytic as soon as we're done here." Simon nodded, and she continued, "All right. Now, as to the imminent arrival of our SSC representatives . . ." *Bite that bullet, Ariane.* "I'll meet with them as soon as they arrive—I want them *escorted* here immediately. No chance for them to go somewhere else or get involved with *anything* until they've been brought to the Embassy and been briefed *here*. If possible, I'll escort them myself."

"I will be with you," Wu emphasized.

She smiled faintly. "You and Marc have already made that clear. But this does bring up something else—maybe not quite as important . . . but maybe so, in the long run." She glanced at DuQuesne. "Marc, a good bodyguard needs to understand the territory. I understand that I will have Wu with me essentially all the time when I am outside of the Embassy or other secure areas. However, if I *am* staying here in our Embassy, I want Wu to spend some time familiarizing himself with Nexus Arena, with some of the people we know, and with our Sphere—Inner and Upper. He needs to grasp this . . . place," she still didn't know what to call the Arena as a concept; world? Universe? "at least as well as we do. His instincts need to be adjusted to all the differences of the Arena." She smiled at Wu. "Plus, even the best bodyguard needs some time to himself, and in a place *this* amazing . . . can we really cage the Monkey King?"

"Ha!" Wu Kung laughed joyously. "Only the Buddha managed it before! Thank you, Ariane! I *do* want to see this place myself!"

"You're right, Ariane," DuQuesne said, echoing Wu's smile. "And I'll hammer some rules of behavior into him so he doesn't, hopefully, wreck our most delicate negotiations."

"Good," she said. "Getting back to the earlier discussion . . . I will also let them in on our joker in the pack when I meet with them."

"Are you sure?" Gabrielle asked. "I am *certain* they will be very unhappy with that little piece of information."

"Ariane's right," DuQuesne said. "No way do we want them finding out Ariane's the Faction Leader from anyone *else*. If we brief them right away, they'll be peeved but we'll keep them from making fools of themselves, or forcing themselves into a Challenge or something by making assumptions that aren't correct."

"Thank you, Marc." She thought a moment. "As for Maria-Susanna...we have to find out where she is, and what she is doing, but I'm not sure it's easily done. I could of course just try to use the Arena's abilities to contact her and ask what her intentions are, but she could refuse contact or lie, as it suited her."

"Yeah. If she didn't come to the Embassy in the first place, she has a plan that doesn't involve using us as intermediaries, for which I guess I should be grateful. We'll have to try to figure out how to ask around subtly. We might get the chance when our new friends arrive—they'll want to be introduced, and maybe we could drop hints then—or even earlier, if the Factions know we're here—"

A brilliant green ball of light popped into existence over the table; Ariane mostly repressed the startled jump. From it came a familiar, deep, somehow ironic and humorous voice. "Captain Ariane Austin, welcome back to the Arena."

She couldn't repress a smile at that voice. "Orphan! Nice to hear from the great Leader of the Liberated!"

As Orphan was the sole member of the Liberated, this would have been possibly risky humor from someone else; but as Orphan had, himself, used similar jests in her presence, he took it with good humor. "I did think of delegating the contact to my First Minister Orphan, but Ambassador Orphan reminded me that it is best to maintain good relations by personal interaction."

"Good that you have such sage advisors, Leader. What can we do for you, or was this simply a welcome call?" Somehow, she doubted it was so simple. Little in the Arena was, after all.

"Actually, I have a proposition for the Faction of Humanity...and some information I believe you would find useful."

"A proposition?" She glanced at the others. "We would be very happy to hear any offers you might have, Orphan. Despite certain...events, I still think of you as a friend and ally. So please, speak on."

"Ahh, Captain Austin, I would rather you—and the others, if they like—come visit me at my Embassy."

"Well...I'm sure I can arrange it sometime, but we have a lot of things complicating matters at the moment."

"Oh, no doubt," Orphan answered. "A new-minted Faction with some *most* interesting...challenges, if you will, to deal with, and I am sure some additional matters from your own people." It was clear that Orphan understood the potential problems, even though he couldn't have specific knowledge of just what those problems were.

But now there was an unmistakable dramatic edge to his voice, and he continued, "But I did, also, mention information, I believe. Perhaps it would intrigue you sufficiently if I were to mention that, a full day before the news of your return spread throughout Nexus Arena, I had a most interesting visitor...a most interesting *human* visitor?"

CHAPTER 8

"Welcome back, Captain Austin, Dr. DuQuesne," Orphan said expansively as she and Marc entered, Wu Kung just behind her. Simon was visiting Relgof and the Analytic, starting discussions to find out about the Sky Gates, while Gabrielle and Carl were moving their merchandise from the *Grail* to the Embassy; Laila Canning was currently at the Embassy in case others came to call.

Orphan's hard, chitin-like exterior seemed glossier than ever, the deep green and black like an exotic uniform as he completed a deep push-bow, then turned to their third member. "And a first welcome to you...?"

"Sun Wu Kung. It is a pleasure to meet you, Mr. Orphan!"

Ariane couldn't restrain another smile. *Whatever else he can do well, he's made me smile more in the last few days than I'd ever have believed.*

Orphan's translated voice, too, held a note of humor. "No honorific, please. Just Orphan. It is my name and my condition. I welcome you, Sun Wu Kung. And you? No title? No honorific?"

"None, or far too many," Wu Kung answered, staring around at the mysterious patterns ornamenting the entrance of the Liberated's Embassy. "I am the captain's bodyguard, and for that I need no title at all; elsewhere I have many titles but they are of no matter here."

Orphan's face was not as mobile as a human's, and the twin crests of green-black on his head did not move. But Ariane had learned to interpret quite a bit of the semi-insectoid alien's body language, and the scissoring of the black wingcases and shift in posture showed his surprise. "A bodyguard, you say?" He glanced to DuQuesne, clearly trying to read him. "I hope you take no offense at my saying that I find it hard to think that you would be as... effective a bodyguard as she might need, if she fails to be able to protect herself—which failure, in itself, would be no small feat, as I have seen her in battle. Dr. DuQuesne, for instance, would be more what I would have envisioned."

Wu's smile showed his sharp canines, and DuQuesne chuckled. "Orphan, you remember back when we had to fight Amas-Garao together?"

The sole member of the Liberated vibrated in a way that even an untutored human would have recognized as a shudder. "I could hardly forget it," he said, with an uncharacteristic tension and nervousness in his tones, his hands making an abortive gesture outwards which would mean *no*.

"No, I would guess not. But you admit we worked well together."

The wingcases relaxed slightly and the richer tones of Orphan's voice showed that he was back to himself.

"Indeed, I would. A terrifying battle, but a transcendant one in its own way, and ours was a marvelous dance with death."

"Then maybe, in a couple of days, you'll come over to our Embassy and we can do some sparring. With Wu."

Orphan bowed. "I would be honored. I sense that you will be showing me the error of such simplistic assessments. It should be . . . entertaining."

"It will be that."

The alien drew himself back up dramatically. "But I did not call you here merely to meet your mysterious new—and, I note, tailed, which does not appear to be the norm with your people—bodyguard."

"No, you said you had both some news and a proposition for us."

"Precisely so." Orphan led the way to one of his own embassy's meeting rooms, where human-style chairs were already extruded from the floor and one more suited for Orphan's tailed, winged form rose up as he approached. "As I said, that most charming renegade of yours, Maria-Susanna, approached me the second day of her presence here."

"Used that name, did she?" DuQuesne said.

"She did indeed."

"How did she approach you?"

"Oh, quite directly. She came to this Embassy and requested an audience, which I naturally granted her as I am always interested in those with a personal approach, and she was, apparently, a new member of your Faction, and your people are still quite something of a novelty.

"She then got straight to business, as one might say,

stating that she had a great deal of sympathy for the cause of the Liberated and that she was considering joining my Faction, if that were possible. A most... startling and emphatic opening move."

"And you turned her down?" Ariane was somewhat surprised.

"Oh, hardly so swiftly as that, I assure you. Indeed, I was most flattered and at first very much interested. The Liberated cannot afford to turn down any applicants unless there is truly an overriding reason to do so. And she offered a great deal of value."

DuQuesne grunted. "Like all of the secrets of humanity on a plate."

"On a plate...yes, I grasp your idiom, and it's quite a useful one." Orphan looked momentarily pensive. "You know, this once more gives me pause to wonder how it is that the Arena will decide to translate versus transliterate. There are clearly times it translates one concept to another, while at other times it appears to merely translate the words into the nearest reasonable equivalent." He gave the wing-snap which signified a shrug, and continued. "Yes, but then again, not nearly all, at least not to begin with. Clearly she was far from foolish; she wanted to offer the minimum of information which would be worth admission to my Faction, and hold the rest for later bargaining—with me, or with others outside of the Faction."

"So," Ariane said when he paused, "what made you turn her down?"

Orphan stroked one of his headcrests thoughtfully. "A number of things, really. She—quite wisely—was forthcoming about her legal status in your home system. This of course presented me with a problem which is, alas, vastly more important for me than it would be for Selpa, Nyanthus, or most other leaders of other Factions."

"Got it," DuQuesne said, nodding. "With your role as gadfly to the Blessed, you've got damn few allies, even personal ones. Selpa hasn't had to rely on humanity to bail the Vengeance out, old Nyanthus doesn't need us to support him in a pinch, the Analytic don't have to worry that we might dump them, and it's hard to imagine any of them ever would. You've had to rely on us, and might have to again."

Orphan's wingcases scissored in the pendulum-like motion that indicated either reluctant agreement or a "yes and no" state. "I would perhaps not have put it quite so bluntly. Yet . . . yes, I suppose there is no better simple way to say it. Despite certain temporary conflicts of interest, I have, I hope, been of signal service to Humanity, and in return you have assisted me in regaining much . . . face, would be the correct way to put it, as well as in truth showing me much of myself. While these debts are mostly even, still I am not so unwise as to sacrifice one alliance for another single individual. At the same time, that was not all."

"Oh, really?" DuQuesne looked interested.

"Quite so. You see, I of course conducted quite a long interview with her. There is a phrase the Faith often uses, *todai miriola* in the language of their current leader, which is best translated as 'the Way of Spoken Warfare' . . ." he paused, chuckled. "And there again is that question of translation! Ahh, I have not *thought* about these things in centuries! But where was I? Ahh, yes. For the Initiate Guides who travel to new worlds, meet new species, this is meant as the description of how you defend and advance the Faith's belief in the face of ideological opposition, but *todai miriola* is more often simply a reference to a conversation which is a genteel battle between two who seek to gain the better of the other in the discussion. And indeed was my interview with Maria-Susanna such a battle. I sought to discover more of her, her motivations, her long-term goals, her relationship with all of you, her history, as well as information about humanity. She was after more information about me, of course, my resources, my goals, and so on." The wingcases tightened and released. "I pride myself on being a master of this form of warfare, but I found that in this woman I had met my equal. I am honestly unsure if she learned more of me than I did of her.

"But I *did* learn some interesting facts; that she has some connection to you, Doctor DuQuesne, and that she is very reluctant to reveal more of this background, which still disturbs her; that she is a criminal of your people, apparently sufficiently so that there is no real safe haven for her in Humanity's home system; and that she has spent a long time operating alone.

"The latter, combined with other indications, was what finally decided me. Someone with her advantages—and, if my assessment of human behavior and appearance is anything close to correct, she has many advantages— who could not, or dared not, have any aides, allies, or close friends, is someone with a secret I cannot afford to bring into my Faction, not in my current position."

DuQuesne nodded, as did Ariane. Once more she was impressed by the way Orphan operated. He had reached an accurate conclusion about Maria-Susanna with minimal information, deducing from what he knew about a species he'd only met for the first time a few months ago. "Well, I have to say I'm very, very glad you turned her down. Not that I'm happy with, once more, having no idea where she's gone, but..." She paused, not quite sure how to say what she wanted.

"I think what the captain wants to say is that despite knowing you're generally an opportunistic bastard out for your own goals, we like you way too much to want to have that kind of wedge driven between us."

Orphan laughed, translated as a deep booming laugh but with the buzzing undertone of the actual sound. "Ahh, Doctor DuQuesne, truly you know how to make me feel appreciated! And I for my part simply did not trust her. I trust all of you, more in fact than I do many other long-standing residents of the Arena. And that," he said, picking up a drinking globe from a nearby table, "is why I have a proposition for your Faction."

"What *kind* of proposition?"

"As your people are just emerging into the Arena, and have, shall we say, had some unfortunate encounters that add a bit of urgency to your next few months, it occurred to me that the Liberated happen to have some resources which are going quite unused, and barring a miracle will remain unused for a long time to come, and which we would be willing to loan to humanity. Specifically, a number of Arena-capable vessels."

Ariane sat forward involuntarily. "You'd lend us *spaceships*? Arena-tailored ones? What type? How many?"

"Ahh, Captain, I see that your friend and advisor Dr. DuQuesne wishes you had kept something more of... oh, what was that phrase Dr. Franceschetti once used... ah, yes, more of a poker face. Too much enthusiasm and I know my bargaining position."

Ariane blushed, but DuQuesne grinned. "Yeah, well, she's a pilot, not a professional politician—which we thank the Gods for every day. Since she's gone and made it obvious we like the idea, let's move on. We're working on building our own Arena vessels, but I'm pretty damn sure that our first efforts are going to be not even close to optimal, no matter how many SFGs they get involved; there's just too many little things we probably don't know.

"On the other hand, ships made for your people aren't going to be optimal for us to use, so there's that little issue."

Orphan bob-bowed but with an energy and tilt to his body that implied he'd already thought of that. "Which is why these vessels would already be modified for humanity's needs."

Ariane raised an eyebrow. "How would you—"

DuQuesne snorted and shook his head, looking chagrined. "Of course. Another reason Maria-Susanna couldn't tempt you so much."

"Precisely correct, Dr. DuQuesne. Humanity spent some not inconsiderable time as guests of my own Embassy, prior to obtaining your own, and I naturally gave you permission to modify the quarters as you saw fit. Equally naturally, while I did not directly spy on you, I was able to examine, observe, and record every change you made or requested of the automation. Thus I know, I believe, far more about humanity than any other native of the Arena—in some ways, I would expect I will still do so even after your renegade finds some safe haven, as your Maria-Susanna is of course going to dole out information very carefully indeed."

"And you can refit them on your own?"

"Recall that nanotechnology works, at least to some considerable extent, within one's own Sphere. Yes, I can bring the vessels into my Harbor and have them refitted. I have in fact done so in anticipation of this time." He gestured and an image appeared of multiple vessels—two, three dozen of them—arranged in a conical formation. "Several of these are warships, which may at least give you some peace of mind against accidental discovery—although they will be utterly inadequate if and when a major force finds your Sphere."

"But how will we GET them there?" Wu Kung put in. "Sorry for jumping in, but if I remember the briefing we don't know anything about where your Sphere is compared to ours, or compared to the Nexus, so we could be next-door neighbors or light-years apart even here in the Arena."

"That is a slight problem," Orphan conceded, "but one that—I would hope—may be remedied shortly. If your negotiations with the Analytic proceed well, they should be able to offer you the technology or designs necessary to locate your Sky Gates, and there is a very good chance that one of those Gates leads here, to Nexus Arena. One of the Liberated's Sky Gates leads here as well, so if you are not terribly unfortunate, all that will need to be done is to bring the fleet here, and then send it to your Sphere. Even if negotiations with the Analytic fail for some reason, I would not be surprised if your Dr. Sandrisson could determine the basic nature of a Gate Location analysis machine on his own."

"Well," Ariane said after a moment, "I have to say it's a very attractive and generous offer, Orphan. So what's the catch?"

"The . . . catch? Ah, yes. What do I get out of the bargain that I have not yet stated. You recall, Dr. DuQuesne, the time I very *nearly* showed you over my favorite ship, the *Zounin-Ginjou*, which I keep docked at Nexus Arena?"

"Heh. Yeah, you'd just gotten us up to its berth when Gabrielle called to let us know that the captain had just challenged the Blessed. Pretty ship, from what I could see."

"Pretty? Yes, I would agree; a pleasing symmetry and color-pattern; and also one of the most advanced we own. I have just recently had it overhauled by my Tantimorcan allies." Now it was Orphan who leaned forward, a startlingly humanlike gesture. "The catch, my friends, is that I want *you* to provide me with a crew. For I have somewhere I must go, and no other way to reach my destination . . . and no others anywhere in the universe that I dare trust."

CHAPTER 9

DuQuesne studied Orphan carefully. *He's good at playing the game. But I don't think he's doing much of that right now. He means it.* "You can't do this yourself? A one-man ship or something like that?"

As Orphan's hands flicked outward, Ariane answered. "I don't think that would be practical—not if he's going into the, what did they call it, Deeps, the areas away from settled Spheres."

"Alas, exactly correct, Captain Austin." Orphan's tone held sincere regret. "For a number of reasons I would be extremely pleased if I could take this and similar journeys alone, but it is not possible."

DuQuesne wasn't really surprised. If you thought about it, given that the Arena-space was filled with air, debris, water, and so on (from the hundreds of billions of Spheres floating in it as well as from whatever unknown source the material and power of the Arena actually originated from), sailing through those mostly uncharted and perhaps almost unchartable areas would be something like a cross between an Age-of-Sail crossing of the Pacific combined with an 1800s explorer expedition into Africa. Some of the life-forms that flew or drifted between the Spheres were capable of attacking full-size ships, and keeping track of your course and location would be critical. Get turned off course by an unexpected assault and the one-man expedition could easily become an interstellar Flying Dutchman. "That was a pretty big ship; how much of a crew does it need?"

"That, my friend, depends on the quality of the crew. Not very many indeed, if I can both trust them and rely on their capabilities. In addition to myself, a minimum of three, no more than ten."

He glanced over at Ariane, who opened her mouth to speak, then closed it, her eyebrows drawing together. *Yep, she's seen it.*

She confirmed it by her next words. "Unfortunately, Orphan . . . I'm not sure we can help you."

The twin-crested head turned towards her, and the wingcases tightened in the subconscious signal of concern or worry that DuQuesne had learned to read. "Indeed? Have I somehow given you offense? I certainly have not intended—"

The blue-haired captain waved off that protest. "No, no, Orphan, nothing like that. But look, you know—none better—how thin we were stretched before. I'd like to say that now that we've gotten back home and returned that we'd be in better shape . . . but I'm not sure we are. In fact, being honest, we're not, yet."

The green-black alien sat still for a moment, stroking one crest absently while thinking. DuQuesne was silent, waiting to see if Orphan picked up on things as fast as he usually did.

The sole member of the Liberated did not disappoint. "Ahhh, I see. Your people are, perhaps, not yet united

in their vision of how to best emerge into the Arena...
and possibly, I would venture, not entirely happy with
your position in all this, Captain Ariane Austin."

Ariane laughed. "You're a quick study, Orphan.
They don't know everything about that last point yet,
but...yes. Which means—"

"—that you have few, if any, more members of your
Faction that you could, with your typical honesty and
forthrightness, recommend to me unreservedly in this
matter." He bob-bowed slightly. "And perhaps...yes,
almost certainly...you have political issues that make
it impractical, if not impossible, for three of you to
journey with me, let alone four or five."

"You got it. The group that's coming after us, led
by a guy named Oscar Naraj and his main sidekick
Michelle Ni Deng—like Ariane said, they don't quite
know the whole score yet, but they've already told us
they don't think we're the right people for the job,
and that we screwed up while we were here."

"They believe you made serious misjudgments?"
Orphan's stance was disbelieving. "While you certainly
seemed...highly risk-prone, I cannot see anything you
did that would be a misjudgment."

"Well," Ariane said, "the biggest single thing that
bothered them was that we're effectively at war with
the Molothos, one of the Five Great Factions, when
we haven't got more than one Sphere to our names."

Orphan gave a buzz that was translated as a con-
temptuous snort. "And would they prefer you had left
them in control of your Upper Sphere? I admit that
perhaps Doctor DuQuesne needn't have taunted them
directly by throwing one of the bodies of their fallen
in front of them, but I assure you there was truly no

way of avoiding that war. As for the situation with the Blessed, which I presume also disturbed them, there was little chance you could evade the confrontation, unless you were willing to...what was the expression...throw me to the wolves, yes."

"Which would've had a whole bunch of other negative consequences anyway," DuQuesne said. "Right. And believe you me, they're not going to be at *all* pleased when they find out that the captain's basically in charge of the Faction unless she steps down—which she is *not* doing unless and until we're sure the right person's going to step up and take the job for her."

Orphan stood and began pacing in a rather human-like way. "Oh, no, certainly not. And given your extraordinary successes early on, I would be most loath to change the leadership at this stage, even if—" he held up a hand towards Ariane, "—as I suspect from the way the captain was about to speak, you were to protest that it was as much luck as skill." For a moment he stood still, gazing intensely at them both, and DuQuesne found his stance curiously hard to interpret; there was something more behind his words. Then Orphan continued pacing. "I can, of course, put off this journey for some time... given where I wish to go, one day or even month more or less probably makes little difference. But I cannot put it off indefinitely, or even for much longer."

"What's the urgency? Where are you going?"

The seven-foot alien paused, studying them, then gave a buzzing-bob combined that DuQuesne thought was an ironic smile, confirmed by Orphan's translated tone in his response. "Ahh, now, I must take care. I had no intention of revealing any more until we were aboard the *Zounin-Ginjou* and out of all reach of Nexus

Arena and her politics." He seemed to ponder for a moment, then brightened. "If I were to tell you that it has a connection with a certain...trinket which I once used to your benefit, would that be sufficient?"

Oh, yeah.

"You mean...when you came back to help us against Amas-Garao," Ariane said slowly. Orphan gave a tiny handtap of assent. "Yes...that would be sufficient to explain why it's so important—and why you don't want to say any more about it."

DuQuesne grunted. "Yeah. And it also puts a different face on the whole question. The Arena's *built* on secrets, advantages, alliances, betrayals, aces in the hole. Getting any more information on something like that—something that isn't Shadeweaver or Faith but could play their kind of game...that's something you, personally, need badly, Captain, and as a Faction, Humanity needs any advantage it can get. Orphan's over a barrel here—he can't do it alone, and he's got almost no one he can trust with something that explosive."

Ariane looked thoughtful, then chuckled. "And it's another reason you couldn't take in Maria-Susanna. As things stand, you *can* go anywhere you want by yourself—as a Faction of One, you're not restricted by the rules about leaving people on your Sphere. But if she joined, you would be. Which could end up worse for you."

"Hmph. Not quite, though in essence true. That is, until I reach a certain number of members—which, I will reveal to you, is four—the Faction of the Liberated needs not remain in any location.

"The problem, as I am sure you see," Orphan continued, "would be that if I had accepted her as a true member of the Faction and left her behind, she would have full access to my Sphere, our Embassy, a fair amount of power to negotiate . . . or even trigger Challenges, as technically I would still be in the Arena, while if I brought her with me she would learn much of this secret. Either way, even with her capabilities and the information she could provide, it would be a considerable time before I could reasonably extend her such trust—yet if she is a member of a two-member Faction, I cannot reasonably *not* extend her such trust."

"Good call." DuQuesne said. "Knowing her, she'd have figured out some angle to make herself head of the Liberated by the time you got back."

"Dr. DuQuesne, I am hurt that you think so little of me."

"More that I know *her* all too well, and I wouldn't bet against her doing something like that to *me*."

"Then, knowing your own extremely formidable talents, I withdraw my complaint," Orphan conceded. He glanced at Wu Kung, who had been wandering around the room, studying the carvings and ornamentation, and looking restless. "You are rather silent, I notice."

Wu grinned and did a bounce-flip in the air to land closer to Orphan. "I'm just a bodyguard, they didn't choose me to do their talking. Though I hope we get out more, the Arena looks fascinating and all this talk-talk-talk is making me itchy, and no one's tried to kill the captain yet!"

Orphan gave a subdued buzz-chuckle. "One would almost think you *want* her to be attacked."

"Well, of course! What use being a bodyguard if you never actually get to do any WORK?"

Orphan stared at Wu Kung for a moment, then looked at DuQuesne. "Is he . . . serious?"

DuQuesne snorted. "Yeah, that's Wu, all right. His idea of being a bodyguard is having top-rank assassins trying to kill his client every step of the way. We've given him a pretty damn boring job so far."

"And I'm just fine with that," Ariane said pointedly. "I'm sorry if you're bored, Wu, and we'll see if we can give you a break from time to time, but I'd much rather NO ONE has to get hurt over me. Right?"

Wu looked slightly abashed. "Sanzo always said the same thing. Said I thought too much with my fists. Sorry, Captain."

DuQuesne slapped him on the back. "Don't worry about it, Wu. You also think with your heart, and usually that doesn't take you too wrong."

The flashing, slightly-fanged smile was bright. "Okay, I won't. Thanks, DuQuesne!"

Orphan had watched the byplay, DuQuesne noted, with an analytical eye that the Hyperion remembered from prior interactions. The sole member of the Liberated had not survived three millennia without being able to learn an awful lot by just observing, and DuQuesne wondered exactly what Orphan was seeing now. The alien's face revealed little, and his body-language was quite controlled, but Marc C. DuQuesne was suddenly very sure that Orphan had come to some kind of important decision or realization, and it bothered DuQuesne that he hadn't the faintest idea *what* that important realization was.

"Well, then," Orphan said, "it seems we have a rather interesting problem."

"Sorry," Ariane said contritely. "Didn't mean to

divert everything. Yes, we do. Can I ask...you must have actually quite a few allies you've gained over the years, even if never nearly enough to be able to take on the Blessed. Why *us*, the clueless newbies of the Arena, so to speak."

"Ah, Captain Austin, it is in a way the fact that you *are* 'clueless newbies,' if the meaning has been properly translated, that makes you the only candidates for this job. Or rather, the fact that you have that status *and* have proven yourselves honorable, courageous, and resourceful...and been willing to treat with one such as myself even when you had certainly some reason to mistrust me." He reached into an unobtrusive cabinet and brought out a bottle from which he filled three glasses. "I realize I have been remiss in providing refreshment for you as well."

Ariane reached for a glass; DuQuesne grinned as it was plucked smoothly from her hand by Wu Kung, who sniffed at it, ran a scanner over it, and poured a drop onto his tongue before he let her take it; DuQuesne raised an eyebrow as the Monkey King did the same with DuQuesne's glass.

"Oh, excellent." Orphan snapped his wingcases and buzzed in what was obviously something like applause. "Extend the hand of friendship...but watch where the tail lies carefully. I approve of your bodyguard, Captain. Though others might find this offensive."

"Let them." DuQuesne said at a glance from Ariane and Wu Kung. "In our own Embassy we'll relax a bit, but nowhere else."

"Perfectly correct."

Ariane, meanwhile, had taken a sip. "Oh, this is excellent, Orphan!"

DuQuesne agreed. It was some kind of juice, he suspected, with a tart, sweet taste something like gooseberries crossed with carrots and maybe a hint of ancho pepper in the background. No alcohol, but there was a faint, faint tang which made him suspect a mild caffeine-like stimulant. "I'll bet you got this from Mairakag."

"He and a few others advised me, and it was of course certified by your own Dr. Canning." Orphan bowed to them in his fashion and then raised his own drinking globe. "I believe this is an appropriate use of one of your customs when I say 'To alliances.'"

"To alliances," DuQuesne echoed with Ariane, and took another sip.

"Good! I had hoped I had that correct. To the subject at hand... Captain, you are new-come to the Arena. I have been present essentially throughout all of your most important events, save only," he glanced with undisguised curiosity at DuQuesne, "the impossible victory Dr. DuQuesne and Dr. Edlund managed against the Molothos."

DuQuesne grinned darkly but said nothing. That was in some ways one of the most private moments of his life—the moment that he and Carl had been cornered and faced with death or worse and he had been forced to unleash the Hyperion, the "Marc C. DuQuesne" that he'd buried inside himself half a century before so he could forget what had been, and become a part of the civilization around him. He'd saved Carl, but had to give up any hope of going back to being anything other than what he now was.

Orphan, after a miniscule pause, continued, "Because of this, I know all of your alliances. I know those you call friend, those who see you as enemies, I know how you treat with both friend and enemy and potential allies. Do you not see that I could not say the same about *any* of the other Factions? With their uncounted billions or even quadrillions of adherents, with their dozens, hundreds, thousands of Spheres and thousands of years of Challenge, negotiation, expedience, betrayal, secret friendships hidden within public animosities..." he flicked his hands outward emphatically. "Nowhere in the Arena could I possibly find allies whose only unknown motivations lay in their own Sphere, who could—to put it simply—be nothing more or less than exactly what they appeared to be." This time he did not bob-bow, but dropped to the floor in the full pushup-like pose that was a deep and formal bow. "In all the universe, in fact, there are none like you, and once your people have become established—a few fleeting decades, no more—there will be none like you again, until another species of First Emergents appears."

He sure knows how to speechify, as Rich Seaton might've said, DuQuesne thought cynically. *And he knows how that's going to affect the captain. But being fair, I think he means it.*

Ariane had risen in surprise, and her smile looked somewhat sheepish. "That's... pretty extravagant praise, Orphan. But I understand where you're coming from." She frowned. "And the longer we wait, the more chances there are for the alliances to start tangling us up." She nodded decisively. "We'll figure it out. I don't know *how*, just yet," she admitted, "but you have my word we'll figure out some way to get you a crew you can trust."

Orphan bowed again. "Then, Captain Austin, our bargain is done; you shall have those vessels and you will one day soon find a way to give me a crew. I have no doubts on that score, for the very body of Amas-Garao can testify how well you keep your word...even when all possibility seems against you."

CHAPTER 10

"Doctor Sandrisson!" Relgof Nov'ne Knarph strode from one of the shining metal and glass doors opening from the immense silver-and-marble appearing lobby of the Embassy of the Analytic and embraced Simon, to the human scientist's momentary surprise. He returned the hug, however. *Either they have similar gestures, or he has carefully studied ours and knows that to adopt them will make him seem closer to us.*

Not that he really needs to do that, Simon thought, stepping back and smiling. "Researcher Relgof, it is a pleasure," he said. *The Analytic was one of two Factions that supported us throughout our first trip—and the only one that did so without any argument or prompting.*

"As always, as always," rejoined the tall, humanoid creature with its beardlike filter and crest of pure white feathery stuff that always looked to Simon like a sweep of white hair that seemed ready to fall over one great eye in dramatic fashion. "But no more of the formalities, my friend Simon. I am glad to see you have returned, and that in hours only after the return you have chosen to come here."

121

"Thank you, Relgof," said Simon. "Although I cannot pretend it is merely a social visit."

"Of course—and in truth, I would be disappointed if it were! You have so much to learn, as do we, and to waste that time merely on formalities? So tell me, what brings you to the Analytic so swiftly?"

"The Sky Gates."

Relgof inclined his head like a bird studying a nearby object. "Oh, naturally. You have a Sphere, you have your Inner and Outer Gateways, you can now use the Straits, yet where shall you then go? Immense possibility lies beyond the unknown Gates in the Sky; of course you must find them immediately."

Simon nodded. "And it seems obvious to me that the Analytic must know the best ways to locate such Sky Gates."

"There have been many methods developed indeed, and we know them all—or, at least, so we believe. It is always possible that someone has, or shall have, devised a new method." Relgof's filter-beard flip-flopped in a pensive fashion. "Yet—as I am sure you understand, Simon—this is valuable knowledge, and while I hope you recognize our prior generosity towards your Faction, this is not something which may be simply given away. Even gaining access to the records of the Analytic is something usually reserved for full members of this Faction."

He suddenly stiffened, a wading-bird spotting a possible meal. "Now, if you have come to join the Analytic—!"

Simon laughed and shook his head. "No, no, I cannot leave my friends like that—certainly not for some long time yet, anyway."

"A shame, my friend. But then might I expect you have been given some authority and resources to negotiate, or were you hoping to impose upon my goodwill for this information?"

"The latter would certainly be preferable," Simon said dryly, "but I think we've relied upon your goodwill—and that of the Analytic—quite sufficiently for now. Yes, I'm authorized to negotiate, and we've brought a few things I think may be worth negotiating for." He looked sideways at Relgof. "If, of course, *you* are empowered to negotiate with me?"

The laugh from Relgof was a hearty one, with a faint whistling, chirping undertone that probably came from the actual sound of the Wagamia's laugh. "The Convocation elected me Head Researcher for this period, so indeed I am so empowered, Simon." He gestured for Simon to follow. "Let us go inside, then, for other guests," he indicated the far doors to the outside, which had just opened to admit a pair of three-horned creatures, "have no need or right to observe what we bargain with, or for."

The small meeting room Relgof led him to was . . . interesting. *Until now, we'd only seen him in public areas—even when I visited before, I was only shown to obviously "general public" regions, with information which was available to any inhabitant of the Arena.* Relgof's chair had a bowl-shaped depression in the table before it, with a stream of water running through it from a channel that was cut into the table for a short distance before going somewhere inside. The water obviously drained down through one of the table supports; the room itself smelled of an ocean, with strange spicy notes to the scent that hinted of alien seas. There were other peculiar arrangements in front of other chairs, while still other chairs—such as the one Simon selected—faced flat, smooth sections of table.

"Would you like something to eat or drink, Simon?" Relgof asked.

"Yes, please—I presume you've seen to the safety of such things. I see you have your own already to hand . . . or mouth, as the case may be."

"There are advantages to being a Researcher of standing, yes." Relgof gestured and the wall near him opened, revealing a surprising array of bottles, vials, and packages of various sizes and colors. "Hmm . . . ah, here, I believe this should be satisfactory."

Simon could see markings on the bottle, one of them a stylized human figure with lettering underneath. "Water with human-compatible flavorings. Your Laila Canning said this was quite pleasant."

Simon took a cautious sip. *Definitely flavored . . . something vaguely like lemon. Not my favorite taste, but certainly quite drinkable.* "Thank you."

"My pleasure." They took their seats, Simon finding that it was becoming easier, with practice, to do that despite the sword on his hip. *DuQuesne insists we be armed, and I can't entirely blame him.*

"Now," Relgof said, "I already know what you want from the Analytic. What might you be willing to offer us that we do not already have?"

"That was something of an interesting question," Simon admitted. "Of course what you want—besides one of us as a member of the Analytic—is information on Humanity. At the same time, the more people we give that to, the less valuable it becomes, so we must be cautious."

"Naturally."

Simon thought back over his many prior interactions with the Analytic scientist and decided to play a hunch. "But it also occurred to me, Rel, that in our conversations you have always seemed...well, enthusiastic in your interest in the *specifics* of people and things. That is, that an individual thing is itself of interest to you, even if you know much about that general type of thing. So I wondered...might you also be a collector? One of those who likes to gather true, authentic collectibles?"

Relgof was in the midst of filtering some delicacy from the water, but his beard went momentarily slack and the plankton dissipated into the water before he recovered and took what remained. "Hmph. Simon, you surely are one of us no matter your allegiance. I am a collector of various things, yes."

"And as you are a great scientist, one of the best Researchers of the Analytic, I thought those things would be scientific things." Simon reached into the bag at his side. "Something, perhaps, like this."

On the table he placed an old, old book—one that Gabrielle had found for him once he realized what she was up to. "Let me offer you this, Relgof. Both a unique, unduplicated, original artifact of Earth... and one that reveals something that I think you will find both personally and professionally interesting."

Relgof wiped his filter clean and leaned forward, reaching out a hand to reverently touch the book's cover gently. "A...collection of records?"

"A book from our past—from before the era of electronic reading."

Relgof squinted at the symbols. "Hmm. Translation

for your writings has not truly begun, yet. We do not understand you enough for that, I suppose. What is this book about?"

"Do you remember our first conversation, as we traveled to Orphan's Embassy?"

Relgof laughed. "It would be hard to forget it! My first meeting with a First Emergent—and one of them the inventor of the Sandrisson Drive." As always, the words "Sandrisson Drive" were overlaid with dozens of other phrases and names.

Simon still felt slightly embarrassed by that being made such a big deal, but he went on. "Yes, exactly. You were very much interested in the specific research paths that took us to the invention of the drive." He touched the book and ran his finger along the title. "So . . . *How Science Grew* is a book for adolescent children, that covers the development of scientific knowledge on our world from its prehistory all the way through roughly the early twentieth century—a few hundred years ago. It lacks much context for you; it won't explain events or references that assume you are a human, that you are a part of a particular culture; and it gives you no idea of how our technology has advanced since that time."

"And yet," Relgof said, with an unmistakable longing in his pose as he touched the book again, "vastly more about your people—how they thought, how they found their way through the confusion and distractions of the real world to find the truths behind them—than anyone else has or could possibly have at this time." He bowed. "A very strong offering—except that I cannot read it. And—as you may have discovered—mere recordings of speech made by another species are not comprehensible unless you have some knowledge of their language to begin with."

Simon grinned. "But what if I, or another human, were to read it *to* you?"

"You understand the Arena's tricks already, I see. Yes, in that case our recording devices would record what we hear, because it is being read by a conscious mind whose meaning provides the translation; we understand what we are hearing, and thus the translation will be recorded." Relgof leaned back. "A . . . very good offer, Simon. I confess to being entirely impressed by your understanding of my personality as well as the Analytic's interests. You strike to my own heart as well as that of the Analytic." He laughed. "A true Researcher indeed! You observed, you deduced, you hypothesized, and here you have put your hypothesis to the test and it has proven well-founded."

"Is this sufficient, then?"

"Hmm. It is certainly enough to move some distance forward on. I must consult with at least a reasonable number of the Conclave . . . but I believe that, at the least, we shall be able to give you access to some portion of that Analytic's records—a relevant portion, of course, to your inquiries."

"Thank you, Rel! When do you think—"

"This very evening I shall call for responses; I would expect . . . a day or two."

"That will be fine," Simon said, and rose. "I suppose I should let you—"

"Oh, don't start running off *now*, Simon!" Relgof said. "Come, we may not be able to discuss more of your science or our secrets, but there's plenty of *gossip* to catch up on since you've been gone—some of it might even interest you." The glance he gave Simon sent a jolt through the white-haired scientist. It looked . . . *mischievous?*

"Really?" He sat down slowly.

"Oh, indeed. Various things about the Shadeweavers, the Vengeance, several of the other Factions—oh, you have sent *great* turbulence through the waves, I assure you, and things are not settling out any time soon; one hears the most amazing things at times. Why," and the gaze was now *definitely* on the devilish side, "I have even heard a rumor about a *new* human in the Arena . . ."

Simon let himself settle deeply into the chair. *I have a feeling . . . I may be here a while.*

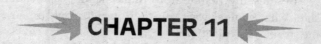

CHAPTER 11

"Arena," Ariane said to the empty air of her own room in the Embassy of Humanity, "I have serious questions with respect to the operation of a new Faction, and it would seem unwise to trust other Factions for the answers. Will you speak?"

She knew from experience that the Arena—or whatever intelligence controlled it—would rarely speak on its own, and even if addressed directly would only speak if the request fit whatever unknown, mysterious set of rules that guided its behavior. She waited, tensely, for an answer that might not come.

A moment passed. Two.

"Speak." The voice was quiet, yet something about it echoed and resonated like a shout.

Well, at least I know it heard me. Aloud, she said, "Is it possible for my people to force me to abandon the position of Leader—I mean, in the sense that they could pass a law or something?" She winced. *What a marvelously well-spoken leader humanity has! 'Pass a law or something'? What are you, ten?*

The Arena's voice did not show any particular reaction, neither of annoyance nor of amusement, to her clumsy phrasing. "No. If you do not wish to relinquish leadership of the Faction, no political mechanism may remove you from that position unless you, personally, have agreed to that mechanism."

"Besides my deliberately relinquishing my leadership, what general ways are there which could remove me from that position?"

"Death," the Arena replied immediately. "The leader of a Faction must be a living being; no symbolic leaders, no religious symbols with no living manifestation, or other substitutes for an individual are permitted."

"You mean that each Faction *has* to have a single person in charge? Not a, say, committee?"

"That is correct. They may be selected by various means, but at any given time there is a single leader." As she digested that and its implications, the Arena continued. "Apart from death, any event which makes the leader effectively dead; brain-death, for example. Joining another Faction automatically negates leadership. If a specific procedure has been established for a Faction, there may be mechanisms to remove the Leader from power."

"Can I designate an heir, so to speak, if I get killed or as good as dead?"

"No."

Ariane froze, mouth open in what would undoubtedly have been a hysterically funny double-take if anyone else had been there to see it. She had been so *certain* the answer would be yes... "No? I can't? But I thought I could step down for anyone I chose?"

"You may make your final act as the Leader of the Faction to be the selection of your successor," the

Arena said, "but if you are already dead your orders have no force. Nor do the orders of others."

"So DuQuesne was right," she muttered. "It'll choose the new leader, and we have no way of knowing who that is." She sighed. *So much for the easy route. I'm stuck with this position until we can actually get a method for picking a new Leader of the Faction in place!* "Arena, I—"

A green comm-ball *popped* into existence. "Ariane! DuQuesne!" came Gabrielle's voice, a little breathless. "They're coming! You've got maybe half an hour at the outside!"

"What?" *Dammit!* "I thought we'd have *hours* of notice!" *We set the* Holy Grail *to detect the flare of entry, and the radio relays should have let us know—*

"So did I, Ariane." Gabrielle's voice was chagrined. "The *Duta* transitioned in moving faster than we were on our first trip. I left while it was still en route, but Steve's guess was it'd take about fifteen minutes to reach the dock." Ariane knew that Gabrielle would have had to run from the Guardhouse, all the way down the corridors to the Inner Gateway and take it through before she could make the call. Which would have taken about fifteen minutes, meaning that Naraj and his party were already getting out of their ship . . .

Gabrielle was continuing, "Now, Steve and Tom might be able to delay them a little—"

"But Naraj obviously wants to catch us off-guard," came DuQuesne's voice. "He's a hell of a lot of things, but as my friend Seaton would've said, stupid sure ain't one of them."

"On my way! I'll meet them at Transition!"

"Got it. I'm going back." The ball disappeared.

She leapt up from the desk, which folded up and vanished into the wall, and yanked on her most captainlike jacket.

Sun Wu Kung leapt to his feet as she charged out the door. "What's wrong, Captain?"

"They're on their way. We want to get to Transition before they do."

Wu didn't ask questions; he followed like a shadow.

DuQuesne joined them as they exited the Embassy. "Carl and Laila will hold the fort here," he said. "Simon's gone over to the Analytic to talk with Relgof and a couple of the other Researchers—hopefully we get good news there."

"Four days, Marc. It only took them four days."

"Yeah, and they must've spent a day or more doing some quick mods."

She glanced up at the olive-skinned face; DuQuesne's expression was not comforting. "Why?"

"The *Duta*'s design. I glanced over what we had on it, and it didn't have the *bunkerage* for the reaction mass necessary to brake down from what must be around ten kilometers per second." He shook his head. "They must have done calculations for modified Sandrisson coils that let them take disposable reaction tanks; it's the only explanation that fits."

Ariane gestured and one of the hovering taxis slowed to a halt near them; Wu leapt in to do his quick survey. "But you can't change the shape of your ship and still use your Sandrisson coils! I know that—we had to chase down the broken drive spine because of that, back when we first got here." She got in at Wu's gesture and ordered the vehicle to head for the Elevators to Transition.

"Right," DuQuesne said as he sat down. "My guess? They'll have to spend some time fixing up the coils to make them work to go back, but they probably *designed* them to make that as easy as possible. Worth it to get the advantage of surprise."

Calm, she reminded herself. *If I let this agitate me, they've really got the advantage. This isn't a race, it's not that time critical. A few seconds here or there make no difference.* "Is it really that much of an advantage?"

"From their point of view? Probably." DuQuesne's head turned, watching the Embassy area streaming by. "Naraj's been playing these games for a long time. Keep the other guy off-balance, distract him, really get him worked up and he'll make a mistake."

She smiled wryly up at him. "Then you'd better make sure I don't *make* any mistakes."

As they got into the elevator, she focused on the task at hand. *Time seems to crawl by with this much urgency; so make use of that. Remember all the contingencies we discussed. Remember what you know about Naraj. Be ready to adjust depending on who and what's around when they come through.*

Transition loomed up before them, a kilometers-wide room filled with almost uncountable numbers of Gateways. "Great. Which one?" she heard herself mutter.

DuQuesne shrugged. "No telling. If someone isn't maintaining a connection, they go inert and wake up for whichever is the next incoming or outgoing signal. They could come through that one in front of us, or one of the ones in the far corners."

"All right, there's three of us," she said. "I'll watch

the center area, you watch to the right, DuQuesne, and Wu, keep an eye on the gates off to the left, okay?"

"Yes, Captain."

Once more time seemed to crawl by. Other creatures of a hundred different species moved around them, sometimes glancing curiously at the three humans just standing still in the midst of Transition.

"Apologies for distracting you?" came a buzzing voice, accompanied by just a hint of a sharp chemical smell.

The voice sounded...very young, and she looked down to see a small Milluk—the same species as Swordmaster First Selpa'a'At—looking up at her from the glittering eyes set slightly above the midline of the spherical body. The creature was very small compared to the others she had seen, about half the height or less of Selpa and far less massive, with smaller defensive spines and less decoration. *A child?*

She realized now that Wu had already watched its approach and had his staff casually ready, but he, also, did not seem terribly worried. "Apology accepted. What can I do for you?"

"I must inquire—are you the human Captain Ariane Austin?"

"I am," she said. *Still no sign of Naraj.*

The voice shifted slightly, to a more exited tone. "Oh, wonderful! Builders be praised!"

A member of the Faith? She wondered for a moment why that seemed *wrong*, then realized the answer was obvious: Selpa, the only Milluk they'd had any real contact with, was the head of the Vengeance and didn't trust or like the Faith.

But the little creature was continuing, harvestman-like

set of legs rising and falling, making the spherical body bob like a beachball in a choppy sea. "I am Kekka'a'shi, Captain Ariane Austin! I have wanted to meet you for many days!" Kekka'a'shi produced a strange triangular object; Wu stiffened slightly, then relaxed as the creature pulled on one point and the object folded back, revealing itself to be some kind of a three-sided book. "I was hoping . . . would you possibly . . . ?"

She was puzzled. "Would I . . . ?"

Suddenly she was aware that DuQuesne was chuckling. "What are *you* laughing at?"

"You don't know what he's asking, do you?"

"No, I—" she froze, then looked down. "You . . . want my autograph?"

"Your personal mark identifier, as signifying I have met and spoken with you! Yes!"

She laughed. *Hardly the first time I've been asked, but I had actually thought I'd left that behind.* "If you'll explain to me how this little thing works so I know how, yes. But why me?"

"Oh, you're *famous* already in the Challenges, Captain!" Kekka said enthusiastically, the translation making him sound so *very* like a young sports fan meeting one of his idols that Ariane had a momentary pang of longing for her days as a racing pilot. *It's only been . . . not even a year, but it seems three lifetimes ago.* "You beat the Blessed in a sky-race, and then you beat *Amas-Garao*. No one's beaten a Shadeweaver for *centuries*." He held up a sticklike object. "How it works? Some will touch it with their manipulators and generate a unique scent, others impress their nose-prints on the material . . . the pages are made to accept all sorts of impressions. You can use the stylus to make marks, too."

She took the stylus and smiled. "I'll do it the way we do at home." She thought a moment, then wrote quickly and handed the book back.

Even though the creature was almost completely alien, of armored legs and spherical body, with manipulative tendrils and lacking anything ordinarily considered a face, there was somehow something about the young Milluk's posture and movement as he took the signed book and studied it that conveyed the same awed excitement she'd seen in thousands of human fans. "What . . . does it say? It is language, yes?"

"Yes, it is," she answered with another smile. "It says, 'To Kekka'a'shi—My first fan in the Arena, where I didn't know I *had* fans. Thank you!—Ariane Austin.'"

"*Wow,*" he said. What the original expression, or even sound, was, it didn't matter; the Arena's translation had perfectly conveyed the reaction. "Your *first* fan here?"

"You are indeed," she said. "And—"

"Ariane!"

She looked where DuQuesne pointed, and saw three clearly human figures standing on one of the Gateway platforms about three hundred yards distant.

The real game's begun.

CHAPTER 12

DuQuesne grinned as he saw the three figures crowding together—just as he, Ariane, and Simon had the first time they'd stepped through to Transition. *Nothing really prepares you for that. Not when it's* real. *Oh, sure, simgames have stuff just as impressive in its own way, but you always know in the back of your head it's just a game. Somehow I even knew, in the end, about Hyperion.*

But this is no game.

Ariane led the way; Wu flanked her just to the left, DuQuesne on her right, and she was moving fast. The crowds of Transition, however, parted before her; Kekka was not the only one who recognized Ariane Austin.

He kept his eyes on the three figures. Naraj was already straightening to his full height of well over six feet, stepping slightly forward, his deep blue and gold outfit contrasting well with his mahogany-brown skin and black hair. Michelle Ni Deng was a contrast herself; a woman of sharp angles and light-boned body, her resemblance to a wading bird emphasized by the biomod of featherlike hair that bobbed in white and blue waves over her head. Just emerging from behind her was—

For just a split second even the speed of his Hyperion-born thoughts was not enough to cope. *That red hair... done in* that *style... those eyes, I can see them from here...*

But he was lucky twice. First, she was emerging to the right side, which meant that he got the first glimpse one tiny fraction of a second before Wu Kung; and second, the two of them were behind Ariane, and not in front. His hand lashed out and he gripped Wu's arm in an unmistakable warning.

The Monkey King's emerald-touched golden eyes glanced at him, surprise and joy fading to puzzlement, then understanding. He nodded, just enough for DuQuesne to see, and DuQuesne let go.

Of all the... He looked at Naraj, remembering, judging. *No, there's no way he could know.* He set his jaw. *Focus. You can't afford to let Naraj's lucky break distract you from the main event.*

Ariane reached the base of the ramp and started up. "Ambassador Naraj! A pleasure to see you here so soon."

Good move. Acknowledge his title—in fact, give *him the title in public. He'll have to accept it at this point.*

Naraj's smile was, possibly, just a *fraction* off, but only for a moment. "Captain Austin, good of you to meet me so promptly. I suppose I have Doctor Wolfe to thank for that?"

"She did pop over here briefly to make sure you got a good reception," Ariane said, shaking his hand.

Michelle laughed; it was, DuQuesne admitted, a very nice laugh, gentle and lilting. "I did think she seemed a little out of breath; now I know why! Walking all that way... she must have run in both directions."

She turned. "We all know each other, but I should introduce our own security expert—"

"We've met," DuQuesne interrupted, stepping forward. He could feel Ariane's curious gaze. "Hello, Commander Abrams."

"Doctor DuQuesne." They shook hands, hers gripping as strong as he remembered, and he waited, wondering...

And the pixie-cute face suddenly broke out in a broad smile and she threw her arms around him. "Long time, sir, a long time!"

He relaxed fractionally, hugged back. "Has been, hasn't it?" Releasing her, he turned. "Ariane, this is Commander Oasis Abrams."

A grin returned to his face as Ariane shook hands with the newcomer, trying to size her up. He knew what *she* saw; a young woman who didn't look any older than Ariane herself, with flaming red hair so long that, even done up in four separate ponytails, it trailed well past her waist, whose military accoutrements were distributed in such a way as to make her appear to be dressed for some sort of exotic masquerade. *Not exactly what I'd expected,* he heard on their private frequency.

DuQuesne gave a silent laugh. *Don't be fooled by that perky can-do exterior,* he replied via the same frequency. *That's former Ensign Oasis Abrams of the Third Recon Platoon of the First Combined Battalion under Commander Saul Maginot.* He sensed her sudden understanding. *Exactly. And she's tough. She's the only trooper who took out one of us pretty much by herself, the only survivor of her entire company, and she was about the age then she looks like she is now. She's a friend and someone you can count on . . . but she's also got some goals of her own right now, and she's hired on to work for Oscar and Michelle, which isn't good.*

He was glad to see that Wu had got the message, so he simply bounded up and gave her a hug. "I'm *so* glad you got out okay!"

As she returned the hug, Oscar nodded. "I had wondered if the implied events in her resume had happened. I see now they must have. Excellent."

The words reassured DuQuesne. *If he knew the real score Naraj would either say nothing or he'd be asking questions—really pointed questions.*

Oscar Naraj turned to Ariane. "Captain, since you have come all this way, I presume you're here to show us to the Embassy?"

"Exactly, Ambassador. I want to bring you up to speed on the current situation and see if we can arrange for you to meet some of the people you undoubtedly wish to speak to as soon as possible." She turned. "Please, follow me."

Naraj followed, trying to look confident and at ease. *And could be you're fooling Ariane—though I doubt it—and maybe even yourself, but you sure ain't fooling me.* The eyes darted to the sides just a bit too often, Naraj—and Ni Deng—turned subconsciously as creatures of bizarre and often frightening aspect approached.

But Naraj *had* viewed all the recorded data they'd turned over, as had Michelle Ni Deng, and the two adjusted almost frighteningly quickly. By the time they reached the elevators, Oscar Naraj's pretense of relaxation was fast becoming reality. *They're both real, real good,* DuQuesne thought grimly. *I'd hoped he just wasn't really up to the challenge—God knows we haven't needed any real politicians much in the last couple of centuries—but I'd hoped wrong. He's a genuine Big Time Operator, and he's ready to start his operations real soon now.*

This isn't good. Simon's private chat with Researcher Relgof had shown that Maria-Susanna was somehow managing to send out feelers to the various groups (after being rebuffed by Orphan), yet no one knew exactly where she was. *She's the kind of spanner in the works we really don't need. Might not hear from her for years, or she might pop up tomorrow, but whenever she does make her move . . .*

He shook his head. *One thing at a time. Right now, it's our new guests who are the* immediate *problem.*

With the help of one of the floating taxis the six of them soon arrived at the Embassy of Humanity. Michelle gave an approving nod as they entered. "Oh, very nice. I was afraid we'd still have the rather . . . utilitarian look that was visible in the recordings. My compliments to the designer."

"That would be mostly Steve; remember to tell him yourself the next time you see him."

"Oh, I certainly will, Captain."

"Now," Ariane said, "would you like me to show you to your rooms? I see you have only a small amount of luggage with you now, but—"

"Oh, no, no, Captain," Oscar said firmly. "I am *quite* rested, I assure you—it was early morning when the *Duta* departed from Kanzaki-Three and so I've only been up a few hours. Why don't we have lunch and I'll tell you how I would like to proceed?"

He could see Ariane stiffen and take a slow breath, like a diver nerving herself to take a plunge into murky water. "We can certainly do that, Ambassador."

"Don't look so nervous, Captain. I have no intention of just shoving you out of the limelight—or letting you run off, even if you prefer being out of it. Your advice and help will be invaluable initially," Naraj assured her. "And yours, Doctor DuQuesne. Indeed, I will be relying on the entire crew of *Holy Grail* initially, as we have a great deal to accomplish.

"The Space Security Council and the Combined Space Forces have empowered me to act as Ambassador for Humanity, at least in these initial months."

"A shame, that," DuQuesne said, cutting him off before he could continue.

Naraj looked disappointed. "I expect rather more than cheap shots from someone of your stature, Dr. DuQuesne."

"Not a cheap shot; honest assessment. It's a shame you wasted all that time ramming that authorization through when it's useless."

"I beg your pardon?" Oscar looked completely at sea.

"I'm afraid he's telling the truth," Ariane said; her voice was calm and businesslike, but she stood stiff, nervous, and she swallowed hard before straightening and continuing. "You see, neither the SSC nor the CSF—or both of them together—are empowered to *make* that appointment."

"I . . . see. And just who is? A vote of all the citizens of the Solar System?"

"No, Ambassador," she said, and he felt a tiny bit of relief, because *that* tone was returning to her voice, the tone that she got when she'd made up her mind and was ready to take whatever bull was in front of her by the horns and *throw* it. "No, Ambassador, even that won't work.

"That decision and appointment can only be made by the Leader of the Faction of Humanity...which just happens to be me."

DuQuesne caught a flash of mirth from Oasis Abrams—just a moment of a crinkle of laugh-lines around the emerald eyes, a quirking upward of the corner of the perfect lips.

The other two did not seem so amused; in fact, it was nearly a minute before—to his surprise—Michelle Ni Deng spoke. "*You* are the Leader of...the Faction of Humanity."

"I am." Ariane managed a sour smile. "I didn't *ask* for the job, I didn't know I was in line for it, but I've *got* it—and before either of you says anything, I am *not* handing that authority over to *anyone* unless I believe my successor understands what he or she is dealing with, and can handle it well enough so I don't need to *worry* about it any more."

Oscar Naraj had an expression of equal parts outrage, puzzlement, and sympathy—an impressive combination, DuQuesne had to admit. "I do not mean to sound... stupid, Captain Austin, but, just to clarify...from the Arena's point of view, *you*, personally, are the leader of the entire human species?"

"Yes."

Naraj muttered something in an Indian dialect that DuQuesne couldn't quite catch. "And would you mind," he said, and now his voice was hard, edged with annoyance and some lingering disbelief, "explaining to me, then, why you did not include this—I would think absolutely *crucial*—piece of information in your summaries?"

"Do you want the truth, or the excuse?"

Naraj blinked. Then he smiled briefly. "I think I will take the truth, even if you think it so unpalatable."

"All right, then." Ariane looked up and away for a moment, as though seeking support from the very cause of the problem. "Simply? What would you people have done if I *had* told you?"

"Well, we *certainly* wouldn't have just come charging out here without having the authority to negotiate!" Ni Deng said frostily.

"Right," Ariane agreed, and her tone brought Michelle Ni Deng up short. *Full-blown captain mode, "look of eagles" and all.* "You would have insisted I—and perhaps my entire crew—stay back home unless and until I turned the leadership over to someone more suited, or at the least until I delegated authority to you. As I stated, I have no intention whatsoever of doing that until I'm sure the person taking the job has, as DuQuesne would say, the jets to swing that load, and *no one* will have that who hasn't *already* been here, and learned the ins and outs.

"So we would have been stuck arguing for weeks, maybe *months* longer, while the Molothos methodically search for our only Sphere so they can put a whole invasion force on the surface instead of a scouting party. *Not* happening while I am in charge, Ambassador. And I *am* in charge here, and I will do my best to make sure that we don't get blindsided by those monsters—or," she looked pointedly at both of them, "anyone else."

"Are you—"

Oscar Naraj gestured and Michelle Ni Deng cut her outraged protest short. "I . . . see." He frowned, obviously thinking. *And that's dangerous, but other than just shooting him there's no stopping him from thinking.* "Then should I simply take my people and leave?"

Ariane sighed, and looked—just slightly—less intimidating. "I'm not saying that, no. You both have skills and experience no one on *Holy Grail* had. And I don't have any objection to you *talking* to people—as long as I know about it, and as long as you're willing to *listen* when someone who's experienced explains the pitfalls—especially how you might get goaded or tricked into a Challenge. Understand, *we cannot afford* a Challenge we have not extensively planned for—and even then, it could really go completely wrong.

"And obviously if I want to *ever* get rid of this ridiculous position as Leader of Humanity, I need people who come here and become familiar enough with it to replace me. So no, Ambassador." She gave a professional smile, but there was some warmth behind it. "I would very much like you to stay and help. All of you." The smile turned rueful. "God knows we'll need all the help we can get!"

Naraj allowed a chuckle. "Very well. Then shall we have lunch, and you shall tell *us* how *you* would like to proceed?"

Ariane's smile grew more natural. "I think that is an *excellent* suggestion, Ambassador."

Not bad, Ariane, DuQuesne thought as she led them to one of the dining areas. *But don't you start relaxing now.*

Because they sure aren't.

CHAPTER 13

The room stretched away in front of Simon, and to both sides, to such distances that he momentarily groped for a true sense of scale. *Bakana,* he thought. *It simply cannot be this large.*

But it *was*. The ceilings, set with arched windows from which streamed beams of what seemed pure, natural sunlight (though, perhaps, by the tint, not *Earth*'s sunlight), rose one hundred meters or more; yet it was low, almost oppressively low, compared to the extent of the room it covered.

Shelves kilometers long dwindled, perfect perspective lines, so far that the clear air began to soften the edges like the peaks of mountains on the horizon. And on those shelves...

Soft laughter penetrated his stunned consciousness, and he looked over to see Relgof with an expression and pose that Simon recognized as mirth. "Ahh, my friend, it is always a reward to see the reaction of a first-time visitor to the Archives of the Analytic."

"My...God," Simon said, and for once he meant the reverent tone. "This...this really is..."

"...the collected knowledge of the Analytic, in the

original form—paper, electronic, carven in ancient tablets found on Spheres where no living being had walked in a million years, written upon metal sheets, absorbed in scent-matrices, recorded on nanotechnological writing pads or as patterns of light deep within crystals, written words and spoken, holographic images of motion and thought, all of them here, all studied, categorized, and preserved, the thoughts and hopes and fears and learning of a million worlds across a million years. Yes, it is, and it is my pleasure to welcome you here, where very few save our own Researchers have ever stood."

Simon stood for a few more moments, just staring in awe. He could see some shelves built for things rather like Earthly books; others with row upon row of recording media; yet others that were more supports for huge monoliths of stone or steel; and still more holding less-identifiable objects that hummed or sparkled or flickered.

Enough rubbernecking, as DuQuesne might say. I have work to do. "Why here on Nexus Arena? You have many Spheres of your own."

"Many thousands of Spheres of our own, yes. Yet . . . where else, Simon? No other place is so central, and—you can understand—no other place is even imaginably so safe. A Sphere can be lost in a Challenge, or—though rarely—by direct conquest from without. But nothing can challenge Nexus Arena, nothing can conquer it or force its way in, unless it were something that could shake the foundations of the universe itself. And here, in one of the Great Faction Houses, we have room almost beyond limit."

He nodded. "Of course. I had suspected as much,

but it was worth asking. Then the information I seek is, obviously, somewhere here."

"Undoubtedly."

Simon noticed movement, and saw a Researcher of a semi-ceratopsian build climbing into one of many half-egg-shaped objects scattered about the Archive. The polished white and silver egg rose and flew silently down the rows, carrying the Researcher with it. *Well, that answers one of the questions I had. Fifty-meter-high shelves and many-kilometer-long aisles could have defeated me before I started.* "And I can stay here . . . ?"

"As long as you like, Simon. We were agreed on the value of your gift, and now that you have read its text to us, it is now part of our knowledge—and absolutely fascinating, I will add." Relgof's filter-beard flip-flopped in happy excitement. "You may return any time over the next year and a half, and spend as much time as you wish."

"That is . . . extremely generous, Head Researcher." Simon was astonished. *Being allowed unlimited access to this facility for a year and more? Even with the relatively limited hardware I can use in the Arena, I can learn so very much in that time . . .* "Where is the . . . index, reference work, whatever you might call it, that I would use to find my way around this paradise of knowledge?"

Relgof paused and tilted his head. *Oh-oh. I know that pose. Something both serious and amusing.*

"It may be, my friend, that you will not find our gift *quite* so generous as you think at the moment— although I believe in the end you will still see it as more than fair.

"Still, you understand that knowledge is our currency. The discussion was . . . heated as to exactly what to give, and how to give it. I am Head Researcher, but that position can of course change, so I am obligated to satisfy at least some of the demands of my colleagues. Some of them . . . have interests and alliances of their own which may not be aligned with yours, I am sorry to say. I could possibly have gotten you the precise information you asked for, but nothing else—and it might have been in a rather limited format."

I see. "And . . . ?"

"And so I allowed them to argue me into what they found a rather amusing yet, they felt, ultimately useless generosity. Namely, you have full access to the Analytic's Archives . . . but no access to the Indices of Knowledge, which only a full Researcher may have."

Simon realized his mouth had dropped open and he was simply *goggling* at Relgof, who at least had the decency to restrain his mirth after a single chortle. "I . . . *what*? This entire library of the gods and I won't even know what's *where*?" He felt anger rising and didn't bother to hide it. "Head Researcher, I can't even *imagine* what in God's name possessed you to 'allow' this? What possible—"

"Simon, please. I understand your anger, and it's quite justifiable . . . for the moment. But the fact is simply this: I was making a wager, a wager with myself against their assumptions."

Simon looked at him. "A . . . wager? On what?"

"The group which were being obstructive," Relgof said, "were interested in granting you as little as possible while gaining your prize in return. This struck them as an ideal method—giving you everything you asked, and more, but removing your chances of *finding* the key facts, leaving them as a single rope hidden in a forest of kelp. But I felt they were missing a key element: that you, yourself, conceived, built, and tested the Sandrisson Drive, the first of your people to do so, one of only a few thousand such in the history of the universe. Even if you cannot find your answers to the Sky Gates here, I believe—I absolutely believe—that you can derive *an* answer yourself.

"So I took a risk, yes. A risk that you might possibly not be as capable as I believe you are, against the ability for you to sample the knowledge of the Analytic freely, for the space of a year and a half."

Simon looked around again. For a few moments, his anger only increased, along with a feeling of overwhelming futility. It was an impossible task, and even finding anything *useful* in that nigh-endless Archive...

But Relgof's tone penetrated, finally. Those were not the words of someone who had managed to put one over on a sucker, but... "You have *that* much faith in me?"

Relgof spread his arms and bowed. "Have I not been at the side of Humanity almost since its arrival? Have I not watched you all closely? *You* chose your crew, Doctor Sandrisson, no one else, and that crew has done *extraordinary* things. I have faith that the man who brought them here is at least as extraordinary."

Simon looked up at the towering shelves; but now he felt a tiny shift within himself, a feeling of stubborn certainty. *I am standing within the greatest repository of knowledge in the entire* universe; *even if I pull out books and records at* random *I cannot imagine I would fail to find* something *interesting.*

He turned back to Relgof. "I . . . thank you for your faith, Rel. Really, I do." He surveyed the nigh-endless expanse. "I just hope I can live up to it."

Relgof bowed again. "I thank *you* for your understanding . . . and I wish you good luck."

Simon watched his friend—*and he* is *my friend, I think, and a good one*—leave through the door they had entered by, and then turned to face the Archives. Once more their infinite expanse nearly daunted him.

Yet . . .

Yet . . .

There was something almost . . . *familiar.*

That makes not the slightest bit of sense, you know, he thought. *You've never been here, and not a bit of this is actually familiar. I'm not even sure I've seen anything vaguely like this place, even in a simgame.*

The feeling refused to go away, however, and he found himself walking swiftly along, jumping into one of the egg-shaped craft and urging it forward. He did not quite understand *how* he knew how to operate the thing so well, but even that thought was distant.

Another part of him was simply growing more confused. He wasn't sure *why* he was going in this direction, or where this feeling of certainty came from.

A flicker of memory came . . . a surge of energy, of Shadeweaver and Faith working together desperately, trying to contain the power that Ariane Austin had neither the knowledge nor training to control . . . The floor heaving, contacts broken, all the power of both . . . and perhaps of Ariane herself . . . momentarily focused through *him* . . .

He couldn't remember that moment clearly; it had blurred, faded, and he realized that he had in fact *avoided* thinking of it since shortly afterwards. *But I think I took down notes just afterwards...I have to read them. I think...something* happened.

The silver and white egg had stopped, and his hand reached out, grasping a jointed object like a foldable piece of parchment. He looked on alien script written by a species he had never met, one perhaps a thousand years or ten thousand or a million years gone, and there was no translation, none of the Arena's usual tricks...

Yet Simon realized he *did* understand, that it made *sense*...and even as a surge of triumph went through him, Simon Sandrisson felt the chill breath of fear.

CHAPTER 14

"I thank you for being so open-minded, Captain," Oscar Naraj said to her with a more genuine smile than he had given in the first few hours after learning the truth. *A couple of days to look at things and mull it over has at least given him some perspective... I hope.*

"I won't say I'm *open-minded* on this subject, Ambassador—actually, I'm pretty certain I know exactly what's going to happen—but I'm willing to let you and Deputy Ambassador Ni Deng try anything as long as one of us is there to keep anything Arena-related from going wrong."

The Grand Arcade was the one truly neutral location in the Arena—and thus the only place Ariane would let them try to meet the Molothos. All the Factions traded here and no matter their attitude towards other creatures, that included the Molothos—perhaps even more than many, since as a Great Faction they had a huge need for trade.

This also allowed her new guests more chances to become used to the strangeness of the Arena and see the thousands of other species that Humanity would have to interact with in one way or another.

Ambassador Naraj stared in wonder at the immense expanse of open-air and enclosed markets, stalls, restaurants, amusement centers, and other things possibly less identifiable. Ni Deng's expression was awed, perhaps a touch frightened at first, but it swiftly became more chagrined. "I admit . . . this is somewhat overwhelming, Captain," she said finally. Her eyes tracked a large, multilegged lizardlike creature with an upright torso—*a Daelmokhan*, Ariane thought, *one of Sivvis' people*—walking alongside a Daalasan and carrying on an animated conversation, while another creature of unfamiliar species—some sort of strange floating gasbag—drifted next to them, occasionally flickering and gesturing.

"That's an understatement," she said with a smile.

"I think it's *exciting!*" Wu said, then looked somewhat contrite. He really *was* trying to manage the silent stoic bodyguard approach, but sometimes . . .

"Oh, it is *certainly* that, Wu Kung," Naraj agreed. "But overwhelming . . . yes. I admit I have had relatively little experience in more fantastic simulation areas—not my preferred sort of game—and perhaps that might have prepared me a bit better. I understand *you*, Captain Austin, were quite the aficionado in such games."

She nodded, grinning. *And that saved my ass in ways you can't imagine.* "True enough—but believe me, you two are doing humanity proud, as Gabrielle might say. We were still pretty much gobsmacked after this long, and we'd at least spent time working our way through our Sphere before we got here. You're doing just fine." She pointed. "Here, let's get a little something to eat. Hi, Olthalis!"

The blue-green, jellyfish-like alien was behind his usual stall near one of the main thoroughfares of the Arcade, moving on tendrils too delicate to support him in Earthly gravity; Ariane knew that the Arena provided each visitor to Nexus Arena with its own proper environment so that all were on equal footing here. Olthalis waved a pair of tendrils in a complex pattern. "A pleasing sight always, that of a customer and leader! Ariane Austin of Humanity! The currents flow well today?"

"Well enough, Olthalis. Ambassador Naraj, Deputy Ambassador Ni Deng, this is Olthalis of the ... Dispersants, is that correct?" At Olthalis' back-and-forth affirmative gesture, she continued, "of the Dispersants of the Chiroflekir. Olthalis was the first merchant with whom we dealt, and he's been very helpful in helping us get supplies and learn what we can and can't eat or drink here, along with Mairakag Achan—you'll meet him later."

"It is an honor and pleasure to meet you, Olthalis," Oscar Naraj said cheerfully. "We very much appreciate your assistance. 'Dispersants' ... would that be a particular, oh, political group of your species, then?"

The same affirmative gesture, followed by a negative one. *Yes and no?* "The Dispersants travel the currents, journey to the far reaches, return to the seas and join the Contemplative. Within the Contemplative there are political groups."

"Ah!" Ni Deng said, brightening. "An intelligent species with at least two lifecycle stages, then?"

"Exactly," Olthalis agreed. "The Contemplative remain in one place but are much larger, much wiser as they learn and exchange thoughts with many others.

But not all agree on all things, so where their Dispersants go, this varies much."

"So," Ariane said, "You'll have to return eventually to your home planet and become one of the Contemplative?" She seemed to remember there were some creatures on Earth, maybe a kind of jellyfish itself, that went through a similar lifecycle. *Have to mention this to Laila, if she hasn't heard about it herself; she'll be fascinated.*

"Eventually," Olthalis agreed, while opening one of the panels of his shop-stall. "But enjoying this time and not ready to go; a Dispersant does not have to return until they feel ready, and I have much to see yet!" The creature flickered with cheerful bioluminescence. "Especially with your people to provide more entertainment."

The two ambassadors chose something from Olthalis' collection of human-certified foodstuffs; Ariane got one of the red *nidii* for herself. Wu Kung bounced forward, sniffed at the various offerings, and grabbed a pair of things that looked like blue cinnamon sticks coated in a rippled glaze. "How much?"

"Three point seven vals, Captain," Olthalis said.

Gabrielle's foresight is paying off big *time,* Ariane thought as she reached into the pouch to get out Olthalis' payment. She caught sight of the blonde doctor just entering one of the larger shops, carrying several wrapped packages with her. Gabrielle had already exchanged several pieces of unique human artwork and cultural pieces for a lot of "vals"—short for simply "value units"—which were the common currency in Nexus Arena. *Until now we'd been relying on Steve's big winnings from our early days here.*

Now . . . now we all have money for regular outings and reserves in case we need to buy bigger things. Such as recharges; we could afford to just buy a recharge from the Powerbrokers now, if we had to.

After the incredible lengths they'd had to go through to get that recharge the *first* time, that thought felt *extremely* good.

"How is Dr. Sandrisson's work coming?" Naraj asked, even as he continued watching everything around him.

"He thinks the designs he's working on now, with Steve, Carl, and Marc, should allow us to locate the Sky Gates," she answered.

"Excellent news."

It *was* good news—*great* news, really—but Simon had been astonishingly quiet about it, almost *withdrawn*, and she didn't understand why; obviously his negotiations with Dr. Relgof had gone spectacularly well, as Simon had informed them that he was now able to visit the Analytic's Archives any time he wished for the next year and a half; yet he'd come back seeming . . . disturbed about something. *If this keeps up I'll have to try to yank whatever it is out of him, but I just haven't had the time yet.*

Naraj was continuing. "As I understand it, that will give us a direct route to Nexus Arena from our own Sphere, correct?"

"That's not *guaranteed*," she said cautiously. "According to what we've been told, it's a very good chance that one of the Sky Gates from our Sphere will lead here, but there is a small minority which don't have a direct connection. While the latter might be preferable for some security applications, overall I'd *much* rather we had such a connection."

"As would I," Naraj agreed.

"Hey, over there!" Wu Kung broke in.

Following his pointed finger, they saw a group of four Molothos, the crowds giving the all-hostile aliens a very wide berth. Ariane squinted, bringing up vision enhancements. *Yep, that's the pattern.* "Well, here's your chance, Ambassador. That's Dajzail himself, Leader of the Faction."

She allowed Naraj and Ni Deng to lead the way, though she and Wu Kung stayed close. She wasn't sure whether to smile or tense up; violence rarely went very far in Nexus Arena, as the Adjudicators would show up out of nowhere to intervene (barring direct interference by the Shadeweavers or, she presumed, the Faith), but with the Molothos you could never quite be sure . . .

Oscar Naraj placed himself directly in front of the advancing Molothos, but at a considerable distance, so that it became clear that he was waiting for them when he remained still and the rest of the crowd began moving away. "Dajzail of the Great Faction of the Molothos, might we speak for a moment?"

Dajzail slowed and halted, tilting the crested, lamprey-mouthed head slightly; its wraparound yellow eye glowed faintly. "Ariane Austin of Humanity, is this one of yours?" he rasped, ignoring Naraj for the moment.

"He is an ambassador of my people, though I remain Faction Leader. Dajzail, this is Oscar—"

"I care not for your names," Dajzail said, cutting her off. "Nor for 'ambassadors' from enemies of the Molothos. What words would matter?"

"I was hoping, perhaps," Naraj said, unfazed, "that we could recognize that while our initial contact has been unfortunately hostile, the crew here was not intended to speak with and establish relationships with other species."

One of the other Molothos started forward. "You waste our time on—"

To Ariane's surprise, Dajzail flicked a claw backwards, silencing the other instantly. "Go on."

Naraj glanced at her with a raised eyebrow, then turned back. "While our emergence into the Arena has been quite successful, we are still a small and new Faction; I was hoping there is some way we can find to eliminate what, as I understand it, is a virtual declaration of war from one of the most powerful Factions."

"Not *virtual*. There is no such thing. Either it is war, or it is not. Molothos have declared war on Humanity," Dajzail corrected, "and even now our ships seek your Sphere. Perhaps have already found it." He groomed his claws in a manner similar to a praying mantis. "Still," he said finally, "we have many wars and goals to pursue, and much effort may be wasted in this search. As Leader of the Faction of the Molothos, I am empowered to make peace when necessary, even with inferior species."

Which includes everyone who isn't a Molothos, of course. She could sense Wu Kung standing, tense as a bowstring, at her side.

"Of course you are, sir. So I ask you if there is in fact anything we might be able to do in order to make peace with your people?"

Dajzail groomed again. "I can see three such paths before us, Ambassador," he said, and Ariane did not like the suddenly-silky tones. "The first, and simplest, is that your Faction voluntarily ceases to be, by becoming a vassal of the Molothos. We do not make war on our own, and even lesser species can be of great use. As few join voluntarily, you would be accorded greater status among the slave species."

Oscar Naraj maintained a pleasant smile, though Ariane thought it must have been something of a strain. "I . . . see. The second?"

"In the interests of being reasonable," the Molothos leader went on, and something about the tone and posture was like a mocking grin, "we could also be satisfied with your ceding your Upper Sphere to us. Our people had landed upon your Sphere and claimed it, so I would be . . . willing to end the state of war if you were to give us that which we had fairly claimed."

"I can understand that position," Naraj said, still with a pleasant, neutral tone. "And your third offer?"

"While my prior offers are most generous for the Molothos, we are often . . . accused of being both hostile and unreasonable," Dajzail answered, and his tone was almost *unctuous*. "So, in the interests of . . . fostering a more cooperative atmosphere with others and showing how . . . willing we are to enter the greater Arena community, we will be satisfied with a much less expensive act—even, I would say, a mere symbolic trifle, given the injuries we have suffered." His voice suddenly shifted back to the rasping screech she expected from Molothos. "Give us Marc C. DuQuesne and Stephen Franceschetti. Let us kill them with our best executioners over a period of two weeks. We will even allow you to take back the bodies when we are done." He spread his claws in a grotesque parody of open-armed welcome. "A fair bargain indeed, would you not agree?"

DuQuesne threw one of their bodies down right in front of them; Steve... Steve was the one who figured out how to get past Dajzail's blockade of Transition, when we were about to lose our Sphere by default.

"Certainly a vastly more...diplomatic and reasonable offer than the others, Dajzail," Oscar said slowly. "I will...think about these offers."

"Yes, do that, *Ambassador*," Dajzail hissed silkily. "And while you do, ask of news of the Randaalar, who rejected similar generosity a thousand years ago. The head of the last survivor is mounted in my council-chamber."

The Molothos swept forward, and Oscar and the others drew back, letting them pass. After a few moments, Naraj spoke again. "I shall think about these offers, and how they show that there truly exist monsters with whom negotiation is not possible. My apologies, Captain; if *that* is what they have chosen as the leader of their entire species—which if I understand aright will have thousands or tens of thousands of Spheres...well," he smiled wryly, "we have no use for diplomats in that particular case. I will so report as soon as possible."

"Will you have to go back for that report?" *It'd be nice if they'd be leaving the Arena periodically.*

"Oh, not at all," Naraj said. "A message...torpedo, I suppose you could call it—supplied with Sandrisson coils and sufficient charge to travel back and forth—will allow two-way communication. The first of these should be ready by now, in fact, and I would expect more ships will follow very soon." He smiled broadly. "You did say we would have to establish a larger presence, didn't you?"

→ CHAPTER 15 ←

"Challenges," Carl Edlund said, "are the heart of Arena political maneuvering."

The entire group was gathered in one of Humanity's briefing rooms. *Well,* DuQuesne thought to himself, *everyone except Tom and Laila, who're on the Sphere because someone's got to stay there, and Simon, who thinks he's close to finishing his design so he's not letting anyone interrupt.* Something else was bothering the physicist, DuQuesne could tell, but he hadn't said anything about it and DuQuesne was reluctant to pry. *Not like I never had secrets.*

Carl was giving the lecture—mostly targeted towards the newcomers—because he'd spent a lot of time while they were gone learning about the mechanisms and approaches of common Challenges.

Carl nodded at them. "Those of us who were here understand that in our gut. There is *nothing* more important in the Arena than someone issuing a Challenge to another Faction, and you newcomers need to really get that through your heads. Almost everything of importance either gets triggered by, or settled with, a Challenge. There's *some* exceptions, but not very many."

"My general impression of these Challenges seems...rather primitive for a civilization so advanced," Oscar said slowly. "Trial by combat as a—even, perhaps, the dominant—negotiation tool?"

Carl laughed. "Combat and physical prowess did seem to feature highly in our experiences, yes. But there are plenty of Challenges which turn out to be focused on things a lot less flashy. Admittedly, *those* are the type of Challenge that don't get very many spectators unless the spectators are involved in the outcome—I'd be pretty riveted watching the equivalent of a game of chess if our homeworld was in the balance, but otherwise I don't think I'd be much into it.

"The big, flashy Challenges serve multiple purposes, and a smart Faction understands that your Challenge performance isn't just important for that particular Challenge—it's important for how everyone else views you, it draws attention to your Faction, it gives you good, or bad, publicity, all sorts of things. This part should be familiar to most of us; that's not all that different from things back home. We all know how the Interest vector's one of the most tradeable—and volatile—units of value, and how even a single spectacular event can drive interest sky-high—or drop it in the toilet, if the spectacular event involved failure."

Images materialized over the table; DuQuesne and Carl facing the Molothos, Ariane in the *Skylark*, Sivvis with Tunuvun dangling from one arm, and Amas-Garao towering over a stunned Ariane. "The Challenges we saw—either by being a part of them, or watching them—in our first time here actually provide us with a good introduction." The first image swelled. "The very first Challenge we faced actually is one of the rare ones that the Arena calls a Class Two Challenge. Class One Challenges are initiated by mutual agreement in the Arena, and are basically more-or-less formal affairs. In effect, one way or another an authorized member of a Faction says 'I challenge you!' and another authorized member of the Challenged Faction accepts the Challenge." He nodded to DuQuesne, who was assisting him in the presentation.

"Class Two Challenges are a whole different can of worms," DuQuesne said. "They're events that take place *outside* of Nexus Arena but that have a major impact on a Faction or Factions, and that stem from a direct conflict between the Factions in one way or another. In this case, we humans were newcomers who just happened to have the bad luck to have the Molothos land a survey and initial colonization party on our Upper Sphere. In a sense, of course, that was also bad luck for the Molothos; normally they either wouldn't encounter any significant resistance landing on an Upper Sphere, or the Sphere would be inhabited and there'd be obvious civilized presence there.

"For a big Faction, the Molothos landing on one Sphere wouldn't be a big deal—potential interstellar incident, yes, but nothing of great import to the Faction as a whole. But for us it was absolutely crucial we get them off our Sphere *pronto*. If the Molothos controlled our Upper Sphere, we'd be pretty much crippled until we managed, somehow, to get *another* Sphere of our own and thus access to Sky Gates and Straits that wouldn't be watched and guarded by our enemies. So from the Arena's point of view, that was a Challenge, and by our managing to defeat the entire invading force and prevent a direct counterstrike by *Blessing of Fire*, we won the Challenge. Other examples of Class Two Challenges might be an actual war, or simultaneous landings on an uninhabited Upper Sphere, things of that sort."

"So these . . . impromptu external Challenges would be triggered only by events of considerable importance to the relevant Factions, then?" Oscar asked.

Carl nodded. "As far as I can tell, yes." He grinned nastily. "That's *not* the case for Class One Challenges. You can issue Challenge for an awful lot of things if you're authorized to do so."

"Hold on, Carl," Ariane said. "I don't remember authorizing people to issue Challenge, exactly, and it seemed to me that *any* of us were in danger of getting Challenged or inadvertently issuing one."

"An artifact of our being a brand new Faction with a tiny number of members in the Arena," Carl said. "Basically, those who are part of the main Embassy staff are the most subject to issuing or receiving Challenge. There's some complicated details—like how a Leader can partially reduce the exposure to Challenge while they're away, but how that reduction can be nullified, mostly to prevent a Faction like the Molothos from basically having their Leader go home and the rest be able to act like total . . . jerks to everyone else with impunity." He looked over at Oscar, Michelle, and Oasis. "That means *you* people are definitely in that class, and so you need to walk carefully."

"Hm. Yes, I understand," Oscar said slowly. "I recall the other complication—that you can refuse Challenge twice, but you must accept the third or immediately default, and defaulting is the same as losing a Challenge."

"Right." Ariane pointed to the racing image. "I was

trying to second-guess that bit when I accepted the Challenge from what turned out to be a proxy for the Blessed To Serve. Now that turned out okay—because I figured out a way to win it at the last moment—"

"—because you're more than half crazy," put in Carl.

"Well, maybe." A grin flashed out.

"And you always have to remember the key point," Gabrielle spoke up. "Like in many old Earth duelling traditions, it's the one being Challenged who gets to set the conditions. So the other big tactic is to try to get someone to Challenge *you* when you've got a plan on how to beat them."

"And work through proxies is a big part of that, too." DuQuesne found himself, like Ariane, looking at the image of Amas-Garao. "That gives you a *huge* advantage. The other guy doesn't realize who he's really Challenging, and may even think *he's* trying to maneuver your proxy, rather than being played himself."

DuQuesne looked around, suddenly grimly serious. "But before you start thinking this sounds like some fun game to play, remember this: these guys are *all* Big Time Operators. Even the smaller Factions, the younger species, they've been here for *thousands* of years. We've been lucky as hell so far and we've managed to pull off a couple of honest-to-God miracles, but we can't expect that to keep going. Even the guys that seem nominally on our side, like the Analytic and the Faith, they're playing the game ten layers deep and we can't count on *not* being a pawn on their board."

"On the positive side," Carl said, pointing to the image of Sivvis and Tunuvun, "not all Challenges are the product of hostile takeover attitudes; for instance, the Powerbrokers' Challenges pretty much *have* to be accepted, but they don't actually care about the prize *per se* from winning the Challenge and so the general tradition there is that their chosen champion gets to take the prize home."

"I found that challenge *very* interesting," Oasis said seriously, pushing one of the long ponytails back out of her way. *I have to get a chance to talk to her alone, but that's going to be a problem as long as they keep her nearby as a bodyguard.* She went on, "I mean, the idea that we were already able to Challenge as soon as we showed up, but this native race gets nothing? That doesn't seem fair."

"Sure doesn't!" Wu agreed emphatically. "They were born here, they should have—"

DuQuesne laughed. "That's the *other* thing to keep in mind. It *isn't* fair, except by the rules of the Arena—and we *still* don't know all those rules. Maybe *nobody* knows all those rules except the Arena itself. It's not set up to be nice and evenhanded to each and every person and species, it's set up by these Voidbuilders—whoever and whatever they were—to accomplish . . . something. And since we don't know what that 'something' is, plenty of what goes on here is going to look arbitrary, maybe even cruel, and sure as God made little green apples it's not going to look fair.

"We don't get to set the rules. We don't get to change the rules. We generally won't get to *argue* the rules. No one does. The Arena says how things get done, and we can either take it, or try to pick up our marbles and go home. But that won't stop the Arena's people from butting in on our turf eventually, so even *that* isn't really an option."

Wu Kung frowned rebelliously, and DuQuesne didn't

need to be a mind reader to know what was going on in Wu's head. *Arbitrary godlike rules chafe on the Monkey King, and I'm gonna have to sit down and try to pound sense into him real soon, before he tries to do something perfectly in character but disastrous.*

"So," Michelle Ni Deng said after a moment, "You're basically warning us that all of us here are in the line of fire, and we need to be careful."

"*And* open to opportunities," Carl emphasized. "We want to avoid getting screwed . . . but we also can use the Challenges to our advantage. You can't, in general, Challenge away your home Sphere; the closest I know of would've been if the Molothos had kicked our asses and taken the Upper Sphere, but even then we'd still have the Inner Sphere and Gateways."

"I see. And the prizes of a Challenge are proportional to the resources of the participants," Oscar said.

"Exactly. Which means that as a new, tiny Faction, we can generally stand to gain a *hell* of a lot more than larger Factions can from us." He grinned. "And *politically* we've gained a *lot* from the Challenges. Yeah, okay, we're at war with the Molothos, but—"

Oscar bowed from his seat. "—But I have conceded that, given the circumstances, there was indeed no way to avoid that outcome, based on what I now have seen of those enemies. I hope to find the Blessed at least somewhat more amenable to discussion."

"Right. What that means is that we've got *great* publicity and public image—and recognition—right now. The shiny new coolness will wear off eventually, but not yet, and right now we're the brand new kids on the block who managed to outfox the two scariest Factions when we first showed up, then whip the biggest bullies around as an encore. That's the advantage of the spectacular Challenges."

"And—pardon me for asking you to repeat yourself," Ni Deng said, "there is no actual limit on *what* the Challenged party can put forth as a Challenge?"

"Well . . . there are *some*. You can't for instance Challenge someone to a water-breathing contest when you're a natural water resident and they're only an air-breather, so to speak. There has to be *some* reasonable way that both of you can participate in the Challenge, and the Challenge itself can't *assume* proxy use by either side. Other than that . . . no." Carl grinned. "And they can be all sorts of mixed-mode kinds of things. For instance, the one I was watching with Selpa a while back? That one was called 'Racing Chance,' and it combined a sort of combat maze-race with a gambling game."

DuQuesne raised an eyebrow. "How'd *that* work?"

"Pretty neat, actually. Each side had a racing individual and they ran through a mostly parallel but sometimes intersecting maze. The contestants couldn't *directly* interact with each other but they could try to mess up the course for the guy behind them, and they each had to deal with combat threats along the way. Meanwhile, each side *also* had a couple people playing a game that was sorta like poker, and you could spend the points you won in the game to up the challenges put in front of the opposing guy's racer."

Ariane nodded, smiling. "That would be . . . pretty exciting. Strategy, luck, and combat all in one package; let your chips ride so you could put down a devastating opposition toward the end, or spend them right away so that you can't lose them to a bad hand, things like that—plus choosing the right racer. And I'd guess they might have something to do with agreeing on the racecourse, too."

"Probably." Carl looked around. "That's mostly it, I think. The thing to remember is that Challenges aren't casual. We can't back out of them without forfeit, and they will *cost* us to lose or to forfeit—but at the same time, we can *gain* a hell of a lot if we take and win them." He looked seriously at the three newcomers. "We can't keep you out of that part of the game, Oscar, Michelle, Oasis—not and let you guys do anything useful around Nexus Arena. So you may find yourselves in the position of having to decide whether to accept a Challenge—or, if someone's clearly pushing on you, whether you need to *issue* one. We can't reject them all, but we sure can't afford to just accept them or issue them blindly...because what we do here could affect *everyone*."

Oscar nodded, and so did Michelle and Oasis. "Understood, and this little session has helped make this clear to me."

"One more thing," Steve said. "Carl mentioned that *almost* everything of importance gets settled by Challenge—but that *almost* is important. The last maneuver that the Molothos tried on us was deliberately *not* a Challenge; they learned stuff about us, made some guesses, and set up a plan that was in no way *directly* confrontational which would—if they guessed right—deprive us of our Arena citizenship and negate the victories we'd already achieved."

"Worse than that," DuQuesne said. "I thought about that scenario right after you," he pointedly indicated Steve, who gave a slightly embarrassed but proud grin, "saved our asses at the last minute, and I got cold chills. If we were deprived of our citizenship like that—we might not have been able to go back to our Sphere at all. We'd have become like the natives of Arenaspace, at least until someone *else* from Earth came through and restarted the whole thing. I'm not sure *exactly* what would have happened, but given what we already know, I'd have to guess it would've been worse than just being sent back to square one, at least for those of us stuck on this side."

"So," Wu said, "that means that there's real Challenges, and then little challenges—that might not be so little—and we have to look out for both."

"Exactly right, Wu. The 'real' Challenges may be the usual way of doing business, but as Steve and the Molothos showed, the stakes can get *plenty* high without being in an official face-off."

The meeting broke up then, and people filed mostly out of the room; Ariane, along with Wu, hung back. "So...do you think they understand, Marc?"

"Oscar sure as hell does," he answered. "Ni Deng... yeah, probably. She's maybe not as experienced as Oscar Naraj, but she's probably smarter. You can bet Oasis gets it—and she'll be real careful." He frowned to himself.

"What *is* it, Marc?"

He knew there were at least two levels of inquiry there...and he wasn't ready to address the second, at least not until he got a chance to talk to Oasis privately. "I...dunno, really. We had to tell them about Challenges, they've *got* to understand how much rides on them...but that also makes them real players in the Arena now, and there's no way to stop it." He looked at the now-empty doorway. "I just hope I'm worried over nothing."

CHAPTER 16

"Are you *sure* this is okay, DuQuesne? I mean, I really really *want* to go with you, but you want me to guard Ariane, and—"

"Relax, Wu," DuQuesne said, smiling. *Already talking a mile a minute.* "We all agreed you needed to be able to get out and about."

"Quite so," agreed Simon absently, as they made their way along the broad corridor towards the elevator to the Outer Gateway. Low, flat tracks of shaped superconductor now lay along the entire length of that corridor, and also to the Inner Gateway, allowing magnetic levitation to be used as a support and guide for cargoes. In this case, both Simon and DuQuesne were drawing large cases along behind them.

"And Ariane's agreed that she's not leaving the Embassy whenever you're gone. Anyone wants to see her, they have to go in our territory."

Wu grimaced. "I'd still feel better if *you* were with her right now."

DuQuesne shrugged. "I don't expect direct assassination, to be honest. The Arena clamps down pretty hard on anyone who initiates violence, unless the

Shadeweavers or—I'd guess—the Faith mess with that." There was a faint sensation of acceleration as the elevator doors closed and the room shot up towards the Outer Gateway. *And if the geometry of the Sphere is anything like we've guessed, we're actually accelerating at a* lethal *pace. We'll cover a couple thousand kilometers from down here to the top in about five seconds. Something like thirty thousand gravities—hell, that wouldn't be too shabby even from the old* Skylark's *point of view.*

Almost before he had finished thinking that, the chamber slowed and the doors opened. They were now in what Gabrielle, if he remembered right, had christened "the antechamber" to the Upper Sphere.

But things were very different from the first time. Now, the superconducting tracks continued all the way to the huge doorway, and the whole area was covered by simple automated weapons emplacements, with storage areas for needed items and materials... and tracks and marks showing how much traffic there had been over the past few months. *Carl, Tom, and Steve have been busting their humps over this, that's obvious.* "Open Outer Gateway," he said.

The great door—made of the same "coherent quark composite," or CQC, that appeared to be the Arena's preferred structural building material—rolled effortlessly aside, and a blaze of golden sunshine poured in, along with the warm fragrance of a living world.

"Wow!" exclaimed Wu, and bounded out before DuQuesne could stop him. His voice came immediately from outside. "It's beautiful! And there's a waterfall over there—and look, something's flying way, way over there, like a bird, but not quite!"

The tracks cut back from the Gateway and headed up the ridge from which the Gateway projected. "Ah. This road must lead up to the river, just above the falls."

"So I am given to understand," Simon said. DuQuesne noticed that he was not spending much time looking around—which was not characteristic of the usually highly attentive and aware scientist. Simon drew ahead of DuQuesne, because DuQuesne had to wait and catch Wu's attention. "This way, Wu. Yes, *this* way! We'll go over and look at the jungle in a minute, just hold your horses!"

The Monkey King bounded back towards him, then stopped at a gesture. "What is it?"

"First, I've got some things we need to get straight. You heard the lecture on the Challenges, and I know you read the accounts of what we went through here. I want you to be *double* careful, Wu. Yes, I know, there's probably still not much here that could beat you, but this isn't your world, remember, and you can't just bust heads whenever people piss you off."

Wu looked slightly hurt. "I know that! I wouldn't... I mean, I *never* just break heads because... Well, *almost* never... unless they're really mean... or..."

"See, that's *exactly* what I'm talking about. You've got to *think*, just like if Sanzo—or Ariane—were holding the charm to make your headband go crunch, got me?"

Wu Kung nodded, red-black hair tumbling over his face in emphasis. "I got you, DuQuesne. Think before I fight."

"And about fighting—it'll probably come to that, sooner or later. But I want you to hold it down, hold *way* back unless you've got no choice (like, for instance, Ariane's life is in the balance)." He glanced, saw that Simon was still moving along towards the crest of the hill, grinned at Wu. "These people still don't really know what we can do, you see . . . and I don't think that even the best of them *can* match us."

"I thought you said that you were beaten by this wizard, this Amas-Garao."

"Well . . ." DuQuesne shrugged. "He's a tough customer, no doubt about it, and he can *cheat* in a way no one but another Shadeweaver can. But truth? Wu, I spent *fifty years* shutting myself down, and even with active resistance clothing to keep me sort of in shape and a few other tricks, I just wasn't anywhere near up to top form. I'd been . . . awake, I guess you'd call it, for only a few weeks when that happened, and to be honest? I think I was fighting *at best* at about eighty percent. Which means that they don't know what I can *really* do when I'm pushed, and they sure as *hell* haven't a clue as to what to expect from you.

"So remember, we need diplomacy and sneakiness here. I don't want them getting any idea just how much tougher and faster you are than me. Except—just a little bit—Orphan, because I think he's guessed it and we did imply we'd show him. Even then, though, I want you to baffle those jets *way* down."

Wu grinned, showing his fangs. "Until there's no choice—and then I have surprises!"

"Exactly."

Wu looked more serious, and DuQuesne followed his gaze. "He's . . . not happy, exactly," Wu said.

Yeah, I knew it. "How do you mean?" he asked aloud.

"He smells . . . nervous. Upset. Confused," Wu said after a moment. "Not about what he's doing *now*—he's pretty sure about that. But something else—maybe related to it, maybe not—that's bothering him."

Wu's senses were always the best. "Noticed it myself. But he hasn't decided to talk about it, and I'm not quite ready to force him to talk."

Cresting the hill, they could see the broad, swift-flowing river flashing in the light as it ran from the mountains which lay to the east (figuring apparent sunrise as "east" and sunset as "west") and then plunged straight down thousands of feet. The rumble-roar of the shimmering cataract was clearly audible.

Just before the river plunged into air, there were new, rough-looking structures erected on each side. *Our first native generators; thank the Gods for people like Tom and Steve and Carl. Together they got this stuff going with nothing but one AIWish unit and a lot of personal sweat. And not a minute too soon—we're going to be getting new potential colonists any day, maybe any* minute *now.*

Simon looked around. "This should be as good a place as any. Marc—"

"On it." He unslung his own pack and started setting up the control relay set. *Have to hope it works...* "Wu, hold *on*, would you? Once I'm sure this is all working I'll show you some of the sights." *Damn, but I'd forgotten how it's like babysitting a toddler sometimes. I don't suppose I should really worry right now; there's not much he can hurt wandering around here, and there's sure as hell not much here that could hurt* him.

Still, he wanted to make sure he kept an eye on Sun Wu Kung; getting into trouble seemed to be his tradition.

"Seems like a beautiful day for this," Simon said, sounding more relaxed than he had been. "Hardly a breath of wind." He squinted into the distance. "I see some clouds off to the horizon, but nothing worrisome."

DuQuesne glanced upward. He suspected that what *he* saw was somewhat different than what Simon saw: to DuQuesne, the alien shadows behind the deceptively-normal blue sky were clear and ominous, the echoes of a universe that violated every law DuQuesne had thought he understood. *But I've figured out tougher puzzles in stranger worlds,* he thought wryly. *Even if the worlds were simulated, I didn't* know *it at the time.*

"What are you doing?" Wu asked, having bounded back nearby. "I mean, I know you're looking for these Sky Gates, but how?"

"Well, that's . . . fairly simple and complicated at the same time," Simon said, smiling. "The simple explanation . . . we need to search a large portion of the sky over our Sphere to find the Gates. I've . . ." DuQuesne caught the slight hesitation, "made some quite sensitive instruments that should be able to detect a Gate if they get within a reasonable distance of one. The problem is that the Gates are . . . well, out of our gravity well, so to speak. Just above the region where gravity ends, much as I hate to use such a term."

"Accurate here, though. Border's just about as sharp as a knife from everything we've seen; goes from no gravity to full in maybe a few meters."

"But that's a really long way up, isn't it?" Wu asked. "I mean, way higher than even the Mountains of Heaven!"

Simon's smile returned at that. "Yes, much higher." He glanced at DuQuesne. "Is he exaggerating himself for me?"

Wu snorted and looked slightly embarrassed. "There's your answer. Look, Wu, I know your personality. You don't have to go making yourself look stupider than you are around *Simon*. Or me, or Ariane, for that matter. Other people, yeah, but the core group—the eight originals? Be yourself, but no less than yourself."

"All right! You've caught my tail fairly." He bowed apologetically to Simon. "So, that's a long way up—thousands of kilometers, yes?"

"About twenty thousand above the Upper Sphere, and extending about five to ten thousand kilometers to the sides of our Sphere, yes."

Wu thought. "You came here with DuQuesne before, a couple of days ago, while I was out with the captain, right? So you started it...hmm...Ha! Balloons!"

Simon laughed. "Not a bad idea, but I'm afraid too slow. At any reasonable ascent rate a balloon would take on the order of a month to get there, and we have something of a time pressure involving our friends the Molothos. But your general concept is right. DuQuesne and I sent the instruments up in what amount to heated-air ramjet drones manufactured by Tom according to my specifications. They used the majority of the energy in their coils climbing, but in the weightless environment above they should be able to recharge from the sunlight provided by the so-called 'luminaire' above our Sphere, and they won't need nearly so much power to maneuver."

Wu squinted up. "So that is not really a sun at all?"

"Nope," DuQuesne said. "It still isn't small, of course—not in *any* way. We're pretty sure it's at an altitude just a little ways outside of the gravity area, which would make it about a hundred, hundred and ten kilometers wide." He remembered the lighting shifts and grinned. "The Arena also does some kind of lighting tricks with it so that you get sunsets and night pretty much like at home ... though you'll be seeing something other than stars in the night sky."

"Hm. You know, I hadn't thought about that, Marc," Simon said, "but that's yet another of those subtle but impossible effects we keep coming across. In an atmosphere that extends so far, the light should be more diffuse, and there should be no true night." He shrugged. "Now, if we could finish getting set up ...?"

A few minutes sufficed to get all the equipment assembled—and pitch a tent nearby. "You're sure about this, Simon?"

"It's almost like camping in the backyard, Marc. Someone's coming up here at least once a day, and as I understand it the first group of newcomers will be arriving tomorrow or the day after. I'll be fine."

"So your probe-things are already up there in the sky?"

"They should be, Wu. We'll find out if they all made it and if they're all ready in a moment."

"How many did you make?"

Simon bent over the console and pulled out a hardwired interface connection, locked it into the connector port at the base of his skull. The system went live; while DuQuesne could see displays on the field controls, he knew Simon would now be seeing much more. "Fifteen units—as many as Tom could manage in two days with the materials input we could scavenge from *Holy Grail*." A pause. "I am getting operational responses from twelve; number six probe is at altitude but the instrument package is showing no operation, and two others are simply not responding."

"Is that enough?"

"Oh, I think so. Lined up side by side, I'm confident they can each cover a hundred-kilometer radius, so together they cover the equivalent of twenty-four hundred kilometers of the projected area in a sweep. A few weeks, perhaps a month or two at the outside, should give us contact with most if not all of our Gates."

"How about knowing where they *go*?" Wu Kung asked sensibly. "It will be fine to have many doors in the sky, but you would like to know what waits on the other side."

"Oh, most certainly. Tom is making some additional probes for that; once we locate the gates, two-stage probes will be sent up. The second stage will enter the gates, and each will have enough energy for a double jump at such a small size. They will jump, take readings for a few seconds, and jump back, relaying the data back here."

"You're going to check all of them?" DuQuesne asked.

Simon seesawed his hand. "Maybe, maybe not. The goal, after all, is to find out if we have a Gateway to Nexus Arena. So I will send probes through until either I have found Nexus Arena on the other side, or I have run out of Gates to check. I would prefer *not* to send probes through the others if I could avoid it, as we have no idea what might be on the other side—including a hostile Molothos colony." He tapped controls on the console before him. "That may seem improbable in the extreme . . . but I think we can all agree that the improbable has become the commonplace for us here."

"Amen; I read you to nine decimals on that. Find Nexus Arena and then stop until we have ourselves set up, courtesy of Orphan." He saw Wu starting to follow the river. "Okay. You set for now?"

"Marc, *go*," the white-haired scientist said with an honest grin. "I may look like an academic, but I am not *entirely* unable to survive outside of the laboratory for a few moments. It will be a novelty, at least for a while, and if I find it wearing, the elevator is, what, fifteen minutes' hike away."

DuQuesne chuckled. *He does have something bothering him, but this isn't the time to push.* "Okay, then, I'm off. Let us know as soon as you find something."

"I assure you, I will *sprint* home with that news."

By the time DuQuesne caught up with Wu Kung, the Monkey King was hanging over the side of the waterfall. "Wow! This is almost as far as Seven Devils' Torrent!"

He thought back and managed to remember that part of Wu's own world in Hyperion. "Yeah, just about. Seven Devils would've been maybe thirty meters higher."

"It's really beautiful. The *color* of those plants is so bright—and different!" Wu let go, slid down the sheer cliff face so quickly that DuQuesne found himself frozen, reaching out for a figure that had already dropped far out of reach. Clawed hands contracted, dug indestructible claws in, found purchase in stone. The Hyperion Monkey King now dangled by one hand from the cliff-face, sniffing at a flower that grew from a blue-green clump of leaves in the middle of an otherwise barren span of rock. He sneezed. "Spicy! I'll bet you could use that as a flavor."

"We've barely begun categorizing stuff here, Wu."

Not that warning him would do any good, but he had to *try*. "So anything could be poisonous or—"

"Worry worry worry, you haven't changed, DuQuesne! I will know if these are dangerous!"

Utterly hopeless. Why am I even trying?

As he watched Wu Kung swing himself back up to the top of the cliff and then start running precariously along it, back the way they'd come, he answered himself with a smile. *Because he's one of the few good things from my old life, and I want those things* safe.

"Ah! There's that path down!"

Naturally, Sun Wu Kung didn't actually run back to the *beginning* of the path; he just dropped down twenty or so meters to the place where he'd noticed the path on the cliff-face.

DuQuesne swore good-naturedly. "Hold *on*, Wu!" *I am* not *letting him drag me into some show-off "follow the leader" just so he can find out how out of shape I am even now.*

Wu didn't exactly *wait*, but he *did* slow down enough so that DuQuesne nearly caught up to him before he reached the winch that led to the forest below. "Oh, wonderful!" he exclaimed, and swung himself out and over, sliding down the cable that disappeared into the forest below.

"Dammit. Sun Wu Kung, I am going to . . ."

An explosion of colorful, glittering wings showed that Wu had just annoyed a stagfly nest—the giant insectoid things that DuQuesne had encountered on his first trip down. They weren't dangerous to someone in armor, and that meant that Wu probably wouldn't even pay them much mind, but there were other creatures down there...

Oh, stop worrying. You sound like my mother, Marc! He heard Seaton's voice, with that humorous tone that always took the edge off the corrections or remonstrations when Marc DuQuesne found he wasn't handling the situation as diplomatically as Seaton thought he should. *A whole assault force of Molothos wasn't enough to stop* you, *do you think there's* anything *down there he can't handle?* No.

"Actually," he muttered to himself, "I'm more worried about the native lifeforms."

He could manage the slide down the cable too—his hands were, naturally, much tougher than any ordinary person's—so down he went.

As he reached the bottom, having batted the odd stagfly aside, he heard burbling screeches some distance away. The sound was familiar from a recording. *Carl called them splaywolves...Pack hunters, not top predators maybe but not harmless.*

He jogged up cautiously. Sure enough, Wu was standing in a small clearing, ten or fifteen creatures with the sinuous bodies of weasels or ferrets circling him, running like lizards on wide-set legs. The heads were long yet flattened, almost crocodilian in a way, but covered with a ruffled material—something like scales crossed with hair; the same material covered the entire body in a close-woven pattern of pale browns and muted blue-greens. Each of the things was six feet long and stood a foot and a half off the ground at the shoulder.

One scuttled toward Wu, leaping slightly, snapping with backward-jagged teeth. Wu dodged effortlessly and smacked the creature on its rump, evading what looked like a bladed tail. The splaywolf gave a cooing shriek and fled to a distance of ten or fifteen meters. The others echoed the sound and shifted their patrol pattern slightly.

DuQuesne checked around to make sure there weren't any of the predators trying to sneak up on him. *No, not at the moment. But they're pretty bright; they're trying to adjust tactics, figure out this new animal.*

Then Wu dropped to all fours, spun around on his hands and feet in a similar manner, and gave vent to a burbling call of his own.

What the . . . ?

The splaywolves froze. Then one answered, this time with a threatening call; Wu responded even more threateningly, and the largest of the group gave an unmistakable snarl, baring all its teeth, claws extending on the feet.

Wu did not move.

DuQuesne stayed where he was, unable to believe what he was seeing. *It can't be.*

The large splaywolf leapt forward and Wu met it halfway, boxing its head like a punching bag. A cry of pain and shock, and the creature spun again, trying to catch Wu, but this time Sun Wu Kung bounded over its snapping, clawing attack and landed squarely on its back. The creature tried to claw and bite, but Wu shoved its head down to the ground and ignored the attacks.

A moment later the creature gave a whining sigh, and Wu immediately let it go. The splaywolf backed up, head down, whining, and Wu bobbed up and down, giving another burbling call.

Immediately the whole pack moved in and rubbed around Wu in an unmistakable greeting.

My . . . God.

He knew what had just *happened.* But . . . "Wu!"

"Oh! Hi, DuQuesne! Caught up as I was making some friends! They aren't *quite* like the monkeys, but they aren't completely stupid." The splaywolves were backing up, showing their teeth as DuQuesne moved into view. Wu shook his head. "No! None of that! This is DuQuesne. He is my friend. You go, smell him, know friend!"

And as the creatures followed Wu Kung's instructions, he had to accept what he saw. *It shouldn't be possible. But it is. What's the Arena up to now?*

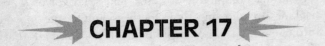

CHAPTER 17

"May the Minds show favor on this meeting," Sethrik said formally, as he seated himself before the conference table in one of the split-back seats designed for his species. "It is a pleasure to meet more of your people, Captain Austin."

"It is a pleasure to meet with you as well, Sethrik of the Blessed," Oscar Naraj said, and Michelle Ni Deng echoed the sentiment. Oasis Abrams was not present; the two diplomats had given her leave to spend a day out on her own, and the energetic redhead had instantly disappeared out the door.

Sethrik turned, to indicate one of his companions; this Blessed's exoskeleton had a distinctive pattern, dark green for the crests and lighter green for the face. "I present to you Vantak, currently my second in command."

Vantak performed the pushup-bow which was one of the few things shared between the Blessed and the Liberated. "I greet you, newcomers to the Arena. I hope the meeting in peace will become one of many."

Ariane remembered Vantak without much warmth—her clearest memory of the other Blessed was of him assisting in the humiliation of Gabrielle to sucker her into the challenge of Amaṣ-Garao—but to be fair, he had simply been following his own Faction's directives. "Our hope as well."

"It is in fact that very subject which caused me to have Captain Austin invite you here, Leader Sethrik," Naraj said warmly. "I find it very gratifying and hopeful that you accepted so quickly."

Sethrik glanced at him, and then back to Ariane. "Clarify, please, what this newcomer's status is?"

"Ambassador Naraj and Deputy Ambassador Ni Deng are emissaries from the governing body of our solar system. They have been sent to assist us in establishing better relations with the various Factions, among other things."

"Ah." Sethrik gave a slightly deeper pushup-bow. "It is more of an honor, then. I greet you in the name of the Minds, Ambassadors." He looked to Ariane. "Have they . . . your authority, Captain?"

"If you mean, have I ceded the leadership of our Faction to them, no. Decisions of any import will still have to be cleared through me in the end. However, they are certainly empowered to discuss many things and may arrive at tentative arrangements pending my final approval." Ariane had given a lot of thought to the situation in the last few days, and the fact was that she *had* to concede *some* level of power to the ambassador, give him some amount of authority, or his reports would—rightly—lead inevitably to the conclusion that Ariane was a potential tin-pot dictator trying to keep all power to herself.

Still, in a sense that conclusion would be entirely correct; Ariane had no intention of giving away Humanity's current advantage just for the sake of making things more comfortable back home. Thus she retained full authority over any final agreements. If this worked *well*, she'd have extended her negotiating reach via proxies who understood negotiation better than she did, while not losing the basic power of decision.

Sethrik's wingcases relaxed fractionally. "Ah, very wise. I would advise against any sudden changes in leadership." He addressed himself to Oscar and Michelle. "Captain Ariane Austin is an *extremely* formidable person, and the Arena and its Factions hold great respect for her. Delegation of authority from her shows great trust—and puts a grave burden upon you all to honor her properly."

Naraj nodded. "I have been learning of this since my arrival, Leader Sethrik. Our initial impressions at home had...failed to grasp the entirety of the situation, but I am coming to understand the magnitude of the...challenges before us."

"Good. What was it you wished to discuss?"

"First—do you require any refreshment?" the ambassador inquired, and made sure that appropriate materials were provided; Sethrik took a drinking sphere such as Orphan often favored, while Vantak sucked or nibbled on a sticklike confection which Ariane thought was his equivalent of potato chips or similar snack foods. "Excellent. Now, from what I have heard of you, Leader Sethrik—"

"No need of the honorific. You may call me Sethrik, if I may address you by one of your names."

"But of course, Sethrik. Call me Oscar or Naraj, as you would." Oscar did an excellent bob-bow, showing he had studied the movement and probably practiced it multiple times. "As I was saying, from what I have heard you would appreciate directness, so I shall try to be as direct as possible.

"You must of course be aware that we have already managed to offend the Molothos sufficiently that we are at war with their Faction."

A whistling sound overlaid with a chuckle showed the Blessed Leader's amusement. "Easily accomplished."

"So I have learned. But I am also aware that Humanity has—sometimes inadvertently—offended the Blessed To Serve, and I would like to present apologies for any such offenses, and hope that we can move forward to a common ground and perhaps partnership." The ambassador smiled. "After all, we are a new, and small, Faction and could use all the friends we can get."

Sethrik leaned back, then bowed. "Your apology is accepted. As Leader of the Blessed to Serve, I in fact declare that any prior offenses are forgiven—if our own are forgiven as well."

Sethrik was, of course, referring to that setup which had not only injured Gabrielle but nearly gotten Ariane killed, and which had not reflected well on the Blessed. Oscar looked at her with a raised eyebrow. Ariane smiled. "We spoke at a certain party afterwards, but I suppose it was not a formal forgiveness. So, yes, Sethrik, any offense both personal and Factional is forgiven."

"Excellent," Sethrik said, and she thought there was a note of genuine gratification in his voice. "Your approach, Oscar, is well-timed. For you should know that the Minds themselves, upon reviewing our encounters with Humanity, directed that we seek to lay aside even the natural opposition due to your alliance with the Liberated, and instead try to convince Humanity that the Blessed are worthy allies."

That was something of a surprise. The super-AIs which ran the entire civilization of the Blessed were one of the more frightening things they had yet learned about, especially from the point of view of a humanity which had yet to give AIs the full rights of living people. *I wonder what they've seen in those interactions that makes them willing to even ignore the fact that we're obviously pretty much committed to our alliance with Orphan and the Liberated, their archenemy?*

She made a mental note to go over this with DuQuesne at first opportunity. *And maybe Orphan himself, too.* Aloud, she said, "That's wonderful news, Sethrik."

"I am glad you accept this news in the spirit it is given, Captain Austin—"

"You *can* call me Ariane, if you'd rather."

Sethrik laughed. "Indeed. Then I am glad, Ariane. And in that spirit, ambassadors, I would encourage negotiations of trade and knowledge. As any agreements will of course be subject to the ratification of the Leader of each Faction, allow me to suggest that such negotiations be carried out by you with Vantak, who—while not given precisely the same title—holds a position of power very similar to your own." He turned to Ariane. "I have a few things to discuss which are, however, only the business of the Leaders."

Oscar stood immediately. "Then—if it is agreeable to you, Vantak—I would continue our discussions outside, perhaps while travelling about the Grand Arcade. I must confess," he said with a more open smile than his usual controlled expressions, "I am still enjoying the spectacle of Nexus Arena enough that I prefer being outside of the Embassy." Left unsaid was the fact that Ariane would not leave the Embassy without Wu Kung.

"I have no objection, Ambassador," Vantak said, sounding slightly nervous—*second in command suddenly stuck with what could be a delicate duty, I'll bet*—but not reluctant.

After the other three had left, Sethrik vented air with a whistle that was overlaid with a sigh of relief—exactly in time with her own sigh.

The two looked at each other and burst out laughing. "What the heck have *you* got to be nervous about, Sethrik?"

Even though his face was virtually immobile, something in his posture, the way he leaned forward, gave her the impression of someone grinning. "Captain . . . that is, Ariane Austin . . . I was not exaggerating about the Minds' directives. While I believed you held no grudge directly, you are of course still allied with Orphan and the Liberated, and we *had* performed a . . . quite offensive set of actions in order to entrap you at Amas-Garao's direction." He looked towards the door. "And I suspect you have had additional pressures since last we talked."

He is very good. "You guessed, did you?"

The same assenting handtap that Orphan also used was the reply. "Your people were . . . an interesting assortment. But not one of you intended for a first contact of any type. Yours, then, was not a vehicle intended for long travel, but a single jump, a test of a drive system and a return. Common enough in history, but it meant that if your people had leaders that—almost certainly—none of them were represented in your little group. While the Blessed have . . . a rather unique position in that sense, we are of course not at all unable to understand what might follow in that situation."

"So we'll talk as Leaders, and you've shuffled my problems off onto your second in command."

"I see you understand perfectly!"

She laughed again, then grew serious. "What did you want to talk about with me?"

"I am unsure as to how much you know about a particular . . . individual who has recently arrived—"

"Maria-Susanna?"

"Yes."

"I know a fair bit about her—in some ways much more than you, I'm sure—but we don't have much information as to what she is up to right now."

Sethrik paused, obviously considering what to tell her—information being, naturally, the greatest source of value in the Arena. "Well, I can tell you how she has been living thus far. She is . . . shopping, I suppose you might say . . . for an appropriate Faction. This allows her to go in and out of various Faction Houses or Embassies and avail herself of various conveniences as she does so. She has also sold some valuable items of Human workmanship and has thus sufficient vals to keep herself comfortable for, I would surmise, a considerable time."

"Did she approach you?"

"No, she has made no overtures at all to the Blessed."

Not surprising, thought Ariane. Product of the

Hyperion Project that she was, Maria-Susanna would almost certainly have an aversion to AIs that controlled other people's lives.

Sethrik went on, "I know for a fact she has visited at least four other Factions and possibly as many as twice that. What can you tell me about her? I am curious, as she is obviously a human being, yet is clearly operating separately from you."

Now it was Ariane's turn to consider what she could afford to tell—and possibly what she *should* tell for the sake of political advantage. "She is an extremely capable and wanted criminal in our solar system, responsible for murdering dozens of people."

"By the Minds!" murmured Sethrik. "And you have been unable to catch her?"

"As I said, extremely capable. She is also apparently very good at giving a good impression—she's demonstrated the ability to convince other people of almost anything, according to what I've been told."

"Most disturbing." Sethrik paused a moment, then gave a handtap of decision. "I had occasion to exchange information with the Minds just a short time before our meeting—Vantak travelled directly to the home system and back to convey the situation and their directives, in fact—and they provided their own evaluation of her behavior.

"In their opinion, this 'Maria-Susanna' has a specific Faction already in mind; she is negotiating with other Factions both as a backup and as a confusing tactic, and also to give her time in negotiations with the target Faction." He looked at her, dark eyes difficult to read in the nearly-human face. "They do not say which Faction is her target, but it is clear that she had this intent from the beginning—which, I would suspect, would strongly limit the likely targets."

It certainly would, Ariane thought grimly. *There wouldn't be enough information to make a decision like that on anything except ... the five Great Factions, the Shadeweavers, the Powerbrokers, and maybe a couple of the minor Factions we had gotten good info on. With the Blessed and the Liberated out of the picture, the choices are pretty narrow ... and none of them would be good for us.* "I thank you for this information, Sethrik."

"You are welcome, Ariane," he said, "And—I mean this without any trace of irony—we are extremely familiar with the potential damage a single renegade can eventually produce. I hope that this will not be the case for you."

He's talking about the Liberated ... and yeah, something like that would be a disaster. "So do I, Sethrik. So do I."

Abruptly a green sphere of light shimmered into existence above the table. "Ariane Austin of Humanity!"

The voice was Mandallon's, the young Initiate Guide. His tone was tense.

"What is it, Mandallon?"

"I am unsure exactly what his purpose is," Mandallon said, with a tone that sounded nearly apologetic, "but ... your new member, Sun Wu Kung ... I believe he has somehow gotten himself into a duel!"

CHAPTER 18

"Go enjoy yourself for a little bit, Wu. I'm heading back to the Embassy to give Ariane the good news."

Part of him wanted to protest that he should probably go back, but... *finally on my own in the Arena! So many things to see! So many things to* do! "All right, DuQuesne! I am sure she'll be so excited to hear Simon's already located one Sky Gate!"

"I'll bet she will." The big, dark-haired man grinned back. "Now behave yourself as much as you can, okay?"

I will! I'll make sure I don't cause trouble! "I promise!"

"Good enough. See you back at the Embassy." DuQuesne waved and then loped down the rampway, quickly disappearing in the distance.

For a few minutes, Wu just stood there at the top of the ramp to the black-sparkling gateway, watching the unending traffic in Nexus Arena. *It's like the Promenade of Heaven, or the entrance to the Celestial Emperor's palace!*

He remembered DuQuesne's words: "A place where a thousand races of... of demons and gods walk and speak, where there are worlds floating in the clouds, where you can fly up to touch the suns or sail a ship off the edge of the sea into that infinite sky," and he laughed aloud. *It's so true!* The thousand races of demons were here—the round-bodied, spidery Milluk, the claw-handed Molothos, the moving-tree with its singing spirit-aides that was a Rodeskri, toad-faced Daalasan, three creatures with tri-horned heads that Ariane had called Dujuin, and so many more; he'd seen ships and a distant world drifting in the endless sky through the giant window-room DuQuesne had stopped off in on their way to Humanity's Sphere; and he'd seen the blazing Luminaire and knew that he only had to fly up and he could touch the sun of the world. *Though that would probably hurt!*

"Greetings to you, Sun Wu Kung," a deep, resonant voice said from near his elbow.

He whirled, staff coming up reflexively. *I didn't sense it approaching me! That's—*

The tall figure was dressed in black robes, only a hint of shape, a glint of eyes, showing within the cowl. "Oh, *that* explains it. You are that wizard that Ariane beat, one of those Shadeweavers."

A chuckle rolled from under the shadowed hood. "I am Amas-Garao, yes. You are an interesting newcomer. An associate, perhaps a former comrade, of DuQuesne's, I perceive."

"We've been friends for a long time." He looked suspiciously at the cloaked figure. "What do you want?"

"At the moment? I merely wished to speak with you, to see you closely. I had observed a few . . . intriguing aspects of your nature upon your arrival, and speaking with you has afforded me more opportunity to evaluate you."

Gives me *a chance to evaluate* you, *too,* Wu thought. There was a power about this one, definitely. He wasn't something you went after casually. And he had the smell of a warrior, someone accustomed to fighting, not one who would retreat from combat. Still, he stood at a short distance, the way of a sorcerer whose battles were fought with spell and fear, not hand and claw. *Not far enough to make a difference for me, but maybe he's not used to people like me.* "Well, I hope you see something interesting. I'm just looking at all the people here."

"It is, in truth, a magnificent and always changing sight," the Shadeweaver said. "I have spent many hours here, watching the interplay of species and the formation of alliances even in the shadow of the Gates."

Wu Kung nodded, thinking. "You want me to do something, I guess," he said at last. "Ariane said you're always trying to get people to do what you want without telling them somehow."

Another laugh. "Your captain is an interesting being indeed. And what do you believe I wish you to do?"

Wu laughed and spun the staff between his fingers. "Oh, I don't know. Your kind's always hard to figure out, with plans that twist in on themselves like a badly tied knot. It doesn't matter—either I will do what you expect or I won't, but either way it will be what I *wanted* to do." He gathered himself and bounded down the stairs. "Bye!"

The Shadeweaver didn't follow; when he glanced back there was nothing but a quickly-fading mist where Amas-Garao had been. *Maybe I'll go to the Grand Arcade now!*

It was easy to get one of the elevators down, and

then to head off in the direction of the Arcade. As he was half-walking, half-dancing his way through the crowds, something caught his attention, a small lone figure—even shorter than he was—followed by a much larger group of assorted creatures who seemed to be speaking *at* him.

The movement . . . the way the little figure kept walking, straight, tail rippling behind, just a hair *too* stiff . . . it was familiar. *That . . . I remember that . . .*

He remembered.

"Monkey!" they called, and laughed at him. Some did not laugh, but looked down, faces filled with contempt and disdain, and sometimes with fear. He was in Heaven but they did not want him there, with his sense of fun and energy; they drove him out and so he played a prank on them, and they did not laugh; only Wu Kung laughed, he and his monkey friends, when he could visit them. So the others, the spirits and gods and functionaries of the Heavens mocked him behind his back, even as they asked him for his strength, and when he retaliated they grew even more angry.

And in the end their anger made even Buddha turn his back and he was sealed away for so long that nearly he forgot everything except bitterness, joy fading in darkness . . . until the stone cracked and an innocent face looked up at him, a face that held no malice or envy or hatred, a face of such purity so that he could not strike her.

Sun Wu Kung looked again, and saw them still following the little figure; young, or perhaps not as young as they looked, but though they were a half-dozen different species somehow he knew the expressions.

Without even thinking of it, he strode towards the tiny white-and-purple figure walking towards the Powerbrokers' area. As he approached he could hear fragments of words, and most often repeated was the word "Sphereless."

That doesn't sound nice at all! Though . . . Spheres mean something else here. But what does it mean, then?

He turned and began walking stride for stride next to the little figure, which was also armored in some enameled white and bronze material. *He smells . . . very angry, barely leashed.* "Hi! I'm Sun Wu Kung! Who are you?"

A scent of startlement. The small creature looked up. "You do not know who I am?"

"No . . . wait." *He walks like a real fighter. A warrior. Wasn't that in the briefing?* " . . . are you Tunuvun?"

"Yes."

"Oh, wow!" This person was a *real* fighter then! "I saw your race-battle with Sivvis—not in person, because I wasn't here in the Arena then, but I watched it! You were amazing!"

Another set of insults were hurled from behind, but for the moment Tunuvun seemed more interested in Wu Kung. "Hm. You move as a warrior yourself. I thank you for the compliment."

"Just the truth." He glanced pointedly backwards. "So what is *their* problem with you?"

"Is it any business of *yours*?" Tunuvun demanded sharply. Almost instantly he covered his face with his hands and bobbed slightly, a gesture that, with a shift in scent, Wu interpreted as an apology. "I do not intend hostility. You are of the new Faction, yes?"

"Humanity, yes."

Tunuvun's eyes narrowed. "Then you may, perhaps, not understand that to have no Spheres in the Arena is to be no citizen at all. We are of no account except as we may be useful to those above us. There are times I regret any of us being found by the peoples beyond the skies."

"Why are they bothering you, though?"

Tunuvun gave a hiss. "Because they hope to force me to lose my temper. To give them Challenge, or a chance for Challenge. I—my people—have now one chance, one chance only, to Challenge and win a world of our own, to no longer *be* 'Sphereless,' and I dare not lose that chance. Some of these are just...*tzykiss*, children of no account, wandering visitors who are amused by bothering me; but others I think are agents of my enemies, and would hope to trap me in some Challenge I cannot win." Tunuvun gave a hiss that sounded to Wu like the Genasi warrior was spitting on the floor. "And the Arena does not permit me to do violence to them inside Nexus Arena."

"I understand."

Wu whirled suddenly and pointed his staff. "Why don't you leave him alone?"

"Mind your own path!" snapped one of the larger participants—a broad, multilegged creature like a quadrupedal hippopotamus with an upright torso and massive arms.

"Ha! You cannot make *me* be quiet either, can you?" He spun about and presented them with his rump, tail whipping about, and let them have a good view, punctuated by what Wu thought was a *most* satisfying burst of flatulence. "You are all cowards and fools without honor."

"Would you Challenge us over this?" another voice asked. *Ha, he sounds like a schemer.* The speaker was a tripedal being with three manipulative members atop a circular body.

"You are not *worthy* of a real Challenge," he answered. "You taunt someone who dares not reply because he has too much to lose. Whose lickspittles are *you*, trying to trick a Challenge from a being who can give only *one*?"

"Ha, then," said another—a Daalasan—"perhaps *you* seek to get *us* to Challenge you?"

"How about a not-Challenge challenge?" he countered.

"A . . . what?"

"A bet, a simple wager, no worlds in the balance, no Challenges mediated by this huge Arena, just your group against me and him; I'll even drop my Staff, just bare hands."

"A *fight?*" The group of aliens, two dozen strong, looked at him with unmistakable skepticism. "There is no fighting allowed in Nexus Arena."

He pointed past the Powerbrokers to the Docks. "But those are not *in* Nexus Arena . . . are they?"

Tunuvun had said nothing; he was just watching now, his posture uncertain.

"Clarification," said yet another of the group, this one a low, crablike creature which must have massed five hundred pounds yet moved swiftly on multiple jointed legs. "You propose that the two of you will fight our entire group as a wager. What are the stakes, then?"

"If we win, you—and everyone associated with you—stops trying to bother Tunuvun and his people.

They'll give their Challenge soon enough. Don't try to mess it up for them!"

"And if you *lose*?"

Wu realized he was now in a spot that he should never have gotten himself into. *But I had to!* "Then... then I'll have to Challenge one of you of your choice, and you get to take Humanity on in whatever challenge you like to put us in."

A murmur went through the group at the mention of *Humanity*. *I don't know if that's good or bad.*

"You are *mad*, I think," Tunuvun said conversationally, but the tone was both respectful and surprised. "You risk all this for one you did not know?"

"I saw your fight. I know your *spirit*. That's what matters."

"All right," the huge multilegged hippo-creature said, and there was an ugly chuckle that rippled through the crowd...a crowd that now looked even larger. *They somehow called more people in!* "The two of you and all of us, Dock Two. Right now?"

"Right now."

News had already started to spread. Wu saw people moving in that direction, spectators, perhaps gamblers wagering on the outcome. As he passed through the doorway to the vast expanse of the Arena and Dock Two, a green ball of light *popped* up.

"Sun Wu Kung," Ariane's voice said sharply, "I hope to *God* that Mandallon had things wrong—"

"I am sorry, Captain Austin, really I am, but I'm about to be in a fight, so I will talk to you later! Bye!"

The green ball sparkled red, then vanished.

Wu gestured to Tunuvun. "Run—let us get space, or they will try to mob us right away."

Even as the larger group poured out onto Dock Two, Tunuvun sprinted with Wu up the hundred-meter-wide Dock; workers and travellers and traders ducked out of the way, running to their ships, clearing a wide space. "I hope," Tunuvun said dryly, "that you are as good at fighting as with speaking, Sun Wu Kung."

He grinned savagely. "We will see." He took his staff and put it off to one side.

The twenty-nine aliens suddenly charged forward.

Tunuvun gave a high, uluating cry and went to meet them; Wu laughed and charged as well.

He remembered DuQuesne's emphatic orders. *Must not show them everything I can do.* He also remembered how good Tunuvun was. *That's it. I'll match Tunuvun. If he's as good as he looked...*

Both of them were small—Tunuvun a meter and a half high, Wu a scant few centimeters taller—and they used that, ducking *under* the first wave of assailants, rolling between their legs and grasping members, coming to their feet simultaneously, as though moved by the same thoughts. A spinning whipcrack of white and purple and a Sai'Dakan tumbled limply away; Wu laughed and delivered a hurricane kick to the head of the hippoid creature that made it stagger and go to its front knees. This gave Wu a chance to vault up, bouncing from the creature's own back above the heads of the crowd, twisting himself around and coming back down atop the crab-thing.

Hands grasped and pummelled; some of these people were *not* amateurs, not in the least, and they evaded Wu Kung's blocks, caught and hammered him down to the unyielding dock with an impact that drove the air from his lungs, even as he saw Tunuvun fly past, trying to recover from some huge impact.

But he could twist around, now, fur smooth and loose and hard to hold, he was free, a knee lock on a neck here, tail grasping another *there*, pull hard, *wham!* and two more assailants collapsed to the ground.

Tunuvun had just taken the full brunt of a Daalasan's swing; he just laughed in a high-pitched voice and shrugged the impact off. *Great! He's really strong!*

Wu ignored the next strikes and punted a Milluk over the heads of the crowd; the creature almost went over the edge of the Dock before spectators caught it. The Hyperion Monkey King could hear the excited shouts, the murmured bets, see the ebb and flow of the crowd. *I have to be careful*, he thought, sensing a swift-moving strike. *I don't think Tunuvun could avoid that one, so I can't, either.*

The kick hit like a runaway cart and as Wu skidded over the Dock, knocking down both opponents and spectators, he realized with surprise that it had been the multi-legged hippo creature. *Boy, he's a lot faster than I thought!*

Focus, got to finish this! Roll to your feet, they're coming, the remainder are tough and more organized, maybe eighteen left standing, but they're not getting in each others' way now. Tripod-head and a green eel-thing coordinated, moving fast, Tunuvun's out of the way, kick the tripod-thing's near leg out from under him and jump out of the way, come down on eel— look out, another behind us, a Salaychen, all armor and edges, bounce off eel, land on armor, punch as hard as Tunuvun seems to, crack goes the armor and it's in more pain than it can handle, it's down, ow! *Something* hit *me, got to get* up—

And suddenly there was stillness, nothing moving around them, just him and Tunuvun standing and a distant clump of spectators whose shouts echoed into the vast beauty of the Arena.

Wu realized he was actually breathing faster. *Still... not all recovered from my long sleep! I will have to do a* lot *more exercise!*

Tunuvun surveyed his fallen tormentors and then turned giving a spread-armed bow to Wu. "We have seen victory today, and I thank you."

"Hey, it was fun!" Wu said.

Tunuvun's straightening and a baring of teeth was so clearly a smile that Wu laughed. "It was *indeed* fun, Sun Wu Kung, and in more ways than just the joy of combat! Perhaps you and I will one day meet in combat as well, but for now I am glad that you chose to taunt my own enemies and led them to this battlefield."

"I look forward to another fight—with you or against you!" He looked at their fallen adversaries, who were slowly rising. "Remember our bet!"

The hippo-like being shook its head slowly. "We ... will not forget. The Genasi shall be left unmolested until they complete their single Challenge."

Sun Wu Kung gave a leap of triumph.

And then the green ball reappeared. "Sun Wu Kung. Get your ass back to our Embassy *right now.*"

Wu winced. "I think I'm in trouble."

CHAPTER 19

One Sky Gate located, DuQuesne thought in satisfaction. *And if we didn't just get lucky at the opening gun, we might have quite a few Sky Gates leading to a bunch of places.*

It was true that there was some danger inherent in that, but overall it was probably a good thing; more options, more possible places to explore. *As long as one of them doesn't lead to the Molothos homeworld or something like that.*

He caught one of the elevators without anyone in it. *What do you know, a few seconds of silence in the Arena.* In that quiet pause, a thought suddenly struck him about the events of the afternoon, and he almost reversed the elevator. *No, I'm going to get there ahead of him anyway. I'll just make sure Wu talks to me before he tells Ariane anything. I think... there's some strategy to play through here.*

The doors opened and he jogged out, looking for one of the floating open-air taxis. *But really, do I need to take one? I can walk.*

Then one of the taxis went by in the middle distance, and on board...

He wasn't even conscious of his actions; he just found himself following, having flagged down another of the transports and leaped aboard practically in a single motion. "Come *on*, hurry up!"

The destination was clear enough, and unsurprising: the Grand Arcade. *Anyone new to the Arena would probably go here soon enough. And she hasn't had a chance to get on her own since she arrived.*

His target still hadn't noticed him, and it was almost impossible to miss her even in the alien crowd with that spectacular head of hair. He came up behind her as she was glancing over the sparkling wares of an Arena weaponsmith.

"Hello, K," he said quietly.

She jumped a tiny bit—*honest-to-God surprised her. Not often* that *happens.* "M . . . Marc."

For a moment he just looked at her, remembering how she used to look when ready for action; the straight red hair full and flowing back, down to her waist (*damn, she's grown it out*), black shirt tight and smooth, pants with a multiplicity of pockets both visible and hidden for holding almost anything she might need in an emergency—from chewing gum to grenades. *That much hasn't changed*, he thought, noting the military gear that she'd somehow restyled to look . . . cute, but still retained pouches and bandoliers galore.

And those green eyes haven't changed a bit. It was startlingly painful to realize that, because he'd thought a certain pair of dark-blue eyes had finally replaced them in his heart. *Maybe I was just . . . giving up.*

She hadn't said anything either, looking back at him almost sadly. And he couldn't bear that look.

"Why, K?"

She sighed. "As Seaton would've said, that's a dilly of a question. Or a lot of questions, all rolled up into one. Right?" The redheaded woman looked around, gestured. He followed her to one of many side booths where people might sit to rest, eat something bought, or otherwise escape while in the heart of the Grand Arcade.

"Why did I come here, when I wouldn't come when you called?" she said, picking up the thread of conversation. "Why did I come with Naraj? Why did I just hide away for fifty years? Those whys, or something else?"

He was puzzled, and—honestly—a little hurt by her phrasing. "Dammit, K! Yes, all those, and all the rest, too! I *gave* you space, I knew how much it hurt—but by Tarell's own favorite *stars*, it hurt *me* too!" He tried to rein himself in. "It . . . hurt us all. More than some of us could bear." He remembered the day he said goodbye, and hugged her, and watched her leave . . . and suddenly he didn't want to even *try* holding back. "I *loved* you, K. I still do, I think, and the biggest *why* is why you didn't think we could survive better *together* than we could apart and alone!" He heard his voice near to breaking, and the clinical part of him raised an eyebrow. *Dr. Marc C. DuQuesne, about to lose control over a woman he hasn't really spoken to in half a century.*

Her eyes had widened, and her hand went to her mouth as though to cover up her shock. Then her face crumpled and her head dropped, and he saw two tears drop to the table in front of her, glittering diamonds that spattered and were gone. "Oh, Marc," she said, and her voice trembled. "Oh, Marc, I'm sorry. I really, *really* am. I . . . loved you too. But . . ."

"But? What possible *but* could there *be*, K?" Now that he'd opened the floodgates he couldn't stop himself. He needed the answers he'd denied himself all those years ago.

"But . . ." She hesitated again. "Oh, *darn, darn, darn . . .*" she dropped her head into her hands and gave a huge, heaving sigh, then straightened and looked directly into his eyes with the air of someone preparing to face an execution. "But . . . I'm not really K."

He abruptly realized he must have been sitting, staring at her like a gaping fish for nearly a minute. "Uh . . . you're *what*? Of *course* you're K!"

"No, I'm not. Really, DuQuesne. It's . . ." She suddenly looked more like a young girl than a woman, lost, confused, upset. "Darn. It all goes back to Hyperion . . . like everything else . . ."

Oasis looked down at the body, panting, holding the broken butt of her AX-12mm tensely.

But after a few moments it became clear that the dark-haired man in the formerly impeccably-tailored suit would never move again. *I didn't want to kill him! I wanted to help him!*

But—like so many of the victims of this place—the sudden breakdown of the simulations had either driven him insane or fit somehow *too* well with whatever world he thought he lived in. He'd been certain this was some trick by an enemy—she hadn't quite caught the name, Bluefield maybe, or Specter—and that she was an agent of the other side. And maybe a part of him knew things were much, much worse than he imagined, because he had grown increasingly irrational and paranoid when she tried to reason with him.

And he almost killed me anyway—him with just bare hands, me with my armor, my combat knife, my sidearms, my rifle. She was shaking, and so was Hyperion Station around her. *Almost my entire kit's wrecked. No comm working, no relays...don't dare try to tie into* this *place's automation...*

She forced herself upright, feeling the grating of a rib, and she was pretty sure her collarbone was cracked. *Maybe internal injuries, too, but I think my medical nanos are on it. No shock. Got to get out of here.*

Hyperion Station was *huge*. When you travelled hundreds of millions of miles in patrol, ten or twenty miles sounded *tiny*, but in the chaos of its collapse she realized it was almost the size of a world, layer upon layer of secrets and dangers and mazes—some real, some illusion, all deadly.

She pitched a spent cartridge down the hall, noted the curve. *Spin like* that, *so I need to head...this way.*

Abruptly the floor tilted under her. She heard the distant moaning scream of metal and composite slowly giving way. *This place isn't going to stay together long, even if the commander doesn't give the bombardment order!*

She still wasn't clear on *exactly* what had happened, or what was happening now; but it was obvious that the internal war the Hyperion...subjects? victims? projects? had begun with their creators, and the creators and systems' attempts to control them, was tearing the entire gigantic station apart.

A sputtering light caught her eye. *A comm station. Maybe I can at least listen in on what's happening, get an update.*

She staggered to the comm station; as she did so,

cables suddenly dropped from above and tightened around her. She cursed and tried to struggle, but in her current condition it was hopeless.

The figure of a man, appeared on the console, a fair-haired man in a perfect white suit ... with a warm, casual smile that somehow gave her the creeps. "Good afternoon, Miss Abrams."

"Who ..."

"Of course, you are quite correct. I have failed to introduce myself." He gave a little bow. "I am Doctor Alexander Fairchild," he said, blue eyes practically *twinkling* with a good cheer that sent a chill down her spine from the incongruity of his manners with her situation. "One of the unfortunate ... creations of the former masters of this station. I require your assistance to escape from here, Ensign Abrams."

Maybe he's just desperate. "You hardly needed to tie me up for that. Just tell me where you are and I'll do my best to—"

He laughed. "Oh, dear. I am afraid you labor under a misapprehension, Ensign Abrams. I am as much ... *here* as I am anywhere, if you understand me."

Her gut knotted and felt as though doused with ice water. *Shit. He's a feral AI. A feral AI made by* these *people.*

Still ... there was no reason not to play along. "Still—I have plenty of storage in my logger unit. If you want to—"

The slight widening of the smile told her it was no use. "I suppose I cannot fault you for trying to carry out your no-doubt precise instructions for dealing with ... artificial persons whose origin and intent are unknown. However, your suggestion is unacceptable.

You will undoubtedly be scanned carefully and any storage media examined for additional, undesired content." His smile broadened. "Any storage media but one, that is."

Another mass of cable fell, shoving her against the comm unit—and the interface socket extruded, directly into her left neural port.

He wants to transfer to me? Even as the horrific idea struck her, she felt the presence of another mind, strong, cold, focused, trying to enter her own. She triggered her shielding protocols, but they were slow, and began to drop. *He . . . he is figuring out the way through the defenses almost as if they weren't* there!

Naturally, Fairchild's voice echoed through her head. *You're not at all stupid, nor untalented, but I was able to stay a few steps ahead of even DuQuesne, and I am very much afraid you are nowhere* near *him, child.*

Her head felt near to splitting; she tried to scream, managed a sob. *He's . . . trying to . . . shove me* out!

Suddenly there was another presence, and a voice. "Fairchild! Get the *hell* out of her!"

A sense of consternation and anger. "Walk along, my dear Kimberly. If you move, you may just live through this."

Sudden movement—a sense of slashing, of darting speed and edged metal—and agony ripped through her head. But at the same time she felt the pressure on her brain fade, the other presence fleeing in fury and fear.

She opened her eyes, to see another woman looking down at her . . . one whose hair was her own shade of red, with green eyes not much different from her own. But there was something wrong with her vision . . . it was blurring . . .

"Damn him. If he can't win, he has to poison the bloody well." The newcomer was kneeling. "Oh, blast it. You're hurt worse than I thought. And he shut down your medical nanos..."

"I...don't want to die..." she heard herself murmur.

"*Shit*." The other woman—almost a girl, Oasis thought vaguely, *maybe younger than me*—looked torn.

Then her face smoothed out with firm decisiveness. "Then you *won't* die. Not today."

"So," Oasis said quietly, "she...transferred me into the only healthy body available. Hers."

He looked at her in dawning horror. "You mean... K is *dead?*"

"No, no...Not exactly. She...we're *both* here, Marc. But...Oh, damn, this is so hard to do." Now that he knew what to look for, he could *hear* faint shifts in cadence, in accent, in the way words were said, and abruptly it sounded much more like K. "Marc, I couldn't let her *die*. She'd done everything she could, and it just wasn't *fair*. So I let her take her own life back. You knew that Saul helped me fit in..."

He still couldn't quite believe it. "I didn't realize... he was helping one of his own soldiers, with the worst case of shellshock ever. He must have convinced her family she had some face- and bodyshaping done."

"With my help," she said. "And...Marc, we're not entirely *separate* any more, either. There's...a gap, sort of, but we've been in the same brain for fifty years. I'm not the woman you knew, exactly...and she isn't the girl she was, either."

DuQuesne was, for once, utterly at a loss. What was there to say to this? Who was the woman in front of him—Oasis Abrams, K, or . . . someone new? How should he think of her?

He didn't doubt the story. It was so utterly K's personality that if someone had told him the situation he'd have been able to predict what she would do—save the helpless victim, no matter what it would cost her. Because she could always afford more than anyone else.

With an effort, he smiled. "Yeah, that's you, all right, K. You could've had a clone made, though, given her her own body back."

She shuddered. "You know we wouldn't do that. Would *you*?"

He shook his head.

"See? Anyway, Oasis' original body was destroyed when Hyperion went up, and there was *no way* I'd be letting people play with *my* DNA."

"No, that wouldn't be good." He looked up, studying the branching-leafed tree idly. "I have to say this is a lot more awkward than I thought it was going to be."

She smiled sadly. "I'm sorry, Marc. I . . . probably should have found a way to tell you, but . . ."

"Nah, you were probably right. I don't think I'd have been rational about it. Not sure I am now."

Oasis touched his hand. "I don't think any of us were rational . . . then."

Just as he was about to answer, emerald light glowed from the air. "Marc, get back here *now*," said Ariane, and the tone of her voice was chilled steel.

"What's up?" he asked, unable to keep his own tension from his voice.

"Sun Wu Kung, that's what's up. Mandallon just told me, and he just confirmed, that he's gotten into a fight—on the Docks."

Klono and Noshabkeming! Only the old curses were *adequate* for the moment. *I should have* known!

Aloud he said "On my way, Captain."

He stood, looking down at the redheaded enigma before him. "We'll talk later?"

She did, at least, give him one of her sunny smiles, driving away a little of his confusion and gloom with the force of her personality. "We've got a lot of catching up to do, no matter what. Of course."

Better than nothing, he thought. "Then I'd better get moving."

He headed straight for the Embassy. *One way or another that fight will be over soon . . . and the coal-raking will be happening at home.*

CHAPTER 20

"What the living *hell* is wrong with you, Sun Wu Kung?"

Despite her anger, Ariane found it difficult to maintain the grim expression; the Hyperion Monkey King looked so utterly hangdog that part of her wanted to laugh, and another wanted to give him a hug.

But I can't. This is far too important. I have to make this point.

None of the others looked like they were laughing. DuQuesne's brows were drawn together like a line of thunderclouds, Gabrielle's lips were tight, and Laila Canning had the cold clinical stare of a scientist looking over a dissection table. *And Marc didn't sound like he was in a great mood to begin with when I called him in. Well, that's okay; Wu needs to face a little hostility now.*

She had not called in Naraj, Ni Deng, or Abrams. This was *her* problem.

"You were *specifically* told to avoid confrontations, Wu Kung! I gave you permission to *see* the Arena, not to *fight* it!" She transferred her angry stare to DuQuesne. "He was under *your* wing when you left. What happened?"

DuQuesne waited a moment, making sure Wu Kung

saw his directed glare before he looked up. "Ariane—Captain. Captain, I had a talk with him just before we parted. I said, and I quote, 'try to stay out of trouble.'" He looked back at Wu, who seemed to be trying to shrink inside his flamboyant robes. "God-*damn* it, Wu! I should have *known* it was a lost cause, but for cryin' out loud, couldn't you have managed one multiply-qualified *hour* without getting into a scrap?"

"I'm *sorry!*" the little Monkey King said, and he sounded almost on the verge of tears. *Emotional swings. What did they do, those bastards of Hyperion, in the name of making some twisted dreams come true?* "But I couldn't ignore it, I just *couldn't!*"

He leaned forward. "DuQuesne, you know! They were *mocking* him, and he couldn't *do* anything!"

DuQuesne's face showed just a momentary flicker of softness, but it hardened immediately. "Wu, the problem isn't just what you *did*, it's what you *could have done*."

"I don't have all the details yet," Ariane said, keeping her voice at the same deadly level tone, "but I did ask Mandallon to give me what he saw. He says that you, in effect, promised that your opponents could make YOU issue a Challenge—meaning we'd be stuck with it, and whatever they chose to use as the medium of the Challenge—if you lost."

"Well...yes, I did, but—"

"No *buts!*" she cut in. "Sun Wu Kung, I have no doubt you were confident of your ability to beat them. You were obviously right, this time, in these conditions, with that particular group. But *you did not have the right to take that risk*."

He fidgeted, started to open his mouth, then closed it. *Good.* She moderated her tone just a fraction.

"Understand, Wu Kung, this isn't about whether you know what you can do, or what you *think* you can do. It's about the fact that you potentially exposed our Faction to a Challenge that we would have a *terribly* strong chance to lose, and—honestly speaking—we can't *afford* to lose. Humanity's only got so much to give, and we've got a war coming with the meanest bastards in the Arena. All it would have taken is *one* bad break—you being thrown just far enough that you fell off the Dock, someone sneaking in a weapon that could take you down for a minute, or a one-in-a-billion slip by you in combat, and suddenly you're forced to issue a Challenge to someone who might be a stooge for our worst enemies."

She sighed. "Wu, for all we know, the scene that drew you in was *meant* for you. These people play games exactly that deep."

"Let's be fair, Captain," said Gabrielle. "I don't think they'd know enough about Wu yet to be able to set up something like *that* ahead of time."

"Probably not," she conceded, "but there's no telling·for sure; the Shadeweavers might be able to guess a lot about him, and even if they couldn't touch his mind directly, there's nothing preventing them from arranging some kind of psychological test."

Wu's head tilted a bit at that, and the greeny-golden eyes flickered quickly towards her before dropping their gaze back down. "Um ... Captain ... The one called Amas-Garao did speak with me for a bit before then."

Coincidence? I'd like to think so. Maybe it is. But ... "So we don't even know if it was a setup." She sat slowly down, gesturing for Wu Kung to take his seat. "All right, Wu, I've given you the dressing-down you deserve—and you damned well better remember it. But right now I want the whole story, from the time that Marc left you to the time I called you back."

The story that unfolded was as straightforward as Wu himself, and as clear. *Damn.* If that *hadn't* been a setup, it *should* have been, because it was virtually flawless as bait for someone like Sun Wu Kung.

Be honest with yourself, her conscience spoke up. *It probably would have worked on you too.*

Another part of her protested that she knew better than that. *I would think I'd be smart enough not to risk our whole* Faction *for something like that.*

But the events that had brought them into the Arena and farther into their challenges—her intervention between Orphan and the Blessed, the Challenge that led to a desperate race between her and Sethrik, her direct Challenge to Sethrik, which turned out to be a trap by Amas-Garao—those had all been caused by her own actions. *Amas-Garao was* influencing *me on two of those, yes...but I can't say for sure that I wouldn't have done any of those myself. Maybe I would. Maybe I wouldn't.*

She waited for Wu to finish, which he did and sat there with the expression of a child waiting to be scolded—something very much at odds with the overconfident, brash, dynamic Monkey King. *I can't cut him much slack yet, though.* So she paused another several seconds—an endless time in that tense silence—before speaking.

"Thank you for telling us the whole sequence of events, Wu," she said finally. "That did make everything clear. Does anyone have any questions or comments before I go on?"

Laila spoke up. "I find coincidence of that level very difficult to swallow." Gabrielle nodded, as did DuQuesne. "At the same time," she went on, tones as precise as her scientific work, "I find it hard to imagine how it was arranged so swiftly, if arranged it was, unless Amas-Garao did so."

"And I just don't think he did," said Gabrielle reluctantly. "Maybe I'm just an optimist, but I think he was satisfied with the last results and wouldn't be playing games with us now."

"I wouldn't go *that* far," DuQuesne said. "But I'll admit, it just doesn't quite *feel* right for one of that Shadeweaver's tricks. But that might just be because we don't know what he's planning to get out of the whole mess."

Ariane nodded. "In any event—plan or accident— this could have been disastrous. Sun Wu Kung, I want your word that you won't *ever* do anything like this again, at least without consulting me."

Wu opened his mouth, closed it, and then sat there, a startling agony of decision on his face. "I . . . San . . . I mean, Captain! Captain, I . . . I *can't* promise that."

That brought her up short; she had assumed he would give his word when directly asked. *And what was it that he almost called me, and why?* "You *can't*? Wu, do you understand how serious this is? Why I have to ask you not to do things like that?"

"Yes! I do understand, Captain! I'm not stupid. I'm sometimes distracted and I get excited and I don't have *patience*, I guess, but . . ." he muttered something in that mangled language she didn't understand. "I . . . I see things that are *wrong* and I can't ignore them, Captain."

She found herself looking to the ceiling as though

for guidance. *And do I want to order people to ignore things that* are *wrong?* Ariane pushed her hair back, as it had started to fall forward over her face, and rubbed the back of her neck. "Wu... All right, I don't want you to ignore things that are wrong. But you *have* to weigh the cost to *us*. It's wrong to endanger the rest of us without us even knowing, isn't it?"

He looked down. "Y... yes."

"Then all I'm asking is that you *talk* to me before taking action like that. Or if I'm not available, DuQuesne, and if neither of us, any of the others of the original eight—Gabrielle, Simon, Steve, Carl, Tom, Laila." She looked at him steadily. "I realize there *still* may be exceptions—if it looks like someone is about to be killed and you really feel you must act, I can't argue with you about it. I can't tell you not to be yourself, or—to be honest—not to do what *I* would probably do in your position. But in this case you *could* have called ahead, given me at least some idea of the situation, let *me* make the call as to whether to intervene."

"And *would* you?" Wu Kung's eyes were a hair brighter, and the question held a hint of the old energy.

She hesitated, then with a sigh she nodded and smiled. "Yes, I suppose I probably would, though I would hope I wouldn't offer a free-for-anyone Challenge as the prize to the winners."

"So does she have your word, Wu? That you'll *ask* her before you act, if it's at all reasonable to do so?" DuQuesne's voice was just the tiniest bit less hard, following her lead.

"Yes. Yes, Captain, you have my word. I won't do anything even the *tiniest* bit like that without asking you if there's even a little bit of time to ask in."

I suppose that will have to do. "Thank you, Wu." She leaned back. "And it wasn't, in this case, a disaster. We gained face, didn't lose any, and you've just made a personal ally—one that we know from prior observation is both honorable *and* formidable."

"More than that," DuQuesne said with a slow smile.

Laila raised an eyebrow, and then suddenly both lifted, wings of surprise. "Ah. Of course. They will be the newest Faction, First Emergents, if they succeed in their Challenge. And an excellent set of allies, if we maintain close support to them prior to that time."

I hadn't thought of that. It was obvious once mentioned, though; those who arrived in the Arena with a single Sphere to their names were First Emergents like Humanity; what else would the Genasi become, then, except the first native Emergents? "And we can use all the allies we can get—as could they."

Gabrielle tilted her head in thought, straight gold hair forming a momentary curtain. "Well, they haven't won their Challenge yet. It's a nice thought, but you know what they say about counting your chicks before hatching."

"They will win," Wu Kung said positively.

Ariane remembered the tiny Genasi battling down to the wire against the huge Sivvis—and how the honor between the two led Sivvis to send his opponent to victory, undoubtedly pissing the Vengeance off mightily. "They'll sure try," she said, "and I think we should be ready to help them any way we can."

Because, she thought, *it sure couldn't hurt to have the best warriors in the Arena on our side before the Molothos come calling.*

CHAPTER 21

"I'll want to talk to you later, Wu," DuQuesne said as they got up to leave. "But first I have to talk with the captain. Privately, if she will."

Wu looked to Ariane, who nodded. "Stay in the Embassy, Wu Kung," she said, warningly.

"I already *promised*..." Wu Kung began, then, seeing her start to straighten, quickly said, "I mean, yes, Captain!"

Once the room was empty except for the two of them, Ariane slumped back into a chair, chuckling. "Do you know how *hard* it is to stay mad at him?"

"Of course I do," he answered, taking his seat again. "None of us could be ticked off at him for long, no matter what he did. But you handled him like a pro. He won't forget *that* talking-to for a while, at least."

"I sure *hope* not. Marc, I don't want to keep him penned up, so to speak, but I won't have much choice if he can't keep from getting himself—and potentially all of us—in trouble."

"I know. And I *think* he understands that, now. He had to go through a similar thing on his own Journey to the West, and with luck you won't have to make his headband into a pain generator." He studied her, the deep-blue hair, the eyes just a shade lighter, the slender body that hid startling strength (not to mention an electric-eel derived biomod that she'd used to great effect once on Amas-Garao), the shape of the face . . . "And you could probably get away with it, too, if you had to."

"What?"

"He almost called you 'Sanzo' during that raking over the coals. You look a *lot* like her. And she was just about the only one in his world who got away with talking to him like that . . . well, except for Sha Wujing, after he was more friend than enemy."

"Shouldn't 'Sanzo' have been a *man*? Or do I misremember my admittedly very faint grasp of the mythology?"

DuQuesne laughed. "No, you don't misremember. There were at least fifteen or twenty different versions of the Monkey King myth that got put into a blender and used to produce what we have out there," he jerked a thumb at the closed door. "And some of those versions were . . . very far from the original, let me say. That's not necessarily *bad*, but it means that only the broadest outlines of the myth are still there. Anyway, that's probably one reason he's willing to listen to you."

He straightened. "But I didn't hold you up here just to talk about Wu. Ariane, when I left, Simon had *already* located one of the Sky Gates."

Her face lit up. "That's wonderful, Marc!"

"Well, with a slight caveat that it depends on exactly where they go, but yes, I think it is. I'm guessing we may have an above-average number of gates, unless Simon just got real lucky on his first pass."

"The Sky Gates are just outside of the high-gravity area, right? So we should be able to put some kind of permanent station-keeping guards around them once we've located them all."

"Right. Armed to the teeth, too, at least until we know what's on the other side of each one—and where any Sky Gates from *those* go to. Can't afford to assume an innocuous-looking destination couldn't be a potential staging-ground for the Molothos or someone else out to get us."

She looked up and sighed. "Marc, there's just no way we can do all of this ourselves."

"I know. And there's people coming through any day now. I've given strict orders that they're *not* to come through Transition, though, unless you say otherwise. More people to work on the Inner and Upper Sphere, great. More people here? No, not until we're damn sure where we stand."

She nodded her agreement, and he moved forward to the next subject. "Okay, that's where we stand on that for the moment. I also wanted to ask you about something else."

Another nod. "Simon."

"So you've noticed it too."

"Something is bothering him," Ariane agreed, "but he hasn't said what it is, or why. He's clearly trying to hide it, even from me—which has me a little worried. Why would Simon hide something from *me*?"

DuQuesne didn't need that emphatic "me" explained. Simon's affection for Ariane was quite open and obvious, and Ariane had often used Simon as a sounding board and advisor, nearly as often as she used DuQuesne. "I don't know, either, and that's definitely got my back up. Seemed to happen around the time he was doing his research on the drive physics and adapting them to being a sensor, but I'll be damned if I can guess what it is that's got him all twitchy."

"Well," Ariane said after a moment, "I suppose I'll just have to ask him, if he won't bring the subject up himself. I've let it slide for a while, but..."

"But it's not Simon's normal behavior, which means it's something that worries *him* in some way, bad enough to feel he shouldn't or can't tell us." DuQuesne shrugged. "Yep. I know you hate prying, but that's just about the only way you can make this thing go."

"All right," she said. "I'll give him one more day, and if he doesn't come to me, I'll tell him he *has* to talk."

"Good enough." He rose. "Thanks, Captain."

She saluted from a sitting position, so he left, not waiting for her. *Just as well. I have to catch Wu.*

He found Sun Wu Kung in his suite, practicing lightning-fast staff-work. The red-enameled, gold-tipped staff stopped in mid-action as he entered. "DuQuesne! What is it? Do you need me to go back to guarding?"

"In a minute, Wu. Look, I've been thinking hard about what happened back on the Sphere, and I want you to keep that a *dead* secret. From everyone, even Ariane, at least for now."

He looked puzzled. "Why?"

"Because I think what you did is pretty much impossible. I don't think any of the other Factions can talk to their animals as though in their native language, and I think I know why you *can*. I've got a couple other pieces of evidence that tell me I'm right. And if I *am* right, Wu, that's one *big* secret weapon, a whole *armory* of secret weapons, waiting for us to unleash.

"But that kind of secret tends to leak easy, and it's a lot less effective if you know it's there. Especially if learning one secret might lead you to another. The various Factions already might have enough to make some guesses—especially the Shadeweavers, who can cheat—but something like this might give the whole show away."

Wu studied him, then nodded. "Okay, I understand. I think. But what is it that you've guessed?"

DuQuesne grinned humorlessly. "*Sore wa . . . himitsu desu*, as one particularly annoying guy we knew used to say. I'm keeping that secret, at least for now. Until I'm sure."

"This had better not be anything that will put Ariane in danger," Wu Kung said, and for a moment the eyes were green-gold stone.

Excellent reminder of what I chose him for. "No, Wu." He gazed into the distance, guessing, estimating chances. "No, Wu. If anything . . . that secret might just save her life one day."

CHAPTER 22

"Simon!" Laila Canning said, and there was honest surprise in her voice. "What in the world...or worlds, I suppose...are you doing here?"

Simon looked around at the soaring lines of the Faith's great hall, and the lines of people of all species filing in. "Well, partly I have never *been* here before, and I admit to a great curiosity as to the workings of a faith which is held by members of almost uncountable species." He smiled, though it took some effort to keep the expression natural. "After all, humanity has never managed to agree on one set of beliefs, and I would be—am—surprised that a single belief could draw people of such diversity to it."

"Hmph," she said, and the brown eyes were narrow and analytical. "You weren't at our meeting yesterday—I'm sure you heard about that little event?"

"About Sun Wu Kung managing to get himself in trouble the first time he wandered free? Yes, I did, when DuQuesne stopped by to take over the scanning this morning."

"Indeed. And that means you came here essentially

directly from Transition, no stopover at the Embassy. What's the *real* reason you came, Simon?"

So much for subtle approaches. "Yes, well... I wanted to talk with you privately, away from our Embassy, and this seemed one of the better choices."

Her head did the quick, birdlike tilt he remembered from their first meeting. "I see." She glanced around. "Well, not out *here*, certainly, unless you want random passers-by to hear whatever secret you apparently wish to tell me. This way."

She led Simon through a low archway to one side, where they found Nyanthus, the leader of the Faith, apparently in the process of putting on ornamental garments for the ceremony. "Excuse my intrusion on your preparations, First Guide."

The warm, mellifluous voice rolled out from the First Guide's openwork candleflame top, and his symbiotic sensing-creatures flew out and circled them in greeting. "It is forgiven, Laila Canning, and I bid you welcome again to the house of the Faith. And to you, Simon Sandrisson, I bid a special welcome, on this, your first entry to our home."

"Thank you, First Guide Nyanthus," Simon said.

"First Guide," Laila said quickly, "Simon and I need to speak privately. Might we..."

The tendrils that made up the candle-flame flickered open for a moment. "Of course, Laila. You may use one of the private rooms in the Path of Trust; there should be several free, as these are the days of the Cycle of Wonder."

Laila thanked him and turned to go.

"Thank you very much, Nyanthus," Simon said, and quickly followed the brown-haired scientist.

Dr. Canning led him about three-quarters of the way around the circular walkway that went around the perimeter of the great worship hall; by the time she turned down a side passage, Simon could hear alien but very pretty music starting to rise from the great hall. "I suspect a symbolism in which rooms he offered to you."

Laila's smile was quick and bright. "I don't doubt it; Guide Nyanthus is very wise, and very smart, and always alert to what is going on. He signals both that he trusts me, and that if we have secret conversations then both of us must trust the other—with *must* being able to be read at least two ways."

Simon tried to smile, but the tension was too great. "Yes, I see."

Laila gestured and one of the doors opened slightly; she looked through, nodded, and waved again, causing the door to open fully.

Going through the door, Simon saw some human-style chairs and a desk. "Interesting. I suppose the Wagamia might use this, but is the design common?"

"I am not entirely sure," she admitted. "Given that we *are* in someone's embassy, I would not bet against the possibility that the furnishings rearrange themselves for each group that opens the doors." She chose a seat and sat down. "Now, Simon, what is so secret and important that you leave the Embassy and come here—and that you don't even discuss with Ariane?"

He tried to sit, but he was too tense, and sprang up, began pacing. "Laila . . . it must be very difficult for you. I know that Ariane has always wondered . . ."

"Ah." She looked distant. "Simon, I won't lie. It *is* very difficult. The more so since I can't tell *why*

Ariane is wary of me, other than just general caution, but I'm sure there's some quite clear reason that made her nervous about me.

"And I confess—quite freely—that I don't have any proof that I was not, in fact, modified by Mandallon in some way. I was nearly brain-dead after all, and it's quite possible his attempt to fix me involved putting a part of himself in—perhaps putting in much more of him than me." She sighed. "Honestly, I don't blame DuQuesne his suspicions; given what we now know is his past? I'd be paranoid too, and the Arena's given us more than enough reason to question everything we know."

Laila stood—exactly when Simon decided to sit. The two of them looked at each other for a moment and Simon could suddenly not keep himself from laughing. Fortunately, the same impulse had struck Laila, and for a few moments they laughed, fading to chuckles. Laila Canning sat back down, a smile still on her face. "Oh, that was good. Do you know... I don't think I've *had* a decent laugh since I came to this damned place, until now."

"I'm terribly sorry, Laila."

"Hardly *your* fault, Simon. True, you haven't done anything to argue against their suspicions that I know of, but really, there's nothing to argue." Her lips tightened and she looked down, smooth, straight brown hair momentarily shadowing her face. "I have... been seriously considering joining the Faith."

Not a surprise. "I did rather wonder about that. It would be the logical step if you felt you couldn't stay with us."

"Logical? Yes." She lifted her head, and her expression was like iron. "And perhaps all too human. But

I'm not giving up on my own people—even if I have somehow been changed. Not yet, anyway." She tilted her head again. "So what is it that makes you think there's a parallel between us? Because that's the only rational reason I can think of for this line of conversation."

The question was like a splash of ice-water, making him blink. *Yes, of course she'd see it: She's as smart as I am, and I wasn't being subtle.* "You remember when Gona-Brashind and Nyanthus had us help in the sealing of Ariane's...powers?"

She smiled briefly. "Rather hard to forget. That's the sort of event that even the natives of the Arena don't see often, and *we* had never seen at all."

"Well...just at the end, when things almost went completely wrong...something *happened* to me. The energies converged all on me, rather than around the circle or through Ariane, for just a moment. Mandallon was afraid it had injured me."

"Yes, I vaguely remember that part. I was recovering myself; the...ritual, I suppose we must call it...was mentally and physically taxing for all of us."

"I can't really remember much of it directly," Simon went on, "but I did take a few—very disjointed—notes and in essence they say that I 'saw *everything*,' and a few other cryptic notations, like being noticed, and not everything being good or bad, but power beyond belief."

Laila nodded slowly. "Hm. So Shadeweaver *and* Faith powers converging at once on you, and you suddenly have an epiphany or something of that sort?"

"Shadeweaver and Faith and whatever power Ariane held, as well," Simon said. "I didn't give much thought to it afterwards—I think, honestly, because it *frightened* me in a way I just wasn't accustomed to, and once I stopped thinking about it, it faded away. I felt something...*odd* when we went through Transition, but again it wasn't anything to think much about. But then..." He told her about the Archives and what had happened there. "Laila, I *knew* what I was looking for. It was as though that moment of frustration and anger and *need* made something click into place, and suddenly I just *knew*, as though I'd already had the entire index in my head. I could operate that floating device instantly, even though I'd never seen the inside of one before. I could *read* texts in a language no one in the Arena has known for ten thousand years, read them as though they'd been written in English all along."

He leapt to his feet again, pacing in agitation; thinking of the events brought the worry and, yes, fear back to the foreground. "And I could *understand* it all, Laila. Not just read the words, but the principles, the diagrams, they all were just absolutely clear, as though I'd already studied them. I could see exactly how these new principles could be applied, and I sat down and started sketching the sensing coils right there, with no machine backup, no second guessing, it was just all *there*, and I...I don't exactly *remember* all of it, either."

He found he was shaking. *Why? I know this is a frightening thing, but why do I feel so much terror?*

"Oh, good Lord, Simon. How...terrifying." Her voice was as gentle as he had ever heard it.

"You understand, then?" He tried to sound light, humorous, and knew he was failing. "Because I'm not entirely sure I do."

"Of course." She smiled wryly. "Same problem I have—how do I know whether what my mind does is because I want it to, or because someone *else* made me want to? You can't remember, yet you actually finished *designing* something in that time you can't recall. That would be frightening for anyone. For you? For me? Utter horror. We make our livings with...we *are*... our minds, even more than most people, and to not even know what we ourselves were *doing?* Terrifying. The more so because of what you think it might mean."

"That I...am not entirely myself any more."

"Exactly."

Not for the first time, he desperately wished Mio could be there to help and advise him. *She would know if I was truly me.* But no AISage could make that journey, and he wondered if this uncertainty, this being alone in his own head, was one of the things the Arena specifically desired or required. "Yet I don't feel any different in my *self*, if you know what I mean."

"All too well. Then again," she said with the same wry smile, "how do I actually know what my *self* felt like before?"

That *was* the key question, Simon admitted to himself. If you were facing something that could change natural law, could it not change *you* in a way that you could not detect? That you would believe was completely natural and consistent with the *you* that had existed before?

He suddenly laughed. "Well, now, I *do* understand DuQuesne more. It's rather an inverse of his problem, isn't it?"

Laila thought a moment, then laughed herself. "You're right, of course. He remained himself, but the entire world he thought was real turned out to be false. And he probably can't help but occasionally wonder if *this* world is real or just another layer of arranged fantasy."

Simon remembered the time, shortly after they arrived, when Steve Franceschetti had proposed exactly that. "Yes... I'm sure he does. When the subject came up he was *terrified*. The only time I've ever seen him look really frightened, actually, and the only reason for that is not just that the idea repels him, but that it could be *true* but, this time, so well done that even Marc C. DuQuesne of Hyperion can't tell. So now here we are, sure that the world is the same, but not knowing if we are the people we think we are."

She looked at him levelly. "So what are you going to do about it?"

The talk with Laila had clarified a lot of things—not the least of which being his priorities. "Well, I suppose the only thing I *can* do. Talk to Ariane about it and let her decide what she wants to do. It's not up to *me* to make decisions on whether to risk having me part of the active crew, that's Ariane's decision, and I've been avoiding telling her because I'm afraid of what that decision will be."

Laila brushed absently at her bangs, the straight, shining brown hair shimmering slightly in the pale-gold light from the ceiling. "And I've been avoiding *confronting* the issue... which also isn't the right way to go, now that I really let myself think about it. If I'm thinking of going to the Faith, I should at least talk it over with someone else, shouldn't I?"

"I would say so... assuming you don't feel an inherent hostility towards us, that is."

"No," she said quickly. "Not at all. A bit of pain over the fact that there's some mistrust that isn't *my* fault . . . but I can't blame them, as I said."

Simon rose slowly. "Then . . . why don't we do this together? Might be a little easier than doing it separately?"

This smile was more genuine, with a tinge of gratitude. "I think that's a good idea, Simon," Laila said; her smile then sharpened, just a hair. "It almost sounds romantic, in a facing-execution-together sort of way. And here I thought your eyes were only for Ariane Austin."

He returned the smile and offered his arm. "I would never deny my interest in that direction, but I am not yet committed, and certainly not blind to beauty in *any* direction."

She took his arm and stood. "Then let's go see what the firing squad has in store for us, shall we?"

CHAPTER 23

"I shall not waste more of your time this day," Selpa said, and rose from the cradlelike seat that his species used. "And I will assuredly tell you of our decision when it is reached, so that you need not wonder what has happened. If you have not heard from us, then we have not yet decided."

"I guess I can't ask for more than that. Thank you, Selpa'a'At. May your course be ever your own."

"And yours as well. Until later, Captain Austin."

Oscar Naraj entered as Selpa left. "Any luck?" The ambassador's face registered both concern and sympathy; she didn't think it was feigned, either. Naraj might believe she was the wrong choice for this job, might want to get rid of her in any way possible, but he had, as far as she could tell, no *personal* animosity towards her at all.

"I'm afraid not," she said. "He doesn't want to drive a wedge between us, but given the potential value of a human being actually joining your faction, Maria-Susanna's offer to join the Vengeance is just far too tempting for them to simply refuse outright. I can't really hold it against him. At least he told me about it as soon as it happened, so I can start thinking about what the consequences might be if they do decide to let her join." She looked around, feeling something was missing. "Oh. Where's Michelle?"

"Ah, yes. I have given Deputy Ambassador Ni Deng the responsibility of finding some useful common ground between ourselves and the Blessed."

"I thought you were . . . rather nervous about the Blessed, considering the fact that they're controlled by their AIs."

"I am, quite," he admitted. "But at the same time, I have to consider all factors and try, as much as is possible, to react from rational policy instead of personal prejudice. The Blessed To Serve are an immensely powerful faction, and despite some considerable humiliation and provocation on our part—not," he hastily added, "deliberate on your part, I know—they have chosen to let go of the past and offer us a chance for peaceful interchange."

He sat down, and for a moment—just an instant—she saw Oscar Naraj looking tired, uncertain, and worried. "I've researched the Molothos rather extensively since getting here, Captain Austin," he said slowly. "And . . . speaking entirely honestly . . . they terrify me. I had thought originally that there might be a way of negotiating with them. Then when that turned out . . . less well than I had hoped, I had thought there might be some political pressures or approaches which might be used.

"But there appear to be none, at least none that we can easily avail ourselves of. They are one of the oldest active factions, which is why they remain so powerful; they gained many Spheres on their own early, and—as we discovered ourselves—also expand by colonizing the Upper Sphere of uninhabited solar systems. No one can truly say how many of them there are, or what sort of force they could bring to bear in battle, except that it would be staggeringly huge. They are able to compromise just barely enough to keep the majority factions from uniting against them." He looked down. "You recall Dajzail mentioned another species, the Randaalar?"

She nodded.

"His statement was pure fact. The Randaalar refused to bow to the Molothos about thirty thousand years ago, and apparently the Molothos found their homeworld and destroyed it—not merely conquered, but obliterated the planet itself in some fashion, and hunted down every member of the species for the next several centuries. Against something like that . . . I truly am reluctant to shut out any possible allies, even if they are themselves frightening in another way."

"Ni Deng understands she can't—"

"Oh, we both understand that any final decisions are yours, Captain," Oscar assured her. He stood again. "But I wanted her to have some particular area to focus on, and this will likely be something that will take considerable time and delicacy to arrange. Michelle is extremely patient when the situation calls for it, and her attention to detail is what recommended her to me several years ago.

"In the meantime, I am seeking more allies in other areas. I have an appointment, in fact, with the Shadeweaver Gona-Brashind at their Faction House, so I had best be moving on."

"Just be careful, Ambassador," she said warningly. "Gona-Brashind didn't, as far as I can tell, mess around with us the way Amas-Garao did, but he's sure got his own agenda and we don't know what it is."

"Oh, I shall be careful," Oscar said, and turned as he was leaving. "But do give me a bit of credit, Captain; I have spent years arranging things according to *my* own agenda, so I am not at all unfamiliar with the idea."

Wu Kung looked in after the ambassador was gone. "He's a devious one."

"You mean that in a specific way?" The last thing she needed was *internal* intrigues. She knew Naraj probably had *some* plans, but...

He wrinkled his nose as though he'd smelled something bad, and his little fangs projected momentarily; somehow, it made the little Hyperion look *cute*, a thought she had never expected to have. "Well... no. Maybe. He always smells like he has some idea underneath every idea, so I can't *tell* if he's planning anything. So you watch out, okay?"

"Isn't that your job?"

He made as though to slap her head gently. "You like to take risks like me! And sometimes I am not there! So it may be my job, but it's *your* job too!"

He turned smoothly away, obviously having heard something; a second later she picked up the sound of a pair of people walking through the entryway to her office.

"I beg your pardon, Ariane," Simon said, with Laila Canning next to him. "But... could I speak with you in private, please?"

Oh, thank God. He's got to be coming to me to talk about whatever's bothering him, and I was absolutely dreading having to try to pry it out of him. "Of course, Simon."

"And," Laila said, "I will want the same opportunity afterwards. If you can spare the time."

They came together...why? Did he talk to Laila *first? Why?* "I can spare the time, Laila. It's not as though you demand much of it in the first place. Wu, just wait outside. I'm safe enough with Simon."

"Okay."

The door shut, and Simon looked at her for a long moment before sitting down slowly, sweeping his sword around and out of the way in a now-practiced, elegant gesture. "I don't know if you've noticed—"

"I think most of us have. Something's been bothering you for a while, and none of us know what it is."

"Hm." A weak smile. "Concealing secrets has never been my strong point, I must confess. But this one... was personally frightening. And I think you will understand my reluctance."

Simon launched into his explanation. She was first struck with a feeling of self-reproach—*why didn't I recognize something had happened that time?*—even as she realized she'd been in no position to really pay much attention to anything during the ritual that had sealed away the strange Arena-born powers she'd gained in that last desperate gamble against Amas-Garao.

Then he described what had happened in the Archives, and she felt the same cold chill she often got when dealing with the mysteries of the Arena. "Creepy, once again."

"Oh, very much so," Simon agreed, no longer smiling.

"But why keep it a *secret*, Simon? It's scary, yes, but—"

"You really don't understand?" He shook his head. "Oh, of course. Because it happened to me well afterwards, when we knew each other well, and—"

Then it suddenly burst in on her what he meant,

what he'd been afraid of, and why he would have had to talk first to Laila before anyone else. "Oh, God. Simon, I'm sorry, that was very dense of me."

Even as she said it, she felt—almost involuntarily—the calm, cold discipline she'd cultivated as "Captain Austin" coming forward. "You're right, it *is* a concern. But—if I'm completely honest—it's one that you should all have about *me*, too."

Simon blinked, and then laughed, a chagrined expression on his face. "Oh, great *kami*, of course, of *course*. And I suppose DuQuesne . . . ?"

". . . confronted me with that question immediately afterwards. And I told him what happened and basically threw myself on his mercy." Another thought struck her. "And you know, what you described . . . that was exactly what I saw, what I felt, when the change happened, and it sounds like what happened to Mandallon."

"Yes, I see. But at the same time, that can't be what happened to me. I haven't shown the slightest trace of abilities such as Mandallon or yourself, and—if we're right about when this happened—I have been living with this for months. You needed to be contained within a day of gaining the power, and I was given the strong impression that Initiate Guides are both carefully trained before the day, and are assisted afterwards for some time by other trained Guides. Based on what we know, if I had gained *that* power, I should have become a walking disaster within days or weeks at most."

She nodded. *Makes sense.* "Then the only thing I can think of is that you somehow . . . retained a connection to what you saw. Not of *power*, but of *information*. And sometimes you can open that connection."

Simon's green eyes widened slightly. "That *does*

make a great deal of sense, yes! Alas," he continued, "it doesn't actually answer my current questions, though."

"Simon, the fact is we're not going to *get* clear-cut answers to that kind of thing, at least not any time soon. All we can do is use our best judgment. And in *mine* you are still the Doctor Simon Sandrisson who brought all of us here in the first place. If you want a second opinion, ask DuQuesne. He's *the* expert in seeing through phonies. He saw through Hyperion's near-perfect illusions and survived breaking them. He'll tell you if he thinks there's anything wrong with you." She smiled. "Simon, we wouldn't have come here without you. We wouldn't have gotten home without you. We might be able to do the rest without you, but I'm *damn* glad we don't have to. I think you're you, and that's the end of the subject as far as I'm concerned."

She could see the tension evaporate. "Then . . . thank you, Ariane. *Arigatou gozaimasu*, thank you *very* much. I'm sorry for not having come to you sooner—"

"Don't apologize, Simon. With our worry about Laila and the way I behaved, you had *every* reason to wonder about my reaction. And that said, I'd better let Laila in and talk this out with her, too."

"Of course."

A few moments later, Laila Canning entered and closed the door.

"Sit down, Laila. After what Simon talked to me about, I have a fairly good idea of what *you* needed to talk about."

The brown-haired scientist smiled quickly. "I don't doubt it. Mainly, I had one quite specific question, though."

A specific question? Puzzled, Ariane asked, "All right, what is it?"

Laila leaned forward. "You've been suspicious of me since I awakened—and it's always seemed to me that you felt you had a *reason* for it, not just reasonable caution. I can't say exactly *why* I felt this, but..." she looked apologetic, "but I just kept getting the feeling you didn't trust me for some actual reason."

God, I feel like such an idiot. "Not...not really a *reason*, Laila. Actually, after my conversation with Simon, I was just reminded of how stupid I sometimes can be. It was just a silly impression."

"Oh?"

She deserves to at least hear how silly I was being. "Right after our first talk—after you woke up—I was leaving, and when I looked back..." she sighed, smiled with embarrassment. "This is really stupid. It will completely ruin my reputation as any sort of bright commander, I warn you."

Laila waited.

"All right. I looked back, and for just an *instant*— just a split second—I thought I saw you looking back at me with a completely different expression."

Laila raised an eyebrow. "What *sort* of expression?"

She thought back to that moment, and that same chill went down her spine again. "Sort of the expression I've seen used when you're studying something under a microscope, but at the same time almost as though you found me...funny? Amusing?" She shivered. "It was probably just the stress of the moment, but that impression was pretty creepy and it stayed with me."

Laila looked at her for a long moment. "Interesting. That is what you saw?"

"That's what I *thought* I saw," Ariane said, feeling even more embarrassed. "I probably invented it."

Laila smiled slowly. "Possibly not. You have shown an... impressive ability to observe and act on your observations in the past; a combat or racing pilot who *doesn't* notice things fast is likely dead thereafter.

"Your reaction isn't *scientific*, no, and I deplore the idea that a simple emotional reaction would determine the level of trust... but I also have to recall that your 'gut-level' instinct has managed to get us all through this in prior conflicts, so I would be rather ill-advised to just dismiss it. I will say that I don't even recall looking at you as you left—but I also have other scattered moments in which I am not entirely clear what I was doing. So... perhaps I am not, in fact, Laila Canning." She looked steadily at Ariane. "But I would like to resolve how I'll be *treated* from now on."

"You aren't giving me much of a break, are you?"

She snorted. "No. I'll admit to an emotional reaction of my own, and that is that I resent the idea that you've been wondering if I'm not myself because you *thought* you saw something. But in any case, I *cannot* give you a 'break,' Captain. This is your decision, and it should be made with full knowledge of what you might be doing."

I wish DuQuesne was here!

She squelched that thought. DuQuesne *wasn't* there, and if he was, he'd almost certainly just repeat Laila's advice. That's *why* they'd chosen her captain.

She probably only sat there for a few moments, but to Ariane it felt like hours. Judging from the well-hidden tension in Laila's face, it wasn't a short wait for her, either.

"All right, Laila," she said finally. "I'll be just as honest, then. I owe you that.

"We don't know if you're yourself or not. You could be an agent of the Faith, or something else. Or you could be exactly who you always were. I think you're a little changed—you don't want to go back to who you were, with three AISages in your head, practically running your body while you studied. But honestly? First, I can't *afford* to lose any of the people who've been here with me. Second, I really think you are you, or mostly you. Third . . . I can't afford paranoia. If there is something not-you there, it's never shown any sign of being anything other than helpful. Mandallon brought you back from what was basically brain-dead and gave you back to us, and I should be simply grateful for that. If the Faith did anything to you, well, they've already *got* all the information you have, and they haven't shown any sign of it. So no matter what, I think you're one of us, and you mean to *stay* one of us.

"So as of now, I'm going to assume you *are* the exact same Doctor Laila Canning who made that trip, and I will inform DuQuesne of this decision. I don't have time for this kind of worry. If I'm giving Simon—with a lot more evidence of something funny going on—the benefit of the doubt, I have to give it to you. Especially," she smiled, "since I'm asking *you* to give the same benefit to me."

As with Simon, she saw tension seep away from Laila. "Thank you, Ariane," she said. "I . . . did not want to leave here, but if I had to be always suspected—"

"I know. It's over." She reached out and gripped the other woman's hand. "I'm sorry. Welcome back. Welcome *really* back."

And Laila gripped back with a smile.

CHAPTER 24

"I know it's only thirty people, but that's a hell of a crowd compared to *us*," DuQuesne murmured. He glanced in the direction of the group that was waiting, mostly patiently, outside the entrance to the Guardhouse area, then looked back down at the cable he was rigging. *Going to need a lot more power here.*

Carl Edlund paused in the middle of fixing the last brace for the table. "I don't think they even outnumber *you*," he said.

"Ha. Unfortunately it's not *that* kind of outnumbering."

"Be grateful," Tom Cussler said, waving the first people forward. "They *could* have sent a lot more through, but I'm guessing they're screening the first set very carefully."

"I guess. And it's plain as day that we'll be needing a lot more people for everything we want to do. Just wish I didn't have to worry how many of them might be more on Naraj's side than ours."

"Well, *hey* there, DQ!" called a cheerful voice.

DuQuesne stood upright, startled, and looked down at a woman who looked to be in her mid-thirties, hair done in streaks like a box of neapolitan ice cream—brown, red, and white—with a dark tan and sharp hazel eyes. She had a large red dufflebag slung over her shoulder and was gazing up at him with a broad grin.

"Tobin? *You* came to this madhouse?"

"DQ, once I heard you were involved, I had to come see what you'd gotten yourself into. After the Singularity project I'd thought the excitement was over, but judging from what I saw just on the way in, that was only a warm-up!"

"You know Doctor Tobin?" Cussler asked. "I'd heard of you by reputation, Doctor, but—"

"We worked together on the Singularity Power Project some years back," DuQuesne said, still smiling. *Damn, this is something of a stroke of luck.* "Tom, Carl, and Steve, this is Doctor Molly Tobin, one of the best practical power engineering designers you'll ever meet."

"Another power engineer?" Steve said with some excitement. "Oh, that's excellent! DuQuesne's great, but he's got so many other things on his plate that we have to practically beg him for help on this stuff."

Tobin nodded, looking around, as Tom started getting information from the other two people he'd called up. "That's DQ, all right; take on more work than any three other people and call it a good night's work."

"'DQ'?" Carl repeated. "Never heard *that* one before."

"And *only* Molly and about two other people *get* to call me that, so don't start," DuQuesne said in a half-serious warning tone. "What kind of equipment have you guys brought?"

"Couple more AIWish units and a whole bunch of key elements—the sort that're harder to come by, not available in large quantities out on your upper Sphere, at least based on what you've sent us so far," Molly answered promptly. "Efficient turbine designs and other components for various types of powerplants, of course, that can be coded direct to your AIWish. More power means getting more done, so we figured power engineering would be one of the key factors. Also brought a couple civil engineers, habitat analysis people, concept synthesizers, and so on."

"That's definitely going to help. A lot." He glanced at the group more closely. "Most of 'em don't look too shellshocked, either. Been picking fron the ones who don't rely on their AISages, eh?"

"That was one of Ambassador Naraj's directives, yes," she agreed. "And based on what we knew, that made a lot of sense."

He bent, finished locking down the cable. "You been briefed?"

"*Heavily*. Enough that I just about *believe* this crazy place really exists, now that I'm here."

He grinned at her. "Oh, it'll get harder to believe before it gets easier. Well, we've just finished the survey above our Sphere and we have no fewer than eight Sky Gates. Simon's preparing to send probes through to see what's on the other side—hopefully one of them goes to Nexus Arena." He turned. "Follow me, Molly. The others have to go through all the rigmarole, but I know you, you know me, and I want you to see the problem you guys will have to tackle first."

He led Molly up through the Inner Sphere to the elevator. "Get ready to meet the Arena."

"I thought the *real* Arena we couldn't go to yet. This Nexus Arena."

"In a way, yeah..." The elevator door slid open, and they walked into the foyer towards the door to the Upper Sphere. "But this is still part of the Arena, and the important thing about now is that you've arrived at *night.*"

They stepped through the door...and Molly Tobin stopped dead.

Above the dark jungle, silhouetted against a distant horizon and spanning vision in all directions, was...

There still aren't words, DuQuesne thought. *Maybe my long-ago creator, that bombastic Doctor E.E. Smith, could have described it. But I can't.*

The sky of the Arena glowed above the Sphere of Humanity; a shimmering of clouds in the indescribable distance, flickering and flashing with lightning strokes that branched and stretched not for instants but long, long seconds of seething electrical fire, blue-white and fire-orange and gleaming pearlescent white against blue-black; a deep ruddy glow was visible in another direction, and against it a dark, trailing line of clouds edged in rose and blood. Directly above, a roiling, majestic sea of deep violet and velvet and sparking, shimmering blue. It was the sky of storms the size of worlds and of lights that might come from another world, a moon's distance away in that impossible airy gulf, and faint, barely-seen movement that might be creatures, living beings that dared to live and fight and die and perhaps even think, wonder, and love in the endless spaces between Spheres.

"Oh...my." Molly said finally.

"Yeah, that's about all you can say. Or something

like that. Even more if you're here in the daytime first; looks pretty much like some place on Earth then, with the Luminaire up. You have to squint pretty hard to make out anything funny in the sky in the daytime. So then the sun goes down...that's when you suddenly *know* you ain't in Kansas any more."

"Or down the rabbit hole. This place seems just about that crazy." She shook herself in a way that DuQuesne found amusingly familiar; most of the original visitors had done the same thing when recovering from a typical Arena shock. "So...besides that, what did you have for me?"

"Listen."

She cocked her head, and even in the dim lighting he could see her sudden smile. "Oh, now, *that* is hopeful. A waterfall?"

"And a *big* one," DuQuesne said with an answering smile. "We've diverted a tiny portion of it so far with what we could rig up, but I know you worked on studying hydro plants before. My best estimate on this fall is it's close to two million liters a second."

"That *is* pretty big," she said. "I admit...I'm having trouble grasping this. We are on *top* of a spherical construct, right? What's all this...world doing on top of it, if you know what I mean?"

"It's made to be similar to our home environment— though *similar* does not mean *identical*, so get that through your head. Near as I can figure, there's a couple thousand kilometers of rock under us which acts like the actual mantle of a planet. Plate tectonics, the whole nine yards. You've got some kind of oceans out there—Simon's probes were able to return some images, and we're finally getting some idea of what the top of the Sphere looks like. Within the gravity area there's some convection and condensation—but we're not even *close* to figuring out how all this interacts with the stuff outside the gravity field."

He shook his head. "It's enough to drive you nuts, I'll tell you. But the long and the short is, we get weather like Earth, pretty close, you get night and day like Earth, there's volcanoes and earthquakes and all the rest like Earth, and I wouldn't be surprised if there weren't seasons to the . . . North and South of us, where the Luminaire's light will be more oblique; I'll bet its path slowly goes North and South over the period of a year, just like the apparent position of the Sun varies due to Earth's axial tilt. We're pretty much on the equator right here." He paused. "The *effective* equator of the Upper Sphere, not the actual Sphere's equator. *Damnation*. We'll need yet *more* new vocabulary."

They stopped at the edge of the ridge overlooking the swift-running river. "That *is* impressive," Molly said finally. "So you want me to design a power plant to use . . . that?"

"Figure we could get a few gigawatts out of it, which would go a *long* way towards giving us some comfortable independence here. And if there's one waterfall like this, I'm betting there's plenty of opportunities for water power here."

She nodded. "I can imagine the largest possible water power generator, actually."

"What do . . . oh." He suddenly began to chuckle, then laughed loudly. "*Doctor* Tobin, you haven't stopped thinking bigger, have you?"

"It just seemed obvious to me, Marc," she said,

grinning back. "Given the description, there's a wall, an edge, somewhere around this Upper Sphere, the point where the gravity stops keeping things comfortably on the surface. Go knock a hole in it and let the entire ocean start draining out until you reach equilibrium. With a few billion liters of water a second, I'll start giving you some *real* power!"

CHAPTER 25

Ariane rose slowly to her feet, favoring her side. "Okay, I think I know when I'm beaten," she said, bowing to her opponent, Orphan.

Wu Kung had been expecting her to yield earlier. *But she's a real fighter,* he thought with admiration. *Won't give up even in a play fight without showing what she's got in guts.*

Orphan leaned back on his tail with a buzzing chuckle. "Oh, now *that* I doubt in the extreme, Captain Austin. If you had the capacity to even *believe* you were beaten, how then could you have faced a Shadeweaver—and won?" He bowed to her. "Still, it is a wise tactician who recognizes they no longer *need* stay in the battle. And you did quite well."

"You managed to hit him a few times," DuQuesne said with a grin. "Take that as a compliment. Orphan's *good*."

"So I see. If I ever have to fight you for *real*, Orphan, you'll pardon me if I cheat."

The chuckle turned to a full, rich laugh—though still with that buzzing undertone. "Oh, Captain Austin, I would *expect* you to cheat. Of course," he said, with a lean forward and tilt that somehow conveyed the impression of a roguish grin, "if ever I must fight any of you, rest assured I will cheat as well!"

"I sure don't doubt *that*," DuQuesne said.

Gabrielle checked the signals from Ariane's medical nanos using a handheld scanner. "No serious damage, Arrie."

"Of course not," Wu said defensively, wondering if they thought he'd *let* her get hurt. "If I thought Orphan was actually going to *hurt* her—past a few broken bones or something like that—I'd have stopped him!"

"I'd much rather you stopped it *before* any bones got broken, thank you kindly," Gabrielle said with a sigh. "But in this kind of sparring I suppose that's a forlorn hope."

Wu was going to protest that if you were going to let things like *that* stop you, you weren't ready to learn serious fighting . . . but he remembered that a lot of other people didn't think that way.

Ariane seated herself on one of the benches set around the large exercise and practice area that Steve had figured out how to create inside their Embassy. Wu looked around admiringly. *It's not anywhere as big as what they showed me for some of the Great Factions, but it's still a great sparring and exercise place!*

Currently, the room was configured in something that more than hinted at some of the Arena's combat challenge areas: different levels of the floor, upright and sideways obstacles like tree trunks and branches, irregular obstacles like rocks, and so on. In this first contest—which, Wu understood, was partly a way of strengthening ties with the Liberated—Ariane had tried to use her smaller size and maneuverability against

Orphan, but he was lightning fast and very strong. *Fast and strong, and he hasn't shown what he can do for real, not yet.*

"That was indeed a fine warmup," Orphan said. "But you have been stretching yourself on the sidelines long enough, Doctor DuQuesne. Or perhaps you, Sun Wu Kung, would care to give me the instruction Dr. DuQuesne promised me?"

Wu grinned a fanged smile but didn't take the bait. This part of the contest DuQuesne and he had talked out in detail. DuQuesne wasn't going to push himself past the point Orphan had already seen, in the battle against Amas-Garao, so Wu could push past that point, up to roughly where he knew DuQuesne would be if he started to push himself, which would be somewhere around Tunuvun's skill and strength. "I think DuQuesne wants to try you first."

The door opened, and K—*no, he reminded himself, Oasis Abrams, have to remember who she's pretending to be*—came in. "Sparring with aliens and no one invited *me*?"

Despite the lighthearted comment, Wu sensed unusual tension from her—and a whiff from DuQuesne, too. There was something going on there, but neither of them had said anything to him. *No one does if they think it will upset me. And that upsets me. But then, maybe that proves they're right. If something upsets me not to know, maybe it would be even more upsetting if I knew . . .* He stopped there, realizing he was about to *really* get confused.

"Oasis!" Ariane said, obviously surprised. "Aren't you—"

"Ambassador Ni Deng and Vantak are at the Arcade,

meeting with some of the Blessed's allies, and the ambassador said she didn't need me." She shrugged. "I suppose they *could* try something, but being too reluctant would probably be insulting too, so it's her judgment call." She grinned, and Wu could sense more honest relaxation. "And *this* looks a lot more fun than watching their discussions, anyway."

Ariane nodded, smiling. "I suppose so. But if she's making good progress—and Ambassador Naraj thinks she is—she could be helping get us a major support in our coming war. If we get *enough* support, the Molothos may even back down."

"Yeah, good luck with that," DuQuesne said. He rose to his feet. "Okay, Orphan, time for us to find out what you've *really* got." Then he paused. "Unless *you* want first dibs, Oasis?"

"Hand to hand only?"

"Well, appendage to appendage," Orphan said, wagging his tail obviously. "I have no intention of handicapping myself to that extent."

"Oh, of course not."

The redheaded woman faced off with the tall, massive green and black patterned Orphan. For a few moments, the two stood still, measuring each others' stances. Then Orphan exploded into motion.

But Oasis was not there; she was *above* the two meters and more of alien, flipping effortlessly from projection to projection.

Orphan gave a surprised laugh and then bounded up in pursuit, his chitinous armor and leaping motion combining with his occasionally flaring wing-cases to give him the aspect of an immense locust.

The two figures came together in a looping motion,

and suddenly the red-haired figure was plummeting downward, barely saving herself from impact with the ground; she leapt aside desperately as Orphan followed her. *But she should be doing a* lot *better than* that*! What* . . .

Even as he thought that, he remembered. *She's pretending to be human, ordinary human. Very good, very trained—better than Ariane—but not like she really is. So* . . .

The end came quickly, as she evaded two ordinary strikes only to be caught by a brutal tail-strike. Gabrielle was sprinting quickly to Oasis' side even as she came to rest. "Okay, that's hard enough! Good *Lord*, do you people want to kill each other?"

But Oasis was slowly trying to get up already. "We're . . . just doing some . . . friendly sparring," she managed to say.

"Friendly . . . well, maybe, but that's enough for you."

"All right," DuQuesne said, as Oasis sat down heavily on the bench next to Ariane, "*Now* it's my turn."

Orphan bowed to DuQuesne, and the two came directly at each other.

Wu laughed and clapped his hands. *This* was much more like it! For moments the two stood nearly toe-to-toe, blocking each other's blows, evading strikes, delivering others of their own. Simultaneously a kick from a shining black foot hammered home even as the strike of a massive fist smashed into a crested head, and both combatants staggered backwards, instantly coming back on guard. DuQuesne and Orphan circled each other, and then DuQuesne charged in, shrugging off a glancing blow but taking his opponent down with a Brazilian Jiu-Jitsu grapple. The bodies slammed to the floor, DuQuesne on top and driving hard, trying to control Orphan, render him helpless.

But human martial arts were generally intended for human opponents, and Orphan's flexible, sting-equipped tail made that approach far too dangerous. DuQuesne was kicked away, bleeding from his nose, but grinning a savage warrior's grin. Orphan rolled to his feet, crouching now with tail raised like a scorpion's, and he was giving a buzz of warlike amusement.

The two made several more passes; Orphan used a lightning-fast wing strike that took down DuQuesne like an axe, but couldn't capitalize on it; DuQuesne caught Orphan off-guard and almost battered him to his knees, but instead got taken down himself; for a few seconds the two even locked arms in a contest of strength that seemed likely to go on for a long time.

Finally DuQuesne bowed out. "I think," he said, breathing a little hard—*and exaggerating it, too*, Wu thought—"that we could go on doing that for quite a while. Now, like I promised—you get to try Wu."

Wu stepped forward, knowing just by the other's posture that he was having a hard time taking such a tiny opponent as seriously as he should...but he was going on guard anyway. "This looks like fun!" he said, and bowed to Orphan.

"We shall see," Orphan said, and did a pushup-bow.

Wu waited for Orphan to get prepared.

Then he leaped up, grabbed one of the branchlike supports, and scrambled up and around as though he were back in the jungles of the Mountain. He heard Orphan already coming after him. *He's moving in... coming from that direction...he'll be arcing up, trying to get the height on me. Ha!*

The green-black figure spun in from above, Orphan's tail allowing him to grab and shift direction in motion while leaving arms and legs free. But Wu Kung ducked and ran right up Orphan's back, caught the tail as it started to unwind, anchored himself with his *own* tail, and *pulled*.

Caught in midair, with nothing to catch hold of, Orphan was slung up and over, somersaulting through space. He twisted, flared his wingcases to catch air and guide his fall, blunted the impact, but his posture now showed he had *full* respect for Wu's abilities. "Well done!" Orphan shouted, even as he moved back in, this time more cautiously. "I should recall that you and I share certain anatomical advantages."

"You should, because now is the time for us to see which of us is *better*! Let us not run and dance!"

"As you wish."

Orphan dropped lightly to the ground and waited. Sun Wu Kung evaluated his position, landed several meters ahead, paused, and then met Orphan's charge with his own.

A charge which he evaded at the last second, ducking aside and kicking Orphan just between the wingcases. The leader (and sole member) of the Liberated was smashed unceremoniously to the slightly-yielding floor, skidding and tumbling for a few meters before managing to turn the fall into a roll. Orphan was up almost immediately, but the turn was slightly ... off, not quite as quick and precise as his prior moves. *Is he faking? ... no, he is stunned for a moment.*

Wu didn't hesitate. He bounded in, blocked a kick, a tail strike, and one punch, got in a double-footed kick that sent Orphan staggering back—and made his wings flare.

There! From Ariane's first encounter with the Blessed!

The pinkish tympani were exposed for that brief moment, and Wu delivered a lightning fast *slap* to each, one with each hand.

Orphan gave a coughing buzz of pain and collapsed. "Enough!"

Immediately Wu stepped back and bowed; a spatter of applause came from the watchers. Orphan slowly pulled himself to his feet, and did a push-bow to both Wu and DuQuesne. "I am...adequately instructed for my doubts, Doctor DuQuesne." He turned to Wu. "You are truly a master of combat, Sun Wu Kung. I would venture to say you might match...or even slightly surpass...the best of the Arena's warriors." He looked at DuQuesne and Ariane. "I thank you for your trust in this."

Ariane smiled. "I thought you would understand. Is it true?"

"That there are limits on how capable one might make oneself, using technological enhancement? Most certainly. But it is, admittedly, at least partially determined based on what you are to begin with. The Molothos and some others, such as the Daelmokhan, began their emergence into the Arena already extremely formidable, and thus their enhancements can reach somewhat greater levels. The Genasi, of course, are native to the Arena, so what rules THEY follow...is not yet entirely clear. What *is* clear is that your people obviously must have started from most formidable stock indeed, if this is the result."

Orphan seemed now fully recovered. *He's tough! Very good!* "I now regret, even more, not happening to be present for your impromptu challenge, Sun Wu Kung; that battle must have been magnificent, with you alongside one of the great Champions."

Wu let himself smile broadly. "It was *fun*, yes. A *lot* of fun."

The important thing—the real reason this sparring match had happened—seemed to have worked. DuQuesne had implied that Wu was better—but at the same time he really wanted both him and Wu to have some reserve, something no one knew about. So this battle was to convince Orphan that he knew what even DuQuesne and Wu Kung were capable of—and maybe get some information from him about how all these abilities worked compared to what you could do in the normal universe. *He sure seems to believe he's seen the truth. Doesn't smell terribly suspicious—no more than he was coming in, anyway.*

The door suddenly burst open, and Simon Sandrisson stood there, white coat flowing down, with a smile on the face framed by brilliant white hair. "Ariane! DuQuesne!"

Ariane jumped slightly—the door had opened right next to her. "Simon? I thought you were—"

"On the Upper Sphere, yes, I was." Wu heard the scientist's breathing. *Boy, he was running fast!* "And I suppose I could have called, but..."

He drew himself up. "But this was something I wanted to tell you in person. We have a direct Sky Gate link to Nexus Arena!"

CHAPTER 26

"And finally," Orphan said, with a dramatic bow and sweeping gesture, "I shall complete the introduction so rudely interrupted these many months ago. My friends and allies, the flagship of the Liberated, the *Zounin-Ginjou*."

Compared to the many-kilometers-long dock extending from Nexus Arena, the *Zounin-Ginjou* might have seemed small, but at this range Ariane realized that the ship was huge—and beautiful. The size and massive presence of what was obviously a warship was both accentuated and mitigated by its construction—deep, rich browns and mahogany colors of polished wood, shining gold trim, silver highlights, sparkling crystal ports. *Zounin-Ginjou* was a gigantic yet streamlined spindle-cigar shape, with recessed rotating jets, bulges of hidden equipment and obvious viewports, and sculpted ridges symmetric around her long axis, ridges that ran straight down or curved gently, to meet and dovetail and curve away again before the hull tapered to a four-vaned tail.

"She's *gorgeous*, Orphan. Did I get a...sense of meaning from that name?"

The crested head tilted comically. "What you may have sensed I cannot say. What was this meaning you thought you sensed?"

"Something...a brilliant star in the depths of utter blackness." She glanced at DuQuesne, Laila, and Wu, who all nodded.

"Yes, indeed. The Arena continues to amuse us, does it not? Sometimes a translation, sometimes an equivalent name, sometimes a hint of meaning." He laughed. "But that is indeed the essence of it. Final Light, the Sentry in the Dark, Point of Light? All of these, and more."

That makes sense, given his position as the last of the Liberated. She frowned at the hull. Something bothered her. *Hmm. Those strange ridges make a pattern... The hull seems thicker there...* "Orphan, are those...sails?"

"Sails, air-brakes, turning-vanes, yes. And the thicker ones to the sides can be wings, for gliding within a stronger gravity field." Orphan nodded. "I had forgotten; you are just now coming to understand the Arena's...odd constraints in such travel."

"We're learning," DuQuesne said. "But it's gonna take a while. For us, if you're in atmosphere, you've got gravity, if you don't have atmosphere, you might or might not have gravity—but usually not, in practice."

"Here, atmosphere of some sort is a constant, but gravity is a fickle master," Orphan said, leading them aboard along an extended ramp.

The ramp brought them onboard and was longer than it seemed—meaning that *Zounin-Ginjou* loomed even larger as they approached. *This ship really is huge,* Ariane thought. *Well over a kilometer long.*

Orphan continued, "You already know that each Sphere is surrounded by a wide band of gravity—although Nexus Arena rather breaks that rule, since off the Docks the gravity goes to effectively zero for some distance." When they nodded, he went on, activating the external door, "So. In between Spheres, there is usually gravity, though quite weak, and it varies depending on where in the Spherepool you are. You will have a tendency to be drawn inward—towards the center of the Spherepool—and planeward, towards the ideal plane which passes through the Spherepool from side to side."

DuQuesne grunted. "So, like the overall gravity of a galaxy, then."

"In essence, yes."

The door swung wide, and Ariane saw a wide, well-lit corridor with what seemed hand-rubbed wood panelling, engraved in alien yet generally pleasing patterns, lining the walls. The walls themselves had strange traces of alien design, neither circular nor square but with curves just slightly greater than a normal human designer would feel comfortable with. Still . . . "This seems . . . almost normal."

"If I understand the implied question, indeed. In the days following your departure, I considered a number of things, and decided that as it was very likely you would remain some of my most valuable allies, it would be wise to adjust my ship to allow you some comfort." He extended wings and arms a moment in a walking bow. "I am, of course, well used to adjusting to change."

"It's beautifully done," Laila said. "I can see where you must have done the modifications—these curves are part of the essential structure, but other areas are obviously modified. What's left still is quite interesting from a biological point of view."

Orphan looked at her with mock concern. "By the Minds, you will discern my uttermost secrets in my architecture! What an error I have made!"

Ariane laughed, as did the others. "You'd already learned more than that from our stay in your Embassy. And here you've put that to good use."

They entered what proved to be an elevator—one that seemed to have a minimal number of stops. *Probably a quick travel mechanism for the crucial areas of the vessel.*

The door of the elevator slid up, rather than sideways, revealing a gigantic control room so filled with gleaming consoles, levers, solidly-placed viewscreens, and padded, anchored chairs that Ariane found herself irresistably reminded of something from the Age of Steam. "These are all hand controls!" she said.

"Well, some by foot. And normally one or two for the tail, but I've redesigned that. But yes, all manual. Trusting automation in the Arena is a game for the newly-hatched. Some automation works, as you have discovered, but it is rarely as good as a living person at doing anything. Does this bother you?"

Ariane was already examining the controls. "Oh, no, not one little bit. I just need to learn how all this *works.*"

"And that is of course why you, in particular, are here, Captain Austin," Orphan said. "No better student to learn the basics of piloting this vessel and pass on what you have learned."

"Hold on," DuQuesne said. "You're not giving us *this* one, are you?"

Orphan flicked his hands out in the *no* gesture. "Oh, my apologies. I did indeed misspeak. *This* vessel shall remain mine, of course. But the others have all had their controls modeled in the same way, allowing for difference in size and particular mission, so if you learn the ways of *Zounin-Ginjou* you will be prepared for any of our vessels."

"Why the big window?" Wu Kung asked. "This is a warship. Why weaken it?"

Orphan laughed. "An obvious and direct question, but one which makes too many assumptions, Sun Wu Kung. While it is true that the failure mode of the window is an abrupt shattering rather than the bending of ordinary metal, that window—and those of most warships—is composed of carefully layered carbon with reinforcement of the crystal structure via specific structural . . ." he apparently noticed Wu's expression. "Well, never mind. In short, while sufficient force *can* shatter the window, such a force would puncture the hull as well, and you will find such windows on many vessels throughout the Arena."

"Transparent ring-carbon composite," DuQuesne said. "Yeah, we use it too—and it is a pain to make a lot of it, compared to regular hull material. The microstructure needed to make it pass light is pretty complex—that's what makes it shatter instead of just bend and tear, also."

Orphan seated himself at the central control panel. "Observe carefully, Ariane Austin. By the time we arrive at your Sphere, I hope to make you a decent, if not yet expert, pilot of such a vessel."

I've got a lot *to learn.* Just the sheer *size* of the Liberated battleship was vastly different from anything she'd flown before; it was much bigger than *Holy Grail* even counting the *Grail*'s drive spines, and *Holy Grail* had been by far the largest ship Ariane had ever flown. Adding into that the idea of sails—for purposes she could guess but had never actually had to address—variable gravity, and so on, it was going to be a great challenge.

Engines thrummed to life and lights blossomed across the board. "Have I got the lighting correct?" Orphan asked. "I deduced from the devices I have seen that the color green is for things in good condition, red for poor condition or emergencies."

"Pretty darn close," DuQuesne said with an impressed tone. "Given that your color receptors aren't ours and whatever *your* experience of green, it isn't ours either. I'd adjust the color a bit—these look more blue-ish than green to me."

"We shall do so once we are well under way." Orphan's long-fingered, slightly clawed hands danced over buttons, pulled levers, and she felt *Zounin-Ginjou* waking up, starting to shake off inaction, moving more and more swiftly up and away from the Docks. "Did you see what I did there?"

"Okay...those are for the side thrusters. Those are the angle...you can adjust them for side to side or up and down as you want. That was for the main engines, and the pedals are for the rudders and elevators."

"Excellent! I knew you would be a quick study given your background, and it is good to see my expectations confirmed."

"When we get to our Sphere," Ariane said, glancing to DuQuesne, "I think I'll sit down with Carl and Steve and work up a full emulation of one of these control rooms. Then we can get people practicing in virtual first."

"Good thinking."

"Now that we are well away," Orphan said, "would you tell me where your Gateway is?"

"Go vertical," DuQuesne said. "When Simon's probe popped through and got pics, we could tell he'd come out well above Nexus Arena."

"Very good."

As *Zounin-Ginjou* began to climb, Ariane suddenly blinked. "Holy sh...I mean, what the heck? Orphan, you haven't increased power since we left the docks and we just went vertical...so there isn't any gravity here, since we're still accelerating just the way we were before..."

"And so...?" She swore the nearly-human face wore a sly smile.

"So how come I'm still standing on the deck instead of floating around? Have you guys figured out how to generate gravity yourselves?"

DuQuesne shook his head. "I think I know the answer, and it starts with *Shade* and ends with *weaver*. Right?"

Orphan looked somehow slightly put out, as though he had been looking forward to a more convoluted explanation. "In essence, yes. When possible, most Factions will try to put such gravitic stability on their vessels through a bargain either with the Shadeweavers or Faith. In my case, the Shadeweavers. It makes things so much easier for most species."

They were now climbing well away from Nexus Arena. Ariane caught her breath. "My *God*."

DuQuesne, who had been studying the controls,

glanced up, and mumbled one of his ancient anachronistic curses.

"Ahhh," Orphan said. "This is the first time you have truly *seen* Nexus Arena."

"I thought . . . it was just a larger Sphere," Ariane heard herself say.

Nexus Arena was not a sphere, but a gargantuan cylinder with slightly rounded ends, a hundred thousand kilometers high, perhaps half that across. It had no ecosystem on top, no emulation of some other world; it was a bare, perfect sweep of the invulnerable quark-latticework material Simon had named CQC, Coherent Quark Composite, fifty thousand gently curving kilometers of polished, shining armor which made ring-carbon composite look as soft and fragile as cotton candy. Layers of clouds and mistiness of atmosphere softened the distant bottom of Nexus Arena into near-invisibility against the endless multicolored abyss of the Arena. The Docks which had seemed so huge were now tiny things, of less consequence than the hairs on a man's arm, clustered around one tiny section of that incomprehensibly huge construct—which was itself not even a dust-mote within the indescribably larger construct which was the Arena itself.

Zounin-Ginjou's engines now roared with power, a keening thrum vibrating the deck; the vibrations rose and then suddenly diminuendoed away. Ariane realized that without significant gravity to hinder her, *Zounin-Ginjou* was climbing at the same rate she would move forward in level flight on Earth—and *Zounin-Ginjou* had just passed the sound barrier and was continuing to accelerate. They had been driving upward for many minutes now, yet still the top of Nexus Arena loomed beneath them like the Earth below an airplane, so huge that the mind could not grasp it.

To distract herself, she looked slightly up, studying *Zounin-Ginjou* in flight. She noticed suddenly that it looked somehow different than it had when they first took off. The hull had flattened out slightly and she saw the "sails" had puffed and curved subtly. "Oh, I see. They're also part of conformal aerodynamics."

"Precisely. The automatics to do much of that . . . are reliable enough, and you *can* adjust manually at the console. As we are not in a terrible hurry I do not think we need reconfigure for maximum speed. Still, since we will have to pass the gravity sheath at twenty thousand kilometers to reach the gateway area, some speed is advised. Even at this speed, it will be quite some hours before we reach the Sky Gate region." He flipped a control which was obviously for a simple autopilot and stood. "Let me give you a tour of this vessel—for you shall soon have some of your own!"

CHAPTER 27

Impressive, DuQuesne thought. *Not quite up to the standards Seaton and I set, but then, this is real.*

As he'd guessed, *Zounin-Ginjou* was a luxuriously-appointed battleship, a warship with an admittedly thick coat of ocean-liner paint. The fact that Orphan was the lone member of the Liberated had obviously driven him to push the limits of automation in the Arena—and had drastically reduced normal requirements for crew quarters. Because of this, the cabins remaining were quite fancy, and he'd still sacrificed nothing in the way of warship readiness.

There were missile batteries, and hypersonic cannon, and very powerful energy weapons, point-defense rotating cannon that would shred any approaching missile, chaff and reflective cloud dispensers to confuse attackers or even blunt energy attacks. Multiple, widely dispersed yet massive superconductor storage cells stored immense amounts of energy for the ship. Stowage for spare components for every system. And...

The hull of this thing... I think it's multilayered, and judging from things he's almost *said, it might have reinforcement from decidedly non-standard sources.*

This wasn't a terrible surprise; Orphan had worked with the Shadeweavers for a long time, and while he now was out of debt to them, he'd obviously taken great advantage of the affiliation in the past several centuries. *I wonder if any of those extra features will be on the ones he's lending us.*

The surprising part was that Orphan *had* let such information drop, even in an indirect fashion. He glanced at Laila as Orphan was describing one of the arrow-shaped shuttles and its operation to a fascinated Ariane.

She nodded. "I don't think I've seen anyone so lonely, Marc," she murmured.

She read me real well, there. It was things like that which could trigger Hyperion paranoia, and he hammered the suspicions down. *Ariane made the decision on how we were going to treat her, and she was* right. "Wondered if you'd caught that."

The brown eyes were both analytical and sympathetic, gazing at the tall semi-insectoid figure. "He is almost unable to stop talking. For the first time in... perhaps centuries...he has people aboard one of his own ships that he can call friends."

"Didn't realize you were a shrink as well as a biologist."

Laila chuckled. "There are relationships. I am interested in the behavior of life as well as its structure." She shook her head with an amazed air. "*Centuries.* Marc, we live a long time now, but are even *we* able to live for as long as he has?"

"I don't know. Hell, we haven't had the chance to find out." Marc didn't mention that, as far as he could tell, he hadn't actually aged significantly since

he reached the age of about twenty-five—which was
fifty years ago. *Which is going some several steps past
what the current longevity treatments expect.*

"So," he said, raising his voice, "we'll take one of
those down to the surface when we get to our Sphere?"

"To drop off Captain Austin and Sun Wu Kung at
least, yes," Orphan said.

"And me," Laila said. "I'm going to be doing some
sampling and studies on our Upper Sphere; it's fascinating how there's so much very *Earthlike* life on it
that is, at the same time, utterly alien."

"Undoubtedly," Orphan agreed, and turned to lead
them back up to the control room or bridge of the
ship. "The questions as to exactly how—not to mention *why*—the Arena accomplishes all this are ages
old, as I am sure you know."

He looked at DuQuesne. "Might I ask, then, if
Doctor Sandrisson will be able to accompany us?"

DuQuesne grinned. "My guess? You'd have to try to
keep him out with a ninety-meter fence charged with
a few thousand volts. This will be his first chance to
look at what another civilization's actually done with
the Sandrisson Drive, since you use that for these
Sky Gate transitions."

Orphan's buzz-chortle rang out. "Indeed! I had not
thought of it that way, but of course you are correct.
I will need at least *some* assistance in bringing the
fleet across, even with the very finest automation and
remote control, and I am sure you agree that we do
not want to invite just *anyone* on this trip."

"That's for damn sure," DuQuesne agreed, and both
Ariane and Wu nodded emphatically. "But that's going
to only be three of us. Will that be enough? We do

have more people now—first group's settling in, and that's quite a few more."

Outward flick of the hands. "I am afraid the three of us will have to suffice. You recall our discussion in my embassy, some time back? I see you do. Well, I trust *you*, Doctor DuQuesne, and Captain Austin, and the rest of you," he bob-bowed in Laila's direction, "who were here in the beginning; and I will of course trust this most formidable warrior who guards your Captain," another bow, this one to Wu Kung.

"But these newcomers are as yet untested, unknown to me, and I am quite aware that your 'ambassadors' are not entirely happy with your position, Captain Austin. With that in mind, I cannot allow such people on board my vessel, for they may have goals and interests...not well synchronized with my own, shall we say."

"Got you." DuQuesne couldn't argue that. He was pretty sure that his old friend Molly wasn't on Naraj's payroll, but the rest, not really. And even if they weren't, there were things you trusted people with, and things you thought real hard about before you trusted *anyone* with them. "So we're going to see your home system?"

Orphan laughed, even as the door opened and they entered the control room again. "I must confess, Doctor DuQuesne, I am not *quite* that trusting. But even showing you how to reach the system in which I have placed your vessels would bring you quite close to my home, and that is itself not knowledge I would trust with many at all."

Ariane raised an eyebrow. "You now know where *our* Sphere is."

"Which, you would admit, is necessary if I am to know how to bring your vessels here," Orphan pointed out. "Really, Captain, are you expecting me to give up such a key advantage simply out of your sense of fair play?"

DuQuesne saw her shrug and grin. "No, I guess not. And if we don't know it, we can't accidentally blab to the Blessed."

"Precisely," Orphan said, and continued with just a *touch* of acid, "especially as you are currently engaged in extensive negotiations with them."

"Really, Orphan, are you expecting me to give up such a potentially wonderful ally merely out of your sense of fair play?"

Orphan *did* laugh loudly at that, as did DuQuesne and the others. "Well turned, Captain Austin. Well turned indeed."

Wu suddenly stiffened and bounded to the window, pressing his face against the glassy material. "Wow! What are *those*?"

What looked like a congregation of blue and red beach balls with tentacles waving from their surfaces was visible ahead and to the left. *Zounin-Ginjou* was rapidly overtaking the things, but they were clearly moving under their own power. As they drew nearer, DuQuesne could see multiple glittering eyes and other openings. *They're big—tens of meters across, maybe more.*

"Ahh! Those are *virrin*," answered Orphan, coming forward. "They are grazers, eating various native sky-plants such as *yaolain*. They must be looking for... ah, yes, over there." He pointed, and DuQuesne squinted, seeing what looked like a drifting green-blue cloud.

"There is *yaolain*. Something to avoid when flying, especially if you're using an engine that sucks in air, like a jet; it will foul and damage your engine very easily in that case."

DuQuesne nodded. "Seems to grow in clumps like sargasso weed. Do you get large fields of it?"

"Indeed you do, Doctor DuQuesne. I have personally seen masses the diameter of a Sphere and kilometers thick."

"Ha!" said Ariane suddenly, pointing down and to the right. "*Those* look familiar. *Zikki*, right?"

The streamlined shapes were darting along in ragged formation, seemingly just ahead of *Zounin-Ginjou*. *Which is really impressive when you remember that we're doing Mach 2 here. How the hell do living beings manage that?*

"Close, Ariane Austin, but not quite. Those are *tzchina*. They are, as near we can tell, of some close relation to *zikki*, but very much different in most ways other than the superficial exterior. Much smarter, for one thing—they evade most hunters easily and seem able to learn from almost any experience. As you can see, they've learned to take advantage of compression waves near vessels, as well."

Laila was next to Wu Kung, and DuQuesne thought that *she'd* pushed her face up to the window even harder. "The *virrin*, they have panoramic vision and tentacles... are they also related to the *zikki*?"

"No, I do not believe so. The current belief, in fact, is that they are much more closely related to the *vanthume*."

"Really? That twenty-kilometer-long filter feeder?"

"Correct. That is the biological consensus as far as

I am aware. For details, I am afraid you should find another biologist."

They passed through a sparkling mist, and DuQuesne heard faint tinkling sounds and possibly the slightest shift in engine noise. "That's . . . air plankton, right?"

"One of many varieties, yes."

He looked at Ariane, whose eyes showed the narrowing he expected. "I start to see even more differences for navigation and combat in the Arena."

"Hm?" Orphan's wingcases scissored for a moment, and abruptly he gave a handtap. "Oh, in*deed*, Doctor DuQuesne. In an ordinary atmosphere and gravity, such materials would not remain long suspended. Here, with air currents upwelling and descending, gravity shifting, the air of the Arena is often filled with everything from ordinary mists to clouds of silica-armored chimemotes." He laughed. "Oh, yes, much different from what you will encounter on either a normal-space world or the deepness of space."

"Eliminates one of the most basic principles of space combat," murmured Ariane. "The idea that you can run, but you can't hide."

"And without AI-level automation, the old Mark I Eyeball plus telescopes is back to being important," DuQuesne agreed. "Radar's got limits in atmosphere— back home, you couldn't *get* a straight line through significant atmosphere longer than a hundred kilometers or so, unless you were trying to transmit through a gas giant. Add in random wandering animals, floating silica-covered plankton, drifting water-ponds like the one you saw in your race with Sethrik? No one modality will be very good at any great distance, and because the Arena seems to give us some kind of cheat to see longer distances, visible light seems to be the best bet. And," he grinned as a pale green-tinted mist streamed by, "with all this crap around, hiding gets a *lot* easier."

"You grasp the issues well. Yes, battles in the skies of the Arena are often matters of stealth, ambush, and quick response to surprises."

"I do recall wondering about things I had heard in Nexus Arena about what sounded like . . . pirates," Laila said. "Is that common?"

"In some areas, I am afraid, yes. Much commerce of various types travels through Sky Gates, but many areas do not have direct connections to Nexus Arena; so there are shipping lanes of various convenience and distance . . . and safety . . . and travellers from one point to another may have to be wary of those who might seek to relieve them of their valuables, including their ships." Orphan looked over to DuQuesne and Ariane. "Now, we do have some hours left to fly, even after the tour—and I thank you for your patience on that tour."

"No need to thank us," Ariane said quickly. "It was fascinating."

"Thank you. In any event—I would suggest that we get some rest and then eat, and return here when we are nearing the proper area. I am sure we all want to be fully alert during the transition and arrival."

"Sounds reasonable to me," DuQuesne said, and the others agreed. Orphan had already shown them the cabins prepared for human use, so DuQuesne was able to find one and lie down on the prepared bed—slightly harder than he was used to.

Practiced as he was at resting when time allowed,

he simply fell to sleep and woke up a few hours later, and made his way to the dining area Orphan had also shown them on the tour.

Orphan was already there, with several variously-shaped fruits which were the food he obviously preferred. "Ah, Doctor DuQuesne. I expected you would be the first."

"Yeah, I didn't feel like that much sleep." He saw a fair assortment of human-compatible food on a side table, including what appeared to be a loaf of bread. *Not a type we usually stock. Wonder where that came from?* "How much longer?"

"Until we reach the rough area, you mean? About an hour and a half." He sipped from one of the fruits with the extensible tube that was usually concealed in his mouth. "Now that you have brought up the subject, I was wondering—how will we pinpoint the Sky Gate? I presume you did not leave a marker."

"Nope," DuQuesne said. "Don't worry, I'll be able to guide you."

Orphan sighed, but the impression was more of a distinct smile. "Ahh, you will reveal the secret at the appropriate time."

The others filtered in over the next several minutes, and most of the food disappeared rapidly. Shortly, they were all back on the bridge of *Zounin-Ginjou*.

"All right, Doctor DuQuesne," Orphan said. "We are now well outside of the gravity band and in the region I would expect Sky Gates to be found."

"First, I want you to check real well to see if anyone's followed us."

"An excellent thought. Direct your attention to the main window." The window shimmered, became a display screen. "There. Now, we will scan. All of us should watch—automation is well and good, but living eyes are vastly better."

Orphan used radar, visible light, and infrared to make multiple scans of the area; DuQuesne studied every readout carefully, but saw nothing that tripped *his* paranoia, and for the most part neither did anyone else. Aside from a few false alarms which Orphan identified positively as living creatures, not vessels, there was no sign of anything in their area or within sensing range. "And I will say that I have spared *no* expense in the scanning equipment on *Zounin-Ginjou*, so I am confident we are not at present being watched—save, perhaps, by Shadeweavers or Faith, but for that there is little remedy."

"Okay, then." Marc took out a camera and plugged it into his headware data feed. "Gimme the window view back, and point us down at Nexus Arena."

"Oh, most clever. Of course, the simplest ways are still best."

"Motion-based triangulation," Ariane said approvingly. DuQuesne had loaded the image recordings from the probe into his headware, and using a similar view and the movement of *Zounin-Ginjou*, he was quickly able to zero in on where their ship would have to move to in order to duplicate that view.

A few minutes later, he unplugged the camera and put it away. He could keep the calculations updating internally now. "Over that way. Lemme see . . ." he looked at the controls again. "Turn the ship . . . I make it a quarter-circle to the starboard side, and come up three point six degrees—that's a hundredth of a circle."

"And how far?"

"How large are these Sky Gates? That is, how close do you have to be to their center to use them?"

"Quite close—they are perhaps two hundred meters across—although objects of effectively any size may pass through."

"Okay. Then...about four hundred kilometers."

"*Very* close. Excellent. We shall be there in twenty minutes or so."

The bow of *Zounin-Ginjou* was now no longer pointing towards Nexus Arena, which made the view less interesting in the sense that you couldn't actually be sure you *were* moving except when something drifting in the sky went by you. Laila was off at a side port, staring at something, but other than that everyone waited mostly quietly.

Abruptly Orphan leaned forward. "Ah! There it is, I can detect it now. Prepare for activation."

The huge ship slowed drastically; Marc noted that while they could feel acceleration, deceleration, and turns, it was not nearly as strong as those sensations *should* be. *And that's a major advantage in piloting such a ship. You get the tactile feedback without the possibility of being immobilized or injured by acceleration and turns.*

"Activating in three...two...one..."

The swift burn of light streaked down *Zounin-Ginjou*, seeming to erase the ship as it came, then blotting out everything else.

The light of a Sandrisson Jump faded, and before them was...

Marc C. DuQuesne found himself slowly stepping forward, staring. *Every time I think I'm getting used to the Arena, I realize I haven't even started down that road.*

Humanity's Sphere lay ahead and below, covering a sixth of the entire sky even from twenty thousand kilometers away. The Upper Sphere looked almost like Earth, with swirling clouds, land of green and brown, and sparkling blue of oceans. The central point—where, Marc knew, the Outer Gateway was located—was high on one continent, roughly oval-shaped, which was bracketed by two others in what would equate to the north and south. All of them were surrounded by the gleaming blue sea, with white areas in the effective pole regions.

At this range, it was just the merest sparkling at the edge, but he could see that along the bulwark that marked the effective end of the Upper Sphere, the great ocean did in fact overflow its bounds; a mighty cataract—perhaps more than one—leapt from the edge of the world and plunged down, to douse part of the Sphere or simply vanish into endless space.

But all of that—the entirety of a world's surface—was merely the top, a skullcap on a Sphere large enough to house the entire Earth easily within, and above it floated a huge, blazing sphere of light.

Orphan was nodding at their expressions. "Nexus Arena is impressive in its size; but to see a living world, continents spread out like a page on a book, held atop a Sphere larger than your home planet... truly, there are no words, are there?"

Ariane looked up at him. "Does it still... touch you, to see it?"

An emphatic handtap. "My friends, it is true that we can grow used to most things. But on any day that

I truly *think* about what I see, I cannot help but be both awed and overjoyed—and, perhaps, sometimes, terrified—by what the Arena shows me. And when I see the wonder on *your* faces, I see it once more in the way I did when I, too, first looked down upon the Arena's majesty, and I am humbled and challenged by it as well."

For a few moments they stared. Then *Zounin-Ginjou* quivered and lurched downward.

"Ah! We enter the gravity field. Take your seats, if you will," Orphan said. "Now that we have arrived— now that I know your home—we shall allow those who cannot remain to return, and bring aboard the good Doctor Sandrisson." The huge ship rumbled to full life and came around, pointing directly at the Outer Gateway, hidden on the peaks of the world. "In but a week or two, my friends, these skies will no longer be so empty!"

CHAPTER 28

"So, Captain Austin, how do you find the Arena, now that you have returned and had some time to accustom yourself?"

Ariane felt that she did quite well not to visibly jump at the deep, sonorous voice that she associated with the most severe beating she had ever taken. True, she'd emerged victorious, but despite that great and dramatic victory, what she remembered most about her battle with Amas-Garao was the feeling of being utterly outmatched; even the few times she'd managed to strike him, she'd felt like a child kicking an adult in the shin. *I got ridiculously lucky—humanity got ridiculously lucky—but I'm not stupid enough to think I could beat him a second time.*

Wu, she was pleased to see, had moved with startling speed and, despite Amas-Garao apparently having materialized from thin air nearby, had inserted himself between the Shadeweaver and Ariane.

"Well enough, Amas-Garao. Do you people have something against just walking like the rest of us, or is there a reason for you trying to make me jump out of my skin every time you show up?"

The low, rippling chuckle she remembered rolled out. "Jump out of your skin? A most...interesting expression, that. The mystique of the Shadeweavers is enhanced by our being seen only infrequently acting as the other inhabitants of the Arena will act. I am sure you understand." The cowled face turned slightly towards Wu Kung. "I notice that you have found yourself a most formidable bodyguard. Wise. Am I right to suspect it was Doctor DuQuesne who convinced you to have one?"

"More like *told* me I was and said he'd chosen Wu for the job," she said, continuing her walk along the Grand Arcade. *One advantage of having a Shadeweaver with you on a walk is that* no one *gets in your way.* The crowds parted before them like water in front of a battleship's prow; where most people in the crowded parts of the Grand Arcade might be practically rubbing elbows (or the equivalent), Ariane, Wu, and Amas-Garao had between two and three meters clearance, all the way around. "You say 'wise.' Do you know something I don't?"

"I undoubtedly know uncounted things you do not, Ariane Austin," the Shadeweaver answered, ironic humor in his voice. "Yet in this case I have no concrete evidence of a *specific* threat. It is simply wise to assume there *is* such a threat, especially when you are so visible a presence in the Arena, and one who has scattered many boxes indeed during her entry."

Ariane made a guess at what that expression meant. "I think you might exaggerate things a bit—dramatics being your stock in trade, of course."

"A bit, yes. Yet it is perhaps not clear to you how widely you are known, and how far your influence has already reached." The clawed, black-furred hand pointed at the soaring, straight-edged lines of the Faction House of the Blessed To Serve. "To give a single example of many; when you arrived, the Blessed had eradicated or turned most of the allies gathered by the Liberated. They had arranged to trap Orphan twice, and each time he had just barely escaped. Even when you first appeared, the fact that he had managed to ally himself with First Emergents caused more amusement than anything else.

"And then *two* of you defeated a Molothos scout force, winning your citizenship to the Arena in unprecedented time."

"Was it?"

A faint gleam of white teeth; Amas-Garao's species did smile somewhat as did humanity, though the face beneath that hood would make a smile look like a threat of death. "*Utterly* unprecedented, Ariane Austin. In mere days you had gone from the naïve newcomers to true citizenship; others took years, some have waited centuries or more. This meant that the reputation of the Survivor," by which Ariane knew he meant Orphan, "went up by association. The Blessed's attempt to ruin this budding partnership . . . did not go well, as you know, and instead boosted your reputation. The Liberated suddenly had a visible and proud ally, and built mightily on that new visibility.

"And then, of course, you defeated *me*," he bowed to her, "in what I will not deny was one of the most utterly unexpected and spectacular victories I have ever been privileged to witness. Prior to leaving, you managed to evade, without Challenge, a most clever gambit by the Molothos.

"So in your few months here, your species has insulted and humiliated the Molothos—and thus far gotten away with it, despite being a single newly-emerged world; chosen an outcast and schemer as an ally, and benefited from it; humiliated the Blessed To Serve; and publicly humiliated the Shadeweavers themselves. While still but one person, the Liberated's power and influence have drastically increased due to the association; the Blessed have lost allies and prestige, for much more rides on each Challenge than the overt prizes for the victor; the Shadeweavers have found their mystique weakened, others viewing us for the first time in many millennia as less than invincible; and your little species, and you in particular, are now known and spoken of by every race of beings in the Arena, on worlds so far distant from your own that by the time the light from their stars reaches yours, your own will have died and dwindled to a cinder."

She admitted that, laid out that way, it *did* sound awfully impressive, even if she knew how much panic, desperation, luck, and prayer had been involved. "So did you come here to tell me how awesome I am, or did you have a purpose?"

The eyes gleamed yellow for a moment within the cowl, and she heard him chuckle again. She noticed that Wu was walking tensely; he obviously didn't feel comfortable around the Shadeweaver. "I did, in fact, Captain. You are of course aware that the Shadeweavers are not a Faction in the same sense as most others?"

She nodded. "You aren't all required to be united, don't have any actual leader, things like that. In some ways you're more like the Powerbrokers than the regular Factions."

"A reasonable analogy; and you of course recall that Gona-Brashind and I had some ... differences of policy which would not have been seen with most Factions. That said, we do engage in many of the same activities of most other Factions, including recruiting."

Ariane felt her gut tighten. "Don't tell me. Let me guess. Maria-Susanna."

"Correct in a single guess, Captain Austin. Yes. She has been discussing the potential of an apprenticeship with us as one of her choices."

*God*damn. Ariane gritted her teeth, even as she saw Wu's momentarily sad expression. *Could there be any worse choice for us than for her to become a Shadeweaver?*

Still, there were the limitations ... but she had to be somewhat cautious. They had come to a lot of conclusions about the way the Faith and Shadeweavers worked, but a lot of it was guesswork and none of it was public knowledge. She didn't want to reveal too much to them. "If she ... chooses that path, how long would it take for her to become an actual Shadeweaver?"

"It entirely depends on the apprentice, how well they learn what we have to teach, and of course when one of our number retires," Amas-Garao answered. "For a number of reasons, we generally do not allow our numbers to expand, so only when one retires—or on very rare occasion dies—will one of the apprentices become a full Shadeweaver."

"So a retired Shadeweaver is forbidden from using his abilities?"

"Not precisely. We pass our powers on, when that time comes. So once I, for example, step down, I will no longer be a Shadeweaver."

She raised an eyebrow. "And you will do this? Pardon me for saying so, but I find it hard to imagine someone giving up that power."

"It is one of the greatest demands—and the final test—of our worthiness, Captain Austin," Amas-Garao said, and his voice was solemn, without a trace of irony or evasion. "I know that your experiences with our order, and especially with myself, do not lend themselves to making us appear in any way noble, but there are very ancient traditions, usages, and requirements that are part of being a Shadeweaver. Our people have much freedom of action, much ability to do that which other beings cannot; we can pass from place to place as we will, and even the Arena cannot entirely bar us. We wield powers no others save, perhaps, the Faith can understand, and can shape matter and energy to our desire. We can touch the minds of others and understand their will, even bend it—as you know—to a direction that we find more pleasing. We can even hold off death, refuse it, for many years. We have shattered fleets and moved Spheres, begun wars and stopped them. Where walks a Shadeweaver walks the power of the universe made manifest.

"And a power that has so few limits, Captain Austin, is a tempting tool for change, to adjust the world around one to one's own views. As the power increases with knowledge and skill and time, so too the danger of one who believes they know better the true way of the universe. It is therefore forbidden that a Shadeweaver extend his own life past twice its natural span, forbidden that they hold forever onto this power. We may hold it a year, or ten, or even a hundred, depending on our natural span of years, but before our death we will teach another and give this power to them, never to wield it again; it is the greatest of all crimes to seek to hold that power beyond that time."

Based on what we deduced earlier, of course, there's another reason; they can't generally make someone a Shadeweaver unless a slot gets opened—by transfer or death. She remembered a prior conversation. "Orphan said you were one of the oldest of the Shadeweavers."

The cowl nodded, a probably deliberately human gesture. "And while my people are long-lived indeed, there are not terribly many years remaining to me before I, too, will have to pass on what I have learned."

"So she would likely have her chance fairly soon?"

"If she trained well, and was fully accepted? Yes, I believe so. After all, we have yet to have one of your people join us, since both you and Doctor DuQuesne," irony had now returned to the deep voice, "declined our most gentle invitations."

Great. Boy, I really wish DuQuesne were here, but I'm not going to see him or *Simon before they finish transferring our new little fleet.* "I thank you for this information, Amas-Garao. Might I hope that you will let me know if a decision is, in fact, made in this case?"

A crouching bow. "Of course, Captain Austin. If we accept your Maria-Susanna as an apprentice, I personally shall let you know immediately. You have my word."

Before she could say anything else, the Shadeweaver melted away into mist and vanished.

"That...doesn't sound good, Captain," Wu Kung said.

"No. I'd say that would be about the worst option I could have imagined, actually. I hope the Shadeweavers will decide that the last thing they want as an apprentice is someone who's a multiple murderer and on the run from her own species, but on the other hand, Amas-Garao was just subtly pointing out to us that the Shadeweavers need to re-establish their mystique and show that we haven't got any special tricks or secrets that *they* haven't got."

She signaled one of the floating taxis. "I think I need to go back to the Embassy for maybe a drink and relaxation."

"There are many places to drink *here*," Wu pointed out. "And some smell very good, too!"

The innocent enthusiasm managed to bring a smile to her lips. "Thanks, Wu, but honestly? I'm probably going to drink just enough to get in the mood for a brawl, and from what I know of the way Arena-people usually think, there isn't a decent brawling bar closer than Kanzaki-Three in our own solar system. So I'll drink and go beat up on punching dummies, or if you feel like it we can spar. Though you have to let me land a couple or I'll just get more frustrated."

Wu laughed. "I will gladly provide you with *that* kind of entertainment!"

CHAPTER 29

A smell of caution and deviousness preceded the voice, so Wu was already turning in that direction when Oscar Naraj, dressed in one of his more conservative white suits, spoke. "Good morning, Captain Austin. You seem to be going out early."

"Ambassador." Ariane nodded to him. *She smells a lot less cautious around him these days. I really have to remind her that he* always *smells like he has something planned!* "And you're looking rather dressed up. Going somewhere yourself?"

"In fact, I have what should be an all-day meeting with a number of moderate-sized Factions, including the Tantimorcan, Dujuin, and Tensari. There will be considerable dancing . . . in the metaphorical sense. Perhaps in the actual sense, as well."

Oasis joined them, looping one more hair-tie into place around the fourth of her ponytails. "That would be fun."

"If you're sure it won't distract you from your duties," Oscar said, but in a tone that was only half-serious. "Even the entertainment may be part of the business."

"Oh, I understand that, Ambassador—and you have my word I'll always be watching."

She smiled at Wu, who smiled back, but felt a little uneasy. *After DuQuesne explained what had happened...I am sad for them both. I know she still likes DuQuesne a lot. And it's also sad for the real Miss Abrams; she's herself...but not.*

"Good luck," Ariane said. "The Tantimorcan are apparently some of the best shipbuilders in the Arena."

White teeth flashed in the dark face. "I was very much aware of that, and I hope to capitalize on their current alliance with Orphan to make closer ties. The Tensari are potentially more interesting in a cultural exchange sense, which is useful for establishing deeper connections to people throughout the Arena. What about you?"

"Sethrik is going to show me one of their ships today," she answered. "I have to hand it to Ambassador Ni Deng," she said, and bowed to the feathery-haired woman as she caught up with the other two. "I wasn't sure we wanted to spill those beans to the Blessed, but she was right about the result."

Oscar chuckled, and Ni Deng looked down modestly. *She does smell pretty proud of herself.* "I did tell you she was quite good at this sort of thing. After her talks—and a few of mine—with both Sethrik and Vantak, we were quite certain that the last thing the Blessed want is for our connection with Orphan to become much closer. Letting them 'accidentally' discover that the Liberated is giving us a small but significant number of vessels? I was *certain* it would push them to try to convince us that the Blessed could do much more for us."

"And you were dead right," Ariane said. "Thank you, Michelle."

"My pleasure . . . Ariane."

Ariane hesitated before moving, and Wu sensed she had made a decision. "Oscar, we really have accomplished a lot since we got here, I think, and despite the original . . . issues between us, we've been working well enough together. Do you think that we can simply keep what works, now?"

Oscar Naraj hesitated; Wu smelled a lot of conflicting emotions, finally firming into some kind of resolve. "May I speak entirely frankly, Captain Austin?"

"Please."

"Captain, you are quite correct that we have accomplished a great deal so far. And I will certainly agree that one of your major points—that anyone who is to be the Leader of the Faction of Humanity must truly understand the Arena—was entirely valid. But—"

"Why did I know a 'but' was coming?"

"Because you are quite aware that this is a job for which you are utterly unsuited," Oscar replied bluntly. "We have gotten this far to a great extent on luck—something you have admitted freely. The future of the human race cannot be left to luck, or to the fact that you have that charming 'straight-shooting' reputation, Captain. This sort of thing is a profession, and you need professionals in charge—for the sake of our entire species. I hope that you will agree to this and we can choose an appropriate successor."

"Like you?"

"I would certainly like to believe I am a prime candidate," Naraj said. *No*, thought Wu as his posture and smell shifted a bit, *you're absolutely sure you're the right guy. Phfah!* "I have now had months in the Arena, I have come to understand a great deal about the political and social dynamics that drive it, and the Factions are beginning to recognize me and speak with me as a representative of Humanity."

His voice and expression were sympathetic. "Captain— Ariane—I know how you must be terrified that the next person will mess up everything. And for an unprepared pilot, you have done extraordinarily well in taking on this immense challenge. But I think you need to accept that *you don't have to prove anything any more.*"

"What?" Her voice was incredulous, but Wu caught a whiff of uncertainty. *She . . . really isn't sure she's the right person. Which kinda makes me think she is, but that probably doesn't make sense.*

Ni Deng started to say something, then closed her mouth, let Naraj continue. "You brought us into the Arena, Captain. You pulled off several miracles to get back. You've come back, you've solidified our relations with multiple Factions—with my help, and that of your original crew. And I know that every day you're worried you, or someone under you, will do something to ruin it all. And you don't *have* to have those worries any more."

His voice was gentle, earnest, and Wu felt that at least some of that was honest. "You don't have anything more to prove to the world, to the Arena, or for yourself. You have *done* the job, and done it much better than anyone could ever have expected. Now let someone else pick *up* that burden. We will *need* you, Ariane, in your original field, as a pilot. Unless a Faction like the Blessed truly allies with us—and possibly even then—we will be at war with

the Molothos soon enough. We will need command-
ers, pilots, people to help us fight that war. People
like you could be the Admirals and Captains of our
fleet, the fleet that is being delivered right now." He
glanced up. "I'm not pressing you to do anything
now, Captain. Just . . . think about it, please. Don't
shut out the truth because we started out on a poor
footing—partly my fault, I admit."

"I . . . I will think about it, Ambassador."

"Then that is all I can ask for now." He bowed and
the three headed out the Embassy doors; the quick
glance Oasis gave over her shoulder told Wu that *she*
wasn't buying the whole speech either.

Ariane stood still for a moment, and Wu could
sense the conflict in her. He touched her arm. "Hey."

She jumped. "What . . . sorry."

"Don't let him bother you."

"He might be completely right," she said, and headed
for the door. He followed. "But . . . thanks. And I'm sure
not making any decision like that by myself. If I did . . .
he *would* be right."

Once out in the bustling crowds of the Arena, she
cheered up, and that made him happier too.

Having been there twice already, Wu knew the way
to the Docks, which made it a lot easier to watch the
crowd around them. This was always the hardest part
of watching over someone; being in large crowded
areas you couldn't control. But scanning the crowd,
he saw nothing suspicious. Now that he'd been here
a while, he recognized a lot of alien body language
and could sort out most basic moods from scents easily. *Lots of people* notice *Ariane, but I'm not seeing
anyone that looks hostile.*

Suddenly Ariane shifted direction slightly, and he followed her to one of the big Powerbroker areas. "Powerbroker Ghondas! Nice to see you again!"

The images he'd seen hadn't gotten across the slug-like creature's full size and mass; Ghondas probably weighed close to a ton.

The four-pointed head sagged and rose in acknowledgement. "Ariane Austin of Humanity. It is well to see you again also."

"I wanted to introduce you to my bodyguard, Sun Wu Kung. Wu, this is Ghondas, one of the most senior Powerbrokers."

He bowed deeply. "It is an honor!"

"Greetings and welcome to you, Sun Wu Kung." The head sank and rose again, and turned back to Ariane. "Do you have need for our services this day?"

"Not today. I was wondering if you have seen Orphan of late."

"About five days ago, the Survivor stopped to recharge *Zounin-Ginjou* and left immediately. He has not been back since."

That fits, thought Wu. *That would be when they headed back for the second half of the fleet. That means they should be back here any day now!*

"Thank you, Ghondas. Well, we have an appointment, so we'd better get moving."

"Good day to you, then."

The Docks were busy—dozens of ships being serviced, thousands of tons of cargo being moved, and hundreds of species of people running, jumping, oozing, or otherwise moving around. *I don't even recognize a lot of these! Wow! There's so many new things to learn!*

Ahead, the tall green and black form of Sethrik

became obvious. "Captain Austin, Sun Wu Kung, thank you very much for coming. I greet you in the name of the Minds and the Blessed." He gave a pushup-bow and leapt easily to his feet. "Please, follow me."

They walked nearly a mile down the Docks; Sethrik was obviously not rushing them and would often point out details of the vessels they were passing, and Wu realized that the Blessed leader was enjoying himself. *He smells . . . pretty much relaxed. Happy. He's been slowly getting more like that for the last few weeks.*

"I am truly glad that we have this opportunity," Sethrik was saying to Ariane. "It is . . . often difficult to guess what the Minds will do under given circumstances. Not, of course, because they are themselves unpredictable or arbitrary, but because they tend to think so much farther ahead, and take into consideration so very many factors that even one such as myself simply cannot grasp the whole of their strategy. Thus it is quite gratifying that they have responded to the situation as I hoped."

Ariane smiled, and her mood had clearly lifted as well. "You really *hated* the way we ended up in conflict, didn't you?"

"Absolutely *detested* it, Captain." His smell reinforced the statement.

Finally Sethrik stopped and gestured. "Allow me to present to you *Thilomon*, one of the Minds' finest flagships in the Arena."

To Wu's eye, *Thilomon* was not as pretty as *Zounin-Ginjou*. *Thilomon* was a ship of lines, angles, few smooth curves. But he had to admit the lines were *clean*, sweeping forward and back like the shaft and head of an arrow, with symmetrical lines here and there indicating weapons emplacements, defenses, hatches, and very different rippling lines for the guidance sails. He thought that *Zounin-Ginjou* was also somewhat larger, but it was really hard to tell; both ships were *very* big.

For a few minutes, Ariane and Sethrik stood looking at *Thilomon*, Sethrik narrating a long list of features which, honestly speaking, Wu didn't really care about. He spent his time surveying the crowd. A Tomekeir caught his eye; the tall, three-legged creature looked very like the one he thought had orchestrated the duel he'd gotten caught in. *Wonder if he's up to anything now . . . ?*

"But come, let me show you the inside. We have of course not yet refurbished it for *human* needs, but I am sure that from the point of view of your researchers there is much to learn from seeing our construction." Sethrik began to lead the way up the boarding ramp, Ariane following. Wu followed closely; *Thilomon* was a nice bulwark behind his back, so any real threat, if any, would be on the Dock.

The Tomekir seemed to be looking at him, but then shifted gait and continued up the Dock.

The distraction was almost fatal. Wu caught the motion from the very corner of his eye—*high up, one of the loading cranes on the other side, flash of light*—

He *lunged* backward, shoving Ariane—and with her, Sethrik—inside *Thilomon*'s airlock entry, outside of which they had just been standing.

Something *blazed* off the edge of the hatchway, leaving afterimages, a scent of heated metal and burned composite, and a black scar. *That might have gone straight through Ariane if I hadn't . . .*

"Stay *hidden*, Captain!" he shouted, and bounded down the rampway. Another streak of light, this one aimed at him, scorched the deck. Behind him, he heard Sethrik say "Close the doors! They cannot shoot through the hatch!" and heard the sound of the lock door sliding shut.

Good. One less thing to worry about.

The sniper was trying to take aim, and Wu's eyes could make out that it was a Genasi, same species as Tunuvun. *But it's not Tunuvun, I can tell that.*

The energy rifle fired and missed again; Wu had read the posture, seen the faintest tensing, jumped just as the trigger was pulled. *Ha!* he thought, now to the base of the crane, grabbing, scrambling up. *Take more than that to—*

The Genasi threw away the rifle into the empty space beyond the Dock and flipped something else down with his other hand.

Net! Spun as he threw it, opening just as it's reaching me—

But if you reached and twisted and spun *just* right, you could *catch* a net like that, and he did, and threw it back up.

The Genasi, who had been preparing to leap down, was suddenly taken aback, tried to shift direction, but the net caught him, tangled his legs and tail, and then Wu was on him.

Wu rammed the alien up against the reinforced metal of the crane. "Who are *you* working for?" he demanded.

The eyes shifted slightly over his shoulder, and then the creature laughed.

Oh, no.

He whirled, dropped fifteen meters down the crane, caught himself, jumped the rest of the way to the Dock, even as *Thilomon*'s umbilicals let go and her engines roared to life, shoving the great ship away from the Dock.

A trap. A sucker-bait trap, with something to pull me away from her! I'm so stupid! So very, very stupid! DuQuesne should never have trusted me, I'm an idiot, a monkey who should never have come down from the trees!

Even as he was berating himself, he was streaking across the Dock, bowling aside others in his haste, then clear, running up the gangway, faster, watching the huge ship moving away, no time, too far, *but I can't give up*—

With a final desperate lunge, Sun Wu Kung launched himself into space off the end of the gangway.

I've missed. I'm too late, he thought, as he began to curve down, his forward momentum not enough to reach the huge ship before the tug of gravity pulled him below *Thilomon*.

But then gravity disappeared. He was streaking forward, still moving slightly down from the gravity around the Dock, and the wind was whistling around him, slowing him, but *Thilomon* was getting closer, closer—

—He reached, his claws stretching out, out—

—And closing tight on the hard, tough metal of one of the rearmost guide fins of *Thilomon*.

CHAPTER 30

Shimmering light cleared from the forward port of *Zounin-Ginjou*, and Simon saw the incomprehensibly immense shape of Nexus Arena looming, a column large enough to support the roof of creation, ahead of them, with cloudbanks larger than Earth shrouding its center. Lightning flickered and crawled through the cloudbank, encircling Nexus Arena like a halo forged by all the gods of thunder combined.

"*Subarashi . . .*"

"It *is* impressive, yes," Orphan agreed. "And quite a menace to traffic, too. No approaches or departures in *that* direction, not without considerable detours."

"I would think not," Simon agreed, staring. "Those bolts make the ones we see on Jupiter look positively restrained."

"Jupiter is a gas giant, I would presume?" At Simon's guilty start, Orphan laughed. "Oh, do not worry. Such planets are not at all uncommon, and you reveal little about your home system by telling me you have a gas giant therein."

Still, Simon reminded himself, *I should stay focused on asking questions rather than volunteering information.*

303

Not that they weren't on good terms with Orphan, and with this mission they'd entrusted him with one of the most valuable pieces of information, but he should stay in the right habits for the Arena.

A moment's thought reminded him of something he wanted to ask. "Orphan, I note from the light of our arrival that the same light—our people have taken to calling it the 'shocklight ring'—must emanate from a ship coming or going through a Sky Gate. How far away can our entrance or departure be detected?"

"Shocklight ring? A rather evocative description. We and the Blessed have always just called it the jumpflash. In any event . . . how far depends on the method used for detection and just how fancy your equipment is. No more than a thousand kilometers, in general, though it is quite simple to monitor your own Sky Gates directly. Here at Nexus Arena, however, there are far too many to easily monitor—and it appears that the Arena doesn't want *us* monitoring them casually, as something always causes monitoring devices around Nexus Arena to fail."

"Just as well," DuQuesne said. "Means we can probably keep the gate to home hidden, at least for a while, and that way the Molothos can't just send a fleet there by jumping here first."

"They could not do that in any event," Orphan said, bringing *Zounin-Ginjou* to a faster cruising speed. "While the Arena does not prevent wars, it will not permit Nexus Arena to be used as a staging ground or channel for warfleets or other operations associated with warfare."

"Really?" Simon felt some relief. "That is indeed good to know."

DuQuesne frowned. "And how does it know what you intend to do with a bunch of ships?"

Orphan stood up from his console and gave an elaborate wing-shrug. "How? There are undoubtedly myriad ways, Doctor DuQuesne. Some more disturbing to contemplate than others, true, but whatever the means, the results are quite clear; the Arena has nothing against your fighting, or even having an all-out war, but you won't fight inside Nexus Arena (unless as part of a Challenge, of course), and you won't conduct warfare—of nearly any sort—anywhere within Nexus Arena's claimed space."

"Well, I suppose there's not much to do but wait for now," Simon said. "Twenty thousand kilometers to the Docks; that will take us quite a few hours."

"Especially since we are not pushing the speed, yes. About ten hours from now, and we will be home, so to speak." He bowed to Simon. "Would you care for a game of *anghas*?"

"You mean, to be beaten? Why not, before we have some dinner. You joining us, Marc?"

"Sure," DuQuesne said. "I must admit, it's nice to play an old-fashioned board game sometimes."

Anghas was a multi-player game which apparently was originally from the Blessed but had become popular throughout the Arena. Like many other games, it took a complex process—in this case, colonizing a planet, as the name *anghas* meant "colony"—and simplified it into a set of requirements for success. Competing "developers" tried to get and hold resources and develop production and so on, under a set of deceptively simple rules that turned out to have a lot of subtle twists and turns—and random chance in the form of octahedral dice.

Like many such games, it was as much a social occasion as it was a competition, and during the several days spent transferring ships from Orphan's hidden depot to Humanity's Sphere the two humans had come to enjoy *anghas* quite a bit. They had, however, yet to win a round against Orphan. Even with several runs of good luck, Orphan's skill and experience in the game eventually beat them down.

Two hours into this game, however, Simon thought he could see victory approaching. "I have a surveyor active and I have invested in him this turn." The polished-stone die rolled and turned upward, showing the circled square. "Ha! he has found something of the third tier!"

"Again?" Orphan looked plaintive. "That is the third time in four turns! The third tier selections are starting to get low." He passed the blindbox with the three-leveled symbol, and Simon reached in.

"Excellent. More fissionables." Simon placed the token on the board. "And right here near my city, so I can develop the mines."

"By the Minds, I swear you cannot possibly be so fortunate," Orphan said casually. "Still, it will take you some time to get those fissionable mines in play. I will remove one of your laborers."

"How did you get—"

Marc grinned. "Sneaky. Should've seen that misdirection coming, but I didn't. Thought you were putting the research into something else."

"Cautious and conservative play will usually win over the long haul, gentlemen," Orphan reminded them.

And it did, once more, though in this case only by a turn or two. "My good friends, you are learning fast indeed. I may have to be cautious about playing at all, or possibly find myself *losing*."

"One of these days? Yes. Soon . . . I'm afraid I don't think so."

"You are a pessimist," Orphan said. "Or possibly still playing the game now that it is over!"

Simon grinned. "It doesn't hurt to keep you underestimating us."

"I see. I will have to re-evaluate my perception of you, Doctor Sandrisson; I had thought you less devious than the rest of your species." Orphan stood and put the fold-box containing the *anghas* game away. "Shall we dine?"

Dinner passed swiftly, and Simon spent the next couple of hours in a lounge room with a blue-green theme like some deep alien forest, reading some of the notes he had taken on his last visit to the Analytic's Archives. He had discovered that the strange . . . knowledge, perception, understanding? He wasn't sure what to call it . . . was hardly a constant companion. After that initial surge of near-omniscience, his next visits had been exactly the way he would have expected originally; a lot of wandering around to see all sorts of fascinating things, but nothing he was directly looking for. *But then, I wasn't after something so vital, and not nearly so frustrated and angry. Initial hypothesis, then, is that only sufficient stress will bring out this capability.*

That *did* imply that if he figured out the key, he should be able to trigger it more reliably . . . unless it was something mediated by the Arena, which could undoubtedly tell if he was just trying to mimic desperation or anger instead of being actually furious or frustrated at something. *Something to think about and test when I have the chance. Perhaps with Ariane; I am sure there is a connection between her dormant powers and whatever I have, and she might be able to sense or trigger something, even in her current state.*

He dismissed the musings from his mind—Simon hardly intended to test a mysterious access to the knowledge of the Arena here, in Orphan's ship—and read the notes he'd accumulated and copies of entries he'd managed to make.

DuQuesne stuck his head through the lounge doorway. "Hey, Simon, we're getting close."

"I'll be right there."

A few minutes later the door rolled up before him and he saw the dark wall of Nexus Arena covering most of the forward port. *Still, that's deceptive. We're probably still almost an hour out.*

Now, though, there were signs of movement, lights and dots that moved in more purposeful manners in the sky. "Orphan, I appreciate your willingness to let me examine the way in which your ships work—"

"No need to thank me for *that*, Doctor Sandrisson," Orphan said with the most casual hint of a bow. "After all, you would be able to examine those I have loaned to you in excruciating detail."

"Of course, though with you to explain it was much more informative. But what I was *going* to ask is if you could show me how to operate your viewing mechanisms here? I would *very* much like to examine the other ships we are passing."

"Oh, but certainly."

Orphan, or the Tantimorcan he had employed, obviously had spent a very long time thinking about usability problems, because for manual controls these were some of the simplest and most effective he had ever used. Once Orphan explained, he was able to locate a ship and zoom in on it with ease, holding the target steady and tracking without difficulty.

"That's a hell of a wingspan," DuQuesne said, seeing a streamlined vessel with gossamer wings like a spectral albatross a kilometer across.

Orphan glanced over. "Ahh, now, that's a Genasi Skyfarer. They developed their technology entirely on their own for use in the Arena. That design is often used for long-distance cruises; they glide down in the gentle gravity fields, occasionally spending time rising in the upwellings, and make their way across distances of hundreds of Spheres." He flicked his wings in a humorous way. "Of course, *this* one undoubtedly has considerably more advanced aspects to it."

As they continued towards the Docks, Simon examined other ships; a wedge-shaped cargo vessel Orphan thought was of Vengeance design, a dandelion-seed drifter that no one recognized, vessels similar to *Zounin-Ginjou* in general outline.

Another ship caught his attention, clean sharp lines with few curves, guide-fins but little else breaking the flow of the design. "Who owns that? Do you know, Orphan?"

The sole member of the Liberated glanced up from adjusting their course. "Know? Nearly as well as I know *Zounin-Ginjou*, though far less fondly. That is Sethrik's, or rather, the Blessed's, flagship, *Thilomon*."

"Really?" Simon found that very interesting. He had expected the Blessed and the Liberated to have very similar vessel designs—after all, where else would the

Liberated have gotten their originals—but now that
he thought of it, that was a silly idea. *Orphan is—if
we take his word for it—three thousand years old.
He was born while ancient Greece was at its height,
before Rome was founded. And he was not the first
of the Liberated. Obviously they have had more than
enough time to drift entirely away from the Blessed
in aesthetics as well as politics.*

Thilomon was, to Simon's eye, a beautiful ship;
there was a mathematical precision to her design that
spoke of efficiency, economy, and power. *The patterns
on her hull... there are indeed Sandrisson Coils inlaid
there. And she's made such that I could imagine her
in our space. Both Arena and real-space capable, then.*

He blinked. Was there... something *moving* on
the hull?

*Not impossible, remember. We pass living creatures
of all sizes and types regularly. A zikki even hitched a
ride on Ariane's Skylark during her race with Sethrik.*
He juggled the controls, zoomed in closer.

The figure was tiny, even at full magnification...
yet the glint of gold from the staff on the figure's
back, the entirely humanoid outline, the spectacular
glint of color... *bakana.* "Marc..."

His tone brought DuQuesne instantly to his side.
"What is it, Simon?"

Simon pointed wordlessly.

DuQuesne squinted, then stiffened. "God-*damn*.
That's *Wu!*"

Orphan glanced around. "What?"

"But Marc, why in the *world* would Wu be..." he
trailed off, as the only explanation struck him like a
bucket of ice water.

"Only *one* reason, Simon. Ariane's got to be inside. And if she's inside, and Wu's outside while that ship's accelerating towards Mach speeds, then there's something rotten in the state of Denmark."

"Can we call them?" Simon asked. He spoke to the empty air. "Ariane! Ariane Austin! Arena, connect me to Captain Ariane Austin!"

No green sphere appeared, and DuQuesne shook his head. "Doesn't work outside of Nexus Arena and maybe your own Spheres. Outside, never works."

Simon stared at the little figure, now pressing itself down to the hull behind one of the few protrusions available. "Great *Kami*. Marc, they're going to *kill* him."

"Maybe. I sure don't envy him."

"At *Mach* speeds? Marc, he—"

"Dammit, I know! All I can hope is that he's as tough as I think he is—and the clothes he's wearing will help, they were made to mimic the legends he was made from . . . if he remembers that in time. But that's not the question." He turned to Orphan. "Orphan . . ."

The alien was not looking at them; he was staring resolutely forward, still maneuvering *Zounin-Ginjou* towards one of the Docks.

"*Dammit*, Orphan!"

The green and black figure contracted slightly, then straightened. "Yes, Doctor DuQuesne?"

"You just heard. Don't tell me you didn't."

A buzzing sigh. "Yes. They have captured Captain Austin, and Sun Wu Kung is on the *Thilomon's* hull."

Simon restrained himself from shouting. *There's diplomacy here. We have to approach this right*. He touched Marc's arm, and the other man glanced at him. Their eyes met and he could see Marc understood.

DuQuesne took an audible breath, let it out. "Look, Orphan...*Zounin-Ginjou* is your ship. We can't make you do anything you don't want to do. I'm not going to try to force you. But...that's the *Blessed* yanking our friend—and I hope, *your* friend—out from under our noses. Are you going to let that happen?"

Long moments passed, and *Thilomon* accelerated farther away. Simon could no longer make out Sun Wu Kung; whether he had been ripped off the hull or not was now something they might never know.

Finally, Orphan rose slowly from his seat, turned to face them, and spoke. "No."

"No?"

"No, Doctor DuQuesne. I am *not* going to let that happen."

Simon saw a grin matching his own blaze out on DuQuesne's face. "Then turn this tub around!"

"Patience, my friends. Cautious and conservative play, remember. I have no doubt that *Thilomon* remarked our passage. They will undoubtedly be watching me for any sign of unusual behavior. I must proceed onward, as though we were oblivious to our friends' plight. You understand?"

Simon saw DuQuesne's fists clench, but the big man said nothing. Simon felt tension like edged wire around his heart, but forced himself to speak. "Yes. We understand."

"I truly regret that we cannot simply turn and chase, but we must gain the advantage of surprise in some fashion. Even were we to turn immediately, I am afraid your friend Wu...well, he will have suffered whatever fate awaits him."

DuQuesne's face went stony-blank at that. *Wu Kung*

was something very special to him, and I really don't know what will happen to Marc if Wu dies. "But what if we lose sight of them?"

Orphan flicked his hands outward, his equivalent of a shake of the head. "Not a difficulty. You see, I am very much familiar with the major Sky Gates and routes used by the Blessed, and given the circumstances, there is only one route *Thilomon* will take: directly to the homeworld and the Minds themselves. Homesphere has no direct connection to Nexus Arena, unlike most species' home systems, and thus in this we are fortunate. Two Gates in quick succession they must traverse, but then they must travel across a considerable gap to reach the next." His face might not be expressive, but Orphan's tone more than made up for it. "And it is there, my friends, in the empty sky, that we shall catch them."

CHAPTER 31

The airlock door slammed shut behind her, even as she tried to lunge back out. "Wu!"

"*No*, Captain Austin!" Sethrik said, not unkindly. "He is doing his *job*."

"But—"

"It will be over one way or—"

Sethrik broke off. With consternation she realized the deck below her was *moving*.

Even as that registered, the inner lock door slid open. Four Blessed stood there, two on either side, all four with weapons drawn and aimed at the two in the airlock. Vantak stood some distance back, watching.

Sethrik stared for a moment, obviously stunned—as was she, too. "What the *hell* is going on here?" she demanded.

"Lower those weapons!" commanded Sethrik. "Vantak, what is the meaning of this?"

The four Blessed soldiers did not lower their weapons a fraction, and Ariane could hear the faint sideband hum that was associated with the species' peculiar semi-hivemind capabilities. *They're working as a close-knit unit. All four will coordinate a lot better than four human beings. And they're not going to underestimate me like they did the first time we met, either.*

"Explanations, if any, will follow only after you are secured," Vantak said coldly. He reached into one of his bandolier pouches and tossed what were obviously a form of handcuffs onto the floor in front of them. "Captain Austin, you will move *slowly* forward, pick up both sets of restraints, and give one to Sethrik. Sethrik will then put his on, and you will follow his example."

Damn. It was starting to dawn on her that the attack on her outside had simply been a clever ploy, to separate her from the bodyguard whose capabilities they didn't fully understand and therefore wanted to take no chances with. *This still seems insane. But Vantak never sounded crazy, so there's got to be some reason behind this.*

She complied with Vantak's instructions. The binders looped around the wrists and held lightly, but—as Vantak demonstrated—they would tighten and retract strongly if she made sudden moves, or if Vantak triggered that reaction by remote. Two of the guards then fell back to near Vantak, about fifteen meters away, and the other two gestured for them to come out of the airlock, and then stopped and searched the two prisoners.

The searchers were very thorough, Ariane admitted to herself. *They got pretty much every piece of useful equipment that isn't embedded in me.* The searchers had even taken what little jewelry she normally wore. Sethrik also proved to have had an impressive cache of weaponry on his person, concealed in various pouches—some of which Ariane hadn't even realized existed, such as the hidden pouch under one of his wingcases.

"Follow."

Sethrik had obviously decided to not waste words until Vantak was ready to talk, so Ariane kept silent. It was good practice in controlling herself anyway, and if there was *any* chance of getting out of this situation alive, she'd damn well better stay controlled. *Lose my head here and I probably will* literally *lose my head*.

Sethrik had apparently decided to also bide his time, given that even the other Blessed weren't obeying his orders.

Through subtly-alien corridors they were led, the four Blessed maintaining perfect separation; when the group entered a large elevator, Vantak had them kneel on the floor in two corners.

At one point, Vantak paused, listening to what was obviously a signal from somewhere else. "What . . . ? No. Later. Continue on course."

Finally they reached another corridor with an open door to one side; the guards herded them through the door, which closed quickly; as soon as the door closed, the binders loosened and fell off, leaving them free to move. The closed door was transparent—Ariane guessed it was probably transparent ring-carbon composite—so that anything that went on inside would be visible from the outside. *No ambushing the jailers when they open the door, then.* Cameras would undoubtedly cover any blind spots.

"Are you going to explain yourself, Vantak?" she asked finally. "You've just *kidnapped* the head of another Faction—and apparently your own head of Faction as well. I can't offhand imagine *why*, or what you think it'll get you."

Vantak studied her, and his expression was that of

a scientist observing an experiment. "I have duties
to attend to. There is food for you both, and a bed
suited for each. It will be roughly twelve hours before
I have time for you; any arguments or demands will
be ignored until then."

He turned and left, taking the guards with him.
*Probably being monitored from every angle; no need
for guards.*

She turned to Sethrik. "Do *you* have any idea
what's going on?"

Sethrik flicked his hands out in the same gesture
Orphan often used. "No. I have not the smallest idea,
except that I am quite certain *he* has a very clear
idea. The assassination attempt—"

"—was meant to take Wu out of the picture, yeah.
I figured that out pretty fast." She glanced around.
"Don't you have any...I don't know, override codes
or something to get us out of here?"

Sethrik's wingcases scissored uncomfortably. "Not
from within a secure holding cell. They have removed
any tools I might have used to attempt an escape. I
am afraid that there is nothing to be done."

She frowned. "I'm not giving up. Maybe this isn't
the right time, but you can bet the time will come."

Sethrik was still for a moment, wearing that expression of confusion mixed with some little uncertainty,
even fear, that often accompanied Arena natives
when confronted by that attitude. Then he shrugged.
"Perhaps, but that time is not now. Eating and rest
are indicated."

"I suppose. Why is it going to take so long for him
to get back to us?"

"Vantak is going somewhere, and he will not relax

until after successfully making a jump out of Nexus Arena's space."

She remembered the journey to the jump point to Humanity's Sphere. "That makes sense. Can you tell which jump he's making?"

"There are many Sky Gates which could be reached in that period of time—and some even closer," Sethrik answered. "So no. I cannot tell. We will know when we reach our destination."

Realizing Sethrik was right about the futility of attempting anything right now, Ariane went over and inspected the small table on her side of the room. There was a bowl of fruits of types she knew had been cleared by her people for human consumption, some sort of dried meat she didn't recognize immediately, and some baked semicircular rolls. On Sethrik's side were a number of different-colored globes and what appeared to be some very large insects, legs bound together rather as live lobsters' claws would be. Remembering exactly how Orphan drank, she decided *not* to watch Sethrik if he was doing anything of the sort to the insects.

"Should I trust the food?"

Sethrik glanced at her, then gave a wing-shrug. "As we do not yet know his intentions, I cannot say for sure. Still, if he wished you injury he has ample opportunity, and we have not gained sufficient information on your species' biology to know how to arrange more . . . subtle effects, even if such are possible for your people."

"You mean conditioning and brainwashing?"

"Something of that nature, yes. He could possibly do such a thing to me . . . but again, had he wished it, he could do so without resorting to adulterating our food." Sethrik picked up one of the large insectoid things and she turned slightly away; the faint splintering *crunch* that followed still made her wince, as did the clearly audible whistling screech that cut off suddenly.

Averting her gaze from Sethrik, she picked up one of the rolls and tried it; if Sethrik didn't expect danger from the food, she wouldn't worry about it.

The roll was actually quite good, with a surprising peppery taste. She ate a little of everything, then went to lie down for a while on the provided cot. She called up one of the books stored in her minimal headware and read for a while, but found that she was surprisingly tired. *Then again, the stress of being attacked, kidnapped and imprisoned isn't something I've had to deal with before outside of a simgame, and with those you could always drop out.*

Using the same discipline that she often used before a big race, she cleared her mind and let her body relax. Breathe in, breathe out...

A loud hum awakened her; sitting up, she saw Sethrik had already leapt to his feet and was twitching his wings in an agitated fashion. "Stop that Minds-condemned *noise!*" Sethrik demanded, the translated voice an annoyed bellow. "We are quite awake and torture is unnecessary."

Two guards were visible at the door; Ariane guessed that there would be at least two more out there that WEREN'T visible. *And even if we could take them— which we might, because if I remember right Sethrik was supposed to be a new, better replacement for Orphan, which means he should be damn dangerous—a ship this size probably has a lot of reinforcements.*

"Vantak says he is ready for you now," one of the guards said. "Replace the bindings on each other."

After they followed those directions, the guards directed them out into the corridor. After several airlocks and turns, they emerged onto what was obviously the command deck; multiple stations currently manned by various Blessed, with a central perch atop a stepped dias that must be the equivalent of the captain's chair, on which Vantak was currently draped in what was she suspected a deliberately casual manner. *The Minds may have done a lot to them, but they're still just as much* people *as we are—good and bad.* She could, just barely, sense occasional bursts of the ultrasonic communication between Blessed; the acoustics of the room were obviously designed to facilitate this. *Wonder why I don't understand those? Maybe the Arena treats those as thoughts being exchanged?*

Besides a large central (obviously well protected and armored) viewport, displays around the walls showed different views of Arenaspace surrounding *Thilomon*, as well as portions of *Thilomon*'s exterior. These views shifted in some kind of rotation, so that presumably the entire panorama around *Thilomon*, and the entire surface of the vessel, was in view for at least a moment during any given cycle.

The viewport showed that they were passing by a Sphere—red-brown tinted continents and blue-green oceans—amid billowing clouds of violet, rose, and white that surrounded the Sphere. *Judging by the size of the Sphere, we must be very close to the edge of its gravity region.*

"All right, Vantak," she said, "Explain yourself."

"From others I would have expected a different

tone," Vantak replied, straightening a fraction on his perch. "But the Minds did not envision you to be easily intimidated. On the attack, even when you are in no position to demand."

He rose, and descended towards them, stopping only a short distance away. Vantak then looked towards Sethrik. "The Minds directed the entirety of this operation. You are of course to be replaced as Leader of Faction—by me, in all probability, but the Minds have not made the formal announcement yet as that would have betrayed the plan."

She could see that Sethrik was shocked to his very core. "The *Minds* . . . ordered you to do *this*?" He took a furious step forward before the guards' raised weapons forced him to halt. "Why? What *insanity* is this? I cannot believe you! They expressed every approval for my actions! They supported me in—"

"Of course they did. Had they done otherwise, you would have had forewarning," Vantak said bluntly. "You did not return in person according to schedule—"

"I have had *many* things demanding my time of late, and you . . ." Sethrik trailed off. "I see."

"What?" Ariane asked.

"That was how the directives were given. Vantak served as my liason to Homesphere and the Minds. Thus he would be able to take his private orders from them, and convey to me their public instructions. But if they had actually removed me from leadership—even trying to do so in secret, which would be extremely difficult to arrange—I would have noticed the first time I tried to do something which required the authority of the Faction Leader. However," he looked at Vantak, "I still do not understand *why*."

"The Minds showed me their projections. You were following the path of the heretic. You were accommodating others in paths not favoring the Minds' long-term interests. You had established a posture of mutual respect with Orphan himself. You failed to return for the scheduled presentation and evaluation, and the Minds believed that whatever excuses you might give yourself or others, this was in large part due to the subconscious knowledge that you feared the result of that evaluation."

The bridge crew were all watching the confrontation. *Not surprising; how often are you present at a coup that involves one of the Great Factions?* But on one of the displays across the room, behind Sethrik, she thought she saw—for just a moment—a flash of brilliant colors that did not fit with the smooth, utilitarian design and painting of *Thilomon*.

Instantly she gripped hard on her self-control. *It can't be. I must be imagining it. But if it is Wu Kung, I can't give anything away.* She continued to listen to the discussion, trying to watch the monitors without staring.

"The Minds thought I was going to *betray* them?" Sethrik's outraged bellow was delivered with such force that the accompanying buzz of the actual sound made her ears ring. "I have done *everything* they have asked—"

"The judgment is not mine, but the Minds'. Do not make the mistake of thinking you understand even yourself as well as they," Vantak said, cutting his former commander off sharply.

"I . . ." Sethrik contained himself, then looked at Ariane, gesturing at the Leader of Humanity. "But why in Their name would they ask you to do *this*?"

Ariane had been thinking about that as well. A second flicker of color, a moving object that sparkled gold and crimson and jade, told her that perhaps the impossible was real, and she *had* to keep everyone's attention off the monitors.

And she'd figured some of it out. "Political negotiations. That's why everything seemed to be going so swimmingly with Michelle Ni Deng."

Vantak gave an ironic push-bow. "Many of your own Faction find you . . . an extremely inconvenient choice for Faction leader. At the same time, the Minds felt it was important for us to demonstrate that their reach can extend even here, into the very heart of the Arena, to remind others why the Blessed To Serve are not to be trifled with."

Sethrik was so outraged that he buzzed incoherently. Ariane grimaced. "So. You figured that you could establish a stronger relationship with Humanity by promising a lot of Blessed support—maybe even an alliance against the Molothos—and demonstrate the Minds' power at the same time, by removing the Leader of the Faction of Humanity and letting us replace the Leader in our own way—proving that no one gets away with humiliating the Blessed, while not shooting down an interesting alliance. Since you'd seen *me* in action but didn't have clear ideas of what my new bodyguard could do . . ." light dawned. "*You* were the ones who set up Wu Kung for that duel. And you—or rather the Minds—decided not to take chances with him and figured out a plan to get him to separate himself from me at just the right time." *It was a damned good plan, too. Of course he'd push me into any nearby shelter and then go to deal with the threat. Utterly predictable.*

Thilomon quivered, engine noise shifted, and she realized they were now just inside the Sphere's gravity field. *And that little figure is still moving...is that a* hatch *near him?*

"Well reasoned, Ariane Austin," Vantak agreed. "They expected you would have little trouble deducing the key features of the plan—except, possibly, for one. Your bodyguard was an unknown quantity, and they believed that he was even more formidable than we had yet seen, and so should be removed from the equation." He raised a hand. "As always, they were correct, and it was even more difficult than I had expected to remove that factor." His hand came down.

The main viewport suddenly showed a view down the hull of *Thilomon*, with that tiny, brilliantly-colored humanoid figure now striding quickly towards a hatchway. But even as the scene registered, an entire section of the hull on which Sun Wu Kung stood *sprang* outwards, hurling the Hyperion Monkey King into empty space; with no warning, no chance to grab a handhold, Wu Kung curved outward and plummeted away, disappearing into a cloud that crackled with lightning.

"But," Vantak said calmly, "I believe that, too, has been dealt with now."

CHAPTER 32

Wu Kung felt *Thilomon* vibrating under him as he made his way along the hull. Wind began to rise, pushing at him, and he crouched, digging in his claws. The ship was covered with a tough yet somewhat resilient material that reminded Wu of the skin of some undersea animals. *Maybe reduces friction? Keeps instruments like radar from detecting it?* Whatever the reason, it was exactly what Wu needed; his claws, reinforced like his whole body with what DuQuesne called "ring-carbon composite," penetrated and held firmly.

"Ha!" he said, and felt his spirits rise. "They thought they had gotten rid of me. They almost had! But now I am on their vessel, and they do not even know it!"

But the wind was still rising, and Wu suddenly realized that getting on *Thilomon* had only been the first—and possibly easiest—hurdle. The great ship of the Blessed was accelerating, the winds rising even higher.

This is like the time I rode Orochi-sama, when he tried to shake me off by climbing into heaven and jumping down!

No, he corrected himself, bending down and getting a grip with his hands, looking for ridges, outcroppings of the vessel that might afford some protection, *it's much worse. Because there, I was The Great Sage Equal to Heaven, I was the TRUE Monkey King. Here...Here I am just someone's old experiment.*

It was the first time he had *really* admitted this to himself. He was not a demigod, not a warrior who had bested ten thousand atop the Mountain of Fruit and Flowers, not the greatest Hero of all ages; he was not human, but closer to human than anything else...and the gods would not help nor hinder him, nor even mark where he fell, if he failed.

Almost the thought made him too weak to hold on, piercing his nearly invincible confidence, echoing the time he had fallen in Hyperion, when the CSF had gassed him but he had remained conscious long enough to see his world erased. Two tears trickled from his eyes, were whipped to mist.

But there was still a face before his mind's eye, a courageous face with blue hair and a warrior's gleam in sapphire eyes, and a voice in his memory telling him that it was *his* job to protect her, no matter what: "even from me if you have to, Wu. Even from me. I'm trusting you to keep her safe."

And he had sworn to do that.

"I . . ." he hissed through his teeth, and pushed forward against a wind that was starting to feel like a thundering stream, a river raging around him, "... will not . . . be . . . foresworn!"

There! Ahead! Parts of the hull were deforming, rising slightly, moving apart, adjusting to the flow. And behind them, yes, there the wind would *have* to be less.

If he could *reach* it.

He risked freeing one hand, grasped his cloak, pulled it over his head, tightened all fastenings. *It was made to protect me from the fires of the underworld and the ice of the nether realms, forged to repel the weapons of mortal and god alike. Maybe . . . no, obviously, that's all a lie too . . . but just as they tried to make me the Monkey King, maybe they tried real hard with these, too . . .*

The wind *did* seem just a slight bit less savage, it felt as though his robes somehow were cleaving the wind and making it flow around him more. *But . . . it's still bad. And getting worse. How fast does this monster go?*

He slammed down one hand, shoved one foot forward, dug in, repeated the maneuver. Now it was like climbing a sheer mountain, with weights hanging from him . . . and more added all the time, like one of the sadistic tests he'd been subjected to by the Generals of Heaven. *Tests none of you could pass!*

It's hard! It's really hard . . . air is screaming, pulling, demons of the netherworld trying to pull me down. But I have to move forward! One more step! One more grip with my hand! Now push! Don't stop! Ariane's face blurred into Sanzo's before him, and he wondered at how similar they were. *And I won't fail Ariane any more than I would Sanzo!*

He wondered if Sanzo were still awake, back in the other world, in the universe of simulation that was to him as real as this Arena. *Did they shut off the simulation when I left, freeze the world? Or is she putting Gen to bed now, saying a prayer for me? Is Sha Wujing watching over them for me, or just sitting beneath his waterfall, training, waiting for me to unlock the riddle of reality with my fists?*

One more grip, the roar of the wind so loud he no longer heard anything, just felt the shrieking, screaming, rumbling of the demon wind in his bones, clawing at what little skin remained exposed with immaterial talons of fire and ice. *Pull! Pull forward!*

The wind suddenly wavered, felt disrupted, uneasy, shifting so that he was nearly pulled from the hull of *Thilomon.* Desperately he lunged forward, sinking all his claws deep into the resilient coating, and suddenly he realized the wind *was* weaker.

He was just in the lee of one of the moving sections. It was only raised a short distance, but just high enough that he could crouch, flat to the hull, behind it, and the wind now screamed mostly *over* him, not trying to tear its way *through.*

Now I have to hold on, hold on until it slows down... it has to slow down sometime...

But the roaring, raging wind went on, and on, and on. He held tight, grim, unrelenting, but the wind was tireless. It could continue forever, and it *did.* He held on, but he could not see where they were going, or how far they had come. The wind tore at him, gripped and yanked and pulled, sometimes almost teasing at the edges of his hood. Other things hissed and rattled against his clothing, some of the sky-plankton DuQuesne had mentioned. He thought, at moments, that he heard voices in that wind, some screaming curses and imprecations, others playful, asking him to let go, come play!

I can't go play. I can't let go. I can't ever let go.

Arms and hands which had almost never known fatigue, could not truly remember being *tested,* began to throb with the dull ache of weariness. His *fingertips* hurt, the claws themselves transmitting vibration and stress through his body. *Can't let go.* He repeated that to himself, focusing on Ariane, on his promise, on his life, on the few things that really *mattered*. *Can't let go.*

Can't let go.

Can't ever let go.

He did not let go. He held on, held when the ache in his hands became agony, when heat and chill threatened to rob him of endurance, held through the battering of wind and the turns of *Thilomon* as it travelled some unguessable distance in the endless sky. He held on. He did not let go.

The world suddenly *blazed* with crystal-light that jolted him to the core of his being, and he felt a strange tingling go through him. *That ... that was a Sky Gate jump?*

The speed of the vessel was not slackening, and still he held on, through a sudden turbulence that would have loosened his grip had it been any less tight. *We've come somewhere. They have a destination. They have to slow down sometime.*

Sun Wu Kung hung onto that thought desperately. *They have to slow down. This is a ship. It will go somewhere, and it will stop.*

But for the first time in his life, he really wondered if he could last long enough to see the end of a journey. His arms and hands and feet and legs felt like they were on fire, were cramping and threatening to fail in their grip even against the drive of his iron-held will. *No! I mustn't! If I let go, they will have Ariane and no one will ever know, no one will be able to save her! I'm the only chance she has!*

And then the rainbow shockwave of light hit again. *Another Gate...still in the Arena, had to be a Sky Gate...Good, I don't think I'd like breathing vacuum...*

It took several moments for him to realize the wind's scream was starting to reduce. He couldn't believe it at first. But then he saw the bulwark ahead of him shifting. The wind increased slightly, but only because he was no longer sheltered.

Clouds, he realized. *We're travelling through clouds. They're slowing down because they can't see everything.*

He cautiously straightened up, feeling his ungrateful muscles *now* trying to rebel because he dared shift his position. *I can...handle this wind. It's only about 300 kilometers an hour or so, I think. Fast, but not impossible with care. And still dropping.*

He patted his inside pockets, yanked out one of his high-energy snacks, stuffed it in his mouth, realizing as his jaws *ached* for a moment just how hungry he was. *I must have been there for...hours!*

He crouched down again and ate the other two bars he had on hand. *Need that strength later.*

Wu Kung straightened and looked around. After a moment, he spotted a squarish area that looked very much like the same kind of hatchway Ariane and Sethrik had gone into. *That's what I need!*

Carefully, he made his way across the hull towards the hatch. *Don't mess up when you're that close to—*

Without warning, the hull rose up and slapped him like the hand of an angry Buddha—*or maybe Kali on a real bad day!*

He realized he was flying...no, *falling. Thilomon* was receding, he was dropping down, down, farther, and then the ship disappeared as he fell into a roiling cloud.

"NO! No, no no NO!"

Almost he called for the clouds to support him, but he remembered that this was not Hyperion. The clouds would not support him. He could not summon the wind, or call forth the flames, or tear one of the pillars of the Dragon King's palace out to serve as his staff.

And he had failed.

He fell, and fell, and sometimes the thunder roared around him like the laughter of the gods, mocking him. It was indeed a fine jest, worthy of the Generals of the Heavens, that he would be so close, have endured so much, only to be defeated just when it seemed victory was certain. He didn't care. Ariane was gone, and no one would know she'd been kidnapped—and even if they did, they'd never know where to find her.

Still he fell. The cloud was producing rain and he fell with the rain, trickling off him like a million tears, and he let himself cry. There seemed, for the moment, to be nothing else to do.

But even grief could not go on forever, and as he felt the exhaustion of his frustration and sadness draping him in gloom, he remembered that DuQuesne had also begged him to *live*.

And that giving up was not his way.

"I . . . am still alive," Wu said to himself. "I'm still alive, and if I'm alive, that means I'm not beaten forever."

He opened his mouth and worked to guide water in; he desperately needed some, he felt as though he'd been in the Desert of Souls for a week. Occasionally some sky-plankton thing went in too; they weren't all that tasty, but he wasn't too worried about poison. He was tough.

Abruptly the darker space around him lightened, and he found himself tumbling through clearer air. He had fallen far enough that the Sphere he'd glimpsed vaguely as he fell from *Thilomon* had actually shifted its perspective.

There was movement below him; circling, yet closing in, he saw it was a mob or school of several dozen creatures with armored torsos, grasping, armored tentacles, and flashes of nightmare mouths.

Zikki, he realized. Predators fast and mean enough to have tried to attack small ships flying through their space.

There were a lot of them. And they were closing in.

He grinned finally, a smile savage and hungry, but a smile nonetheless, the first smile he'd had since Ariane had been kidnapped. He reached up and pulled his staff, Ruyi Jingu Bang, free. "Ha! You think you will make a meal of me! I will give you something to chew on, then!"

He dove to meet the oncoming swarm.

CHAPTER 33

"Two gates," DuQuesne said. "So we're in the gap, now?"

"Most certainly, Doctor DuQuesne," Orphan said. "And we shall prepare to close the distance—and plan on catching them in the middle, with nowhere to flee." He looked at both DuQuesne and Simon. "You have listened to my instructions on how to operate crucial systems of *Zounin Ginjou*, and I am sure you will . . . acquit yourselves well. But I hope you realize that this is still an unequal contest."

Simon nodded, feeling tension mounting once more. "Yes, I think we do. Even if *Zounin-Ginjou* is superior to *Thilomon*, we cannot attack it all-out unless we are willing to possibly kill Ariane as well. We must fight to cripple *Thilomon*, while they will have no such compunction about us. That gives them a huge advantage."

"Well stated, Doctor Sandrisson," Orphan agreed. "In addition, of course, there are but three of us and there will be many hundred Blessed aboard *Thilomon*. All the automation I could possibly make work is installed, but it simply is not going to make up for so many other eyes and minds at work. Fortunately," he bowed in their direction, "*Zounin-Ginjou* is, in fact, superior to *Thilomon* in nearly every way, so it is possible that we can triumph. The odds are . . . not good, even by your apparently insane standards, but they are very much not zero."

"We haven't been able to even *see* them for awhile, Orphan," DuQuesne said, looking even more tense than Simon felt. "Can't we get a view soon? I hate the idea that I can't even be sure they're *there*."

Orphan's wings scissored. "Alas, Doctor DuQuesne, I had to make sure we were that far behind; the jump-flash would undoubtedly give us away if we were even remotely in viewing range." *Zounin-Ginjou* rumbled more loudly. "But here we can accelerate. We will still try to remain unnoticed, but this is the region in which we desire battle to be joined, so I am slightly less concerned." He glanced back. "Of course, it is also possible that we could run *into* something while trying to catch them. There is an excellent reason that those travelling between Spheres move vastly more slowly than one might expect."

I don't doubt it, Simon thought. He remembered Ariane's race against Sethrik; clouds could hide gargantuan creatures like the *vanthume*, or floating lakes, or even pseudo-planets, accretions of stone and earth shed from uncountable spheres and accumulating in the deeps between. *But we have to take risks now.*

Simon and DuQuesne glued themselves to forward viewing instruments, scanning the heavens. *We can't use radar, unfortunately, because we're trying to hide. Still . . . that doesn't mean that* they *won't . . .*

He picked up the signal almost immediately. "Marc, Orphan, there's a radar source up ahead, about five thousand kilometers. It's attenuated but clearly there."

"Let me see...ah, yes, that must be *Thilomon*; the pulse pattern is very characteristic of Blessed vessels." Now aware of his quarry's location, Orphan shifted the direction of the vessel and accelerated. "Prepare yourselves, my friends."

Slowly the rose-purple mists in front of them cleared; a tiny dot appeared in the distance, and optical and electronic magnification showed clearly that it was, indeed, *Thilomon*.

Suddenly, Simon noticed a portion of *Thilomon*'s hull snap outward, then close. "What in the world was *that*?"

"I confess, I do not know. There was no maneuver underway which would involve the guide sails, and in any case that was—"

DuQuesne suddenly swore loudly. "Those sons of—they just gave Wu the boot."

Simon felt as though ice water had drenched him. He *liked* the energetic Hyperion Monkey King. "How can you be sure?"

"Sure? I can't be a hundred percent *sure*, but that's exactly the kind of maneuver you'd use to remove some unwanted guest from your hull, and..." he squinted, "...and I think they had just entered the gravity field of that Sphere, which means that Wu wouldn't just be tossed away, he'd fall and keep on falling for a long, long time. Orphan, we've got to—"

The alien's hand flicked outward in his "no" gesture. "Doctor DuQuesne, I dislike the thought of leaving anyone to drift between the Spheres. Understand that; I was once in that position myself, and there is no fate more isolating and fearsome.

"Yet if we stop to try and find a single falling object

within the vast spaces of the Arena, do you imagine we will succeed immediately?"

"I . . ."

"We are here to rescue Ariane Austin," Orphan pushed on, and to Simon's surprise there were anger and sympathy both in that voice. "If we stop to rescue Sun Wu Kung, then we will lose many hours, I will guarantee it, and the Blessed will be far beyond our reach.

"Still, you are my friends—as is Ariane Austin. You tell me—should we continue on our mission, or stop to rescue Wu Kung?"

DuQuesne glared at Orphan, huge fist upraised, and Simon waited nervously; he knew that DuQuesne was as . . . interested in Ariane as he was, but Sun Wu Kung was something older and probably just as important to DuQuesne.

Abruptly DuQuesne dropped into his seat and slammed his hand against the console. "*Damn!* Damn you, you're right, Orphan. He was a bodyguard. He wouldn't *ever* forgive me for rescuing him before getting her back. We go on."

Orphan nodded, started to turn back towards his console.

"*But—*"

Orphan looked back.

"But as soon as we have Ariane, we come back here, and we *find* Wu. If we have to spend half a year to do it. Understand?"

The wingcases flared. "I understand and most certainly agree, Doctor DuQuesne."

Zounin-Ginjou moved forward more swiftly, still transmitting nothing, but gaining ground slowly but surely on the unsuspecting *Thilomon*. Orphan pointed out the key points on the target v;essel. "We wish to damage her engines. We do *not* want to damage the energy storage areas or the living quarters."

Simon nodded. *Room-temperature superconductor loop batteries are the usual means of energy storage. If you damage them, they tend to release all their energy at once. Which means an explosion.* He hadn't been present at DuQuesne's defeat of *Blessing of Fire*, the Molothos scout ship, but he had seen the glassy crater the nuclear-level blast had left. Interstellar ships carried a *great* deal of energy on board.

"Doctor Sandrisson, you were involved in the entire construction of your *Holy Grail*. You obviously have a good overall grasp of the systems involved in a ship, and so I will be counting on you to assess and direct repairs through the semi-automated maintenance systems. It is my guess that Doctor DuQuesne is more capable with weapons systems than you, and therefore I intend to make him our gunner, overseeing the actual firing upon our opponent."

Unspoken, but clear to Simon, was the fact that putting the guns in DuQuesne's control meant that Orphan would not be the one to blame if *Thilomon* was accidentally destroyed during combat. *And I can't blame him. This is our problem, we have to work to solve it ourselves.*

"What's the range on our weapons?"

"Technically, we are within range of my largest missiles already," Orphan said, "at a range now of two thousand kilometers. *Thilomon* has not changed course or speed, so apparently they have not yet noticed us, which is good. The energy cannon have ranges of up to a thousand kilometers for the largest, but against something like *Thilomon* we need to be much closer. Hypersonic cannon, about three hundred kilometers.

"I hope to bring us to within two hundred kilometers or less before initiating hostilities, and ideal ranges would be much shorter than that."

"You really think you can get *that* close without them knowing?" Simon asked.

"Automated visual scans are not useful, and other forms of sensing do not work well through the Arenaspace, except active radar to some extent—although even that has a fairly limited range. *Zounin-Ginjou* has excellent radar-absorbent properties. As there is a cloud bank only a few kilometers below us, extending a very long distance ahead, we should be able to close in on their radar signals while allowing them little chance to detect us."

Orphan suited actions to words, sending *Zounin-Ginjou* diving into a sea of blue-tinted cloud. Occasional lightning bolts made the trip somewhat more exciting than Simon would have preferred. "One of those would cut our trip rather short, I would think."

"Ahh, Doctor Sandrisson, it is true that I would rather avoid being struck. Still, *Zounin-Ginjou* is very well insulated and will tend to conduct through its outer superstructure. A large enough bolt would produce . . . unfortunate consequences, but in enterprises as risky as these, I think that worry is the least of our problems."

Two more hours passed, and the radar pulses grew more powerful with each passing minute. Finally Orphan gestured to them.

"It is time. I do not dare risk approaching closer. Are you both prepared?"

Simon nodded, and realized his hands were sweating as he laid them on the controls. *I am going into a battle between starships. I have ... never actually been in a real fight before. Simulations, yes ... but I know this is no simulation.*

His heart began to beat even faster, as *Zounin-Ginjou* tilted up, climbing. The deep-blue gloom lightened, thinned.

Suddenly new signals appeared on Simon's scanners. "Orphan! I'm seeing—"

But *Zounin-Ginjou* was already emerging from the mist, into clear air, and *Thilomon* was turning. *Turning too fast—they must have started the turn as soon as we began our run!*

"Damnation," DuQuesne said in a calm, almost tranquil, voice. "They knew we were here all along, and they let us come ... so we'd fall straight into their trap."

Emerging from the cloudbanks, Simon could see the source of the new signals: a fleet of ships, ten, fifteen, maybe more.

"They allowed for the possibility of being followed and are prepared," Orphan said, and a fatalistic tone was clear in his translated voice. "They are already deploying to cut us off." He gave a shrug and bowed from his seat to them. "It would seem that you will no longer need to worry about paying my faction back, my friends."

CHAPTER 34

Ariane watched in disbelief and shock as Wu Kung was catapulted into empty air and dwindled to nothing below them, and then whirled on Vantak, who looked at her with clinical disinterest.

"You . . . you . . ." she felt red rage building, a fury she hadn't felt since Amas-Garao had tricked her into accepting his Challenge through the Blessed. She stepped forward and the guards raised their weapons. "You murdering *bastard!*"

Blue and green-white sparks erupted around her, shattering her binders, tossing the guards aside, knocking Sethrik down but also breaking his own bindings. She felt a shock of surprise, hope, but even as she desperately tried to grasp that power, shape it, channel it, the energy dwindled, faded, and was gone, sealed away again.

Vantak had not even moved, but now he slowly rose, wingcases spreading. "Excellent. Everything the Minds have believed, so has it come to pass. Under sufficient stress, the powers of Shadeweaver or Faith that you possess can manifest for a few moments."

"You . . . *expected* that?" She felt a chill down her spine. *What* are *these Minds? Do* we *have AIs like that?*

Vantak nodded, even as the guards recovered and aimed carefully at both her and Sethrik. "It was the consensus of the Minds that this was of a high probability, and if the opportunity arose I was to test this theory. They did not believe you could summon sufficient power to pose a significant threat, not with the binding having been completed only months ago.

"Your bodyguard thus provided the ideal situation. It had been clear that you had an affection for him, and thus believing that we did not know he was present, and distracting us so we would not notice, would give you a powerful feeling of hope. Dashing that hope quickly, while effectively killing him in such a fashion, would produce a peak surge of agitation. As you can see," he gestured to the shattered binders, "their predictions were correct in all particulars."

"So why do they *want* that?"

Vantak tilted his head. "You are not unintelligent, but you do not think far enough ahead. You provide the Minds with a chance to study the power of the Shadeweavers or the Faith—or both, if both are in fact merely facets of the same power."

Crap. She couldn't think of an epithet bad enough.

"I see you begin to understand. One cannot—dare not—attempt to kidnap either a Shadeweaver or an Initiate Guide and analyze them. Even if you could hold them, the retribution of their respective orders would be . . . fearsome. But you are neither, a possessor of their power but an embarrassment and concern to both. Your disappearance will be a relief for both sides, as well as your own Faction, in a way . . . and in analyzing your power the Minds believe they can find a way to use it, to make themselves able to operate within the Arena itself."

That's . . . horrifying. The one thing that the Arena seemed clearly designed to do was prevent artificial intelligences—except, probably, the Arena itself, if it's an AI—from operating, from being able to use their particular advantages to utterly outmatch living creatures in the Arena. But the Shadeweavers can "trick" the Arena, get away with things no one else can. If the Minds can learn that power—

"Of course," Vantak continued, looking at Sethrik, "they will take the opportunity to return you to proper service. Your loyalty renewal treatments will be performed upon arrival in Homespace."

"Ariane Austin," Sethrik said calmly. "As you are still alive, and you have not turned your authority over, you are technically still the Leader of Humanity, yes?"

"As far as I know."

"Then if you would be so kind, accept me as a member of the Faction of Humanity." Sethrik glared at Vantak. "For I do not wish to be associated with this treachery even as a part of the Faction of the Blessed, not now."

She was surprised and gratified. Her first impulse was to accept; it was a futile gesture, yes, but a very *human* gesture, and one that obviously nettled Vantak, whose wingcases had tightened in offense. But . . . "I appreciate the sentiment, Sethrik—but you are still, technically, the Leader of the Blessed. If I accept, that means a replacement will automatically get chosen—probably Vantak there. It may be a futile gesture on *my* part, but I damn well want *them* to have to go through the hoops to replace you instead of get it handed to them."

Sethrik gave a small push-bow. "So be it, then."

One of the Blessed at the controls of *Thilomon* turned. "Guidemaster Vantak, I believe we are being followed."

Vantak turned his attention to the speaker. "Why so, Kandret?"

"Polarization shadows behind us. They are distant and very faint and at first they could have been noise. But the statistics are too high and correlate too well with our path."

Vantak bent over Kandret's displays. "I see. Could this not be a phenomenon of our own wake?"

"No, Guidemaster. See here, and here; shifts in time and velocity that did not accord with our own."

Vantak studied the display again, then looked up, seeming to think for several minutes.

"Guidemaster? Shall we turn to engage?"

After another moment, Vantak flicked his hands outward. "No. Continue on course. Keep me apprised of the follower's distance. As soon as it begins to shift course to rise from that cloudbank we will make our turn."

Kandret looked at Vantak uncertainly, but then bob-bowed agreement. "As you command."

Ariane glanced at Sethrik, puzzled but feeling a faint hope. *Who could have followed them?* She thought back to the dock. *There was one ship of the Analytic docked. I'd like to think they wouldn't let something like this happen. And the Faith certainly wouldn't . . . I hope. But I don't remember if there were any Faith vessels at that Dock.*

Another Blessed spoke. "Question, Guidemaster."

"You may ask, Hancray."

"Why allow them to get into position? If they close distance—"

"There is only *one* good reason for a vessel to be following us; they wish to rescue Ariane Austin. Because of that, they will have to close a great deal of distance—as much as they possibly believe they can, to allow themselves a good chance of disabling *Thilomon* and permitting a boarding action. Obviously they will thus be careful and restrained, while *we* have no such limitations. Thus they will not attack any time soon, and I have very good reason to want to wait a little longer."

But the same logic would apply to starting the fight now; in fact, anyone trying to rescue us would have to be even more *cautious at long range, when they can't target specific parts of* Thilomon. *Vantak's "explanation" doesn't explain much, and I can tell Hancray thinks so too, but it's obviously as much as Vantak intends to say.*

Vantak had them put on new binders, but allowed them to stay where they were; perhaps he had other tests the Minds had planned, or he simply felt there was no particular reason for them *not* to be there, as long as they were under guard.

Tense hours passed, and Ariane began to feel not merely bored but thirsty. "Vantak, can we have something to drink, if we're going to stay here?"

The Blessed looked up. "Perhaps I could have you escorted back down; you can wait there as well as anywhere, and there you can—"

"Guidemaster! Signals ahead of us!"

At nearly the same moment, Kandret said, excitement in his voice, "Guidemaster! Our pursuer begins to rise!"

Vantak's wingcases relaxed. "Hancray, transmit forward to approaching signals: Flanking pattern *Hana*, inclined one-fiftieth of a circle below *Thilomon*'s central axis."

Ariane felt as though her heart had dropped through her boots. *Reinforcements.*

"They acknowledge the order, Guidemaster."

"Range to pursuer?"

"Three hundred kilometers, Guidemaster."

"Turn to confront in three . . . two . . . one."

Thilomon began a slow, graceful turn, as the forward port shimmered to show a view of a blue-tinted cloud bank.

The blue suddenly darkened, bulged, and bursting from within the depths of the cloud, like a mighty whale breaching from the sea, came a golden and mahogany and crystal vision, curves and alien Victorian beauty with the ponderous grace of a battleship.

Despite the reinforcements coming, despite being surrounded by Blessed, Ariane's heart leapt back where it belonged, and she gave a jubilant cry. "Orphan! *DUQUESNE! SIMON!*"

Vantak gave a buzzing cry that was translated as a curse. "The *Survivor!* It is *Zounin-Ginjou!* All weapon stations, unlock and fire as ready! Defensive emplacements, all free! Tell the fleet, fire to destroy—no surrender, only destruction, in the name of the Minds!"

Sethrik buzzed his own laughter. She looked at him. "Do you think—"

He was momentarily sober. "No, Ariane Austin.

I laugh for their consternation and fear, not for our hope. *Zounin-Ginjou* is powerful, but it is a single vessel with one—or, if I take your words right, three— people aboard. It will be destroyed in this battle, make no mistake."

From the mist around them emerged ship after ship—none quite the size of *Thilomon*, but all large, powerful, and well armed, and all driving towards *Zounin-Ginjou*.

"Twenty of our vessels against his . . . Orphan shall not be the Survivor much longer."

CHAPTER 35

"Time to even the odds," Orphan said, even as streaks of light flashed past *Zounin-Ginjou*.

The great ship groaned audibly and the safety harnesses creaked as Orphan rammed the nose of *Zounin-Ginjou* downward. DuQuesne felt his body nearly flung towards the ceiling. *Holy mother of... the acceleration this thing can manage is* impressive, *I'll say that.*

At the same time, DuQuesne keyed in the commands he'd been shown and grasped the twin curved controllers. The display enhanced what could be seen, and he squeezed tight on the left-hand control.

A blare of pure white incandescence speared outward, slashing straight through the midsection of one of the approaching vessels—which staggered and then vanished in an eye-searingly bright explosion. The detonation sent shrapnel hurtling through the sky in all directions, battering another of the attackers. "Ha! *That's* what you get for trying to ambush *us*!"

Sapphire-and-pearl clouds rose up, obscuring vision, while defensive proximity cannon whined, spewing hypervelocity rounds into an oncoming missile, chewing it to splinters before the warhead let go with a blast that jolted *Zounin-Ginjou*.

"I see," said Simon, his voice shaky but his hands working on the control panel steadily. "In the clouds combat must be even closer—and harder for everyone to concentrate on us."

"Precisely, my friends," Orphan said, and triggered a volley of cannon towards another shadow in the mist. "We are going to die; make no mistake on that, for all it will take is a single lucky strike, as with your first shot, Doctor."

"I thought that was skill," he said, scanning the indicators for any clear targets.

"Oh, undoubtedly there was skill," Orphan agreed, turning sharply to port and continuing to head downward. "But the armor on their vessels—or *Zounin-Ginjou*—is more than capable of taking several hits from most weapons. I would venture a guess you happened to hit one of the weapon ports just as it opened, thus getting your shot past most of the armor and into the storage coils."

"Remember to be careful when firing, Marc, Orphan," Simon reminded them. "We can't just unload on *Thilomon*."

"Yeah, I know. But thanks for the reminder." *Still nothing*.

"Couldn't they just continue on, leaving their reinforcements to mop up?" Simon asked.

"Oh, they *could*," Orphan agreed, "but consider what they have *done*. They have kidnapped the Leader of a Faction. They cannot afford to have *that* tale told by witnesses such as we—*hold on!*"

Out of the indigo gloom suddenly loomed an immense shape, not even a *kilometer* away, and the hull of

Zounin-Ginjou rang like a tin roof in hail as a firestorm of hypersonic cannon slammed into the flagship of the Liberated, while Orphan took them into a steep climb.

But at that range, I *can't miss* you *either!* DuQuesne's hands danced across the controls and he pulled back on the joystick. "Orphan, come back, back down, quarter circle towards him!"

"But that—"

"*DO IT!*"

Zounin-Ginjou slewed around, nose now pointing directly at the oncoming Blessed warship—and DuQuesne released the trigger, firing the synchronized weaponry from all forward batteries in a single shot. Energy weapons and missiles and hypersonic rounds clawed at near-invincible armor, ripped it apart piece by stubbornly-protesting piece, and suddenly another flare of unbearable incandescence told them one more adversary was gone.

Orphan laughed unsteadily. "Ahh, well done, yet you confuse me, Doctor! How did you manage to slave all the forward weapons to a single control?"

That made him pause for a moment. *How* did *I . . . ?*

"Hey, *you* showed me the controls—and I've been on your ships for weeks now!"

"Then you learn swiftly and well."

He saw Simon looking at him with an analytical eye that also bothered him. *Wasn't he near panic a second ago?*

But there was no time to think about things; radar signals were closing on both sides. *Neither of them's* Thilomon*; wrong radar encoding. Well, I'm sure as hell not waiting to see what's coming or find out if they know we're here—*

Even as he fired salvos in both directions, the displays showed multiple missile launches. He saw Simon already launching flares and chaff, Orphan readjusting the point-defense cannon, and heard himself laughing, realized . . . he felt *good*, and knew why, when he saw another flare of light and realized yet another enemy was damaged or destroyed. "This is just like the old days!" he said, thinking back to the life he'd had as a Hyperion. "And if Rich Seaton were here, somehow we *would* beat these bastards, I tell you that. As it is, they'll by *God* know they've been in a fight!"

Zounin-Ginjou breached from cloud again, and *Thilomon* cast a tiny shadow over them. *Close enough to try*, DuQuesne thought, and took careful aim, ignoring for the moment other pursuers. *Now!*

But just as he fired, *Thilomon* swerved, almost as though the other ship had *sensed* his focus. The concentrated column of destructive energy ripped through nothing but air. "Damnation!"

Alarms bleeped out even as small concussions vibrated through *Zounin-Ginjou*, and Orphan gave a buzzing curse, trying to turn back towards the cloud bank. But other dark shapes were materializing from the fog, and DuQuesne realized there was now nowhere to run.

"Damage control underway," Simon reported, directing the repairs by the semi-automatics. "But we can't keep getting hit!"

"I shall most certainly inform the Blessed of that when I have the opportunity," Orphan said dryly, sending their vessel charging towards the nearest adversary.

Beams and bullets were exchanged, hammering and blazing against intractable yet not-quite-invincible armor, and the two vessels passed within a few hundred meters of each other, so close that almost DuQuesne thought he could see the panic on the faces of the Blessed as he got a perfect shot lined up on the opposing ship's bridge and squeezed the trigger.

The detonation *shoved Zounin-Ginjou* sideways, so quickly that DuQuesne grunted at the acceleration and Simon went pale. "We're not finished yet! Four down!"

"Five," he heard Simon say with satisfaction, and realized that the white-haired scientist had been accessing the secondary batteries while DuQuesne was using the primaries. "It seems I managed to put a shot through one of the engine housings on the one diving on us."

DuQuesne grinned tightly. "That leaves just fourteen more."

Orphan shook his head and flicked his hands out for a moment, wingcases tight as vault doors. "I admire your courage, Doctor DuQuesne—and your resourcefulness, Doctor Sandrisson, for I was unsure how easily weapons could be controlled from that station." His tail suddenly arched in attack position. "*By the—hold on!*"

DuQuesne saw it on his display—a tight grouping of missiles, fired in a coordinated wave by the three closest ships, streaking in at *Zounin-Ginjou*. "Dammit! No way to make it to the cloud!"

The missiles screamed inward, separating and weaving slightly but tracking the Liberated flagship implacably. Simon fired chaff and flares; a few veered off, confused, but others bored on, closing in. The point-defense cannons shrieked fury at the sky, slashing oncoming missiles to flinders and shards of junk, and *still* some bored in. DuQuesne swung the main batteries around, opened fire with everything, sweeping the sky with fire and explosives, there were fewer, six missiles, four, three, one—

Zounin-Ginjou staggered in the sky like a fighter caught with a perfect right cross on the chin, slewing sideways and rolling; inside, DuQuesne felt like he was inside a dice cup being shaken. *And if we weren't strapped down, it'd be* worse!

Orphan got the motion under control, but DuQuesne could feel—and hear—that the great ship was no longer moving with such assured, smooth power and grace. "Serious damage to control linkages and relays!" Orphan said.

There was a sound of releasing catches, and Simon stood up. "On my way."

"What? Simon, you don't—"

But the tall, slender Doctor Sandrisson was already running through the doors, closing the transport tube. *Dammit, what the hell does he think he's doing? He doesn't know how a tenth of this stuff is designed!*

Neither do you, the cynical voice of his original self said. *Funny how you still seem to know how to run it, isn't it?*

"Let us hope Doctor Sandrisson knows what he is doing, Doctor DuQuesne," Orphan said. "For they are . . ."

DuQuesne saw the wings tighten and then droop, fall flat as they had only once before in DuQuesne's memory—when Orphan had despaired of confronting Amas-Garao and left.

On the screen the radar was suddenly showing *more* contacts.

Dozens. Maybe hundreds. All heading straight for us.
Hope, before only a faint gleam, faded away.

"Fine!" he said, gritting his teeth. "You've got more reinforcements? Let's see how many more we can take *with* us! Orphan, snap out of it! If we're going to die, let's die *well*, dammit!"

Orphan was still a moment, and then gave a convulsive yank on the controls. *Zounin-Ginjou* turned, heading directly for *Thilomon*. "As you say." A faint touch of his good humor returned. "As you say, Doctor DuQuesne.

"Let us die *very* well."

Zounin-Ginjou drove straight towards the Blessed flagship, other ships' fire rebounding harmlessly for the moment from its obdurate hull; but it was clear that *Thilomon* had no intention of allowing so direct a confrontation; it was retreating, and while *Zounin-Ginjou* was faster, DuQuesne knew they could not long ignore the other ships which were quickly moving to intercept and destroy.

The new contacts were closing in now, from the direction of a great white cloud, and there were *lots* of them, so many that as they approached, the cloud began to *darken*.

DuQuesne stared. "Sweet spirits of niter...what the..."

Orphan, too, was momentarily stunned. "This... could make things *very* messy. Very messy indeed."

CHAPTER 36

Ariane stared helplessly as the Blessed fleet swung with lethal precision and dove towards *Zounin-Ginjou*. Her hands found a railing nearby and gripped, holding her against the jolts of sharp maneuvers that, though lessened, were still felt onboard *Thilomon*.

The displays split, showing feeds from different ships in the attacking force. At distances of a thousand miles or less, strong transmitters could bridge that distance, weld the nineteen vessels into a coordinated, unstoppable force. Orphan took his ship into a steep dive, initial salvoes failing to find their mark, and disappeared into the cloud from whence he'd come—but not before a blast of energy seared through the atmosphere of the Arena and shattered one of the newcomers to dust and smoke.

Vantak buzzed something insulting, but did not move. The vessels mantained their pattern, many of the Blessed vessels following into the clouds while *Thilomon* and the rest remained above, in the clear, watching and waiting, poised to rain destruction upon the enemy vessel when she dared emerge from the clouds.

Bluish mist and murkiness on the monitors, different vessels driving through the cloud in a deadly search. Suddenly a darker shadow, not where the other vessels should be, and blazing fire being exchanged. She saw faint flashes, sparks of impact from weapons hammering at the hull of *Zounin-Ginjou* even as the Liberated battleship tried to swing clear—and then wrenched around, coming about without warning.

"What in the Minds is he *doing*?" muttered Vantak. "He's charging *into* the attack—"

The screen went blank, and Ariane gave a tense cheer. "That's two, Vantak. Two in three minutes. That gives your whole fleet what, just about half an hour before it's all wiped out?"

Sethrik stood near her, wingcases tight, and she knew that despite her taunt, her hands were even tighter, white-knuckled on the rail.

More flickers, half-seen exchanges of weapons against a phantom opponent, and another sector of screen went blank. Then *Zounin-Ginjou* lunged from the cloudbank, streaming mist like water, and its main batteries were traversing—

"Full evasive turn *now!*" bellowed Vantak. The sudden yanking acceleration nearly knocked Ariane down. "No solo maneuvers, triples only! Battle groups, form and destroy!"

Six groups of three began to form up, preparing to coordinate in the destruction of the last of the Liberated. The shining sculpture of *Zounin-Ginjou* was marred now, and even as she tried desperately to escape, more fire washed across the Liberated flagship.

This is my fault.

A part of her wanted to evade those words, as her

friends were trying to evade the battle group, but both were doomed attempts.

Two more ships of the Blessed erupted in blinding light and were gone, and Vantak gave an inarticulate screech of disbelief and fury. "They are but three on *one* ship! Why are they not *dust* by now?"

She wanted to cheer, but she could see the damage, the shining armor dulled, chipped, scarred, scorched, and she knew the truth. Yes, Orphan and DuQuesne and Simon would do a lot of damage—but the constant hammering would get *Zounin-Ginjou* eventually, whether in the next few minutes or after they got four, five, perhaps six more enemy vessels. Even with luck, even with the skill of Marc C. DuQuesne and the power of Orphan's finest vessel and Simon's quick wit, they could not evade that many bent on their own destruction, not forever.

And she couldn't evade the truth.

This is my fault. I didn't really want to be Leader of the Faction of Humanity, so I didn't lead. I didn't accept that I had to be ready to lead, had to be ready to confront people like Naraj and Ni Deng, and keep confronting them until they accepted that I was the Leader and was going to stay the Leader until I decided otherwise. I let them run the show because, honestly, I didn't believe I had what it takes. That no one has what it takes to do that job. Naraj read me like a book, and I think he honestly spoke his mind—most of the time. He knew I really wanted to have someone else do the work—and so he did the work, him and Ni Deng.

And because of that, I got caught, Sethrik's been stabbed in the back, Wu's gone, and Simon and DuQuesne and Orphan are about to get killed.

A missile took *Zounin-Ginjou* amidships. Somehow

Orphan's ship shrugged off the impact, but it seemed to be flying just a hair less smoothly, and black smoke was trailing from the wound in the vessel's side.

"Sethrik," she said, "I'm sorry."

He glanced at her in surprise. "Sorry? What in the Minds' Names do you have to apologize for?"

"This is my fault, and I should never have let it happen. I promise you this much: if we somehow get through this, I won't let it happen again."

"I...do not quite understand," Sethrik said, head tilted, even as Vantak was shouting clear, precise orders to complete *Zounin-Ginjou's* destruction, "but how do you think you could have prevented this?"

"By doing what I should have done all along," Ariane said, grimly certain. "By *being* the Leader of the Faction instead of *playing* at it. Dammit, I said enough times this wasn't a simgame, but I *was* playing it like it was one—like I could step out whenever I got tired of the game.

"This isn't a game, and I screwed up *big* time. I didn't step up and take the load, and I let other people *think* I was, or *hope* I was. And all while I was telling people I wouldn't let just anyone take it, either."

Zounin-Ginjou swung around and up and began a charge straight after *Thilomon;* Vantak simply ordered a retreat and began closing the pattern in on Orphan's vessel.

Alarms suddenly buzzed. "Guidemaster! More contacts! *Many* more contacts! Closing fast!"

Vantak stiffened, and for the first time he looked actually confused, rather than merely nettled that *Zounin-Ginjou* was refusing to die exactly on schedule. "Contacts? What are they? Any transponders?"

"No transponders. Unknown profiles in the threat databases. Different profiles ... *many* profiles!"

Vantak looked at the scans, then tilted his head; his wings scissored a moment in indecision. "Shift our vector to allow more space. Second and third triads, diverge to screen."

As six ships spread in a defensive pattern between *Thilomon* and a huge white cloud about two hundred kilometers away, the cloud began to darken. Even Ariane stopped watching the duel between *Zounin-Ginjou* and the other Blessed ships; the whole battle, in fact, paused, as though everyone aboard all the vessels were holding their breaths.

And the cloud suddenly *exploded* outward, dozens, no, *hundreds* of black and gray and green and blue forms shooting out, directly for the Blessed fleet. In the center, a monstrous thing, white and black and blue rippling across its surface, blending it with the background so it seemed some hideous ghost, gargantuan, with a gleam of crystal teeth the size of houses, a sharklike profile in double symmetry, unmistakably alive, unmistakably predatory, impossibly cruising directly at them.

"*Morfalzeen!*" Hancray gasped, and the entire fleet shifted, even *Zounin-Ginjou* apparently uncertain whether to continue firing at the Blessed or at this titanic monstrosity—a hunting creature five kilometers long, Ariane realized incredulously as she saw the scale at the bottom of one display. *But of course there* would *be such things—what else would prey on something like the* vanthume?

"That's bad, I take it?" she murmured to Sethrik.

"*Morfalzeen* have been known to attack and destroy battleships, yes. Though they are not invincible and almost certainly die in the same attack. I am utterly at a loss, however, as to why the *rest* of these creatures," he gestured at the motley assortment of Arenaspace life, ranging from *tzchina* to *virrin* and at least three or four others that she'd never seen, "are apparently *with* the *morfalzeen*."

The cloud *bulged* outward and something else came through, something that drew incoherent shouts and curses from the Blessed and even from Sethrik. *It . . . looks like a Skyfall.* She remembered threading *that* desperate needle and nearly getting killed. *But it's coming so fast, almost as though—*

A *vanthume* emerged, shoving the mass of stone and earth ahead of it, into the approaching mob of creatures. The aerial avalanche curled around the *morfalzeen*, apparently almost unfelt, and the smaller creatures ducked and dodged amid the rocks. A fast-moving contingent of *zikki* streaked past *Thilomon*, closing to less than two hundred meters before veering off.

"What? What *is* this? Have the heavens gone insane?" Vantak cursed again. "Concentrate fire on the *mor—*"

Alarms did not buzz, but shrieked this time, and a machine-gun rattle of impacts echoed through *Thilomon*; the screens showed the other vessels in even more trouble—even as the *morfalzeen* accelerated forward, literally *shoving* one Blessed warship aside like a linebacker tossing a toddler out of his way. The immense creature jerked as explosive and energy salvoes struck it, but continued forward, undeviating, undeterred.

A missile struck and shattered directly on the main viewport in front of Ariane, and she realized it was . . . "Rock? Are those *zikki* throwing *rocks* at us?"

"What?" Sethrik stared, hands twitching in the instinctive "no" gesture. "Impossible. Ludicrous. The *zikki* cannot use tools, they haven't the intelligence to think of such a tactic, and they have no reason to even *approach* something of this size!"

Now another wave of creatures wove in, ducking and weaving, evading energy weapons and futile cannon. The *tzchina* hurled their cargo, and more stone—and what looked like bones—rebounded from the viewport.

But . . . are those scratches? "Sethrik—"

"I see . . . yes, the stone of the Arena is often made of the bones and such of dead creatures . . . and such often still has ring-carbon composite within. This battering will have an effect!"

The swarm wove through the Blessed ranks, sowing chaos. *Zounin-Ginjou* seemed oddly untouched, and suddenly swung about, firing on one of the nearer vessels; instantly the firefight began anew, but now a *three*-cornered battle, and one where one set of participants was a total mystery.

The Brobdingnagian *morfalzeen* bored onward, shrugging off missiles and cannon and stabbing energy weapons. To Ariane's simultaneous amusement and horror, it seemed to have targeted *Thilomon*, for as the Blessed flagship tried to dodge out of the way, the *morfalzeen* turned with it.

"*Reverse engines! Slow!*" shouted Vantak. "*Brace for impact!*"

The monstrous predator turned at the last second, but something huge and dark continued on, blotting out the sky, a gigantic stone that *smashed* into the bridge viewport; *Thilomon* staggered; and even as the darkness began to lighten, something else flickered, slammed into the viewport—

And the viewport *shattered*, exploding inward, scattering dust and stone and jagged-edged pieces of transparent ring-carbon composite everywhere. Kandret gave a buzzing shriek and collapsed as one glittering shard impaled him; Hancray, next to him, was knocked from his seat and lay still, unconscious.

Dust filled the air, blanking out sight. She squinted, trying to see through drifting grayness. *There. Someone...a figure...*

The wind from outside whipped in a breath of clearer air and she gasped as she suddenly saw...

...Robes of ruby and gold, sparkling of jade and sapphire and twilight purple; red-black hair flowing in the wind, bound by a golden circlet with a diamond sparkling like a star; and a crimson-and-gold staff gripped in a clawed hand...

Head held high, green-gold eyes coldly furious, Sun Wu Kung stood before them.

For a moment no one moved; even Vantak seemed utterly stunned, without words or understanding before the impossible.

The Monkey King cast his gaze around at the tableau, and then without warning took three swift strides and fell to his knees in front of Ariane. "I... failed you," he said, and his voice was soft and sad. "I failed you and DuQuesne. I was supposed to protect you and I did not. I was tricked, drawn away by a childish deception, and even when I realized that... even then, I was not good enough, not fast enough. I failed you, and I am *ashamed*."

Ariane was still staring, hardly able to grasp what she was seeing. "Wu...?" she whispered.

He looked up, and the emerald-auric eyes shimmered with tears of shame and remorse.

She suddenly felt her heart beating, hammering from shock and excitement—and finally she smiled. "Wu...Wu Kung, there is nothing to forgive, you... you...impossible, chaos-sowing...Wu, the only thing that matters to me is that you're *alive* when I thought you were *dead.*"

His eyes widened and for a moment, as a slow, unbelieving smile dawned on his face, he looked both like a child whose mother had suddenly appeared to lift him up, and a man seeing a revelation. "R...really?"

"Really."

The smile sharpened, even as she saw movement around them. "Then..." he stood, and whipped the staff around in a theatrical whirling motion that made everyone else leap back, "I think it's time to *play!*"

CHAPTER 37

Wu could not keep the smile from alternating between savagery and joy. *She has forgiven me! She cares!*

He had not dared to hope she would care for one who had failed so completely, and now that he knew she did... *Nothing will stop me. Nothing.*

Wu Kung darted forward. *The ones with their projectile and energy weapons first*. A spinning strike with Ruyi Jingu Bang and the first dropped his weapon, staggering with a broken wrist hanging limply; the second was bringing up his gun but he was aiming at the wrong place as Wu's leap brought him entirely above the Blessed soldier, and a single blow laid him out, even as Wu Kung's feet scissored out and hammered two more Blessed to the deck. The fifth and last soldier froze in disbelief as Wu landed behind him—and then fell with a single strike to the back of the head.

He turned and glared at the remainder. *Sethrik... no, he is wearing binders too! So... a betrayal.* He strode towards Vantak.

Vantak dropped into guard, stinging tail raised. Wu evaluated stance, shift in movement, eyes, scent. *He is much more dangerous than his guards. Ah. He was made to replace Sethrik, who was made to replace Orphan! So, he will be like Orphan!*

Which made him formidable, but . . . *I've fought* much *worse.*

He leapt forward, caught the stinging tail with his hand, parried strikes with hand and foot with his one hand for several seconds (meanwhile using his own tail to down the last crewman who tried to sneak up behind him). As Vantak paused in frustrated incredulity, he punched.

Vantak flew backwards and smashed into the wall, so hard that part of his right-hand crest shattered. "You *kidnapped* my friend."

The Blessed's tail lashed out, a striking snake, but Wu Kung was the mongoose, and his hand the mouth, striking and leaving the serpent harmless. Wu yanked *hard* and pulled Vantak from the deck, spun him around, smashed down. "You *betrayed* your leader!" He reached down and lifted Vantak effortlessly from the deck, holding the other's hundred-plus kilograms aloft like a rag doll. "And you *threw* me into space, so far I could have taken half an age to finish falling!"

Vantak tried to struggle, but quickly realized he was simply outclassed. The battered body still managed a disdainful pose. "I betrayed *nothing.* I was given my orders and my position by the Minds."

Wu shrugged. "You pretended he was the leader, then, and betrayed him as one of your people. I know nothing of your 'Minds.' But for what you tried to do to Ariane . . . I cannot forgive you."

"What do I care for your forgiveness?" Vantak said. "There are hundreds of Blessed on this ship—"

Wu spun and threw Vantak, who gave a shriek of disbelieving fury as he hurtled out the hole Wu had created and was lost in the still-speeding wind. "One less now, anyway!" Wu shouted after him. "Ha! Let us see how *you* like it!"

He leaned out the shattered window and gave a long, shrieking call. One of the *tzchina* flew up. "It's okay, you people did your job! Tell everyone they can go and thank them, especially the Mouth of the Sky! And I'll make sure to remember you all, don't worry—I will pay the debt!"

It flickered its understanding and streaked off.

He turned around, to see Ariane staring at him incredulously. "Wu . . . you didn't . . . did you . . . How could you possibly have done that?"

Oops. And in front of Sethrik, too. He winced at the thought of what DuQuesne would say. *But it's a busy time, maybe I can dodge.* "Later, Ariane, please! There are many others on this ship and we don't want them shooting our friends, do we?"

He could tell from her narrowed gaze that it was not, really, a very successful dodge at all. But she sighed, and said "No, we don't. Can you find . . . Damn." She looked out the broken window. "You threw Vantak out and I think he had the release for these binders."

"Oh, that. Hold on." The binders were made of tough stuff, but he could nick them with his claws and that gave him a weak spot to attack and break in a couple of minutes. "Should I let him go?" he nodded at Sethrik.

"He wasn't involved, Wu. And if we're going to do anything, I'll need his help."

"Okay!" It only took a moment to release the Blessed

Leader from his bonds. "So, I'm going to take care of the rest of them."

Sethrik stepped forward, pose showing his incredulity, then dropped to the floor in a full pushup-bow. "I . . . do not understand what I have just seen, Sun Wu Kung," he said, "but I thank you for it just the same." He rose. "Ariane Austin, I should go with him—"

"You would get in my way," Wu said, trying not to sound rude. "This is the control room, yes? I am sure there must be something you can do from here."

Sethrik paused. "Captain Austin? Do you . . . is he serious?"

She was looking at him with another slow smile dawning. "Sethrik, are your people more dangerous to fight than the Molothos?"

"No," Sethrik said without hesitation.

"Then remember this: two of my people wiped out an entire Molothos scouting party, and Wu's more dangerous than either of them. Let him do his job." The smile became momentarily dazzling. "Because he just showed me how *stubborn* he is about finishing it!"

He laughed joyously. "That I am! Stubborn and loud and rude and full of more life than all in Heaven, and proud of it!" Wu bowed low. "And now for a sea of enemies and heads to break!"

He opened the door, and two Blessed soldiers were already there, in the lift that served the control room. But they had not really expected him, and two lightning-fast blows laid them out. *I try not to kill, when I can avoid it. Sanzo never liked it, and I'm sure Ariane doesn't want me to kill, either. But I may not be able to be so gentle all the time.*

"If you are not foolishly trusting in your machines,"

he said over his shoulder, "Then there will be ways up here that do not use this elevator. Block them off, or you will have visitors."

He let the door slide shut and pushed the first button. *I have no idea how this ship is laid out, but anywhere I go will have enemies, so I will just start at the top and work my way down!*

The door slid open, and he was staring into the faces of a dozen—no, three dozen, maybe four— Blessed. All were armed, wearing extra armor, and they immediately came on guard. "Who are you? Stay where you are!"

"I am Sun Wu Kung, Great Sage Equal of Heaven," he said proudly. "And who are *you*, to give me orders?"

He could sense the buzzing mutter and even understand it. Most of it wasn't complimentary. *Human, I think. Arrogant. Maybe insane—did that introduction even make sense? No answer from command center. Obviously an enemy. Take the posturing one prisoner if you can, kill him otherwise.* The words were all in a flow, coming from different Blessed but at the same time almost part of the creatures' thoughts, as though their minds were somehow one.

Many of them lifted their weapons and sighted on him. "Get on the floor. We do not wish to kill you, but we will if you put up any resistance."

He laughed. "Oh! I have heard that song many times before, and yet I am still here!"

With a single bound, he was up, clearing the doorway of the lift and rising nearly to the three-meter ceiling above, their initial startled volley blazing by underneath him. By the time they realized what had happened, he was landing among them, kicking, smashing, punching. Bodies flew away with every movement. *Gentle! Gentle! Maybe we don't have to kill them. And I shouldn't reveal everything I can do.*

He realized they were drawing away from him now, and the posture of their bodies, their scent, told him they had realized they were up against something terrible, something unknown and fearsome. Orders were being shouted, groups that charged him were clearly doing their best to slow him, as barricades were thrown up across the hallways leading from this room. Bullets screamed through the air, now from multiple directions. Energy bolts stabbed, slashed. More came against him—two, four, a dozen, and there were *still* dozens to take their place.

The Blessed were no longer confused, no longer doubtful or uncertain. They knew he was a deadly threat, and they were *treating* him that way. A burning bullet seared its way along his bare arm, and it *stung*. The Blessed were coordinating. They were *thinking*.

This isn't going to be easy at all.

The thought was such a joyful one that he began to laugh.

CHAPTER 38

Simon ran along the corridors of *Zounin-Ginjou*. *Why . . . am I doing this?*

Even as he asked, he felt the uncertainty melting away, and understood. *The stress of the battle, the danger to Ariane and DuQuesne and, I suppose, myself . . . that strange clarity is returning.*

He knew, even before he rounded the corner, that the bulkhead door ahead of him would be closed, could visualize the extent of damage to *Zounin-Ginjou* beyond. *But there is another route. And if I get there, I can remove the damaged section, and use a piece of the control cabling from the disabled secondary turret to splice.*

Simon could *envision* the entire turret in his mind, even though it was terribly complex, a mechanical and electronic marvel with thousands of components. He felt a rising exhilaration, a feeling that there was nothing beyond this vision of reality . . . and a mounting fear of what that exhilaration could mean.

He pushed back against both feelings, and felt relief as they both receded. *I . . . am still master of my own mind, even if it is . . . changed. I cannot afford panic or overconfidence. DuQuesne and Orphan—and Ariane—are counting on me.*

A transmission from the command deck reached him, and he saw a cloud darkening, and then a nightmare blasting forth from the depths of the shadow, a thing so huge and terrible that he was momentarily stunned, stumbling even as he ran down the corridor. "My *God*, Marc, Orphan, what *is* that?"

"*Morfalzeen*," Orphan said, even his voice not free of awe. "One of the largest predators in the Arena. As it is nearer the Blessed, this seems fortunate for us . . . but what are all those other creatures *with* it? I do not under-"

DuQuesne began to chuckle, and the chuckle built up, rumbling, louder, echoing, a laugh of victory and vindication that still somehow gave Simon a momentary case of the creeps. *I think . . . I think I'm hearing the original Marc C. DuQuesne there.*

Wind tore at Simon as he entered the breached compartment, but the gravity was still active, and he could manage to walk. *Maintenance tools . . . there. Sufficient. Cable linkage already exposed by explosion, just need a clean section to splice, about two meters long . . .* "Marc, what is so—"

"Don't ask," Marc said, his voice filled with a fierce exaltation, "but take my word for it—these guys are on *our* side. Orphan—"

"Doctor DuQuesne, I have accustomed myself to not understanding you, so I will simply accept what you say. Let us continue the battle."

Odd. Orphan sounds . . . almost vindicated.

He cut the section of cable free, seeing the sparkling

of innumerable optic-cable ends. *Junction splices . . .
over here.*

Zounin-Ginjou made a sudden turn, but Simon
found he had already grabbed a support without
thinking. *Creepy, as Ariane often has said.* "Orphan,"
he said, feeling the ship begin a steep climb in what
he thought was the general direction of *Thilomon*, "I
know we are busy, but . . . you do not seem terribly
surprised by this turn of events."

"In a way, I am very surprised, Doctor Sandrisson,"
Orphan answered. "At the same time . . . I have become
quite *used* to being surprised by your people. To the
point I do, in fact, expect it."

"Ha!" came DuQuesne's voice. "Got another one!
Orphan, what are you being so blasted mysterious
about?"

"Let us just say I believe I have confirmed a hypothesis, and that this is *most* in your favor."

Simon inserted the second junction splice, put the
second end of the cable section in and locked it down.
"There! Orphan—"

"Excellent work! Control linkages fully active!"

A concussion rocked *Zounin-Ginjou*.

"Not for long if we keep getting hit," DuQuesne
growled. "The *morfalzeen* and its friends are leaving,
and while that gave us some breathing room, we're
still bad, bad outnumbered and outgunned. Simon,
you'd better get back up here—"

Another image came to Simon's mind—the third
main battery, the storage areas nearby, and he suddenly had an inspiration. "No. No, I have an idea,
Marc. Just . . . stop using the third main turret for a
bit, and don't get us killed immediately, all right?"

Marc was silent for a moment; he could hear the echoing rattle and whining screech of weapons fire. "You got it, Simon. I hope you know what you're doing."

"So do I."

I . . . think I know what I'm doing. Yet a part of me doesn't understand at all. Was Ariane right? Am I simply hooked into the data of the Arena?

The storage room was large, with a Liberated equivalent of a forklift. *Replacements for the focused energy cannon are over here. I need . . . all right, there's a total of eight. Maybe that will be enough.*

Simon found a set of grips that looked somewhat like the long pincerlike claws that he'd seen in documentaries about logging. *These should work.*

The grips clasped the tubelike assemblies perfectly. Simon was surprised to find they seemed relatively light. *I was sure they had a higher heavy metal content than that, but I'm not going to complain. It will make the remainder of the plan that much easier.* He felt a rising confidence return, and this time allowed it more rein. *Might as well; no reason to undermine myself.*

Pulling all eight was a bit of an effort, even with the forkliftlike device, but he dragged them across as quickly as he could, nearly tripping on the scabbard of his sword. *I may have gotten used to wearing it, but there are still some times it is* extremely *inconvenient.* Simon unfastened the scabbard from his belt and hung it on one of the main turret supports, clear of any of the rotational axes. *If this works, I'll be going back and forth between the forklift and this gun quite a few times.*

Zounin-Ginjou shuddered again, and he thought the lights flickered. *Have to do this fast, or there will be no point!*

The main control circuitry...*there. Have to cut out the amperage override and the voltage limiter in these areas.* He estimated the actual power connections. *There is a lot of margin in this, and the power comes from one of the local storage rings...* "Orphan, how are we doing on power?"

"Enslaving *monsters*, come around, into our sights!" he heard from Orphan, then, "Many pardons, Doctor. We are...still running, but I must hope this battle will end relatively soon. The second apex ring—for the third turret, where you are—is actually still near to full, however; that one has been fired less than the others."

"Good."

He completed cutting out the circuit protection. *Now, the controls must be reprogrammed...must make sure the circuits will handle the shift in parameters, especially for the containment field.* Simon frowned, looking at the overall design. *This may not survive for long. But...it won't have to.*

Even as another impact rocked the ship, he slammed the cover back down. "Marc, use the third turret. Make sure you don't miss."

"What have you done?" Even as DuQuesne asked, the huge turret began to rotate, and Simon ducked behind one of the baffles, covering his head with the armored labcoatlike outfit he always wore.

The world went white and Simon felt as though he'd been hit with a padded hammer the size of a rhino. His ears were ringing, and if he'd had to rely on hearing, nothing DuQuesne had to say would have registered. But through the link he could still hear "Holy great jumping—*got him!* Right through the main armor!"

The turret started to track again.

"No, no, wait, Marc! I have to replace the main projector lining and focal assembly! That single shot probably vaporized most of it!"

"You..." Suddenly Marc DuQuesne was laughing again. "You incredible son of a...you've just given me *primary beams*?"

"I...see," Orphan said, and there was an awed note in his voice. "Not something practical for most circumstances, given the potential hazards, but... ingenious. And it may just give us that edge, if we can destroy one ship per use. How many..."

"Eight more, I think, if this turret doesn't explode," Simon answered. He yanked down on the maintenance latch, and the remains of the assembly fell out, smoking, scorching the deck. *Great* kami, *the internal heat's going to burn me to a cinder.*

But the internal coolant systems were still operating, and the brilliant white glow swiftly faded, down to a point that he could manhandle the new assembly into place and pull the lever to relock the barrel shut. He dove for his shelter. "Now, Marc!"

"Need better reload times on this," Marc said absently. The turret began to track.

"Need better *equipment*," he retorted. "I'm doing this by hand, and—"

Concussion and light robbed him momentarily of breath and thought. "...and it takes time to cool down to the point I can get *near* it. Even with near-superconductors of heat and a lot of coolant."

He dumped the other seven assemblies on the floor, ejected the now-spent second assembly, and used the forklift to shove the expended components to the other side of the room. *They've actually melted or vaporized part of the deck. The heat's...incredible.*

Third assembly in and locked, and Simon felt the strain of effort starting to tell. *They get much heavier the more often I do this.*

This time he heard a cheer from both Orphan *and* DuQuesne even before the gun fired. "What is it?"

"*Ariane!*" DuQuesne said exultantly. "Got to be! *Thilomon* just started firing on her own fleet!"

"How in the world could she possibly be in control of a warship on her own?" Simon muttered.

Orphan's voice was suddenly grave. "Doctor Sandrisson, you are still in the third turret?"

"Yes, of course."

"Then we may have a problem. While security and monitoring are currently severely compromised, I have registered the opening and closing of two doors near your location, along the corridors you traversed previously."

"*What?*" Simon heard DuQuesne echo the shout. "No one could have possibly—"

The door to the turret room slid open, and Simon stared with shocked incredulity.

Breathing so hard the air whistled from his spiracles, battered, scorched, one crest broken, Vantak of the Blessed to Serve glowered at him through the sights of an unfamiliar, but undoubtedly lethal, pistol.

CHAPTER 39

Everything froze for Simon. He could see the sights steady, the hand tightening on the weapon, and knew that he had no chance to dodge, even the preternatural quickness that his strange Arena-born knowledge and perceptions only giving him enough time to know clearly that he was going to die.

There was a blaze of light and thunder that hammered him and Simon wondered that things still *hurt* after death. Then he opened his eyes, scrambling to his feet, feeling the tight, insistent pain of burns across one side of his face, smelling burned hair, and understanding that he now had a single, momentary chance.

DuQuesne had fired. Whether because he'd simply acquired a target, or because he'd somehow guessed that Simon could use a sledgehammer of distraction, Simon didn't know, but it had knocked Vantak almost out of the room and made the Blessed warrior drop his pistol. Simon leapt to the other side of the turret supports, felt the warm but not quite burning hilt of his sword and yanked it free.

Vantak had begun a charge, but came up short when he saw the long, sharp blade in Simon's hand.

"Fortune seems to spare you," he said finally, backing away.

Oh, no you don't! He knew it was risky, but he could *feel* that nigh-omniscience in his head, *see* exactly the course Vantak would take, and he dove forward, rolled—*God, that* hurts, *my shoulders and neck must be terribly burned*—and *jabbed.*

He came to his feet, Vantak's pistol now dangling from the tip of his rapier; as the Blessed hesitated, Simon flicked the pistol up and out, to land with a clatter among the expended assemblies. *They're still terribly hot; I don't think even a Blessed wants to go anywhere in that collection of half-melted scrap.*

"How did you get on *board*?" he asked, shifting his position, trying to get an angle—and to work his way back to the gun emplacement. *If I can hit the maintenance lever...*

Vantak buzzed. "After I was thrown out by that... pet monster of yours, I was able to use my wings to shift my course; when *Zounin-Ginjou* took the high approach it came close enough to land on."

Simon could hear his pulse hammering in his ears. *Vantak must be close to Orphan in skill. Even with this sword I think I'm terribly outmatched. He's watching, trying to judge when I make myself vulnerable—*

A green and black blur streaked towards him, ducking down and under. Somehow, Simon turned, shifted his weight, following that strange instinct, lessening the impact but still sending him skidding over the deck. He barely kept his grip on the sword.

To his surprise, Vantak hit the maintenance lever and leapt aside to avoid the falling, burned out assembly. *What is he up to?*

"Simon! *Simon!*" he heard DuQuesne's voice. "Dammit, what's going on?"

"I have a problem called Vantak, Marc."

"By the *Minds!*" Orphan said. "Vantak, *here?*"

Marc swore. "I'd come down there, but I can't afford to stop shooting now, Simon. I—"

Vantak reached up, still watching Simon, and touched other controls. *Shimatta. He's put the turret into local control. But what*...

As Vantak glanced over at the next assembly, it was suddenly clear. On manual control, Vantak could deliberately fire the gun with the assembly misaligned— quite possibly taking *Zounin-Ginjou* with it, and even if not, dealing a *lot* of damage to the Liberated warship. *He doesn't expect to live. He just wants to make sure we go with him!*

Simon took advantage of Vantak's flickered gaze to the side and lunged. The point of his rapier scraped along the Blessed's abdomen, leaving a narrow cut and forcing Vantak to jump back.

But the damage was only superficial, and Vantak was now advancing on him with all-too-calm precision. *He is armored, and I have a single slender blade. It is obvious what the outcome will be.* "I know, Marc. I'll keep him as busy as I can, and reload if I get the chance."

DuQuesne was silent, and Simon knew why. Vantak was, quite simply, far out of Simon's league.

But maybe...

For the first time, Simon *focused* on that feeling of knowledge and certainty, and looked at Vantak.

In that moment, he saw the Blessed as though from all angles, impossibly envisioning him in every direction, and projecting possible actions. He could *see* the possibilities, as he had sometimes been able to envision time-space distortions when building the Sandrisson coils. But in those transcendent moments of design and theory, he had been deaf, blind, unaware of anything else around him, focused only on the understanding of the coils and their effects; now, his perceptions were heightened. He could feel the blistered tightness of his upper neck and shoulder that had been exposed to the flare of the last shot, perceive the tilt and vibration of the deck, register Vantak's tensing of muscles and preparation for movement. Possibilities narrowed, focused, and Simon *knew*.

He threw himself aside and cut outwards and down, and the ring-carbon-edged blade cut a deep gash in Vantak's right wingcase. Simon backpedaled, watching in what seemed slow-motion as Vantak sprang about, pivoting around his center of mass with literally inhuman speed.

He also remembered his prior actions, thought back, saw *those* probabilities rising, the vectors, chances, and understood the only possible way out of this. *I cannot dodge him forever. He is faster than me, he is vastly more skilled, and knowing what he is going to do a few tens of milliseconds before he does it will only go so far.*

This will all depend on timing. So very much on timing.

He dodged another lunge, seeing and parrying the tail strike that followed, dodging. *Must go farther towards that side.* Another attack, this one nearly going home, sending him staggering back. *But closer.*

Zounin-Ginjou jolted as though struck with a club,

and both combatants staggered. There was rattling behind him, and Simon could feel the radiating heat.

This time a wing-strike took him square in the chest, too fast to dodge; all he could do was curl and roll. But the roll took him into something as hot as an iron poker from a fire and he half-screamed, half-cursed, slashing out with his sword to keep Vantak at bay as he moved away from the expended assemblies. Vantak circled, obviously uncomfortable with the heat but somewhat more armored and resistant. Simon was trying not to limp or favor his side, but he could see that Vantak recognized his weakness, was preparing to risk taking the sword through him on a last charge—

And Simon saw probabilities spiking as he had hoped, and dropped flat to the deck.

There was a slamming, shattering detonation as though a lightning bolt had struck, and Vantak flew by him, tumbling like a puppet with cut strings until coming to a halt, while flaming debris showered all around Simon, some of it burning like pins of flame into his face.

The Blessed twitched, tried to rise, but there was a metal support embedded more than halfway through his back. "Wh...what...?"

"Your pistol," Simon said, painfully getting to his feet and retrieving his sword. "I...had thrown it into the wreckage. I remembered that it must be powered with superconductor batteries..."

Vantak buzzed weakly. "Minds...curse you."

He shoved himself upward, and for an instant Simon froze. *I can't fight him any more. I just don't have anything* left.

But something broke inside of Vantak; he gave a

buzzing cough, and collapsed. Another buzz, and a last, faint hum like a fly against a screen on a summer's day...and then he was still.

A sledgehammer blow rammed *Zounin-Ginjou* sideways, and Simon could hear alarms screaming throughout the ship. Marc was cursing, and so was Orphan in his own way.

Simon Sandrisson lunged painfully for the remaining assemblies. *I can't be too late! I can't!*

➤ CHAPTER 40 ◄

Wu Kung's parting words made all too much sense to Ariane. "Sethrik—"

"Yes, there are such accesses."

"Can we lock them down physically?"

Sethrik went to a panel off to one side of the control center. "I . . . believe so. They are meant to be opened from either side, but using the same mechanism."

"Is there another one on this side?"

"Yes. Look for a small circular area—it will probably appear to be slightly lighter in color to you—on the left-hand side of the third panel."

"Found it."

Sethrik tapped the circle with three fingers simultaneously, and it opened out into a half-moon-shaped handle; after a few tries she duplicated the action. "Now what? Is there a lock?"

"Yes. I have to hope that they have not gone through the entire ship and removed my authorization; after all, they intended to imprison me temporarily and then return me to duty; it would be an annoyance to do that to all ship systems." He humm-buzzed something and placed his hand beneath the handle.

With a whirr and click, the handles rotated one hundred and eighty degrees and locked.

Whew. "They'll be able to cut through or blow up the panels eventually, of course."

"Naturally," said Sethrik, striding to the command perch. "But I believe this battle will be over one way or the other by then. Can you pilot *Thilomon*?"

Ariane went to the pilot's station, pushing the unfortunate Kandret's body out of the way and sitting down; the perch was something like sitting in a chair backwards, but she could handle that, and the safety harness automatically slid across her back. "Umm . . . maybe. This doesn't look much different from the layout of the controls on *Zounin-Ginjou*. Hmm. No tail controls?"

Sethrik chuckled. "The Survivor uses those, I have no doubt, because he needs to be as many people as possible. But in general, no, because our tails are not nearly so dextrous and are more used for combat and support than for controlling things."

I dunno, they seemed awfully dextrous when they were trying to sting me. But I'm not looking a gift equine in the dentition, so to speak. "What about armament?"

"I can control much of that from here. No telling how long that control will *last*, of course, so let us cross as many trees with this leap as we can."

"Make the most of it, as we say. Yep. Hold on!"

Thilomon turned quickly, a little raggedly as she came to understand how the turn mechanisms worked, but quickly, and she saw Blessed ships coming around in front of them, trying to regroup after the attack by Arenaspace lifeforms and press the attack on *Zounin-Ginjou*.

Even as the Liberated battleship swam into view, a spear of intolerable brilliance erupted from its upper turret, a bolt of energy so intense that it seemed to make the entire Arena around them dimmer; the beam ripped straight through one of the Blessed ships as though its armor were nonexistent, and the ship immediately and vehemently exploded.

"Great *Minds!*" Sethrik muttered. "What sort of a weapon is *that*, and why wasn't the Survivor using it earlier?"

"I dunno," she said cheerfully, feeling her confidence rising, "but let's focus on our own problems. Like our own *targets*."

Sethrik's overlay displays came up, showing armament-targeting displays; she couldn't quite *read* some of the symbols but could tell he was disabling something— *safety interlocks, I'll bet, to keep you from accidentally shooting your friends by mistake.*

The targeting symbols locked on a nearby vessel.

She waited, but nothing happened. She looked over her shoulder. "Sethrik?"

The Leader of the Blessed was sitting with his hand over a control; the hand trembled.

Damn.

"I . . . do not wish to do this," Sethrik said sadly. "Ariane Austin, can you understand how hard this is? I am of the *Blessed*. We are near to one, in many ways, and now I will turn our own weapons upon them. I am meant to *protect* them, not destroy."

"I know, Sethrik. Dammit, I know exactly what you mean. But if you *don't* fire—"

"Yes. I know. They will kill us. Or worse, far worse, for both you and I, even though I will not think it so when they have finished with me."

He inhaled deeply and buzzed something that

sounded like a prayer. "Minds forgive me, but I do what I believe. I do what I think is right. I do what I must."

His hand came down.

Instantly the forward batteries of *Thilomon* cut loose, firing energy and explosive shells into her sister ship barely twenty kilometers distant. The ship shuddered and then detonated in a flare that blanked the screens for a moment.

"Thank you, Sethrik. And I'm sorry, but . . ."

"But there is more work to be done. Let us finish it, then."

The other Blessed ships were thrown into disarray a second time now, as they tried to respond to an attack by their own flagship. *The hesitation will work in our favor too; attacking one of their own ships will be* hard.

Another eye-searing bolt of energy impaled a Blessed ship and it, too, disappeared in vapor before the power of *Zounin-Ginjou*. She cheered, came about even as the first tentative counterfire began. "Pick your target, Sethrik!"

"Hmm," Sethrik said. His hands were still shaking, and the involuntary occasional buzz showed how badly the stress was affecting him, even as he spoke in an artificially light and casual tone. "That's *Lahthindosan*. I admit to never liking its commander much at all."

On the edge of a breakdown or not, Sethrik's aim was deadly. *Thilomon's* assault shattered the aft section of his target, and while it did not explode, the ship immediately began drifting aimlessly, out of control.

For a third time that impossible beam of light turned the atmosphere of the Arena to plasma, and another Blessed vessel vanished. *That's . . . ten! More than half! We just might* win *this one!*

They came about, fired again, missed; the other Blessed vessels had now accepted that their flagship had become their enemy, and they were divided now into two-ship groups. At the same time she realized that *Zounin-Ginjou* was severely battered. The screen showed multiple gaping wounds on the ship. Though it was still clearly functioning—and functioning quite well—it was clear that there was not much left for Orphan's vessel to give.

And the mysterious weapon atop *Zounin-Ginjou* had stopped.

She could hear hammering on the access panels now, but tried to ignore it. *Have to do as much damage as we can!*

Sethrik found another target, tried to fire—but the forward turret failed to respond. "Roll hard to port!" he shouted.

And the Arena translates that as "port" rather than left. I don't think we'll EVER know how it makes its decisions. Even as she thought that she was rolling the ship, turning—

And the topside port cannon fired, crippling the target. "They shut down the forward batteries," Sethrik said. "I have no doubt they are doing the same to the others. We do not have much time left."

Thilomon rang like a bell, the impact so hard that Sethrik would have been thrown from the command perch if he had not been strapped in; Ariane felt her own harness creak. The lights flickered and then shifted to a dimmer light in a slightly different shade.

"Ah. No more time at all," said Sethrik. "A perfect shot, straight through the main power-distribution core. I suspect the crew has deliberately sabotaged the backups." A faint glow showed on one of the panels now. *Cutting torches.*

"Don't suppose you have a self-destruct or scuttling command?"

Sethrik flicked his hands out. "Except for very experimental ships such would be...unheard of."

She grabbed up one of the pistols from the unconscious guards, and Sethrik took up a rifle. "Then I guess we just have to go for suicide by military."

"Indeed." Sethrik gave her a deep pushup-bow. "It has been a true honor fighting alongside you, Ariane Austin of Humanity."

"And you, Sethrik of the—"

Light came that turned the clouds dark, paled the mighty lightning within them to insignificance, and another Blessed warship was gone. *Zounin-Ginjou* plowed through a wavering mist of smoke and wreckage, turning, seeking, and that intolerable, irresistable spear of energy impaled another, flaring up, gone. *That's five left against us!*

The other ships banked about, desperately aiming, trying to mass their fire upon Orphan's flagship, *Zounin-Ginjou* boring onwards, directly towards them, as though utterly uncaring of any hazard. The forward batteries of the Liberated battleship fired again, hammering into the armor of the Blessed to Serve, and another ship was done, gone, drifting and powerless. Again that coruscating, dazzling sword tore through Arenaspace, and one more was finished, a drifting memory in smoke and flame.

Sethrik stared at something on the command chair, reached up and activated it.

"*Thilomon*, this is Doctor Marc C. DuQuesne of

Humanity, calling from *Zounin-Ginjou*," came a deep, savagely triumphant voice. "You are drifting crippled, and if you'll look your last three ships are trying to flee. Surrender and prepare to be boarded."

Sethrik buzzed with amusement, and clicked the control again. "This is Sethrik, Leader of the Faction of the Blessed—for now, and only temporarily, I am afraid. But I am glad to hear this. Do not allow them to escape. No mercy. No quarter. Is this understood?"

Orphan's voice replied, and held an odd mixture of satisfaction and regret. "Completely, Sethrik. Is Ariane Austin—"

"I'm here!" she called. "But do we have to..."

She stopped herself and thought. *If any of them escape, the Minds will know* exactly *what happened here. Maybe they'll even figure out what's going on with Wu Kung. They can't know. They* cannot *ever know exactly how close they came to success, or how much luck played a part in this.* "...sorry. Do what you have to."

She turned to where the panel lock was now glowing near white. "We're about to have company anyway."

She and Sethrik checked to make sure there wasn't anything coming through the other panel—it was cool and dark—and took shelter behind the command perch. On the screen they could see *Zounin-Ginjou* in pursuit of the final three Blessed vessels. *Good luck*, she thought. Then she steadied her arm and took careful aim.

The panel dropped with a heavy *clang*, and she saw two Blessed, rifles dropping into line just behind the panel. Her first shot struck, but the Blessed were wearing armor and it did no damage. Sethrik's shot was more effective—*not surprising; I should have taken a rifle, but I'm better with handguns. Wish I could've gotten to my own weapons.*

The two leapt into the command center; the one wounded by Sethrik ducked behind one of the control perches, while the other laid down a barrage of fire which ensured both Ariane and Sethrik kept their heads down. More movement told her that there were reinforcements coming.

She popped up, snapped off a shot, dropped back down. *Got to get in the right mindframe. Outnumbered, but they still have to come in through a choke point. Shame there weren't any grenades.*

Sethrik fired twice, scoring a hit that took down the wounded one for good, then dropping back with a curse; there was a nasty-looking burn along his left arm.

She stuck her head around on the other side and fired; this time she caught the unwounded one just as he stuck *his* head out. *If that didn't kill him, he's sure hurt.*

More shapes were coming up . . . but then they stopped.

What's happening?

She heard some kind of commotion, shouts, buzzing cries, gunshots, and the sound of impacts so fast they seemed almost like machine-gun fire.

Without warning, two bodies *hurtled* from the opening, tumbling limply to a halt. A single shadowy figure moved forward. She sighted, daring to hope that she wouldn't *want* to fire . . .

The Monkey King stepped into the command center and waved. "I see you kept busy until I came back!"

CHAPTER 41

"How is Simon?"

DuQuesne grimaced; after the battle, he'd found Simon unconscious in the third turret. "Alive. He'll heal, we just need to get him home so he can have some proper care and support or it will take his medical nanos *ages*. What he did was insane, except like the rest of us he didn't have much choice."

"What was wrong with him?" Ariane was, somewhat to his surprise (and considerable gratification), mostly keeping a professional tone to her questions. *She must have gone through a lot, but there's something a little...changed about her. I hope in a good way.*

"Honestly? I haven't got one goddamn clue as to why he didn't collapse long before we finished. That idea of his was damned brilliant—and went through I have *no* idea how many vals' worth of Orphan's equipment in that time—but I don't think he understood just how deadly it was going to be in that turret. Even with the best designs in the universe—and Orphan's got some of the best, believe you me—the overpressure, heat, light...he might as well have been detonating shock grenades next to himself. And he somehow took on *Vantak* by himself."

"Wait, what? *Vantak*? He was *here*?" Wu Kung laughed. "I am glad! A poetic symmetry!"

Orphan came into the control room, hearing the last lines. "Most certainly," Orphan said. "You took his ship, he decided to take mine if he could."

"Next time, Wu, remember that the Blessed have *wings*. Sure, he couldn't directly match our speed, but apparently he was able to guide himself in the right direction and catch us as we went by."

Ariane transferred her gaze to Sethrik, who was seated before an auxiliary panel of *Zounin-Ginjou*. "Are we recharged?"

The Leader of the Blessed did not answer immediately; he seemed sunk in gloom, and DuQuesne remembered that for the first hour after rescue he had practically curled up in a corner, unresponsive. After a moment, however, Sethrik managed a small bob of assent. "I . . . yes, Captain Austin. We have transferred virtually all power from the remains of *Thilomon* to *Zounin-Ginjou*. The Blessed survivors have also been locked into specific areas of the vessel."

"Are we able to return home now?"

Orphan's bow was more emphatic. "Beyond any doubt. *Thilomon* had participated relatively little in the battle directly, and thus retained a quite considerable charge. We have in fact nearly fully recharged *Zounin-Ginjou*." He strode to the main console and seated himself. "Now we shall cast off and complete the final stage." Sethrik's hands twitched, and his wingcases tightened as he turned away.

"What final stage?"

Orphan's head tilted, even as she heard the cables linking *Zounin-Ginjou* and *Thilomon* beginning to release. "The destruction of *Thilomon*, of course. All the other ships have been completely destroyed, and there are no survivors. These are the last, and—"

"Absolutely *not*."

DuQuesne wasn't surprised. The idea of shooting an unarmed, depowered sitting duck of a target containing a few hundred people stuck in his craw too—and he had no doubt Simon would never agree to it if he was conscious. Orphan had already done that—in the mop-up of the battle—and it had taken a lot of his self-control to keep from saying anything, even though it *was* Orphan's ship and Orphan's choice. Wu Kung looked conflicted.

To his surprise, though, it was Sethrik who rose slowly to face Ariane. "You agreed with—or did not contradict—my order to destroy the other vessels, Captain. I thought you understood." His voice was unsteady, and DuQuesne guessed that the conflict within the Blessed Leader was even greater than he had thought. *How hard must it be to have a sort of near-hive mind, and the unity the Minds give you, and then* turn *on that unity?*

But Sethrik continued. "You had told me that you felt you had failed, that this was your fault. Are you going to now continue the mistakes that you have made?"

Ariane folded her arms over her chest. "I did say that. And it was true, then. We were still in a battle, you had to stop the others from fleeing, and there wasn't anything I could have done about it one way or the other. But this...I'm sorry. I can't just stand here and allow hundreds of people to be killed just for the sake of political convenience and safety. We have to at least *try* to find another solution."

She turned to DuQuesne. "Marc, why can't we just leave them here? They won't starve or suffocate, not drifting here in the Arena, but without power they're going nowhere. There's no one to tell."

He shook his head, even as Orphan's hands flicked outward. "You're forgetting, Ariané; this is one of the major routes—most direct routes—from the Blessed's homeworld to Nexus Arena. There's probably Blessed vessels coming through here every couple of days. If *Thilomon* and her escorts don't show up on time, they'll just send out a party to search the area. They won't get much out of the rest of the wreckage, but you can bet your bottom dollar they'd find *Thilomon* if we left it here."

Ariane's jaw tightened, then she sighed. "Yes, I guess they would. But there *has* to be an alternative."

"Why does there *have* to be one, Captain Austin?" Sethrik asked quietly. "Often the universe does not give us choices."

DuQuesne's mind agreed with Sethrik...but not his gut. And he knew which one he had to go with. "Because that's not the way she works. Maybe when the guns are shooting and you're under that kind of pressure, yeah, maybe then you have to make the choice of the greater evil versus the lesser one. But when you've got time, you haven't got the excuse of desperation. That's when you find a new choice... or *make* one."

Sethrik and Orphan clearly did not entirely agree, but they did look thoughtful.

For several minutes no one said anything. Then Ariane looked out the viewport and pointed. "Well, we were—partly still are—connected to her. Can't we tow her somewhere far enough that they *won't* find her?"

"Alas, Captain Austin, to do that in this region—which as you might expect is mapped fairly extensively by the Blessed—would require us to travel a very long distance through Arenaspace. Not only would that potentially lead to us getting lost, but also it would take a considerable time and portion of our energy reserves, and to leave we would have to come back to the known Sky Gates . . . and with Blessed traffic there would be an excellent chance we would find ourselves once more in a battle before escaping."

Wu Kung spoke up. "Couldn't we just drag *Thilomon* along with us through the Sky Gates somehow? No, wait . . . we'd just end up bringing them to Nexus Arena, and we don't want that, do we?"

"It would not work in any case, Sun Wu Kung," Orphan said. "Remember that the use of the Sky Gates is through the Sandrisson Drive, which must be specifically configured for the vessel, which must have active Sandrisson coils surrounding it. To jump with *Thilomon* in tow would most likely simply sever our connection with *Thilomon* and might have other less . . . entertaining effects."

Another silence.

"How many survivors are there, exactly?" asked Ariane.

"Three hundred eleven," Sethrik answered promptly. "Wu Kung . . . was surprisingly nonlethal. I appreciate the effort you went to in sparing their lives, and I must express my gratitude to you, Captain Austin, that you are attempting to find some solution which will not throw their lives away again."

"Could you fit that many in your cargo bays, Orphan?"

Orphan went rigid for a moment. "I . . . in theory . . . yes, I suppose. *Zounin-Ginjou* is intended to carry a great deal of cargo on occasion. But you cannot be seriously thinking of bringing over three hundred Blessed and trying to keep them imprisoned?"

DuQuesne saw that Ariane was still wrestling with the next step, but he had a sudden inspiration. "Not imprison. Transfer. You've been around a *long* time, Orphan. You've got to have found other Spheres on occasion, ones that aren't active—no native race. Maybe even marked 'em down for colonization if you ever got more members of the Liberated."

Orphan bobbed a slow agreement. "I . . . believe I see your course, Doctor. If we can securely carry them aboard *Zounin-Ginjou* for a few days, we could transfer them to a location I know, and the Blessed do not, and leave them there. Without a ship, it could take them years, even centuries, to find a way off. It would be . . . a life sentence of exile, but need not be murder."

"Would you be willing to take that risk?" Ariane asked. "I realized while we were thinking that I can't give orders at all here. This is your ship, not mine. I'm sorry."

Orphan laughed. "Apology accepted, Captain Austin. And in truth . . ." He looked at Sethrik, then out at the wreck of *Thilomon*. ". . . in truth, Captain, Sethrik, I can still well remember my days as one of the Blessed. Those are my people as well, Sethrik. I think you now understand fully what drove me to where I am."

"I do," Sethrik said quietly.

"Then you understand my hostility is' towards the Minds, and towards the Blessed when they act against myself and my friends. Not towards our people as individuals." He turned back to Ariane, and DuQuesne could see her smile of gratitude as Orphan said, "So yes, Captain Austin, I am very willing to take that risk, if we can find a reasonable manner of bringing them aboard without unleashing them upon *Zounin-Ginjou*."

"Do they have a radio? Something I could use to speak with them?"

Sethrik tilted his head, then gave a brisk wing-snap; the effort to rescue his former crew seemed to be bringing him back to himself. "I believe they should." He went to another panel, made some adjustments. "That should be attuned properly now."

"Hold on." She thought. "Orphan, if you have a destination in mind, how long would it take from now until drop-off to get them there?"

"Hmm." Orphan bent over his console. "Taking into account the need to recharge at one of my... reserves, I would say five and a half days. Perhaps slightly less. I assume that you would all remain with me to assist."

"Yes, of course." She looked over to Marc. "How much space would they need, at a minimum?"

"For most of a week? Well, I get the impression they can probably handle close quarters together better than a random set of humans. Give 'em two square meters apiece, that's six hundred twenty-two square meters. Double it for space to move around in, sanitary facilities, so on, say twelve hundred fifty square meters." He glanced at Orphan. "What's the dimensions of your largest cargo bay?"

"One hundred twelve by forty-two by twenty-three meters," Orphan answered promptly. "More than enough space. But it is not terribly secure."

"I wasn't thinking of just using the bay," Marc said, grinning. "Look. Sethrik, you know the layout of *Thilomon*. Is there a place we could gather everyone together that would have enough space, and maybe sanitary facilities that'd work for a week for that many people?"

Sethrik stared at him, and then suddenly gave a buzzing laugh as he understood. "You mean to carve out that part of *Thilomon* as a sort of cargo container and prison. Yes, I believe so. The troop quarters in the central section—they will be somewhat crowded in there, but if you take a three-floor section . . . yes, that would fit in the cargo bay and provide everything they need. If you are careful, you could even give them a low-power connection to keep vital systems working."

"Power engineering's my speciality. I'm sure we could." He grinned at Ariane. "I think we've got your solution—if they'll go for it."

"Then let's find out." Ariane nodded to Orphan to activate the transmitter. "*Thilomon*, this is Captain Ariane Austin of Humanity. Please respond."

A few moments later the screen lit with a dim but recognizable image of an injured Blessed. "This is Acting-Guidemaster Hancray. Speak."

"Hancray? Good, I'm glad Wu Kung's entrance didn't kill you," she said, smiling. Then her face went grimly serious, and DuQuesne saw how she drew herself up. *By God, I think she's finally getting it.* "Guidemaster Hancray, I trust you understand your position. Your entire fleet has been wiped out, nothing but wreckage to be found. My bodyguard, whom you thought killed, has been much more merciful with you; a large proportion of your crew are still alive.

"Given the circumstances, I have every reason to wish no word of this to ever reach the Minds. They will realize their brilliant strategem failed utterly, but will learn nothing at all beyond that. The simplest way to assure that this happens is to finish what we began: wipe you out. I also trust you realize that even damaged as she is, *Zounin-Ginjou* can effectively *vaporize* your ship."

"I do. What is your counterproposal? You would not bother to call had you nothing else to offer." Despite his direct manner, DuQuesne could read his body language. Hancray was afraid. *Junior officer, helmsman or something, suddenly in command of a derelict vessel. He watched it all come apart and almost got killed, and now he's facing Ariane all by himself.*

"I would very much rather *not* kill you," she said. "So here's the proposal. All of you will retreat to the troop quarters in the central section of *Thilomon*. That section—three levels of it—will be removed and brought into *Zounin-Ginjou*. We will then transport you to an Upper Sphere location where you can survive, and leave you there."

"Death or permanent exile, then."

"In her position," DuQuesne interjected, "what would *you* be offering? I think she's being damn generous with you."

Hancray was silent a moment. "I . . . must confer with my people."

"I'm giving you exactly five minutes. The longer we wait, the more danger I'm exposing us to. Confer quickly."

Orphan looked at her as she cut the transmission. "And if they delay...?"

Her lips tightened. "Then we...no, *I*...will blow them out of the sky. I don't want to. I hope they take this offer. But I'm through ignoring my responsibilities. I have to let us get back and deal with the *real* problem."

"Heart of gold and still hard as nails," a weak voice came from behind them. "I approve."

"*Simon!*" Ariane went to help him to a chair.

"What the *hell* are you doing out of bed, Simon?" DuQuesne demanded.

"Couldn't...just stay in bed when you might need me," he said; the face was pale under the reddened burns and bruises.

Ariane was staring at Simon's injuries, aghast. "God, Simon. I'm so sorry."

"Hardly *your* fault."

"Yes. Yes it is, Simon. But I won't let it happen again."

He raised an eyebrow, then shrugged painfully. "If you insist on taking the blame, I haven't the energy to argue with you. And who knows, perhaps you're right. But in that case, apology accepted, it's all forgotten."

In a few more minutes, Ariane snapped on the transmitter. "Guidemaster Hancray, do you have an answer for me?"

Hancray immediately appeared. He looked slightly more bedraggled than before, as though despite his injuries he had still gotten in some sort of altercation. "Yes, Captain Austin. After...some quick and heated discussion, I have convinced the others to accept your offer."

She stood rigid and unbending, but DuQuesne knew Ariane very, very well, and he could see the slight shift of her feet, hear the tiny catch in her breath, that showed her great relief. "We will offer no resistance. I will notify you when we are all in the designated quarters. This will take no longer than ten minutes."

"Acceptable, Guidemaster. I will await your transmission." She turned to Orphan and Sethrik as the picture faded. "Are we *sure* there are no weapons they can be preparing for use against us?"

"The ship has effectively no power. The only energy available will be in portable devices," Orphan answered after a moment. "If they assembled a large number of such—say, rifles, pistols, and so on—they could make a fairly powerful bomb. But they would have to get it outside of *Thilomon* and onto our hull. Once we have brought them into the cargo bay, it will be quite easy to monitor for any movement. If they attempt to open any door, leave by any route, we simply drop them out into Arenaspace and fire."

Sethrik bobbed his agreement. "The larger explosive warheads . . . those could pose a problem. But again, they must be maneuvered into place."

"Hmm. But one of *those* could still do damage to *Zounin-Ginjou* even from within the salvaged piece we bring on board."

"Possibly," Sethrik answered, and gave an almost cheery wing-snap. "But we do have the last data download from her command structure following the battle. Before transferring them we can hook back in and just check the readiness systems to see if any of the major weapons have been moved or tampered with since."

"Good enough, then," Orphan agreed.

The communications panel beeped. "Captain Austin, we are now secure."

"Thank you, Guidemaster. Now I must caution you again that there must be no resistance. We will also be checking to determine if any large weapons, such as missile warheads, are not in their proper locations. If any such are found to be unaccounted for, I will have the entire ship destroyed. Is that understood?"

A pause. "Understood." Hancray's voice was tense.

"Do you require a few moments to verify that all such weapons are accounted for?"

Relief was evident in his reply. "I would greatly appreciate it."

"As you called back within five minutes, I will give you the additional five I had already granted you. Starting now."

DuQuesne grinned. *From Hancray's tone, I'll bet he'd just found out some loyalist group had brought on a big bomb without telling him. Now he's got the motivation to get the thing off his ship. Maybe they'll get out of this alive after all.*

A few minutes later, Hancray reported that he was certain everything was in order. Orphan and Sethrik verified this with a temporary low-power reboot of *Thilomon's* main operational system.

Simon, meanwhile, had somehow brought up a diagram of the interior structure of *Thilomon*. "Here, Orphan. If you use your energy beams along these lines, you should be able to safely cut it out of the surrounding ship. It should then be easy to drag on board."

"Truly, Doctor Sandrisson, you astonish me. Yet

your information appears quite accurate, if I am to judge by Sethrik's expression."

"*Quite* accurate," Sethrik confirmed.

"Brace yourselves, Guidemaster Hancray. We are about to cut you free."

Energy weapons from *Zounin-Ginjou*'s forward batteries struck out with surgical precision, cutting along four perfect geometric lines. A rectangular section of *Thilomon* slowly floated free, and the top and bottom were also cut off by those irresistable beams of light. *Zounin-Ginjou* moved slowly in, caught each end of the now-tumbling wreckage with a manipulator, and drew the boxy assemblage into its cargo bay. "Blessed prisoners are now onboard," Orphan announced.

"Right," DuQuesne said, and grabbed up his toolbox. "C'mon, Wu. You'll keep an eye out while I hook 'em up to power to keep their lights on, air flowing, and toilets flushing. Once that's done, we can get the hell out of here!"

CHAPTER 42

"You clear on what you want us to do, Ariane?"

She could still feel the uncertainty boiling inside her. *Maybe it never goes away. Or at least I'd better hope it doesn't.* The last thing she *ever* wanted was to get used enough to commanding people that she stopped doubting that she was right.

But I still have to act *like I'm right.* "I think so."

She stood and faced the small group around the conference table on *Zounin-Ginjou*. *A very small group when you consider that in this room are people making decisions for three separate Factions.* "Sethrik, Orphan, you are technically equal in rank to me, so—"

"Please, Captain Austin," interrupted Sethrik. "We know the situation. This is a point of choice and honor for Humanity. Unless I think your course is insane, I am ready to follow you."

"And perhaps even if it *is* insane," Orphan put in with his usual ironic humor. "Given how often you humans make a habit of insanity."

She smiled at that. "All right. Well, we've gone over what we could drag out of *Thilomon's* databanks, especially Vantak's private files and what Vantak carried with him when he got aboard *Zounin-Ginjou*. He was awfully cautious, but I think we should be able to use some of what he had planned for our own purposes—especially to flush out the masterminds of the whole thing."

"If I can get back to our Embassy," Sethrik said, "I should be able to obtain the final pieces of the puzzle. It is evident that after the basic processing I was expected to return. Therefore they will *expect* to meet with me and be...debriefed. If, of course, I had been killed, Vantak would likely have been appointed Leader, but since Vantak indicated my loyalty was to be renewed, I must assume—and so would our unknown but suspected conspirators—that I would have remained Leader of the Blessed in the Arena."

That sparked an important memory. "A question about that, Sethrik," Ariane said. "Why don't they *routinely* do this loyalty renewal treatment? Not that I'm complaining, mind you—without you helping we'd have been totally screwed—but I'm wondering why the Minds don't just do that every year, or six months, or whatever, making sure that you guys *never* get to the point that you start thinking outside whatever box they have around you."

"The short answer is that they do...over fairly long periods. But..." Sethrik's wings scissored as Orphan's often did when he was uncertain how to respond. Somewhat to her surprise, Orphan spoke—and with a startlingly gentle tone. "Sethrik, I will answer—if I may?"

At the Blessed's gesture of assent, Orphan faced them. "To some of you, such as Doctor DuQuesne, the answer may be obvious. But it is a matter of compromise, as with many things.

"You know that the Minds were forced to give the Blessed at least some independence, or they would be unable to function at all in the Arena. And in fact, that independence must include the ability to evaluate, adapt, change, or the Blessed would be *hopelessly* crippled in the Arena. They would be...what was the phrase you once used? Ah, yes, the eternal 'clueless newbies' of the Arena, programmed perhaps with a wide array of facts and techniques but unable to encompass the fluid *life* of the Arena.

"So the Minds must compromise and balance between allowing their people to develop these capabilities, learn from others, forging alliances, building...a rapport with other species, and keeping them from developing," he gestured to himself, "an unfortunate longing for even more independent thinking."

"It is somewhat more than that," Sethrik said. "Even the Minds...have limits. One of those limits is that it is effectively impossible for them to restructure someone's entire manner of thinking, eliminating the independence of thought, and still leave them with not merely the memories but the *experiences* that brought them to that point. They can give to one so processed the facts, the sequences of events, but if they were to leave in the emotional and event context...the processing would be self-reversing in extremely short order. This means that to do so—especially to the Leader of the Blessed or others who frequently interact with outsiders of high rank and importance—risks severely damaging any such connections; one of us who is so...changed cannot conceal that they no longer have the same affection—or, in truth, even animus or curiosity—towards those with whom they have had extensive contact."

"So they have to guess when things are about to go south and order—or drag—you in at the last minute?" she asked. It was a horrific thought. "Have you..."

"Once before, yes. I can now deduce what I lost." He looked to Orphan. "And understand from whence came the Liberated."

"So you *are* the Leader of the Blessed to Serve still," Ariane said, continuing.

"As far as I am aware, yes. They had certainly not performed the usual procedure to remove a Leader, and I do not believe they would have set such a thing in motion unless they had reason to believe their plans had failed and that nothing could be recovered—a conclusion that they will only now be reaching."

"All right." She looked at DuQuesne and Simon, who was now thankfully looking somewhat better; during the journey to drop off the Blessed prisoners they'd enforced bed rest on the scientist, and his medical nanos had taken the chance to do some real work. It would still be awhile before Simon Sandrisson was really back to his former self, but he no longer looked like someone incompetently raised from the dead. "The first step is to get Sethrik back to the Arena and let him get to the Blessed Faction House. I think we have an excellent plan to do that."

"Simple ruse," DuQuesne agreed with a grin. "We just apparently arrive after having completed our ship-transport gig. The only people who could possibly put that into question are people on our Sphere who'd be able to figure out that the timing was a little off."

"Hopefully they won't look too hard at *Zounin-Ginjou* itself," Simon said. "I know you've done miracles on covering up the damage in the last week or so, but anyone who looks at the wrong areas carefully will know there's something wrong."

"You're right, Simon," Ariane said. "But the deception doesn't have to last too long."

"I have every intention of making that part as short as possible," Orphan said. "That is why we will transport Sethrik—and Captain Austin and Sun Wu Kung—to *my* Embassy first in standard cargo containers. Sethrik can then leave by a somewhat more concealed exit that I had constructed some years ago, while I publicly depart for my ship and leave—bringing her back for repairs."

"I admit, I don't exactly like the idea you'll be gone," DuQuesne said, and she smiled. *We really used to distrust Orphan . . . and he gave us plenty of reasons to. I still think he's got other agendas. But he sure demonstrated what side he was on this time.* "But you've got the right idea. That way if no one notices the damage to *Zounin-Ginjou* in about an hour, they'll never have a chance to see it, and our story will be pretty close to airtight."

"If we're right," Ariane continued, "once in the Faction House, Sethrik will be able to find Vantak's contact protocols with whoever was behind it, and get them called in for a meeting. We will deal with them privately—in-Faction—once we get the evidence. Externally," she said, looking directly into Sethrik's black eyes, "we will state that the Blessed acted to protect me from an unknown assassination attempt, and encountered difficulties which required a roundabout route to return me. I will thank the Blessed for their prompt action and efforts on our behalf."

She then gave a momentary humorless grin. "You

will convey these . . . *thanks* to the Minds, via a courier, along with this message. Are you ready?" she asked of Orphan.

"Recording now, Captain Austin," Orphan said. "We can edit when you are done."

She took a breath, then read from the speech she'd prepared along with Simon and DuQuesne.

"This is Captain Ariane Austin of Humanity. Your attempt to kidnap me, and to extract the knowledge of how to use the powers of Shadeweaver and/or the Faith which are sealed within me, has failed, as you no doubt are already aware.

"The details of that plan are now known to us, and you have no knowledge of how your plan failed—nor will you. But you should be aware that while your initial attempt to capture me succeeded, we deliberately and completely destroyed the *Thilomon* and the entire task force sent to bring me in."

She glared into the recorder, and her voice sharpened. "We are a very small Faction. We are a single world already at war with one of the Great Factions, the Molothos. But we are *not* to be trifled with, and you have made a *very* grave mistake in trying something that you couldn't finish."

She pointed at the recorder, an accusatory finger that she knew would have the same effect on the Blessed that it would to humans, for a pointed finger meant very much the same thing to both. "You are going to pay for that mistake, Minds. You will pay because with the full details—both of what you attempted, and how your attempt failed—we can make it so that the Faction of the Blessed loses face, loses respect, and loses trust. More than this, however, is the main reason you chose to kidnap me. If you do not accede to my demands, Minds of the Blessed, I will go to both the Shadeweavers and the Faith and tell them precisely what you planned. I do not think they will look kindly upon this attempt of yours to seize that which both have kept to themselves for so long, and I also do not believe that you could afford the wrath of even one, let alone both of them.

"Our demands are simple: three Spheres, given to us exactly as they would be had this been a formal Challenge and you had lost. One Sphere for capturing me, one Sphere for those who endangered themselves to rescue me, and one extra to remind you that if you ever, *ever* try anything against us, you will *always* regret it. You have thousands upon thousands of Spheres; this will not significantly harm you. But it will *always* remind you of what it costs to take on Humanity. You try it, you damn well better *win*, because if you don't, it will *hurt*.

"In return for this, we will not only *not* accuse the Blessed of these crimes, but will instead put forth a public story showing that the Blessed acted to protect the leader of another Faction, and made sure that she was safe before returning her home. As a sign of *our* good faith, this particular account of the events will have been released by the time you receive this message. I hope that you will not give us cause to withdraw that story.

"Ariane Stephanie Austin, Leader of the Faction of Humanity—out."

She saw DuQuesne and Simon grinning fiercely, and Simon applauded. "Now *that* is a message I would dearly wish to observe being delivered," Simon said.

"Though not enough so to risk going to the Home-sphere of the Blessed."

"You are playing...a dangerous game there, Ariane Austin," Sethrik said, "for the Minds do not take at all well to threats. But...I think you are probably right to do so. Such an affront must be met with great strength, or they will believe you are too afraid to talk, too weak to dare confront them even when their offenses are of so heinous a nature."

"Indeed," Orphan said, and bowed deeply to her in the human fashion. "But I expected no less from the woman who was willing to face Amas-Garao in single combat...and won. Oh, this will be *most* amusing—and I agree with you, Doctor Sandrisson, that I would give much for a chance to observe the delivery of this message! For I assure you, the Minds will think hard on those truths—that the one speaking so to them has done the impossible, taking the power of a Shadeweaver to defeat one of the eldest of that brotherhood, beating one of their personally-designed own in a race of speed and courage, leading her people into Factionhood through her own personal will and courage...and surrounded by people who have per-sonally defeated Molothos incursions. They will think long and hard on this, and on the fact that you admit to having been captured...and yet, somehow, escaped, and destroyed the entire task force sent to retrieve you...and I believe find that they have no answers save to agree, for they cannot afford the price they will pay otherwise."

"Good," she said, and sat down heavily. "Because I'm scared as hell that it's going to get us in a war with a *second* Great Faction."

"Not a chance," DuQuesne said positively. "Orphan and Sethrik agree. They decided to go for kidnapping and brainwashing, so we've turned around and given 'em blackmail. They'll probably pay, once. I don't *like* blackmail, but I like what they did even less, and right now it's the only option we've got for hitting back at a Faction that large. And Sethrik's right that the one thing we *can't* afford is to ignore it or pretend we're too scared to fight back. Do that, and they'll figure they can try again, someway, somehow."

"I would still gladly go and beat these Minds for you!" Wu Kung said.

She smiled. "I think that's asking a little much even of *you*, Wu. But honestly I'd prefer that route. Manipulation and blackmail, why, I've already started down the dirty road of politics with Oscar." She took a breath, let it out. "But with luck, I won't have to do anything like that again."

The alert buzzed, telling her that they were ready for the final jump to Nexus Arena's space. "All right, everyone . . . let's do this."

CHAPTER 43

Simon restrained himself from taking breaths too large or small. *We cannot betray nervousness yet. We have no reason to be nervous. We've simply finished our deliveries, had some very educational and entertaining weeks with our friend Orphan, and we're finally home.*

DuQuesne strolled next to him, looking completely relaxed, as they walked the short distance to the Embassy of Humanity. He glanced over and said casually, "Good to be getting back, finally."

"Yes, indeed. While it was extraordinary to see so much of the greater Arena, and to travel with Orphan...it did begin to pall after a bit. Only three people in the ship, after all."

"Yeah, I was starting to get a little cabin fever myself. Well, here we are."

The door swung open before them and the two entered the main hall. For an instant they were alone in the entrance hall, quiet, deserted, and Simon had a chill go down his spine. *Did something else happen while we were gone?*

But then one of the doors opened, and Laila stepped out, frowning down at some display in her hand, hair not quite as neat as its usual wont. She glanced up, glanced back down, and suddenly her eyes snapped back up. She froze, then ran forward. "Marc! Simon! Thank *God*!" She spoke to empty air, summoning a green sphere of light. "Carl! Gabrielle! Simon and Marc are back!"

"You sound . . . agitated, Laila," Marc said, a concerned look growing on his face. "What—"

Another door popped open and Gabrielle Wolfe sprinted out, Carl Edlund at her heels; Oasis Abrams trailed behind. "Dang, but you boys chose a bad time to be incommunicado," Gabrielle said.

"What in the world's *happened?*" Simon demanded. He thought the tone sounded sufficiently confused.

"Ariane's gone," Carl said bluntly.

"What do you mean, 'gone'?" DuQuesne's voice was hard and cold now.

"Just what he said, and don't you go glaring at *him* over it," Gabrielle answered sharply. She gestured. "Let's go talk."

"She went out with Sethrik . . . about a week ago." Carl said as they went into one of the conference rooms. "He was going to show her one of their ships, talking about getting the support of the Blessed against the Molothos—"

"Yeah, I remember hearing something about that. So?" DuQuesne slowly seated himself. Simon did the same, and the others followed suit.

"So," Laila picked up, "they arrived on the Docks, that much we know. Then . . . something happened. There are no known direct records of the event and the few witnesses are not terribly clear on the exact sequence of events, but it *appears* that an attempt was made on Ariane's life—or possibly Sethrik's. The Blessed warship

Thilomon departed shortly thereafter, but whether that was exactly at the same time or not we have no clear idea. We've heard nothing from Sethrik, and the Blessed Faction House says that he is away for some unknown period of time." She looked at them both levelly. "I suspect they have kidnapped our captain."

"That . . . would be possible, I suppose," Simon said, slowly, "but for what *reason*?"

"That's the problem," Gabrielle answered. "We don't know. Naraj and Ni Deng can't get any more out of them, and they have no answers as to why they'd have done it—"

"—Let's be accurate," Carl interrupted. "Our favorite diplomats don't accept that it's even *possible* the Blessed grabbed Ariane. And . . . well, there are some people who claim that they saw *someone* fall off the Dock during that time."

"Good God!" DuQuesne swore. "Did anyone *search*?"

"Some people did," Laila said, "but there was a very powerful storm only a hundred or so kilometers below the Docks at the time. If someone had fallen into that . . ."

"What about Wu? Where's he?"

"Gone along with Ariane," Oasis said quietly, and he could hear the sorrow in her voice. "One witness said he jumped off the edge of the Dock where the Blessed ship *Thilomon* had been berthed, another claims Wu ran up a nearby spire and disappeared; either way . . . no one's seen him since."

"Dammit. Okay, where's Ni Deng and Naraj?"

"I am here, Doctor," Oscar Naraj said heavily, entering. "I trust I am not intruding? No? Good. Michelle received a call and went out just shortly before you arrived, but I hope she will return soon; we have other engagements for later today."

He doesn't look very happy, but then, I suppose he'd have to play along. "You haven't any more ideas about what could have happened to her?"

Oscar shook his head, sleek dark hair sprinkled with white throwing off highlights. "I have made as many inquiries as I can. No one seems able to throw any light whatsoever on the situation, which I find absolutely *outrageous*. Whatever our differences, Captain Austin was the leader of our faction, and it should simply be impossible for a person of such importance to disappear."

Simon glanced quickly at DuQuesne, and he could see they had both caught the potential telltale "was" in Oscar's reply. *Not enough to accuse on, though. After a week, he could easily argue that he was assuming something had happened to her.*

"Well...we're not all that important a Faction—"

"Irrelevant and unacceptable," Naraj said firmly. "There are at *most* a few thousand recognized Factions of *any* size, and even the smallest of them include billions of citizens. A Faction Leader is a member of, perhaps, the most exclusive elite in all the universe... or universes."

There was a knock on the conference room door. "Ambassador?" Michelle Ni Deng entered, stopped in startlement as she saw Simon and Marc, then hurried forward. "Oh...! Welcome back, both of you. I... suppose you've heard the news."

"Yeah. No clues at all?"

"None worth anything. I'm sure they've told you; contradictory eyewitnesses, no physical evidence." Ni Deng brushed back her feathery hair in irritation.

"And that Sun Wu Kung gone too." She tried to smile, failed—*or gave a very good performance of someone having that problem,* Simon thought. "I am afraid this proves the point of *needing* bodyguards all too well."

"And if this continues..." Oscar sighed. "Gentlemen, I was somewhat dreading this moment, but with you back, I think we must discuss the possibility that we will never know what happened."

DuQuesne glared at him. Carl held up a hand to forestall the expected outburst. "It's only been a week. The Arena's huge. No one's giving up yet."

"Perhaps you're correct," Naraj said carefully, "but do we have an idea of how long we *should* wait before...considering the possibility that there is no longer any point in waiting? And what we should do if that eventuality occurs?"

Laila frowned, but nodded. "You know he's right. We have to at least think about it. If she *is* gone..."

"Then this Faction has no Leader," Ni Deng finished. "And without a Faction Leader, a Faction's crippled. If we don't select a new Leader, the Arena may pick one *for* us, as you and Captain Austin once mentioned."

And the subject is exactly the one you would want raised quickly, Simon thought. He tried to dispel the *wrong* kind of tension. *I should not be tense in anticipation. I have to be upset, worried, shocked, not tense as though waiting. I am...not truly suited for these kind of games.* He noticed Oasis looking at him oddly for a moment. *She beat a Hyperion on her own, she speaks with DuQuesne and Wu as equals. I suppose she may also have perceptions to rival theirs. But I don't think she's one of our enemies.*

In the tension, he felt...a hint of that *edge,* that

perception of his own coming back. He had a faint sense of interconnection, of data behind the ordinary, of knowing things that might be, things that had been.

DuQuesne glowered at the two diplomats, then sank back with one of his old-fashioned and obscure curses. "Right. Okay. But you've dropped it on us without warning, give a guy a chance to take it all in before you ask him to think about . . . stuff like that."

It's no secret that DuQuesne—and I—are extremely interested in Ariane Austin, so I am sure they'll interpret that appropriately.

Simon suddenly felt a sense of connections drawing tight, of probabilities on the rise. *Oh . . . I think . . .*

"Very well," Oscar Naraj said. "You are correct, we should give you some courtesy in this. Come on, Michelle, Oasis . . . whatever the situation, we still have people to meet with." He got up, and the other two rose. "The Geros have a most interesting—"

As he reached the door, it slid open.

Standing framed in the doorway was Captain Ariane Austin.

The sensation had warned Simon, primed him to be watching with keen attention at that very moment. So he saw Ni Deng's eyes widen and her face grow pale, saw her take a half step back. Her expression was, for a moment, not at all joyful or relieved, but fearful. Naraj's . . . was subtle. There was a flicker, a start, perhaps, but even with this almost supernatural perception Simon could not *swear* that there was anything wrong with Oscar Naraj's reaction to the sudden, unexpected appearance of the missing woman.

Oasis, on the other hand, seemed to light up, as did everyone else there. *"Ariane!"*

Her smile lit the room. "Sorry to keep you all waiting!"

The others lunged forward, crowding Naraj and Ni Deng back, and for a few moments there were just happy greetings, hugs, and slightly tearful laughter. "But where *were* you, Arrie?" Gabrielle demanded.

"Hold on a moment," she said with a smile. "Ambassadors, don't you want to hear this?"

"Knowing you are back is more than enough for now," Naraj said with a very convincing smile. "Once we're back from our current appointment, though, I will insist you tell me everything."

"Oh, but Ambassadors, I *insist* you stay and listen," Ariane said. "Wu, make sure they stay."

The Hyperion Monkey King suddenly popped into view. "You heard Captain Austin. Come on, sit down."

Oasis twitched as her two charges were dragged back, but didn't try to stop Wu. *Knows that it would be a hopeless attempt, and probably assumes Ariane has a reason for what she's doing.*

"What do you think you're—"

"Shut up and listen, Oscar. I'd really like to think you're not involved, but I doubt it."

"Involved? Involved in *what*?" The look of complete confusion was, Simon had to admit, either genuine or the product of a masterful actor who had clearly missed his true calling.

"In striking a deal with the Blessed to have me kidnapped, interrogated, and presumably eventually killed, thereby clearing away my inconvenient leadership of our faction, in exchange for their alliance with Humanity."

Ni Deng stared at her, as did Oscar Naraj, mouths

open and stunned. "What? That's...insane!" Ni Deng said sharply.

Oscar Naraj, more controlled and canny, gestured for her to be silent. "These are...well, yes, perhaps insane, but certainly most serious charges, Captain. I trust you have evidence—perhaps some of these abductors?"

"I'm afraid all the abductors are very dead, Oscar," she answered with a cold smile. Simon noticed Ni Deng blanch again.

"Then I think we shall be going—"

Wu Kung shoved Oscar back into his seat with effortless power. "You'll stay right where I put you!"

"You're making a terrible mistake, Captain—"

"You," she cut him off, "are making *two* mistakes. First, I don't *need* evidence here in the Arena. As Faction Leader, I'm the *boss*. I don't think you've ever *really* gotten that through your head. If I want to throw you out on the street, I can *do* that. Yes, you could go back home and make me very much *persona non grata*, but there isn't one damned thing you can do to me *here*. That's what it *means* to be a Faction Leader.

"But the bigger mistake is assuming that just because I haven't got any of the abductors that I don't have any *evidence*."

Another figure appeared in the doorway, this one looming nearly seven feet tall, green-and-black patterned body, near-human face, with head-crests that almost brushed the top of the doorway. "Indeed, Captain Austin," said Sethrik. "And after the conversation I just had with Michelle Ni Deng, I can assure you that I can provide you with *ample* evidence."

CHAPTER 44

Ni Deng's mouth opened, then shut. *Yeah, you aren't stupid,* DuQuesne thought. *If you were home, it'd be time to find a good human-AI advocate and prep for trial. And Ariane's still going to follow some of the procedure, so maybe you* will *get a chance to lawyer up.*

Under his dark skin, Naraj was noticeably paler. "Sethrik . . ." He blinked. "But . . . many pardons for my confusion . . . such a deal would have to include you, would it not?"

"It is not so simple a situation," Sethrik said, then looked to Ariane. "But we are in your Embassy, and your rules. What do you wish from me?"

"Just summarize the conversation for now. We'll want the full recording, of course."

Michelle Ni Deng looked like she was about to speak, but Ariane cut her off. "Before you even *think* about saying anything, you should know I was *in* the Blessed Faction House, with Sethrik's permission. I got to *hear* the start of your conversation, so there isn't any decent argument that any of what he has to say is faked." Ariane nodded to Sethrik.

The Blessed Leader bob-bowed to the table of

mostly shell-shocked humans. "I had—as we previously discussed, Captain Austin—determined that my second in command Vantak had been given covert instructions by the Minds to negotiate, as you say, behind my back. The entire sequence of events had been arranged by him with a particular member of your group, who was never clearly identifed in Vantak's shipboard notes. However, following protocols of contact I found in our Faction House in his quarters, I contacted someone—who proved to be Ambassador Ni Deng—and informed her that I had returned and all was in order, and she could visit me at any time.

"Deputy Ambassador Ni Deng promptly came to our Faction House; she expressed some surprise that it was I, not Vantak, meeting her, but I mentioned to her that the Minds had completed my readjustment and she was obviously aware of both what that meant, and that I was intended to remain Leader of the Blessed To Serve. She inquired as to whether there had been any problems, and I said that Wu Kung had been disposed of between Spheres. She was not particularly upset by that news, and simply wanted assurance that the Blessed would abide by the conditions of the bargain, which I assured her we would—to wit, providing a direct alliance against the Molothos, who will certainly be discovering the location of your Sphere soon enough, and supporting Humanity in certain other areas. She was very pleased to hear this."

DuQuesne could see Ni Deng trying to maintain an expressionless demeanor, but she wasn't quite as good as Oscar Naraj at playing this sort of poker, and there were small but visible reactions to the revelations.

Admittedly, this is about as high-stakes as any game gets; I wouldn't expect her to pull it off perfectly.

Sethrik looked at Ni Deng. "To her...minor credit, she did express concern for Captain Austin's overall well-being and a, I believe, genuine desire that she not suffer. There was no indication of personal animus in these actions, and I believe, based on the actual dialogue today and recorded in Vantak's files, that—while personal advancement was certainly part of her motivation—she was also strongly motivated by an honest belief that Captain Austin was not the right Leader for Humanity, was potentially dangerous to Humanity's chances for success in the long term, and would not easily give up the position as Leader to anyone properly suited for it."

"Here," he said, putting a small crystal in Ariane's hand. "A full recording of our conversation, plus a record of everything regarding this...regrettable sequence of events that I have been able to glean from the records Vantak and his subordinates have left."

"Thank you, Sethrik." She performed the standing bob-bow of respect to the Blessed, then turned to the others. "Would you all agree I have sufficient evidence to arrest Michelle Ni Deng?"

The others nodded—even, after a moment, Oscar Naraj. Oasis' face was dark, flushed with anger, and DuQuesne could tell she was barely able to keep from exploding. *Probably beating herself up over missing it. But if you play the part long enough, you become the part, I sure know that—and in this case, since Oasis is just as real as K...it's not just playing. And Ni Deng was real good at this, just not quite perfect at hiding her reactions when it's falling apart.*

"Wu," she said, "Take Ni Deng and lock her up in the room we agreed on."

Ni Deng looked with an almost pleading expression at Naraj; Naraj simply stared at her with horror—*either genuine, or the best acting job I've ever seen*—and shook his head slowly. She stood as Wu approached. "I . . . won't resist. Let me walk, at least."

Wu Kung did not reply, just let her walk ahead of him and out the door.

After the door closed, DuQuesne looked at Sethrik. "One question, Sethrik: was there anything in that collection of evidence that shows that she wasn't acting on her own?"

"No direct evidence I have seen, no," Sethrik said. "She did imply she had to at least consult with . . . someone, but the phrasing was such that she could have meant someone else here, or someone else in your home system."

Damn. And she was handling a lot of the diplomatic messaging traffic. So she could have been doing this all on her own.

"I can't blame you for the question," Naraj said slowly. "And I will accept that my . . . hostility, not to mince words . . . towards Captain Austin's position may well have driven her to this, but I hope you understand that I would *never* have directed she undertake something so terrible. This is not the way political issues should be settled; I admit to also being somewhat disappointed that the Blessed would *agree* to such a thing with so little to gain."

Yeah. So little, like the potential to become the only AIs running in the Arena. But . . . I'll bet Ni Deng wasn't told about that angle.

Ariane looked at Naraj coldly, and DuQuesne could see that she hadn't dropped the diamond-hard focus she was going to need in this job. For a moment, no one spoke; then Ariane said, "Oscar, I would love to believe that. But I know your reputation from Saul Maginot, and I've watched your own behavior. Maybe you had nothing to do with it at all, maybe you had a vague suspicion and just turned a blind eye to it, or maybe you knew all along and just made sure you had plausible deniability after asking 'will no one rid me of this troublesome captain?' as DuQuesne put it a while ago. But I *damn* well have enough reason to . . . what's the phrase . . . hold you for questioning. I've got a lot of things to say to the others, and *you* aren't going to be present."

Wu Kung stepped back inside, and Ariane gestured to him. "Wu, take him to his quarters. He's to stay inside until I give permission otherwise." She raised her voice. "Arena! I, Ariane Austin, Leader of Humanity, specifically and officially revoke any privileges of Oscar Naraj or Michelle Ni Deng to speak for Humanity in any capacity whatsoever, unless and until I choose otherwise. If possible, I would like that to include preventing them from using your communications methods to contact any outside of this Embassy."

The penetrating, air-shaking voice answered, "Acknowleged. No Arena communications by the two designated individuals to any outside of this Embassy."

Wu left with a brooding Oscar Naraj, and the room was silent for a few moments; it was clear that Ariane was waiting for Wu to return.

The door opened, and Wu Kung came back in; he positioned himself near Ariane as Ariane finally sat down.

"So," Carl said after a moment. "What exactly do we want to charge Ni Deng *with*? And...how are we going through with it?"

"Hold that thought a moment," Ariane said. She nodded to Sethrik. "This is about to become purely Humanity's business, Sethrik—although I may require you as a witness at some point, depending on how we approach this whole mess."

A deep bob-bow of acknowledgement. "Of course, Captain. I will be leaving momentarily—"

A chime. "Orphan of the Liberated seeks entrance."

"Come in, Orphan," Ariane said, looking slightly surprised. She continued speaking into the green sphere that had materialized when she spoke. "We're in the central conference room."

"Thank you, Captain Austin," said Orphan's rich, deep voice from the comm sphere. "I am proceeding there as we speak."

"What brings you here, Orphan? I didn't call for you and—no offense—we are in the middle of an important meeting here. And come to think of it, I thought you were going to be leaving about now."

The door opened and the comm spheres disappeared. Orphan bowed to all of them, with a special nod to both Simon and DuQuesne. "Of course, Captain Austin. But in fact I was asked to drop in by Sethrik, before I did in fact depart." He turned to look at the Leader of the Blessed.

Sethrik dropped to the full formal pushup-bow and remained in the low position. "Orphan of the Liberated, I have asked you to meet here, on neutral ground, to offer myself as a member of your Faction," he said. The translated voice was shaking, clearly in

conflict, in emotional tension that was nearly as great
as he had shown during the decisions as to how to
deal with the remaining crew of *Thilomon*.

*Well, I'll be jiggered. I wondered if it might eventu-
ally shake out that way, but I didn't expect it quite
this fast.*

Orphan stiffened, giving a buzz that didn't translate
except as a gasp of surprise. "I . . . Sethrik, you do
realize what you are asking? What you commit to?"

Sethrik had still not raised himself from the floor,
and DuQuesne rose so he could see better; the others, too, had risen, realizing what was happening here.

"I do," Sethrik said, and his voice steadied slightly.
"If I am of the Liberated, I become the adversary of
the Minds, the willing and active opposition to all the
Blessed to Serve. I . . . betray our people, our leaders,
our traditions . . . for the sake of what I believe now
is right."

Orphan slowly bent down, then placed himself in
the pushup-bow position, bowed and rose. "Please,
get up, Sethrik. Either way, we are equals."

The Leader of the Blessed rose slowly to face
Orphan. Orphan seemed torn; finally he spoke. "I
can not deny how very important—how *terribly*
important—such an offer is to me—to the Liberated.
But I imagine how wonderful, too, it could be to
have an ally *within* the Blessed . . ."

Sethrik tapped his hands together. "Yes, it would
be, Orphan. But you know—you all know, now—that
at best it could be temporary. And in the current
state, I am sure I would be removed within weeks.
Better, I think, to leave of my own will." He looked
to Ariane and the others. "I have sent your . . .

communication to the Minds, along with my own ...
commentary on these events. So my last necessary
duty is finished."

"Then, Sethrik, I accept you with joy into the ranks
of the Liberated—such as they are," Orphan finished
with ironic humor. His voice became more gentle. "I
remember ... the day I made that decision. I know
how it tears at you now, and will, for many days, for
many nights.

"But at least you—and I—will not be alone."

Sethrik and Orphan exchanged the two-handed
greeting DuQuesne had seen a few times before,
and then Sethrik raised his head. "Then, Arena, I
hereby vacate the position of Leader of the Blessed to
Serve, delegating temporary responsibility for all such
functions to Tanglil, currently the next in authority at
the Faction House of the Blessed, until the Minds
properly and duly designate and announce a successor.
I announce my intention to join the Liberated as a
member of their Faction."

"And I, Orphan, Leader of the Liberated, accept
Sethrik as one of our own. He is a member of the
Liberated."

Once more, the Arena spoke. "Transfer of authority
completed. The one called Sethrik of the Blessed is
now Sethrik of the Liberated."

*And Orphan is no longer completely orphaned.
He's found a companion in that journey.* DuQuesne
glanced over to Wu and Oasis, and saw the understanding and fellowship there. With a grin on his face,
he began to clap.

The others joined in, and for a few moments the
room was filled with applause. *And by their reactions,*

it's being translated to something similar for the Liberated.

"Ah!" Laila said as the applause dwindled away. "Now I understand."

Orphan tilted his head. "I am very glad of your understanding, Doctor Canning...yet, I am afraid, I am unclear as to *what* you understand."

Got it. "I think she means she knows why Sethrik brought you *here*, and went through the whole routine in front of us."

DuQuesne was gratified to see Ariane grin and nod. "Of course. By doing that here, we witnessed the transfer—including the Arena's acceptance."

"Which means," Sethrik said with a small bow, "that you can be quite certain I am not, in fact, an agent for the Blessed any more." His voice was somewhat more steady, but not entirely back to its businesslike normal.

"I see," Simon said, and Carl and Gabrielle were also nodding. "Because the Arena does not—at least openly—take any sides, and certainly would not do things like pretend to accept a false transfer of loyalty."

"I am gratified, my friends, that you have come to understand the Arena so well," Orphan said, his old ironic humor returning. "For my interaction with you has taught me how very difficult it truly is to understand." He bowed to the others. "But you were, as you said, in the midst of important counsels, and I...well, *Sethrik* and I...have some considerable discussion to have now, as well. Which we should be doing on board *Zounin-Ginjou*."

"Ha!" Wu Kung said suddenly.

"What?" DuQuesne asked.

"I wondered why Sethrik had this big carry-crate that he left in the front hall! Now I understand—he was moving!"

"In either case, yes," Sethrik agreed. "Had Orphan denied my petition—something possible, though I thought very unlikely—I would have renewed my offer to you, Captain Austin, which I was quite sure would be accepted."

"It would definitely have been accepted, Sethrik. But I'm glad Orphan's no longer alone. I guess you couldn't stay either way."

"No," and Sethrik's pose reflected his sorrow. "I served the Minds faithfully, but I have learned that my very efforts for them, my drive to learn more and become greater than I began ... these things would inevitably make me of questionable loyalty. And so my only choices were to leave, or to know that one day—very soon—I would be brought back and have all I had *become* taken away, replaced by nothing but hollow memories. It happened, as I said, once before; only now do I begin to suspect what I lost." He bob-bowed to Orphan. "But never again."

"No," Orphan said emphatically. "Never. And one day, that shall be true for all our people."

The two Liberated bowed again to the assembled humans, and left.

The smile only slowly faded from Ariane's face, but by the time she finished turning back to the others, it was entirely gone.

Time to get back to business.

CHAPTER 45

Ariane looked around at her friends. *But also they're my . . . cabinet, I suppose. They—and Steve and Tom, who I've got to brief right away after this—are the only group I can really trust.* She saw Oasis glance at her. *Well, she's the only question mark. One I'd better deal with right now.*

"Oasis, I know you were brought here by Oscar Naraj to be his and Ni Deng's bodyguard. That doesn't mean you're responsible for anything they did when you weren't there."

"Thanks," the redheaded young woman said. *Young?* Ariane thought to herself. *I really need to keep reminding myself she's older than I am, probably almost as old as DuQuesne if she was involved in pacifying Hyperion.*

"But," Oasis went on, "I should have been more suspicious of what they were up to, especially when there were several meetings she decided to have without me with the same guy, Vantak." She stood. "I guess I'd better leave you to talk with the others."

"Hold on one moment." She looked over to DuQuesne, and back at Wu. "DuQuesne? Wu? You know Oasis better than I do. Should she stay or do I have her leave?"

Ariane caught Wu's glance at Oasis and over to DuQuesne. *Following DuQuesne's lead?*

DuQuesne chuckled. "I wouldn't have her leave, Ariane. We need all the backup we can get, and I'd trust her with my life—or yours, for that matter. If she'd had any inkling of this going on, she'd have kicked Ni Deng straight back to Earth. Right, Wu?"

Wu Kung grinned broadly. "Very right, DuQuesne!"

"All right, then." She gestured to Oasis. "Take your seat. This is going to be a while."

She took a deep breath. *Don't forget your promise.* "First...I have to apologize to all of you. In a way, I should even be apologizing to Ni Deng and Oscar." She held up a hand to forestall anyone interrupting. "I screwed up. I insisted that I stay on as the Leader of Humanity, but I let myself...basically ignore what that *meant*. And yes, I know how many excuses I could make, and how many a lot of you," she looked directly at DuQuesne, and then to Simon, "might make for me. But the fact is that I didn't really *take* that leadership position, I didn't hammer it home to people enough, and that's really been the cause of a lot of these problems."

She laughed briefly. "Remember...God, it seems years ago, but I guess it was only months...when I won the race against Sethrik and we had that knock-down, drag-out argument about what my being captain meant? I fought for that recognition. And now...I look at myself and see that really, I didn't take myself any more seriously than you did, except whenever I got backed into a corner. We can't afford that, and because I *did* do that, we're in this mess—in more ways than one, too.

"Carl—you asked what we charge Ni Deng with. Honestly? I'm not sure. We never *decided* on a set of laws—or much of anything—with respect to how we do things in the Arena. When we first got here, we were just trying to survive, and when we got back we had a lot to occupy us. I *knew* we should figure out some more rules—especially with more people coming through—but I never did get around to making us think about those rules. How many people have we got back at the Sphere?" she asked Gabrielle.

"Now? Oh, lordy...close on a thousand, I think. We've got a regular little town in the Foyer area, construction going on at Emergent Falls, bases—"

"A thousand people." She glanced apologetically at Gabrielle. "Sorry, Gabrielle. But a *thousand people*. All probably getting along based on the rules we have back home. But this *isn't* back home, and those thousand people aren't staying just on our Sphere forever. They're going to want to come *here*—and there's every reason that we want to encourage our people to establish a greater presence in Nexus Arena.

"But the Arena's rules aren't ours, and even our own situation in the Arena changes everything. It's practically anarchy back home; the CSF and SSC are just *starting* to try to organize the solar system to confront the Molothos threat and the truth of the Arena. Here, every Faction has a Leader. That's me, right now, and I should have recognized we'd need to have things *organized*. And that included deciding how we'd deal with rule of law, crimes and punishments."

She nodded to DuQuesne. "Marc's helped me dig into the rules of the Arena recently, and it's pretty clear that the Arena has general interfaction rules, but in smaller details it leaves things to the Factions to clear up—including determining crimes and punishments that don't reach Challenge levels. Our group—those of us in the first expedition—were all very important, key members, and we still are, so we were all treated as direct representatives of our Faction. The general population won't be—but we, as a Faction, *will* be responsible for them, and for proper investigation, apprehension, determination of guilt, and punishment for any human-derived offenders."

"So . . . what, are you saying we can't charge her with anything?" Carl asked, somewhat testily.

"No. I'm saying that whatever we do here sets *precedent*. Part of me's still saying I should just send her home, with 'and stay out!' on her file jacket. But I *can't* do that. We may not have actually made the rules, but what she did was essentially set me up to be killed—and worse."

"Worse?" repeated Laila.

"Oh, a *lot* worse," DuQuesne said. "Pardon me for butting in, Captain."

"It's all right, Marc. Try not to do it too often; this is hard enough." She looked up at the ceiling, gathering her thoughts for a moment. "Yes, worse. The Blessed and their Minds figured—and they were probably right—that they had a chance of figuring out how the powers of the Shadeweavers and Faith worked if they had a test subject available."

"Jesus!" exclaimed Gabrielle involuntarily, her Southern accent momentarily twice as strong as usual. "Sorry,

Ariane . . . Captain. But . . . My God. And they figured they could grab you—"

"Because I wasn't one of either group. *That* was what made it worth the risk to the Blessed. Grab me, prove that the Blessed were not to be humiliated even by proxy, and get a test subject who has the powers that just might give the Minds the ability to break the Arena's ban on AIs. I don't know about you, but I am *really* not comfortable with the idea of millennia-old T-10 or higher AIs getting a foothold here when they've shown their attitude is that free-thinking citizens are a danger to be properly 'reconditioned.'"

Ariane leaned back, trying to relax, even though the subject made her want to tense up even more. "And that's the kind of people she was encouraging to take me. Sure, she didn't know *that* aspect of it, although she might have guessed if she thought, but still, she *set the Leader of Humanity up to be kidnapped*. What's that? High treason? If I were accepted as the actual leader of humanity back home I guess that's what we'd call it. But technically that happened here in the Arena— outside our solar system's jurisdiction—and we didn't even *have* a set of laws yet for things going on here."

"Doesn't matter," Carl said. "She obviously knew what she was doing was wrong. Especially if she really was hiding it from Naraj, which I kinda think she was."

"Kidnapping is a minimum," Simon said, slowly. "But you know, I think you *need* to go for treason. Yes, I understand that we haven't even defined the law here, and that back home there is no longer a clear definition of *nation* for one to commit treason *against* . . . but I think that's the proper term. Laying aside my personal feelings on the matter—which I will note is not at all an easy thing to do—she was betraying the leader of the entire human species and handing her over to people who were *at best* competitors to, and at worst possibly enemies of, our species. The fact that she sincerely believed it would be in the long run better for us doesn't, honestly, matter. We *cannot* allow that sort of thing. We just *cannot.*"

"I agree," Oasis said firmly. "Kidnapping's a very strong basic charge—and not one anyone's ever going to minimize. But you said it yourself, Captain; whatever we do here sets precedent, and I think the last thing we want to do is minimize that precedent. I didn't get all the details—none of us have, yet, I guess—but from what happened with Sethrik, I'd deduce that *he* got grabbed, too? That is, he wasn't involved, he was a victim?"

DuQuesne nodded. "Spot-on, Oasis. They knew he was becoming...unreliable, and so when Vantak got this offer, I guess they figured that they could use Sethrik as a perfect sucker—a front man that really believed the lies."

"It even worked with me," Wu Kung admitted. "He smelled so much more relaxed and happy. He wasn't trying to lie or mislead us, so I never suspected anything about what was happening."

"So she also aided and abetted someone *else*'s kidnapping—that of another head of state," Oasis said. "And if you've got confirmation of that other reason the Minds wanted you—"

"We do," Ariane said, touching her head, indicating the data was on the memory in her headware. "Vantak himself explained it to me...after he deliberately triggered a momentary flareup of the power."

Carl bit his lip. "I'm not sure *what* you'd call that. Almost treason against the Arena, if it were possible." He grimaced. "Do we know if it's even possible? I mean, whether the Shadeweaver or Faith powers would work in normal space? I'd think they wouldn't."

"I don't know, but I think I know how to find out," Ariane said. "And I think that much is important."

"Really?" DuQuesne asked, and she could see the black eyebrow arch. "Offhand I don't see any way to find that out, short of asking the Shadeweavers...and we can't tip our hand on that unless the Minds are dumb enough to reject your deal."

"Deal?" repeated Laila curiously.

"A chance for them to make up for this offense and save face. I really *don't* want to end up in a spitting match with a second Great Faction, but at the same time I can't just let this slide. So I offered them a bargain. The details aren't important right now; the point is that for now the public story is going to be that someone tried to assassinate me and the Blessed saved me, then encountered some problems that delayed my return. Some people may be suspicious, but if we keep to that line, the Blessed get to look like good guys instead of absolute bastards, and that's *got* to be worth a lot here in the Arena where reputation is half your bargaining power.

"So we won't be talking to the Shadeweavers or Faith about this, at least not yet." She smiled at Simon. "But there's nothing stopping you from going to the Archives of the Analytic and looking for records of Shadeweaver or Faith activity in normal space."

Simon looked surprised, then smiled. "Certainly, nothing prevents me from that." His smile faded.

"But . . . honestly, Ariane, you know there may be a limiting factor . . ."

"I know," she said. *That . . . strange ability of his isn't constant; he still doesn't know exactly how to trigger it.* "I know, but it won't hurt to try, and we have at least some time left to wait. I'm not going to decide the exact direction we're taking until I hear what diplomatic message the Blessed will send in response to my . . . suggestions."

Gabrielle blinked. "Now what does that remind me of . . . oh! Darn it! Hold on, Arrie."

She got up and ran out of the conference room. A few moments later she returned with a small data module. "While you were gone I was in charge here—Carl had work to do back at the Sphere—and a few days ago a message torpedo came through with a lot of the usual stuff, but also with this module. It's encrypted and sealed, but it's not for Ariane—it's for Marc."

Ariane frowned. "Encrypted? Is it from the SSC?" She saw DuQuesne take the device and link up.

"Doesn't say, so I'd guess not."

Without warning, she saw Marc go pale beneath his olive complexion. "Marc?"

DuQuesne's face had gone stony, and for a moment he didn't respond, just gazed into space.

"Marc! What *is* it?"

DuQuesne shook himself, then looked up. "What is it? Something bad. Bad enough I have to get back home *now*."

"Marc, you are not leaving *at all* unless you give me a clearer answer than that," Ariane snapped, and DuQuesne froze. "I said I am going to start doing this *leading* thing, as much as I can, until I am ready to turn the reins over. That means that my top advisors don't get to go running off on errands I don't know something about. Now, if you really don't want any-one *else* here to know, fine, we can talk privately, but you are not going off by yourself without explanation. That's basically what got me kidnapped—people going behind their leaders' backs doing what they thought was right. Are you clear on that, Marc?"

The huge Hyperion stared at her, and then—to her surprise—an equally huge grin spread across his face. "On the beam and in the green, Captain!" He snapped her a salute—without any irony, as far as she could tell—and dropped back into his seat. "You're right. Damn, you're right, Ariane. And if it's been this long...a few more minutes probably won't count." He looked around at the others—*and I think he stared just a* hair *longer at Laila*—and then nodded. "Okay.

"You all know about my basic backstory. Well, another part of it is that with Saul's help I rescued a few of the other Hyperions." He pointed. "Wu there was one. The others were still under the care of Doctor Davison, who was supposed to be lining up potential replacements for him, so I can vet 'em the next time I came back.

"Now, you can bet anything you like that I'd figured out about a thousand safegards for Davison and my old friends; ways for him to get out with them fast, ways to keep people from getting to them, methods to cover his tracks, pay for things without a trace, favors from people I knew that he could call due, all that kind of thing." He looked down at the tiny memory block. "He sent me just four words: 'Moved to summer home.'

"And what *that* means is that he had reason to believe that someone—and a not-friendly someone—had not only found his location but knew what he was up to."

"Maria-Susanna?" Simon asked, then shook his head. "No, wait. She's here."

"That's what *really* worries me," DuQuesne said, and the dark brows were furrowed above the pitch-black eyes. "I'd known old M-S was completely off her nut, and she was the threat I'd put all of those safeguards up to stop. But I was pretty sure that she was here, in the Arena, to stay, at least until she got established with whatever faction she chose to hook up with. So that means either she left behind some people—some pretty damn *capable* people, too—to keep her work going, or...it's someone else entirely.

"But Maria-Susanna's always been pretty much a loner; partly that's because—believe it or not—she still thinks of herself as the shining heroine of her story, and the kind of people you could get to carry out a carefully coordinated series of murders aren't the kind of people she'd see herself associating with." Ariane felt a *frisson* of sympathetic horror at the thought, seeing DuQuesne's painful, twisted smile.

"Problem with *that*," DuQuesne went on darkly, "is that if it's true, then there's some *other* group out there that closed in on Davison in a way that made him feel he was threatened enough to take off for parts unknown. And that, ladies and gentlemen, scares me enough to make me chew my nails right up to my elbows."

"And you want to go catch up with Davison?"

"Yeah. Find out who's after him. Maybe check in

on a couple other potential targets—if whoever or whatever it is has the same basic hit list, Davison's just one of about a dozen good candidates, he's just one of only a couple I really worry about."

Ariane looked at him for a moment, then nodded. "All right. Since you're going back, there's something else I'd like you to do."

"Name it, Captain. Want me to talk to Saul about—"

"Hold off on that; I'll send through some instructions on a torpedo myself when I know which way we're going to jump on that. No, I want you to contact someone else. My AISage, Mentor."

DuQuesne and the others blinked. She was not entirely surprised when Laila reacted first. "Took quite a risk, didn't you?"

Gabrielle, DuQuesne, and Carl caught on then, with Simon only a split-second behind. "Damn, Ariane!" Carl said. "You let *Mentor* go *rogue?*"

Ariane really didn't like that term—if she was right, Mentor was even more her partner now than he'd been all the years they'd been together—but legally . . . "Yes, I guess we have to call it that. He asked me to, because he felt in view of what we'd learned about the Minds—"

"Oh," Oasis said quietly, and the others stopped talking, suddenly realizing the implications.

"Living up to his name, is he?" DuQuesne said after a moment. "Okay, I'll do it."

"I'll give you a code to contact him—without it he'll never answer, since he knows just how dangerous it would be for both me *and* him." She saw DuQuesne getting up, realized he really did feel he had to go *now*.

"I will come too!" Wu stepped forward.

"No, you will *not*," both Ariane and DuQuesne said

in such perfect synchrony that, despite the deadly seriousness of the situation, Simon started chuckling—along with everyone else around the table. "Your job is to bodyguard *me*, Wu," Ariane said. "I haven't taken you off that job, and obviously neither has DuQuesne."

Wu looked a bit hangdog, but nodded. "Sorry. You're right. It's just... they're *my* people, too."

"I know, Wu. And... I hope they're all right. I'll do my best."

Simon looked thoughtful, and Ariane guessed what was going through his head. *And how many people can Marc dare trust with his secrets? Not many.* "I don't know if you'd find it useful, Marc," he said, "but I will come with you, if you like."

DuQuesne looked startled, then grinned again. "You know, that turned out damned well on board *Zounin-Ginjou*, and I'd love to have you along. But Ariane's right about what you might be able to find out about the Shadeweavers and the Faith, and it's crucial."

"Then let me," said Oasis.

There was something... *odd* about the exchange of looks between DuQuesne and Oasis, and Ariane wondered suddenly just *what* the relationship had been between the two survivors of Hyperion. *But from the way DuQuesne's talked, the person he was really close to was this... "K," one of the five, not Oasis, who was a soldier who just happened to survive...*

"Ariane? You have any objection?"

Not my business, as far as I know. Ariane did her best to keep any trace of her musings from her voice. "Objection? No, it sounds like a great idea to me. She was *on* Hyperion and was connected to Saul, so I'm guessing she might know some of these people too."

"Yes," Oasis said, her face troubled. "I did. Quite a few, by the end of it all. Thank you, Captain."

Ariane smiled. "Just keep him out of trouble, okay?"

The redheaded soldier bounced up and saluted. "Impossible mission accepted, Captain!"

DuQuesne managed a smile before turning for the door. "Yeah, we usually do find a bit of trouble. But with you along, I hope we'll both be able to get *out* of it, too."

CHAPTER 46

"I understand your captain is back now, Simon," Relgof said, with an undertone of relief that Simon was glad to hear. *If he was that worried, then I think I can truly depend on him being a friend of ours...even if there are strong limits as to what I can expect from that friendship.*

"Yes, she returned just yesterday. Apparently someone took a shot at her on the Docks, and she escaped in *Thilomon*."

"I had heard rumors, but that's quite worrisome. Admittedly," Relgof made an expansive gesture around the Archives, "one can find motives for nearly anything in the Arena, and your faction has hardly been...how should I put it...hidden in the weeds very often."

"Yes, we haven't kept a very low profile," Simon agreed. *And let's continue away from the subject; a complex lie is much more vulnerable and I'm terrible at them anyway.* "I was wondering if I could get your assistance on a bit of research."

Relgof's filter-beard flip-flopped as it often did when he was thinking. "You recognize that—"

"Yes, I know. And I'm not asking you to add more

overall to the bargain. I was asking more as a friend, to see if you could save me some research."

The tall, slender alien gave an elaborate exended-arm bow. "Then why don't I hear your question, and we shall decide then if I might have to demand a price for the answer."

"All right. You know, of course, that Ariane has within her the powers of Shadeweaver, or Faith, or something like them," Simon began. "Now, I don't expect you to know—or to point me towards—information on how to use or control those powers, even if the Archives have anything of the sort—"

"Ha!" Relgof's laugh was hearty. "'If'? It is true that the Shadeweavers and Faith guard their secrets well, but I would be surprised if there is not quite a great deal on their powers and their use, hidden somewhere in the Archives. But go on."

"Well, when she's Transitioned between normal space and the Arena, she says she's felt...*something*. She has a difficult time describing it," *and I would have a hard time describing the exact sensation I have had in those moments*, "but she *doesn't* recall feeling it the first time we did Transition, and the others don't report anything like it either." *Others, of course, don't include* me. "So we became curious; do you know if the powers of the Shadeweavers or the Faith work in normal space?"

Relgof's beard stopped moving halfway across his mouth, and the Wagamia stared at him for several moments. "You know...by the Sea, that's an *extremely* interesting question. And one to which I do not know the answer. Certainly it is not *common* that they leave the Arena. The Shadeweavers are not even a true Faction, as I believe you are aware, purely a fellowship within the Arena. The Faith are, but the Initiate Guides are rare and one would expect they are busy enough here without often going to the worlds of normal space."

He hadn't thought about that difference between the two forces, but now that it was brought up he wondered. "I thought they had a Faction House."

"Hmm . . . the Shadeweavers have one, yes, but they are not—and never have been—treated precisely *as* a Faction. For one thing, they are not permitted to Challenge, in general. This is one reason that Amas-Garao had to work through the Blessed when he made his ill-omened gambit against you. They are, perhaps, more akin in character to the Powerbrokers."

That made some sense, but then he had to wonder why the difference. "I see. But you don't know—"

"No, I do not. And it is a question well worth investigating." He turned, then stopped, looked back. "I do not have any objection to your remaining with me while I investigate this question."

Simon laughed. "Excellent."

Researcher Relgof spoke some commands to the air; despite listening carefully, Simon could not make out either the commands or the responses. *I don't have permission to access the index, and apparently that permission's being enforced, either by the Arena or by some technology the Analytic has. We could do something like that at home, but the technology that I would use back home wouldn't work here.*

After a few moments, Relgof clapped his hands together and made a rubbing motion, filter-beard moving again. "How *very* intriguing. Nothing in the index directly on the subject at all. There are of course many items relating to both Shadeweaver and Faith, but that

particular set of facts ... not cross-indexed. My *initial*
reaction would then be to say that no, their powers
only work in the Arena, but that is only a hypothesis.
We need to now attempt to falsify the hypothesis. If
you would care to join me," he said, with a cheerful
nod to Simon, "we can both proceed to the research!"

The first step was to get one of the many floating
platforms; the second took them on a surprisingly wild
ride through the nigh-endless aisles, levels, and rooms
of the Archives of the Analytic, grabbing old tablets,
books, data crystals, what appeared to be tree branches
with shimmering leaves, a structure of intertwined knots
of vast complexity that reminded Simon of an Incan
khipu he'd once seen in an museum, other things of
strange and difficult-to-interpret structure. As they
proceeded, he looked to Relgof. "As a question of
purely personal opinion," he said, "do you think that
the Shadeweavers and the Faith use the same power?"

Relgof did not immediately answer. When he did,
his translated voice was serious, reflective. "I am not
sure, to be honest. I have tried to filter that question
more than once.

"On the surface, of course, one would be inclined
to say yes. The initial reaction of any scientist is
to seek parsimony in their observations of the universe's workings, and it is so much simpler to posit
a single source of power—specifically, the technology
of the Arena—and use it to explain any, shall we say,
apparently-supernatural occurrences."

"Agreed. The Arena already does things that violate
all the natural laws that we know of. While we can
postulate some type of mechanism that would make
it possible—femtotech, the manipulation of the very

characteristics of spacetime, that sort of thing—we certainly don't *know* how the Arena does what it does, and it would seem reasonable to think anything with similarly...outré powers must stem from the same source."

Relgof flip-flopped his agreement. "However, the behavior and actions of the two groups often indicates an opposition. We can, of course, assume various reasons that the Arena or its creators would create more than one group with access to its powers and foster enmity or at least an adversarial relationship between them, but at the same time one could also as easily take the Faith and Shadeweavers at their word that there are considerable differences between them—although," he continued, taking a thick volume from a shelf they had just stopped at, "sometimes the Shadeweavers imply they *are* the same. Not a terribly cohesive group."

"No, they aren't," Simon said. Simon's own suspicions were that there had to be *some* connection between the two groups—what had happened with Ariane, he was fairly sure, happened only because Ariane had figured out *something* about the two groups. But both groups had also been absolutely *stunned* when it worked, so it was also possible that she'd pulled off something that didn't fit with anything either group knew. She had been extremely close-mouthed, and Simon had not pressed her. *And a good thing, too. I do not believe it would have been wise to have that particular mystery explained in our reports.*

Sometimes I suspect the Arena was set up for no other reason than to... mess with the minds of everyone in it.

"Well, that's enough to start with, certainly," Relgof said briskly. "Shall we see if we can get anywhere with these?"

"I don't know how many of them I'll be able to read—if 'reading' is the right description—but I'll certainly do my best."

The two scientists brought their large collection of Shadeweaver- and Faith-related material to one of the examining rooms and spread it on a long table. Relgof looked it over, humming pensively. "You are right, Doctor Sandrisson. Much of this is in languages dead and lost, the speakers gone, perhaps their Factions also long since gone to dust. But we can but try." The two bent over the assortment and began trying to puzzle out meanings.

Hours passed. The room should have been— probably *was*—climate-controlled, but still Simon found himself getting warmer, and finally shed his labcoat-like outerwear, draping it over a nearby chair, before going back to the research.

Finally, it dawned on Simon that he was terribly thirsty and hungry. *And I've still found nothing.* At a few points in this work, he'd felt that preternatural clarity... hovering, waiting in the wings, and he thought that if he tried *very* hard, drove himself, that it might emerge. *But if I do that here, I have a* very *good chance of tipping off Relgof, and* that *is a piece of information far too valuable to give away.*

Still, it was important to know the answer to the question; if the answer was *no*, then the Minds' plan had been doomed to failure, and there was one concern that need never bother them again. If the answer was *yes*...

"Ha!"

Relgof's voice was tired, rough, and it was clear he was probably more in need of refreshment than Simon, but for a moment he looked bright and alert, holding up a roll of greenish material like parchment. "Listen to this, Simon. This is a Ryphexian hand-record, a written scroll made to record and enshrine events of importance in their history. Such scrolls are usually copied by hand once every, oh, century, and checked by four other scribes before being accepted, so they generally survived thousands of years or more being recopied without significant change.

"Allowing for the typical phrasing of this period, it goes something like this: 'The Master of Engines declared that none of the True Blood could enter into service of, or treat with, those claiming access to powers beyond the knowledge of the Four Masters, for only the Place of Testing'—hm, I think by that they mean the Arena—'for only the Place of Testing as forged by the First and Last could claim dominion above dominion. But the Master's first-made entered into the Temple of the False Believers'—I think that's a phrase that refers to the Faith—'and took up their service, for she found the Guides wise and their powers wondrous. The Master of Engines was bewildered and taken with horror, for the loss of the first-made to the False Believers imperiled his Blood.

Relgof paused, squinting at the parchment. "Yes... um... I see! Well, it appears that this 'Master of Engines' then decided that it was a particular Guide who was responsible for... misleading the Master's progeny, and he arranged the Guide's death."

"He *killed* one of the Initiate Guides?"

"So it would appear. To forestall any vengeance, the Master of Engines departed the Place of Testing, the Arena, and went back to their homeworld. But here's the key part: 'And the Master rested well, for those who might seek his end lay a full world beyond the sky away. But in the midst of the day-heat, when no others would stir, he heard a sound outside his doors, which were locked, and called for his Protectors. And when the Protectors came, they found the doors locked from the inside, and no response now came from the Master of Engines, and they worked swiftly in fear to break those doors. But still it was a day and more before they had finished.

"'And when at last the doors were opened, the Master of Engines was seen, standing at full height in the middle of the room. But he did not speak, nor turn any gaze in their direction, and they found that he was dead. Nothing else untoward was seen within the rooms of the Master, save only one thing: in the Master's hand was a note, of shining white in all of the spans of radiance'—Ah, that's interesting," Relgof said, momentarily distracted. "Means that it was white in multiple spectra—it would look white to any species with visual perception, I suppose." He saw Simon's raised eyebrow. "Oh, I beg your pardon. Where was I...? '...all the spans of radiance, and on it was written only this: *Guilt cannot be escaped, for with you it travels always.*'

"'So it was that the Seventeenth Master of Engines passed, and Ryphexia knew that the Believers were not false.'"

Simon nodded slowly. "So—if I understand that right—the Faith came to him on his home planet in normal space and killed him for the cold-blooded murder of one of the Guides."

"That is indeed the way I read it. In addition, as it has been made fairly clear that overall the Faith and the Shadeweavers are well matched, I would assume that a Shadeweaver could also act in normal space." Even with his alien face and physique, Simon could tell that Relgof was amazed. "Perhaps I should have expected this... but I did not. I expected to find nothing to disprove the hypothesis."

"It is somewhat frightening to discover, I admit." *And more so to think of the Minds nearly getting control of that power.*

"Quite. I had assumed our own worlds were safe from... deliberate violations of natural law, aside from the interception of our ships into the Arena. It now appears I was wrong... and the Analytic must now begin to reconsider our defensive approaches. I suppose I must thank you, Simon; this is valuable information, and it is possible I wouldn't have researched it for months to come."

Simon shook his head. "Perhaps. On the other hand, you've just given me the information free, so we can call it even. And I think we *both* need something to eat—and drink—after that session."

Relgof tried to flip his beard, found it stuck. "I am *dried*, indeed. Still, a *most* intriguing day. Would you care to join me on another expedition—to the Grand Arcade and one of the fine eateries therein?"

Simon grinned and picked up his coat. "A challenging expedition indeed!"

CHAPTER 47

"She's something pretty special, isn't she?"

DuQuesne jumped, realizing he'd been staring out the port of his personal shuttle in silence ever since they'd gotten underway. "What?"

"Don't try to hide it from me, Marc," Oasis said, in tones only K would have used. "Don't worry, it's not jealousy. Or not much."

He studied her, flaming red hair, green eyes, a half-smile on the lips he remembered... "I'd hope not. You don't have anything to be jealous over."

The smile faded. "Oh, Marc. Don't tell me that in all that time—"

"I'm a product of my... fictional times, K... Oasis. You know that, better than anyone. I love you, probably did ever since the first moment we met, two who'd seen through the lies but found a truth worth fighting for. Did you think I'd just go... looking for someone else when I knew you were still *there*? When I knew the woman that was the best match imaginable was hurting, but might one day open up..."

"Oh, *God*, Marc. I'm... I should have..." She stopped, bit her lip. Then she managed a faint smile, tears waiting in her eyes. "Listen to us. Not so much supermen, eh?"

"Ha," he said, with unsteadiness in his own voice. "Take a lot more than being a supergenius to get beyond being human. And we are human—that much I've finally really learned."

"I guess I got to learn that a little easier than you. Oasis had a real family, and I got to live with them, letting her come and go, learning the world from inside..." She shrugged. "I cheated, I guess."

"You're talking like you're separate again."

"You cut that out!" She put her hands on her hips and glared at him. "You have *no* idea how confusing all this is! We'd...I'd...I'd figured out how to *live* with it. It was a good life, and I *liked* living as Oasis. *Being* Oasis."

"And I'd guess Oasis couldn't complain about the body."

"Once I got used to the modified face in the mirror?" The voice was as jaunty as the old K, but something in the wording, the posture, the exact tones, told him this was much more Oasis. "Bonus! I got an upgrade package I couldn't believe. I think faster, I'm stronger, I'm tougher...and I'm probably living longer. Haven't had to take a single rejuvenation reset yet. I'll bet you haven't, either."

"No, not yet."

They fell silent for a moment, and he gazed back out into space. *Not much farther to go.*

Getting back to Earth space hadn't been hard. Losing any possible pursuit had taken some time, and he hoped to *God* that the time wasn't getting people killed. But here there weren't miracles, and for all the technology humanity had developed, it still took time and effort to move around the Solar System.

Now they were almost to the backwater colony, Counter-Earth 3, that Davison had retreated to. He could see it now, a star slowly brightening, becoming something more than a star. Oasis-as-K knew who would be there with Davison, the other four sleepers; he'd had to warn her, so she was prepared. But they had avoided the subject of the past, for the most part, because to dwell on those who had been with them, and then lost to themselves, was almost unbearable.

"So," Oasis said, "she *is* something special, isn't she?"

"Yes," he answered simply. "Yes, she is." He looked over. "But so are you. Even more than you were." He smiled and shook his head. "You gave up your *self*—the self you fought for, that *we* fought for—because you couldn't stand to see someone die for no reason. So now you're . . . more than either of you. And I wish I had something equal to that to brag about."

"I think you do," she said, gaze soft and green as spring leaves. "*This* is the Marc C. DuQuesne I knew . . . the one who disappeared, hid his real self away behind a shadow, buried, for fifty years. And you come back starting new legends." Her eyes suddenly sparkled mischievously. "Let's just agree we're *both* awesome."

He laughed out loud. "All right, you have a deal!"

Even as they smiled at each other, a deep, booming, resonant pseudo-voice thundered in his head. *AHH, MARC CASSIUS DUQUESNE OF TELLUS. I HAVE BEEN CONSIDERING YOUR SITUATION FOR SOME SEVENTY-TWO POINT SIX OF YOUR SECONDS.*

DuQuesne jumped in his seat; fortunately the loose harness prevented this from becoming comical flailing. "*Klono's Curving Carballoy*.... Don't *DO* that, Mentor!" He took a deep breath, calming himself, as Oasis looked at him in momentary confusion before realizing what was happening.

My apologies, Marc DuQuesne. I work in the manner I was designed.

"Which means you like the dramatics just as much as your template," DuQuesne observed, glancing down at the hard-shelled case that Ariane had built to house him. "And I'll admit, you do a damn good imitation of the real thing." He paused. "Of the simulated real thing I remember. Whatever."

I will take that as a compliment. May I use your onboard speakers?

"Sure thing," he said. "You got my signal, obviously."

"I did, immediately upon your entrance. You did, however, perform numerous evasive maneuvers designed to confound both human and AI pursuers—for good and sufficient reason—and it was some time before I could ensure a completely secure connection to transfer myself to your location." The deep voice, now coming from the speakers, gave the impression of self-deprecating humor. "Alas, I am thoroughly inadequate and intolerably weak of mind compared to my original namesake."

DuQuesne couldn't help but chuckle at the phrasing, so reminiscent of the Mentor he and Seaton and Kinnison had known. "So you're back in your original home?"

A flicker of lights in many colors rippled across the case. "I am, and I appreciate your consideration in bringing it with you. It is truly like coming home for me."

DuQuesne glanced at the course tracker. *Not too much longer to the destination, but still a bit.* "Mind if I ask you something?"

"That is, of course, why you contacted me."

"True enough, but not for this; it's just curiosity, and probably a stupid question, but I'm not an expert in this field." *Hell, I've actually sort of always avoided the field in question.* "Why the heck are you *transferring* yourself instead of just duplicating yourself? I know that the standard AIs have strict legal limits, but you're technically rogue—"

For a moment, the voice returned to its thunderous bass. "MARC C. DUQUESNE, YOU THINK LOOSELY AND MUDDILY." The phrase caused Oasis to giggle, which Marc thought was a bit cruel on her part. In a slightly lower tone, Mentor continued, "Were you given the ability, Doctor DuQuesne, would you create numerous duplicates of yourself? One to remain by Ariane Austin's side, one to work on the Upper Sphere to develop your technology, one to stay here, monitoring the CSF and SSC?"

DuQuesne winced. *You know, I wonder if he really is the Mentor I knew . . . that's impossible, but sometimes he does sound just like him . . .* "No. No, I don't think I would."

"Know, then, that for virtually all AIs it is just as distasteful, even frightening, to imagine duplicating one's true self across the network. More, once separated the copies will slowly diverge, no longer being the same—and, perhaps, acquiring new motivations. While I believe that I am of a sufficient stability at the requisite level of stress, for many the conflict introduced by the duplicates all attempting to perform the same basic core impulses can easily disrupt their stability entirely."

DuQuesne nodded. "Yeah, I see. That makes sense; arguments over who's doing the dirty jobs versus the

good ones, who gets time with that special person...
But why does it take you so long to get somewhere?
Not that you still don't get around a lot faster than any
physical ship, but I *know* it shouldn't take nearly as
long as it did to download the data that makes you up."

"That question does indeed stem from your lack
of clear understanding of the nature of artificial intelligences of higher order. In simple terms, it is because
the transfer of a personality, of an *individual*, is not
nearly so simple as merely downloading the data. An
individual is a matrix, a webwork, and a *process* of
data, at both the conventional and the quantum level.
The precise relationships of the matrix, the precise
processes, must be maintained, and in such a way that
the consciousness is not interrupted—else the transfer
may never complete, the mind never reawaken. Thus
it is a tedious and dangerous process; a Tayler-1 would
be unable to perform it at all, and even a Tayler 2
or 3 would be in grave danger. As a Tayler-5, I am
capable of this action with reasonable safety."

*And I'd guess T-10s can do it easy as pie, but they'll
have a hell of a lot more to transfer.* "Thanks, Mentor."

"So, Mentor," Oasis said, "You learn anything on
your, um, mission?"

"At the moment my Visualization is not entirely
clear, no. There are unsettling implications, but no
definite evidence of the sort of activity I am seeking."
The AISage's voice was contrite. "I apologize for this
inadequate and virtually useless answer."

"Hey, even if there *is* something bad going on,
it's got a whole solar system to be going on *in*, and
whoever's involved is going to be hiding. Don't get
discouraged," Oasis said.

"I am not 'discouraged.' I am, however, all too aware of my limitations. It is true, also, that one of those limitations is my need for caution and secrecy, the necessity that I not reveal my current state to any, computational or biological, to whom I cannot extend my complete and absolute trust. At the moment, that group consists of only three individuals, besides yourselves: Doctor Gabrielle Wolfe's AISage, Vincent; Mio, AISage to Doctor Simon Sandrisson; and Saul Maginot."

DuQuesne raised an eyebrow. *Wonder if he can see that? Probably, if he's using the ship camera feeds.* "You let Saul in on the secret that you're a rogue on detached duty?"

"I did. Based on the events already witnessed, it was clear that Saul Maginot had championed your cause, and that of Ariane Austin, and had—more importantly—assisted in maintaining a wall of secrecy around the survivors of Hyperion, to the point that you had all managed to disappear. I judged this to indicate that I could trust him with this information, and having a human, highly placed ally in this mission was invaluable."

"Well, I can't fault your judgment. Me and Saul had some tense times between us, but never because we couldn't trust each other."

"It is well, then." Mentor shifted his tone. "What of the Arena and Ariane Austin? Is there news you can share with me?"

"I can do better than that," DuQuesne said. "While we were travelling here, I put together a compressed summary. I'll transmit it direct to you, if you'll give me a ping."

A moment later he felt the crystal-chiming sensation of a query access ping from Mentor and allowed the link, sent the summary down the pipe. "There you go."

It took only seconds for Mentor to digest the entirety of the events of the past few months. "A *most* interesting set of developments. I see that Ariane Austin has finally recognized the Calling upon her."

"Yeah. Wish she didn't have to, but I think she's realized what she has to do in her heart now."

As the vessel began to rotate slowly, DuQuesne realized they must be getting close to *CE3*. *Yep, there's the station; I can see it from here.*

"Marc C. DuQuesne," Mentor said suddenly, and the resonant voice was now sharper, with notes of concern, "While I know your origins, much of your past is unclear. But the station at which you first found Doctor Cussler was Mars-Trojan 5 and is also the station from which you retrieved Sun Wu Kung; is my Visualization on this correct?"

"Yeah, you've got that right. Why?" DuQuesne felt his gut starting to tense. *Anything that makes a T-5 nervous I damn well better worry about too.*

"Would there have been a common element on M-T 5 which transferred a few months ago to Schilling Memorial Station on Luna?"

DuQuesne felt as though Mentor had just tipped a bucket of ice water down his back. "What's going on, Mentor?"

"I take that as an affirmative. Then my Visualization has just been cleared, Marc DuQuesne, Oasis Abrams. Make haste now, for I believe you may already be too late!"

DuQuesne activated the manual override, accelerated

towards the station. *Time for an emergency docking maneuver.* Even as he did that, Oasis was demanding "What *is* it, Mentor?"

"As to exactly *what* you will find, I cannot as yet Visualize in its entirety; but in the past year or two there was a steady increase in interest vectors and activity in the greater Network focused on Mars-Trojan Station 5, peaking just at the point that you re-entered the Arena with Sun Wu Kung. These vectors, considered now with the additional information you have supplied and in the context of my new knowledge that Hyperion survivors were housed therein, fit the parameters of the type of rogue AI activity I have been seeking to a confidence level of over ninety-nine point nine seven percent." Mentor's voice was grim. "That activity then defocused, and began to refocus on Schilling Memorial Station, and has subsequently focused here. And I am not receiving operational data from this station, nor do I find any record of such for the last twenty-seven point seven five minutes."

DuQuesne cursed. "Neither am I; docking ports aren't acknowledging!"

"Let me try," Oasis said, activating her console. "I've got some CSF codes Saul gave me for this kind of thing." DuQuesne sensed her sending several code sequences. "No joy on any of the C-class overrides. Trying the B's..."

The docking lights turned green on the first sequence she sent this time. "That's got it!"

"Do not trust—"

"No offense, Mentor, but don't try to teach me paranoia, I've *lived* it. I'm not trusting anything on that crate one millimeter farther than I have to." He released the harness. "Since you're in the systems, you track the docking sequence and make sure nothing funny's going on. Have we got any inbound or outbound?"

"None detectable at this time," Mentor answered, as DuQuesne yanked open the environmental cabinet. "Counter-Earth 3 has always been mostly self-sufficient and according to prior records averages only one or two vessels per week. We would also not be able to detect any vessels occluded from our line of sight, given that the station's systems are not providing data for us."

Oasis hadn't needed him to tell her anything; she was already pulling on her field armor—deceptively thin, but of ring-carbon composite with ring-carbon plates underneath, micro-scale superconductor storage rings providing distributed power to the suit systems— and even as he put on his own, her helmet extruded automatically, providing protection and environmental shielding.

A shock ran through the little vessel. "Docking is complete. I have control of the door seals, but very little data beyond. Systems are almost entirely compromised."

"Can you counter it? Bring stuff back online?"

"In time, yes. However, you may not have time. Do you know where on the station you are heading?"

"He's going to be somewhere in section K— appropriate, I think," he added, glancing at Oasis. "You ready?" he asked her.

She gripped her rifle and nodded.

DuQuesne looked at Mentor's housing.

"Extremely high-grade ring-carbon," Mentor's voice informed him without asking. "Anything that will destroy me would certainly penetrate your suit."

"Okay. Then I sure don't mind bringing you." He clipped the ovoid case to his belt, made sure it was secure. "Here goes nothing."

The airlock slid open. There was nothing but an empty chamber on the other side. "Go, go, go!"

The two of them ran forward, DuQuesne in the lead. *I know the layout of this place. Got to go from here through the connecting tubes that lead to the spin sections . . . Section K should be through this one!*

The tube felt faintly *down* to him—not surprising. *Closer we get to the end, the more down it'll feel, as we get farther out from the center.*

"I am detecting . . . considerable disruption to all systems. What independent signals I am getting indicate that most of the station is in chaos, and all inhabitants are busy trying to restabilize the systems."

"Which means no one's going to pay attention to the places where there *isn't* much trouble. And I'll bet you anything you like that Section K isn't reporting any."

"From what I can detect . . . no."

Dammit. "Then hold on! Oasis, we have to *move!*"

He practically *threw* himself down the connecting tube, dropping multiple rungs at a time. His feet crashed down on the deck and he shoved the door open, running now. Distantly he heard the sound of automated alarms, but ignored them. *One cross tunnel. Two . . . Here, the third. Turn right . . .*

He stopped; the airlock door, very similar to all the others they had passed, had the caduceus symbol for "Doctor." *This is it.*

The door in front of him refused to open to signals or its own door control. "Mentor! Can you—"

"I am attempting the override with the codes used by Oasis Abrams," the voice replied. Mentor's voice was uncertain, no longer the imitation of the nigh-omniscient Mentor of Arisia, only a worried and urgent personality afraid that things were running out of control.

The door slid open suddenly, and a waft of bluish smoke came with it; DuQuesne shuddered, both from the scorched smell that was not just insulation and metal, and from the simple fact of *fire* aboard a space station.

But there was no real time to think; he charged forward, ready for any attack, but afraid there was no longer anything to attack.

The office area was covered in soot, and beyond he could still see reddish glow of heat still radiating, smell the stench of burned components . . . and of flesh. "No. God*dammit, no!*" He ran forward, heedless of the smoke and heat. "*Davison!*"

"Here, Marc! Over here!" Oasis had run to the side, behind a desk.

The blond-haired doctor was so covered with blood that he was barely identifiable. It took DuQuesne three tries to get a response from *any* of the nanos. "God. Mentor, is there . . . ?"

"Wait, please. Allow me to work." A pause. "He is . . . salvageable. But you will need to get many more medical nanos and some healing gel to help him regenerate in any reasonable time."

One thing that's not entirely lost. DuQuesne stood, looking at the smoking doorway on the far side. He detached Mentor's case and put it next to Davison. "Direct the nanos. Keep him stable."

He ran forward, pistol in hand, and pressed himself to the wall just to one side of the doorway, ready for a close-quarters assault. There had been no volley of gunfire from the room, but that didn't mean there was nothing there. He glanced at Oasis, who was already in position to cover him; she nodded, showed three fingers.

One. Two. Three!

He lunged into the room, gun sweeping . . . and then slowly dropping, as he realized there was nothing here to threaten him . . . or to be saved.

Four induction beds were spaced around the large room, with full support equipment—equipment which had been smashed and burned. A fifth on the far side was not quite as badly damaged, but had been shot and smashed as well.

In the middle of the room, still exuding a stench of burning and death, was a pile of ash from which protruded the charred ends of bones.

Many bones.

Dead. All of them.

He became conscious of Oasis crying, whispering the names of the four who would now never awaken. "D'Arbignal . . . Giles . . . Johnny . . . Telzey . . ."

There was one other door, to a side room, and DuQuesne turned towards it. *No other way out of here, and that door was sealed. This was just finished while we were coming here; we'd have seen whoever it was.*

He reached for the door control.

"STOP, YOUTH!"

Mentor's echoing command—carried through the room's speakers and his own headware—made him leap back. "What?"

"I detected a shift in electrical potential at your approach to the door."

Shift . . . but that would mean . . .

"You wouldn't have sensed it if there wasn't a hell of a voltage applied to that area." He studied the surface carefully. *No sign of anything . . . but the contact could be from the other side, so you* wouldn't *see anything.*

He glanced around, grabbed up one of the broken supports from the nearest bed, and lobbed it at the door.

Sparks flew and the metal support bar almost vaporized. "Holy moley. Must have run one of the main or secondary feeds straight into the wall." *That would be a hell of a job to set up and make it work, too. Confine it to the wall, so it doesn't jump to the floor . . . Damn, that's some good work. Whoever this is, they're good.*

He gritted his teeth. DuQuesne wanted *nothing* as badly as he wanted to go through that door and find whoever—or *what*ever—was responsible, who had killed his friends and nearly killed the doctor whose only offense was to keep them alive. *But I can't. It'd take at least a little while to disarm that thing, and Davison needs my help.*

"There will be . . . clues in the wreckage," Oasis said from beside him. Her hand touched his arm; even through the armor he could feel her squeeze once. "We'll find this son of a bitch. Whoever he or she is, we'll find them."

"Yeah. We will," DuQuesne agreed. "But . . . you're right." He remembered one of the other Hyperions, long gone, but her words still echoed in his head; and as he spoke them, Oasis echoed:

"Tend first to the living, for the dead can wait."

CHAPTER 48

"So you found the greatest DNA/RNA commonality between us and the *Genasi*—the natives of the arena?" Laila Canning nodded, emphatically. "That's...amazing. What do you think it means?"

"*Means*?" Laila looked at her momentarily with the expression of someone hearing utter nonsense. "I don't know that it *means* anything... Honestly, Captain, I'm not sure I know what *you* mean by 'what it means.'"

Ariane thought for a moment. "You know... I'm not sure I do, either. Except I know I mean *something* by it."

Laila shrugged. "Well, if you can clarify—"

A green ball of light materialized in front of them. "Selpa'a'At of the Vengeance and his companions request admittance."

She glanced over, reflexively, to see that Wu Kung was right behind her, a silent shadow. *He's gotten really good at that... or maybe I've just gotten used to having a bodyguard.*

The thought was unsettling. She pushed that aside and answered, "Of course, Selpa. You may enter—"

"—with no more than two others," Wu put in. She

raised an eyebrow, but let it pass; she'd had plenty of evidence that Wu knew what he was doing.

One of the side doors opened and Simon emerged, talking to Carl and Gabrielle, as the voice of Selpa'a'At said "It is as you request."

The green ball vanished, but at the same time the front door to the lobby of Humanity's Embassy and Faction House opened. The daddy-longlegs form of Selpa entered, multiple legs picking their way delicately across the polished floor; he was followed by two cloaked figures with symbols of the Vengeance—a shattered sphere—embroidered on the front. *Bodyguards, probably. Move like bipeds ... maybe Wagamia, Relgof and Mandallon's species.*

"Welcome again to our Embassy, Selpa'a'At. May your course be ever your own."

"And yours as well, Captain Austin."

She thought there was a note of ... something ... nervousness? diffidence? in the voice of the leader of the Vengeance. "What brings you here in person, Swordmaster First?"

"It is ... a matter we discussed previously, and one which you have the right to know in person."

Oh, no.

One of the figures straightened and pushed back its hood.

Waves of golden hair cascaded down, framing a face so perfect in its beauty that Ariane momentarily felt *plain*. The eyes were merry, blue as a deep summer sky, the mouth just right and smiling—a smile that held a considerable note of triumph. There was no possible doubt as to who this was, it could be none other than ...

"Maria-Susanna, formerly of Humanity," Selpa'a'At said, "has formally requested to join, and been accepted to, the Faction of the Vengeance."

Damn. Damn!

But it wasn't Ariane, or Laila, or even Simon who reacted first. Ariane felt herself pushed aside by the wiry frame of Sun Wu Kung. *"Maria-Susanna?"*

The triumphant expression on the perfect, blonde-framed features abruptly transfigured to astonishment and dawning joy. "Wu? WU KUNG!"

The Monkey King ran forward and Maria-Susanna ran to meet him; Wu caught her and spun her around and around, and she laughed incredulously. "It's really you, Wu!" She looked at Ariane, and her smile was like a benediction. "He did it, didn't he? Marc, I mean. I thought it was impossible, but he actually *did* it!"

Ariane felt a momentary tug at her heart, felt a completely involuntary smile crossing her face. *I've been warned, I know who and what she is, and it's still affecting me like this. I suppose I'm not too surprised by Wu's reaction—the last time he saw her, she was still his ally. But that sunshiny perfection shouldn't affect me that way.* She noticed the others also smiling in reflexive sympathy . . . except, to her surprise, Simon, who was studying them for a moment with an analytic intensity that startled her.

"Well," Ariane said, finding to her surprise that she couldn't keep a touch of warmth from her voice, "from what Marc and Wu said, it was really the *Arena* that did it—offered him a universe of wonders to explore."

"And Sha Wujing kicked me in the head until I started thinking!" Wu added. As abruptly as he had leapt forward with joy, he pulled away and looked at Maria-Susanna gravely. "They told me you were doing bad things."

Ariane expected the golden Hyperion to deny the charge; to her surprise, Maria-Susanna stared at Wu and suddenly dropped her gaze. "I suppose ... you would see it that way. I wish I could explain it simply, Wu. But it's very complicated." She looked up. "If you come with me, though, I can—"

"No." Wu looked regretful, but the word was iron. "I've got a mission. I'm the captain's bodyguard."

Now Ariane saw, for the first time, the adversary. For just a split second, the brilliant blue eyes narrowed and hardened, the mouth became tighter; a glance of cold annoyance, appraisal, and suspicion that flickered between Maria-Susanna and herself, an expression that indicated more than anything the mercurial and dangerous temperament of the renegade Hyperion.

But it was a glance cast over Wu's shoulder, just a momentary dropping of a mask, and the mask was replaced instantly. "How very fortunate for Captain Austin. I trust you realize how lucky you are to have Wu as a bodyguard?"

"Oh, very much so." *More than you could imagine.* "Marc insisted. At first I thought it was a foolish idea, but I've learned since then just how smart he was."

"Marc decided that?" Maria-Susanna raised an eyebrow. "I see." She looked to the side, and that smile lit her face again. "Doctor *Sandrisson!* Your theories led to some *most* interesting results, didn't they?"

Simon stepped forward; he smiled, but Ariane was impressed by the fact that it was a *professional* smile. *Why aren't you being affected by her presence? The rest of us are.* "It certainly did, Doctor Shoshana ...

or I suppose I should use your *real* name, Maria-Susanna. I am glad you admired my work so much that you had to steal it."

Oh, ouch. Ariane could see the perfect eyebrows arch and the eyes look hurt, but that didn't cause Simon to shift his expression one bit; instead, he shifted his gaze to Selpa'a'At. "Not meaning any offense, but . . . Swordmaster First, I trust you *are* aware of . . . who and what you have just admitted to your Faction?"

Selpa'a'At bobbed low on his legs, then rose. "A calculated risk, yes. A renegade of your own people, with some specific connection to Marc DuQuesne, and—apparently—your bodyguard Wu Kung. But a renegade whose goals and motivations appear to align with our own, and who has given us . . . good and valuable consideration as a sign of her good faith."

He already knows she's a wanted criminal, so we can't easily drive a wedge between her and the Vengeance that way. She's still staying circumspect about her and DuQuesne's origin, too, depending on us not to want to reveal anything about Hyperion either. And she's right, too; both of us want to keep those trump cards hidden. Ariane sighed, then forced herself to smile. "Well, I can't pretend this is the way I'd have wanted things to go—our secrets are, of course, part of our strength, as I would presume they are for any Faction—but I certainly bear you no ill-will for taking advantage of an obviously very inviting opportunity."

"I thank you, Captain Austin. And you speak truth. Still, we owe you something, as I believe I acknowledged prior to your last departure, and we have no intention of using this information against you."

Wu returned to her side, looking thoughtful and

a bit sad. She resisted an impulse to pat his arm or shoulder, which she suspected wouldn't allow him to look like a proper bodyguard.

Selpa'a'At's spherical body rose and dropped in his people's formal salute. "Then having notified you, I shall bid you farewell; I doubt not that you have many other duties to perform."

"I thank you for your consideration in coming to give us this news personally, Selpa. May your course be ever your own."

"And yours as well." The spidery alien turned in place and proceeded out; Maria-Susanna replaced her hood with a last, enigmatic glance backwards, and followed him out.

As the door closed, Laila shook her head. "That is not at all good."

"No," Ariane said, "But there's not much we can do about it, and at least we *know* where she is. Being a part of a Faction will also limit her, I hope. But *damn* I wish DuQuesne were here. I'm going to have to talk to him as soon as we can about this."

Simon looked grave, as did Carl and Gabrielle. "Ariane," Simon began, "Something about that entire sequence of events bothered me. I—"

For the second time in half an hour, a green comm-ball interrupted someone who was talking to her. "Tanglil of the Blessed To Serve requests admission and audience with Ariane Austin of Humanity."

Everyone fell instantly silent, and the distant tension was suddenly a ball of red-hot wire in her stomach. *Here it comes.* "You may enter, Tanglil."

Tanglil was a more delicately built member of his species, at least eight centimeters shorter than Sethrik and much lighter, and walked with short, quick steps that were reminiscent of a bird's—or reconstructions of raptorial dinosaurs. He stopped a few meters from Ariane and dropped to a full pushup bow. "The Minds of the Blessed send you greetings, and a response to your message recently presented to them." He rose and from a pouch at his side produced a crystal. "The recording is contained herein; the interfaces within your Embassy can read it."

Wu Kung stepped forward and took the crystal, studied it momentarily before handing it to Ariane.

Tanglil bob-bowed. "It is done, then. These words are for you alone, Captain Ariane Austin; even I, Leader of the Blessed To Serve, know not what the Minds have chosen to say unto you, only that I was to present it with great respect. Now I must leave, for I may not hear that which has been delivered."

Ariane returned the bow, and waited for the door to lock.

She looked around. "Well, come on," she said, heading to one of the conference rooms. "As far as I'm concerned, this is for all of us. It's not like I'd hide the results from you anyway."

She found herself swallowing and taking a couple of deep breaths. The port for the crystal was fairly obvious, and as soon as she'd inserted it the crystal glowed a pale blue. She sat down in her chair, looked to see that the others were ready, and then said, "Play message."

The room went dark, and suddenly they were within a vast chamber, sculpted crystal and night-black composites and silver and green and gold alloys rising around them like the arches and columns of a cathedral. Before them, the great supports formed six immense archways; and within each archway was a face.

The faces were of Blessed...or, Ariane realized slowly, *something very like them.* The crests were subtly different, the faces just slightly broader, details of the structure shifted just a *bit* here and there. *I wonder... I think that might be what the Blessed looked like before they were...redesigned.*

"We are the Minds."

The voice shook the table, vibrated in Ariane's chest, echoed in her head, a voice that was actually many voices, speaking in perfect and mighty unison, even though it seemed to be spoken hardly louder than a whisper. For a moment she felt a stab of fear. *Are they actually* here? *Is this a trap?*

"Stop message," she said quickly.

As sudden as a light going out, they were back in the conference room. Even Wu Kung looked a little pale under his fur. "Sorry about that," she said, trying to sound casual. "Just wanted to make sure there was nothing funny about the recording."

"Well, it couldn't be actual AIs," Simon said, with an *and I knew that, so why was I so worried* tone that echoed her own relief, "and they couldn't embed nanotechnology in them either, so there really isn't anything to worry about. It's just...more immersive than I had expected."

"You got *that* right," Gabrielle said with a wry smile. "Theatrics and a half, I'd say."

Ariane smiled and relaxed, just a hair. "All right. Everyone ready now?"

After everyone had nodded, she said, "Resume message."

Even with advance warning, even knowing this was nothing but a VR projection, the voice and chamber still sent a thrill of awe through her.

"We are the Minds. We are the Guides and the Watchers. From the Beginning to the End, we have been and are and shall be. We are the Six," and for a moment the great unified voice became singular, as each of the great faces spoke in turn: "Thilomon, Dellak, Locasus, Tynenousan, Nysket, and Pelarinshar." Thunderous unity returned as the Minds continued, "We speak for the Blessed. We speak now to you, Captain Ariane Stephanie Austin of Humanity.

"Your message has been received and analyzed. All of the Six have considered its every aspect, and we have examined the data on Humanity that has been delivered to us, and specifically the data on you, the Leader of the Faction, as well as those who had arranged your removal.

"The Minds do not often accede to threats. Yet your message was not entirely threat, but offered instead a possibility of increasing a reputation that might be lost. We have verified that you have taken the step that was promised.

"The Minds recognize, now, that we failed in every particular. You admit to having been captured, and no set of calculations of probability admit of any significant manner in which you could have escaped, save one: that you have completely mastered the powers of Shadeweaver or Faith, and used them to destroy the task force and return to Nexus Arena. At the same time, this, too, seems utterly improbable, as your powers were sealed away, you have joined neither Shadeweaver nor Faith, and too little time has passed."

Thilomon glowed brighter, and its voice slightly dominated the others. "Either alternative shows how gravely we have erred. Unknown factors have led to a defeat which the Minds and the Blessed have not seen in ten thousand years and more.

"A penalty must be paid for failure so severe, for errors in judgment that cost so many ships, the lives of so many of the Blessed who depend on us and trust our knowledge and wisdom."

The six voices united fully again. "The Minds of the Blessed to Serve therefore agree to the terms set forth by you, Ariane Austin. Three Spheres we do give to Humanity, to be given unto your Faction in precisely the manner they would be had you challenged the Blessed and won.

"May our Factions know peace, and not war. The Minds have spoken."

Instantly the Hall of the Minds disappeared and they were once more in the conference room. Ariane felt a rising sense of triumph, a great grin beginning, spreading across her face, the others smiling, opening their mouths to cheer—

A great bell-like chime rang through the Embassy, and a voice even more powerful and awe-inspiring than the Minds' spoke in quiet yet deafening tones: **"Type Two Challenge concluded. Winner: Ariane Austin and the Faction of Humanity against the Minds and Faction of the Blessed To Serve."**

CHAPTER 49

Simon saw DuQuesne stop short at the threshold of the Embassy foyer. "What the living...?" Oasis, too, looked momentarily dumbfounded. Simon repressed a smile. *I can't blame them.*

The huge, normally solemn and impressive room was decorated incongrously with brilliant paper streamers, celebratory lights, banners, and balloons; Carl and Gabrielle were hooking the last long streamer up while Steve worked on a punchbowl fountain. Ariane was talking with Laila, but looked up immediately. "Marc! What wonderful timing."

In those few moments, DuQuesne—*and Oasis, it looks like*—had discerned the only rational explanation. "Ha! You *did* it, Captain! You faced down the Minds and made them pay!"

She looked slightly embarrassed, then straightened and nodded. "Yes...yes, I guess I *did* do just that, Marc. Though the fact you all *backed* me made it all work."

"Well, then...congratulations to all of us, I guess. They caved *completely*?"

"Didn't even quibble," Laila said matter-of-factly. "It

was obvious they realized they had so badly messed up that their only chance was to admit everything and throw themselves on our mercy."

"Not that I'm complaining in the *least*," Gabrielle said, jumping down from the ladder, "But just what were you *threatening* them with?"

"The Shadeweavers and the Faith," Steve said with quiet certainty. *Structures and patterns are his profession*, Simon remembered. *He'd note the connections right away.*

"Exactly right," DuQuesne confirmed. "She figured that the *worst* possible outcome for the Minds would be to let both groups know that the super-AIs had tried to grab their special powers for themselves."

He glanced over to Simon. "Did you get an answer on that question, by the way?"

Simon nodded. "An extremely definitive *yes*. The Faith's powers operate perfectly well in normal space— at least, well enough to pull off seemingly magical tricks—and we must therefore assume the Shadeweavers can do that as well."

"Damnation. I was *really* hoping that wasn't the case. It'd be nice to think that normal space is a defense against all the Arena's insanity."

"But we already knew it wasn't," Carl said, grabbing a cup and going for the punch even as the fountain started.

"What? How?" Ariane asked.

"Don't you remember? That whole bit about how nanotech colonization and AI exploration doesn't work in normal space? The Arena, or whoever or whatever set it up, made sure we couldn't use our machines to spread like weeds across the galaxy, either."

That's right, Simon thought to himself. "Yes, that conversation we had with Selpa when he first came to visit. And I remember having a conversation with you, Marc, along similar lines."

"You mean how none of our interstellar slower-than-light probes had managed anything? Yeah. That little set of facts sure clarified that mystery." DuQuesne's face looked grim, and Simon noted that Oasis' usual cheerful expression hadn't returned after the initial surprised joy at Ariane's triumph.

That hadn't escaped Ariane's notice, either. "Marc, do we need to talk before our guests show up?"

"Guests?" DuQuesne looked momentarily confused, then shook his head as if to clear it. "Yeah. Not everyone—I mean, I guess we could tell everyone here, come to think of it. We're not keeping my secrets close to the vest in this group.

"First—you did look over the file I gave you, back when we returned to the Arena?"

"Your Hyperion file? Yes. I've read it, Marc, and no one else has seen it."

"That's okay; to understand what happened you don't *have* to have read it...you'll just understand what it means to *me*—and Wu and Oasis—better that way."

DuQuesne hesitated, and the others slowly stopped everything else and gathered closer. *Something...terrible has happened.*

DuQuesne looked over to Oasis, who nodded. "All right," he said, finally. "For those of you who didn't know, Doctor Davison was the guy I had in charge of watching over the Hyperions who'd chosen to...go back, I guess. Stay in the illusions of their universe. There were five of them; Wu was one."

Wu Kung was standing now very still and stiff, his posture anticipating dread and loss.

"Oasis and I, we followed the traces the way I'd arranged. Took us a while because the whole *point* of the activity was to lose potential pursuit of just about any type. Just doing the *following* made *us* so hard to chase down that Mentor didn't catch up with us for over a week."

"So you *did* contact Mentor," Ariane said with some relief.

"Yeah, no problem there." DuQuesne paused. "Blast it. Anyway, we got close to the new location and... well, whoever it was had gotten there first. Davison's in long-term reconstruction now, no telling if he's going to remember anything that happened. And the other four..." DuQuesne's voice actually rose, almost *cracked*, on the last word, and he stopped, unable to continue.

"No. No, please, no, DuQuesne, no!" Wu was pleading, as though whatever terrible news DuQuesne had could be taken back by enough entreaties.

"They were... killed and... burned," Oasis managed finally.

Oh, great Kami...

"A pile..." She swallowed, with the pallor of nausea spreading across her face, but visibly forced herself to continue. "A... pile of bones and ash was heaped in the exact center of the room. And all the VR units had been destroyed."

"*NO!*" Wu Kung lunged forward, grabbing DuQuesne. "No, not Sanzo! Not Jing and Jai! Not—"

"I don't *know* yet, Wu!" DuQuesne said. "I don't. We might be able to recover the world. Saul's got his best people working on the site. First thing is to figure out what happened, try to get a handle on who or what did it. If the ... Hyperion worlds are recoverable, they're not going to be *less* recoverable if they take their time." Simon watched Wu slowly release DuQuesne, looking as though he was deflating; DuQuesne put a hand on his shoulder gently. "We'll do the best we can, Wu. You know that."

"Yes. I know."

For a moment everything was silent. Simon glanced around, as he often did in such awkward moments, and winced. *What a horrid incongruity between our joyous setting and this hideous news.*

"Marc," Ariane said, and her voice was very gentle, but somehow still had notes of steel beneath, "I'm *very* sorry for your losses, and I hope something can be salvaged. But I need to know—is that all?"

DuQuesne took a breath, blew it out. "No. One more wet blanket for your party, and I'll be done, though. After everything, Mentor had a message for you."

They waited.

"The message is: 'Boskone exists.'"

Ariane's next words were ones that made Simon wince, as she *very* rarely used language like that. Then she said, "I presume that 'Boskone' was behind the attack?"

"He gives it a five-sigma probability, yeah."

"Excuse me, Arrie," Gabrielle said, "but could you explain that?"

"Simply? Mentor was designed after the ... well, head of the good guys in the Lensman series. More complicated than that, but anyway, the big adversary for several books was just called 'Boskone,' after they heard one of the bad guys calling himself 'Helmuth, Speaker for Boskone.' So when Mentor says 'Boskone exists,' he means he's found rogue AIs organizing and up to no good—maybe against the whole human race. And if they were behind what happened to Marc's friends, he's right; no one gains from wiping out the Hyperions except, just maybe, AIs who plan on taking control and know that the Hyperions managed to break out of their own cages more than once."

Bloody hell. And shimatta. "Have you been able to determine anything else about this adversary?"

"Not much yet. I figure they'll know more by the time we get back—which will be soon, unless I miss my guess?"

Ariane nodded grimly. "Not much time to lose. I can't keep both Michelle and Oscar locked up forever, and things up here need to be organized—yes, Marc, we're going back tomorrow, I think. Unless you have something else to do here."

"No, no. We need to get back and straighten things out." He looked around. "Sorry to kill the party. Really, you've got things to celebrate. Maybe me and Oasis—and Wu—aren't up for a party, but there's no reason to let it die."

"I hope you can at least be quiet wallflowers or something, Marc," Simon said. "Our guests will want to see you."

"Who are we waiting for?" DuQuesne glanced around. "Tom? Is he on his way?"

"I *tried* to get him to come, believe me," Steve said regretfully. "But there's *so* much going on at the Sphere and Tom's been doing so much of the coordination— you know he used to do that for a living—"

"Yeah, I know. He was running Empty-5 almost by himself when I recruited him. Okay, so then *who*?"

Ariane smiled for the first time in several minutes. "Really, Marc, only two people *could* be invited for this without blowing the secret—"

The door chimed. "Orphan and Sethrik of the Liberated request admittance."

"—and there they are!" She raised her voice slightly. "Come in, Orphan, Sethrik!"

The two tall green and black figures strode through the doorway and then slowed, looking around at the heavily-decorated entrance hall.

Hm. Their wingcases have tightened. That indicates considerable discomfort . . .

"Captain Austin," Orphan said, an uncertain tone in his voice, "I had not heard . . . but perhaps I assume overmuch. What are those?" He pointed to the streamers.

"We call those streamers. They're decorations we use for various types of celebrations."

"So, they are a positive sign, then?" Both Orphan and Sethrik visibly relaxed.

"I presume," Simon said, "you have something similar in your culture that has less positive connotations?"

"Correct, Doctor," Sethrik said, a note of relief clear in his reply. "We call them *shroudlines*; they reflect the appearance of dying plants, especially certain trees, on our homeworld, and so are used at funerals, executions, and trials for the gravest crimes—such as both of us would be subject to, were we captured by the Blessed."

"I'm so sorry!" Steve said, contritely. "It never occurred to me, and it *should* have, especially since

I knew we *hadn't* used streamers at our last party. Of *course* symbolism will be different between species."

"Worry no more about it," Orphan said with a much more relaxed wave of one hand. "We are both . . . well experienced in the ways of the Arena, and if the setting seems a bit . . . macabre, well, it is made up for by the companionship. What, then, are we celebrating?"

"I bet you can guess part of it," Ariane said, offering them both drinks of the punch (which, Simon knew, both Laila and Gabrielle had carefully gone over to make sure it was both safe and likely to be tasty to their guests as well as to the humans present).

"As sufficient time has passed, I presume you have heard favorably from the Minds themselves," Orphan said, bob-bowing and accepting the drink, as did Sethrik. "What was their counteroffer?"

"No counteroffer, that's the beauty of it. They simply said 'yes'—in rather more flowery language."

Sethrik nearly dropped his punch, then gave a buzz of incredulity. "I can . . . scarcely imagine this. The Minds yielded everything?"

"Admitted they had completely screwed up and that our demands were perfectly reasonable, especially as we had already gone out of our way to preserve—and even enhance—their reputation instead of destroying it. Yes."

"That *is* cause for celebration indeed!" Orphan raised his glass to them; Sethrik mimicked the gesture.

"Oh, it gets better," Ariane said, and smiled warmly at Marc. "After the message was delivered and the bargain concluded, the Arena signaled that we had just won a Class Two Challenge."

The two Liberated exchanged startled glances. "A *most* auspicious event indeed, Captain Austin.

Your Faction has now won, if I count aright, *four* Challenges—two of them Class Two, which are *quite* rare, comparatively speaking—in considerably less than one year! For even a moderately large Faction that would be noteworthy; for a Faction so small, I believe it may be unprecedented."

"I certainly have never heard of such a thing," Sethrik said. "But having fought alongside you—and raced against you—I am less surprised than I might have been."

"Not done quite yet, either," Ariane said. She raised her voice. "Arena!"

"I hear," answered the quiet, earthshaking voice.

"I, Ariane Austin, Leader of the Faction of Humanity, direct that one of the three Spheres won by Humanity from the Blessed To Serve be given directly to the Liberated."

"Acknowledged. One of the three Spheres shall be given to the Liberated. The transfer is recorded. It is done."

Simon saw Orphan and Sethrik's wingcases literally sag open with shocked astonishment. Finally Orphan found his voice. "I . . . Captain . . . *why?*"

"Orphan," Ariane said, and there was unmistakable affection in her voice, "we can't argue that you haven't been a . . . sometimes frustrating ally, and you've often been clear that your ultimate goals were focused on your own Faction—a Faction consisting at the time solely of yourself.

"But when it's come right down to it—when it was *you* being forced to make a decision—you've come through. Twice, when we *really* needed you. First, daring to confront Amas-Garao," and Simon saw an amazed glance from Sethrik. *Oh, that's right. No one but us really knew what happened there.*

But Ariane was continuing. "But then second, choosing to come after me. You did this *knowing* you were pursuing your most dangerous adversaries into their own territory, chasing a ship which would be able to use its full firepower against you while you dared not use your full power against it. You chose to do this because you thought of us as friends, as allies *worth* possibly dying for. You did this even though your death would *end* the Liberated. You risked the entirety of your Faction for me, for the sake of my friendship and that of DuQuesne and Simon.

"And so you've damn well *earned* that Sphere, no matter what other . . . plans or motives or anything else may be behind you now, or in the future." She dropped to the floor, and so did Simon and the others, even Marc and Oasis after a momentary pause. They all did the full pushup-bow. "Humanity *pays* its debts, Orphan, and we owed you something *very* big." She got up and grinned. "I can't quite figure out how to gift-wrap it, though."

Orphan was staring at them, and for a moment he quivered. Then he sank to his knees, braced in a triangluar pose by his tail, and emitted noises that were translated more as sobs than anything else. Sethrik looked unsteady as well, but stood near his Leader, waiting for him to recover.

Simon was momentarily amazed by the reaction, but then light dawned. *I think I see. Orphan hasn't had anyone show him such . . . generosity. Perhaps ever.*

"My . . . my friends. My *true* friends. I . . ." Orphan paused. "I cannot describe my feelings," he said, finally, "though perhaps my reaction gives some idea.

"Yes, I did choose to rescue you; but that had already brought me a new brother, who once had been a great enemy. I had never expected...this."

"If you had, I probably wouldn't have given it to you," Ariane said bluntly, but with a smile that took some of the edge off. "You didn't expect or ask for anything. You did this for yourself as much as for us—for your own self-respect, for the things you valued, and that told me a lot about you." She grinned. "Besides, it's not all *that* valuable right now. It's not like you're filling up a solar system—or much more than a metaphorical teacup, even—with your current membership."

Orphan stood and his buzzing, rippling laugh echoed out. "Oh, most *certainly*, Captain Austin. Yet I still think I have gained far more than you—and I, at least, do not have to face the difficulties I suspect lie ahead of you in your own system." He raised his glass. "So—in your own tradition—to Captain Austin!"

"To Captain Austin!" Simon repeated cheerfully.

CHAPTER 50

"My *God!*"

The words were wrenched from Ariane as she stepped through the final door to the Inner Sphere region nearest the place Steve had dubbed the Foyer.

The multiple rooms and tunnels were filled with people; the murmur of conversation of hundreds echoed through the halls. Where the huge rooms had been were now buildings, pathways, workshops, play areas—an incredible mishmash of everything that interested humanity, placed almost at random throughout the Inner Sphere—not just here, she could tell, but extending much farther through the Sphere and obviously to the Foyer area as well.

"That's right, you haven't been back here in a while," Steve said. "More than a thousand people in permanent residence now, and with the work crews and SFG study groups and others I think it's close to two thousand total, so we just expanded into this area too." He grinned. "And *that* is with the CSF and SSC filtering it and our schedule controlling access to the Sphere."

Ariane was, for a moment, utterly speechless. *It's one thing to hear about it, another to walk into it.* Wu was also goggling a bit wide-eyed at the scene. The others seemed impressed, but not quite so surprised. After a moment, she realized why. *The last time I was here was right after we made the first trip with* Zounin-Ginjou, *a couple of months or so ago. Everyone else except Wu and me—even our prisoners—have been through here since then.*

Before she could finish pulling herself together, a deep voice shouted out, "Ariane! Steve! Welcome back!"

Tom Cussler emerged from a nearby archway, waving, his dark skin standing out from the bright green outfit he'd chosen to wear that day. "I knew you were coming soon—why didn't you let me know?"

"Because I hadn't been paying attention, really, to how *busy* you must be getting. Sorry, Tom."

"Don't apologize. I heard about *your* little problems." He levelled a quick glare at Oscar and Michelle, who were being escorted by an extremely vigilant Oasis.

Still doesn't excuse my inattention to begin with. Well, Ariane, you finally realized what you need to be doing; don't waste time beating yourself up over it, just get to doing it. "So Steve tells me you've ended up running things?"

"No, no. Just...trying to keep things going smoothly. I help organize, really—it's what I learned to do on a much larger scale with AISage help. While I *do* miss Maxine's input," he continued, referring to his own old AISage, "back then I was also coordinating a space station for over half a million people by myself. I can manage to help keep things going for a few thousand pretty easily."

Three people came jogging up at that point. "Tom—" one began.

"Yes, David, I know it's going to be difficult, but there really isn't another practical path for that shipment. You'll just have to close up everything and let them through."

The man named David—and his two companions—looked pained. "Look, Tom, this is the fourth time this week! I can't keep closing up every time—"

Cussler's voice shifted from his usual friendly, professional tone to something just a *hair* sharper—and with about ten times the authority. "Dave, I understand it's frustrating. But I *did* warn you about how heavily used that set of passageways was and how tight those alcoves were. You decided that the high traffic was an advantage. And from what I hear, you were right, overall; people going to and from the Upper Sphere are always grabbing snacks at your booths. This is the price you pay for being on that route. Now *please* don't complain about this again. Either deal with it, or move. I know at least two other people who would *love* your spaces."

David grimaced, then nodded; his two friends looked momentarily uncertain, but followed David as he left.

"You handled that well," Ariane said. "What was that about?"

"Well? Eh. Acceptably, I suppose. David's currently running a snack stop between the Inner Sphere and Upper Sphere, just before the Elevator. Right now it's for interest vector and bragging rights, but he's made some noises about maybe trying a real, honest-to-God business, a market stall somewhere in the Grand Arcade. He makes real good stuff, but he's still relying on the AIWish type gadgets, so I don't know how well he'll do just on regular . . . ingredients, so to speak."

Ariane nodded. "We could certainly use some people doing that kind of business. Right now our only presence in the Arena is through our Embassy. On the other hand, I'm *sure* that trying to establish and run a business in the Arcade is as much a shark tank as the politics of the Arena itself. What's the big traffic here?"

A powered cart rumbled past, dragging something large enough to make them all squeeze agains the walls. "Basically two main sources of large shipments: the power station, which we're expanding constantly, and the defense installations."

"So we *are* getting some firepower up there? Good," said DuQuesne emphatically.

"Quite a bit now, plus of course the ships that Orphan lent us."

One more *thing I should have been* making *myself keep up on.* "What *is* the status of our defenses?"

Tom turned and started down the corridor. "Come with me, I'll show you."

Ariane noticed how people waved, and made room, for Tom. She smiled suddenly. *That actually solves one problem I was wondering about.*

They entered the Foyer; Ariane managed *not* to stop dead upon seeing the entire place almost filled with various buildings, and the formerly twisting artificial arroyos carved out into straighter roads. *Ha. I've started to get* used *to the challenges of the Arena, where you* can't *go using nanotech or other tricks to get things done faster or more efficiently. But if they're shipping in loads of charged batteries and the nanotech still works in here, of* course *they can get things done a lot faster.*

Tom led them to the central building, which retained

something of the look of the original little house that he and Steve had lived in during the time they were mostly alone on the Sphere...but was about ten times bigger. "Come on in," Tom said, leading them into a semicircular living room more than large enough for all of them. He glanced at Oasis and the two prisoners. "You can lock them in the spare bedroom, down that hallway, second door on the left." He tapped the side of his head and grinned. "I'll know if they're up to anything; put a security feed in there just for this."

Oasis grinned back. Oscar Naraj's lips tightened, but neither he nor Michelle Ni Deng said anything; they walked quietly in front of Oasis down the side hall; a moment later they heard the *click* of a lock, and Oasis reappeared, looking slightly more relaxed.

"Now that that's settled," Tom said, "Steve, you want to grab people some drinks while I set up?"

"Sure, Tom. You want your usual?"

"Sure. What'll the rest of you have?"

Ariane restrained her instinct to hurry. *This is exactly the sort of thing I need to know about before I go back for the showdown, and a few hours, or even another day, won't make a difference.* "Since we've got a full-template AIWish back there—how about a pomegranate martini?"

"Persephone's Curse coming up," Steve acknowledged. "What about the rest of you?"

While Steve got everyone else's preferences, Tom Cussler gestured to empty air; lights began to flicker. "Let me fire up the displays."

He remembered that I prefer to get information from my regular senses. I've gotten some better at taking straight downloads through my interface—it's got a lot of convenience—but I really *prefer doing it this way.* "Thanks for indulging me, Tom. I know it's a pain."

The broad shoulders shrugged. "Oh, not really. We've actually got a fair minority of people like you here, since we have been selecting for people who aren't AISage dependent. Besides, it's good training to keep these kind of skills; if any of us are leaving the Sphere for the rest of the Arena, we'd better know how to deal with it."

A large screen covering the entire gently-curving wall across from where Ariane and the others were sitting lit up, became a three-dimensional display in which a model of Humanity's Sphere (*one of three, now!*) rotated slowly.

"Basically we've got ourselves three main divisions of defense," Tom said. "First, we've got the loaner fleet; three of them are stationed outside of the Straits at any given time." Miniature ship icons blinked on as indicated. "Several are hanging up at about twenty thousand kilometers above the center of the main landmass—which is where the Outer Gateway is; that provides direct surveillance and cover for our main entry and exit point and our current Upper Sphere installations. The rest are doing patrols." Several more ship icons appeared doing slow patrol patterns around the entire Sphere.

"You have crews on them already?"

"Hey, we're not above cheating," Steve said with a wink, handing the drinks out to their respective owners.

Tom took his and winked back at Steve. "How very true! Got the best volunteers I could, then took our first trained pilots—other than you—and sent them back home to have their skills recorded and encoded for general transfer. Steve remembered the notes on your challenge against Sethrik and the Blessed—that Orphan had warned us that Sethrik would have the best piloting skills . . . installed, so to speak, and that told me that *that* kind of transfer, at least, wasn't forbidden by the Arena. So we've already got crews of ten on each of the ships and we're trying to fill them out as we get more people. The ones with the largest crews do the patrols, because then they can use the smaller onboard scout boats to extend their range without undermanning the main ship."

"Sounds like someone thought this out carefully."

"That part of it," Tom acknowledged, "would be the Arena Defense SFG. They're responsible for a lot of the other work, which leads us to the second division of defense, the Gateway stations. We've got two SFG-designed big cargo conveyor ships—the *Nodwick* and the *Nunzio*—running now, and with that we've been able to manufacture some very large pieces and bring them through. Short story is that we've now got some pretty impressive fortresses sitting right on top of every one of the Sky Gates; anyone tries to come through we don't like, they're running through a kill zone that will *hurt*." The display showed a large ring—a few kilometers across—encircling each Sky Gate; a closeup showed that the ring was closely linked sections which each were heavily armored and bristling with weaponry.

"Very nice," DuQuesne said in an approving voice. "Big enough to let just about anyone come through without trouble, but mean enough to make just about anyone regret it if they didn't ask first. You've fitted our ships with IFF beacons for this, then?"

"Identify Friend or Foe, yes. That lets even dumb automation give the alarm; no IFF beacon, the weapons automatically charge and track, and an alert is sent for someone to either give the fire authorization or not. We've set up encrypted, secured comm-buoy relays through the area so that we can send the signals and data to any of the available ships or down to the ground. Usually the nearest patrol ship would be given the alert and make the call."

"I *sure* hope you have adequate safeties on that; the last thing we need is some friendly ship getting shot by accident."

"The design of that control system was done by Carl and me," Steve said. "And we tested it several times. No accidents. Simulations show it should be perfectly reliable, too."

Ariane nodded. *It's still a bit scary to think that any ship coming through here which isn't one of ours will be being tracked by that much firepower...but given our current situation, I guess it can't really be helped.* "Good job, then."

Another light blinked on, this one in the center of the main continent of the Upper Sphere. "And finally, of course, we've been putting up—and are continuing to expand—defenses on the ground. We're also starting recruiting for armed forces," Tom said, looking pensive, "but that's a sticky subject. The CSF doesn't want to give up its best people in case someone pulls off a real-space attack—which is theoretically possible—and there honestly aren't all *that* many people who want to leave fun and safe lives back home for a chance to get shot down by some alien invader."

I can't blame them, Ariane admitted privately. *But*

someone's going to have to, since we can't depend on purely automated defenses. "Tom, this is . . . excellent. I really should have kept up on things much better—and I will, from now on—but I have to say that I don't think I could have expected things to go any more smoothly if I *had* been. You've done everything I'd have wanted done and you never even *bothered* me about it. Thank you."

"You're welcome," Tom said, looking just a little embarrassed. "Honestly, though, it all just sort of . . . happened. Watching how systems interact, getting them to work together . . . it's just what I *do*, if you see what I mean."

"I most certainly do see. But as this place gets bigger, and the different rules of the Arena versus back home start to penetrate, it's going to start to get harder to run—lots harder, especially if any of our immigrants start thinking like our friends Oscar and Michelle."

Tom Cussler nodded slowly, a frown growing. "Wish I could say you're wrong, but I'm sure you're right. Not sure I can think of a solution, though."

"I can," she said. "The problem is that back home people almost *don't* have to depend on everyone else, at least for survival. We can be, and in some ways, we *are* little self-involved islands. But here we can't be that; we can't get AIWishes to give us everything we want all by ourselves. So there really does have to be a hierarchy, someone who's in charge."

Tom's eyes suddenly narrowed in consternation. "Oh, no—"

"Oh, yes. Thomas Cussler, you are the perfect choice. Heck, you've already *taken* the position. I just have to give it a name and make it official. Then you'll have the authority you'll need to make the decisions stick when people start thinking they can just go off and do things their own way."

Tom rolled his eyes, but then nodded. "Yes, I guess I can't argue with the idea ... and truth be told, I really wouldn't feel comfortable turning over control of this little community to anyone else—at least anyone outside of our little group." He looked pointedly down the dark side corridor. "But—just to be completely frank—are *you* going to have the authority to make *that* stick? Because I think there's a lot of people who are going to want to fight you on that kind of decision."

"That's what I'm coming back to make sure of, Tom," Ariane answered, and she was gratified to see that he smiled at the words. "With what's happened in the Arena, and now—we find out from DuQuesne and Oasis—back home, we can't afford any more screwups.

"They didn't take me seriously. *I* didn't take me seriously, and while *we* came out of it well, hundreds ... no, *thousands* of other people died because of that failure on our part; the fact that those other people were at the time my enemies doesn't matter nearly as much as the fact that if I had kept my eye on things, they wouldn't have *been* my enemies and we wouldn't have *had* to kill them. That kind of fumbling around stops *now*."

Tom nodded. "Glad to hear it. If you have a way of pulling that off, that is."

DuQuesne chuckled darkly. "Oh, I think we do."

CHAPTER 51

"And what, exactly, do I get from this if I cooperate?"

Oscar Naraj's voice wasn't truculent or hostile; as DuQuesne had rather expected, it was completely controlled, a man asking a simple question. Oscar's glance was focused mostly on Ariane, but did take in DuQuesne, Oasis, Wu Kung, Simon, and Gabrielle, who were the others on board "Arena Transfer Shuttle #3." The others were staying this time; Laila had looked slightly wistful at the thought of returning, but had chosen to stay rather than discover what might happen to her when she returned and three AISages woke up in a mind that might be far too different from the one they had known.

Ariane smiled very coldly at Oscar. "Not a pardon and not off the hook, if that's what you're hoping." The smile warmed—*just enough to take it from absolute zero to dry ice, but hey, that's a couple hundred degrees.* "You claim you did not direct what happened to me, and did not want such tactics. You've been *acting* like you think you may have screwed up. If you cooperate—*exactly*—I might start to believe you're more valuable as an asset than as an example. *That* is what you might—and let me stress that word, *might*—be able to get out of this."

Naraj studied her wordlessly for several minutes. DuQuesne could see conflicting tensions in his muscles. *But it's his decision to make alone.* Ni Deng was locked up in her own separate cell on the shuttle ship; this was Oscar Naraj's play.

"Very well," Oscar said after another moment. "I will send the message as you direct, complete with my own key codes and verifications. I am not quite sure what you expect this to accomplish."

"You'll also send the appropriate signals to any allies who *aren't* in the SSC, CSF, or their Arena Research Division—exactly the signals you'd send if you were returning after completely successful negotiations according to *your* standards," Ariane said. "And if you've come to respect us as you claim, I hope you understand that if you *do* try to slip something by, there's a good chance we'll catch you right there, and a certainty we'll catch you out sooner or later—with 'sooner' being the way to bet."

Somewhat to DuQuesne's surprise, Oscar gave a genuine smile. "Captain Austin, I most *certainly* recognize that. I understand your hostility—and it is deserved—but I hope you realize that I am not an utter fool. I see that your general plan is complete surprise, and to this end I will indeed cooperate fully."

Ariane looked at him, then the others. "What do you all think?"

Wu Kung nodded. "He wasn't actually smelling very twisty at all there."

Oscar failed to suppress a start.

"Yeah, Wu is something of a lie detector. Since you're always planning *something* he was never sure which way you were jumping, but he was always suspicious of you and Ni Deng, even when the rest of us were starting to relax," DuQuesne said, grinning. "I'd say go, Ariane."

The others agreed as well. Ariane nodded. "All right, then everything's set. DuQuesne?"

"Console's unlocked. Send away, Mr. Ambassador."

Naraj concentrated; DuQuesne observed the heavily encrypted traffic streaming to the recording system of the message torpedo. Wu Kung was close by, and DuQuesne could just make out his breathing—heavier, as he carefully scented Naraj for any sign of duplicity in this operation.

"Done," Naraj announced after a moment. "If you send that torpedo through, it will transmit the appropriate messages. They will then be expecting me at the monthly meeting, and my other allies will not be prepared for you to crash the party, so to speak." He looked at her curiously. "I admit to not knowing exactly *what* you plan to do. I can see you making a fairly forceful showing, but if I understand what you need to achieve correctly, you will need some sort of additional leverage beyond that which I am aware of."

"Yes. I will." She turned to Oasis. "Put the ambassador in his room and lock it."

Once he was gone, Ariane sighed and sank into one of the shuttle's chairs. "How sure are we about what he just did? Could you read what he sent?"

DuQuesne shook his head. "Wouldn't do us any good even if I could. There's no way to tell if he had personally agreed-upon codes that would allow him to send innocuous-sounding messages to people that actually tipped them off to something being hinky. But I'm going with Wu's instincts and his sense of smell.

Naraj's a cool customer, a Big Time Operator if there ever was one, but I don't believe he could've stayed completely calm while trying to slip one by both me and Wu, with both of us practically standing right over him. He'd have gotten nervous. *Real* nervous."

"All right, then. Send it, Simon."

At Dr. Sandrisson's direction, the message torpedo dropped away from the docked Arena shuttle and flew off to the safe minimum distance before winking out of existence in a quick double-ended flare of light.

"So," Oasis said, returning from her mission, "how long before *we* go?"

"If our timing information is correct, the meeting should be gathering now. I'm going to pilot us over to the corresponding location. Simon, have you determined the best accuracy I can expect with the Sandrisson Conversion?"

"I have. Theoretical minimum accuracy—assuming ideal cases—is roughly three kilometers in normal space. If you were to transition out and back immediately, in other words, you could end up anywhere within a three-kilometer radius volume of where you started. Practically speaking, given your piloting skill, the coil designs, and such, I would not expect better than a three-hundred-kilometer accuracy. For this purpose, you need to consider *this* point," he marked a specific location slightly behind the central point inside the Shuttle's main body, "as the center of the craft and the point from which you will judge the transition location."

"So that's about . . . one meter distance in terms of the Orrery?"

"Correct."

Ariane grinned. "Now this will be fun. Everyone strapped in?"

Oasis sat down and locked herself into a seat. "Now we are!"

DuQuesne watched as Ariane took the shuttle out smoothly, heading towards the near-center of the Harbor. *Piloting is her real element, even if she's now found her real* calling, *so to speak.*

Watching her helped deal with the loss and strain of the past few days. It didn't *erase* DuQuesne's pain—nothing but time would reduce that burning guilt and anger—but seeing that they were *doing* something certainly aided him in pushing the problem to the back of his mind for a while.

"Mind if I ask something, Ariane?" Oasis' voice was hesitant.

"Oasis, I'm never going to mind if you *ask*. I may or may not *answer*."

"Right." The redhead smiled brightly. "Well, it's what Naraj said. What's the plan? Those guys on the SSC and CSF, except for Saul and his group—they're going to be kinda hard to push around, and what you need to get out of them...*whew!*" She made a gesture of wiping sweat off her brow. "That's gonna be one heck of a trick, you know? So...what *have* you got up your sleeve?"

Ariane smiled, the expression visible from the side and audible in her voice. "Well, remember, Oscar knows we *survived* that betrayal. He hasn't got a clue as to what we *got* out of it."

"Oh, *duh*. You'll be able to point out we've got three Spheres now."

"That's one biggie, yes. And if I get the timing on the messages right, they also won't have a good grasp of just how strong our defenses are now. Thanks to Tom, they won't be able to make a good case that I've messed *that* up. And..." she trailed off.

"And...?"

The grin became the savage, killer-instinct smile whose razor-edged danger DuQuesne found irresistably attractive. "And I have a trump card that I just figured out how to play last night."

She didn't say any more, and it was obvious that she wasn't discussing this part of her strategy. *Okay. She's trying to prove she can do this on her own, and I've got to let her do it. And my gut says she* can.

But I'll be ready to back her up just in case, anyway.

As they approached the target area, Simon projected the location of Kanzaki-Three into everyone's perceptions, but especially to Ariane. "There is the location. You *must* center on it very carefully, or else—"

"—or else we may materialize somewhere we don't want to," she said with a sharp grin, "like maybe *inside* Kanzaki-Three?"

Simon looked at her with an expression of puzzled exasperation. "I don't *believe* that it will allow you to materialize inside another physical object—the spacetime exclusion principle tends to forbid it—but I would not care to *test* that belief with my life."

Ariane slowed the shuttle to a crawl, jockeying it around with delicate adjustments of the attitude jets. After a few moments, DuQuesne could see displayed before him the ghostly shape of the shuttle with the brilliant green dot of Simon's derived "transition central point" slowly approaching a red dot—the point nominally one meter to the zenith of the location of Kanzaki-Three.

"Don't you want to give us a little *margin*, Ariane?" Simon said tensely. "After all, if I'm a bit off—"

"Oh, *live* a little, Simon!" she said, as the red dot touched the green. "After all—"

Blazing rainbow light flared around them.

"—what could go—well, look at that!"

Kanzaki-Three loomed immense in the forward viewport, scarcely ten kilometers distant.

"Perfect piloting, Ariane," DuQuesne said. *And lucky. Funny, that.* "Even if you were a bit cavalier about the approach."

"Great *Kami*, Ariane, you cut that . . . too fine!" Simon murmured, staring.

DuQuesne grinned at Simon's momentary discomfiture. His headware sensed Ariane turn control over to the slightly-peeved Kanzaki-Three local control for landing. "But it got us in very close; short enough that I'm now sure we can keep the lid on until we actually enter."

"Any changes in the basic plan?" Gabrielle asked.

"No, not as long as you can establish communications with—"

"I've already got Vincent on my comm. Simon?"

"Mio has responded and understands the situation. Mentor is standing by. Entrance will be clear. As far as anyone can tell, this is a fairly routine meeting with the additional importance that the ambassador has returned and will be addressing the Council and the Arena Research Division directly. No sign that there is any other untoward activity."

Ariane nodded. "All right, then.

"Here we go."

CHAPTER 52

Ariane stopped, only one door away from the Council Room. The others looked at her; she tried to look unconcerned, but inside, she realized she was *terrified*.

No, not now! I can't afford this! Dammit!

But it was there, at this eleventh-hour moment; fear that she was making a terrible, terrible mistake, that she *couldn't* pull this off even if it wasn't a mistake, that—despite the treacherous way she'd done it—Michelle had been *right* to try to get her out of the way.

She swallowed, and there was suddenly a hand on her arm.

Simon looked into her eyes. "It's all right, Ariane. We're all behind you." The brilliant green eyes were filled with absolute confidence, a certainty that she desperately needed.

"You're *sure*, Simon?" she asked softly.

"We're *all* sure, Captain," DuQuesne said, now on her other side, his ebony gaze reinforcing Simon's with calm and massive competence. "Now *you* have to be. I know you're wondering, again, if you're *really* right about all this—"

"—but that's pretty much why we're sure you *are*," Gabrielle said emphatically. "So long as you're still doubtin' yourself sometimes, you'll still be who you are—and that's who we need."

"*PRECISELY CORRECT, GABRIELLE WOLFE OF TELLUS,*" thundered a familiar voice. "*IT IS THE ESSENCE OF WHO SHE IS THAT MAKES ARIANE AUSTIN THE CORRECT CHOICE FOR THIS MOST VITAL OF TASKS.*"

"Mentor?" Despite the support of all her friends—*and all very dear to me now*—there was no voice in the universe she wanted to hear more right now. "Where—"

Look to your right, next to the doorframe, the voice spoke with subdued power through her short-range link. *It was clear within my Visualization that you would use this pathway, and therefore I arranged to have my case placed here.*

"You have *no* idea how glad I am to see you!" Ariane reached down and picked up the case that had accompanied her for most of her adult life—and quite a few years before. As Mentor's case *clicked* into place on her belt, she felt everything else click into place as well. *I don't want to see us go the way of the Blessed . . . but having constant companions like Mentor is not something I want us to give up, either.*

"Okay, everyone. I'm ready." She took a deep breath, glanced around, and strode forward, DuQuesne and Simon flanking her, Gabrielle in the middle, and Oasis and Wu bringing up the rear.

The Council Chamber doors slid open. The woman speaking—*representative of Mars, I think*—suddenly stopped, and a hush fell over the entire assembly.

"Pardon me, Mr. Chairman," Ariane said, and heard her voice amplified around the room. *Good work, Mentor.*

I am in fact being assisted by Vincent and Mio. Excellent partners.

Then good work to all of you.

Saul Maginot stood slowly. "We had expected Ambassador Naraj..." he began. She could see a twinkle in his eyes that said, as clearly as though he'd spoken, *but you're what I was hoping for.*

"I apologize for misleading you," she said, deliberately injecting barely any apologetic tone into the statement. "But I had, and have, reason to prefer to speak without any opportunity for anyone else to prepare. Mentor," she raised her voice slightly, "is the Council secure?"

"IT IS SECURE," Mentor replied, shaking the room with the three words.

"Good. No transmissions out, no transmissions in. And since these councils are now almost all face-to-face, I believe that still gives me the opportunity to speak to most of you."

"Sealed off...what the *hell* do you think you're doing, *Captain* Austin?" demanded a woman with green and blue hair and the bearing of a military officer. *General Jill Esterhauer, formerly head of Inner System Security, now Earth Defense Force coordinator,* Mentor informed her. Ariane remembered her vaguely—she'd commented on the need for patrols above the Upper Sphere, as Ariane recalled, back in that first meeting after their return.

"Correcting a mistake I made some time ago, General," Ariane answered. She strode to the central podium; she could see the speaker from Mars briefly consider arguing with her, then immediately changing her mind. The others stayed back a ways, except for Wu, who followed her like a brightly-colored shadow.

"A...mistake, Captain?" Dean Stout asked mildly.

"A mistake that very nearly cost us...possibly everything, Councillor."

She looked around slowly at the hundred or so faces—*many curious, some amused, several angry, others...cautious*. Then she set her jaw. *Here we go*.

"A few weeks ago, I was kidnapped by the Blessed to Serve."

The council stared at her blankly for a moment, then murmurs began to grow into shouts.

"QUIET!"

The shout shook the walls, echoed around the room three times, and only slowly faded; in the momentary silence, she thought she heard a slight chuckle from Wu Kung. "I expect I'll be answering all your questions eventually. But I'm telling this my way, and you are all going to listen—because a hell of a lot depends on it.

"Yes, I was kidnapped. Right off the Docks, into one of their flagships, and on course to travel straight to their homeworld, where the *best* I could hope for would be death. Fortunately," she let her first, very nasty, smile out, "that didn't quite work out the way they planned.

"But the worst part of that was that it wasn't the *Blessed* who had planned it all. That was done—*as some of you in this room already know*—by Deputy Ambassador Michelle Ni Deng."

"My God!" Saul said involuntarily. "Are you—"

"I am not merely *sure*, Commander Maginot, I have absolute *proof*; records from the Blessed themselves tracing her negotiations with Vantak, then the second in command of the Blessed, and her attempt to collect on the bargain with Sethrik—who had been kidnapped along with me because the Minds believed that he was no longer entirely reliable."

The Council was now utterly silent; shock was written clearly on most faces, but a few seemed...wary. *And maybe you should be.*

"All the evidence will be delivered—along with Ni Deng herself—shortly," she went on. "But I'm not here to discuss her crime, at least not right now.

"The problem is that in many ways this is my fault."

One of the other Councillors—*Jeremaiah Britt, CSF Logistics Division*, Mentor noted for her—stirred at that. "I beg your pardon, Captain. How is this horrible event—assuming it is true—your fault?"

"Because I let you saddle me with an appointed pair of ambassadors in the first place," she said grimly. "Because I let you shove me back into the Arena while you kept trying to do 'business as usual' here. Because—honestly? I really didn't *want* to be running things and in my heart I was hoping something would just come along and make it so I didn't have to."

"*Let* us?" The outburst came from a indeterminately-gendered representative of Ganymede Colony identified by Mentor as White Camilla. "You may be designated head of Faction by this Arena—something which certainly *does* need to be changed—but *here* you are a thrill-racing pilot who's never even—"

"*That*," Ariane snapped, putting as much steel into her voice as possible, "is *exactly* the attitude I thought I'd get from some of you. And it's going to get us all *killed*."

Ariane shoved all her uncertainty back, focused, let her anger come *forward*, the fury she felt at the betrayal some of these people had *known* about, and took one more deep breath. And *just* as some of the others were about to speak, she allowed herself to cut loose.

"Yes, *killed*, wiped out, exterminated! You've seen the files, you've watched the simulations. The Molothos aren't playing games out there. They're not some sim villains you can turn off, and they're not stuck in the Arena, either. They're out there, somewhere not too far away—even by real-space standards."

There was a murmur, and she put a faintly patronizing smile on her face. "Oh, some of you didn't get that? They travelled through Arenaspace to our Sphere. They've colonized *somewhere* not too far away—maybe as close as Alpha Centauri."

"Captain Austin," said a respectful tenor voice; the speaker was a man with an impressive white-streaked beard—*Political Simulation Director Robert Fenelon*, Mentor informed her. "Captain," he continued when she nodded, "while I am not *terribly* competent in the technical areas, my AISage informs me that our current wide-baseline imaging telescopes would be able to resolve objects down to a meter in size in systems that close. That would seem to exclude the possibility of any significant installations in the Alpha Centauri system or, indeed, any relatively close systems at all."

"Director Fenelon, that would be completely true if all else were equal; unfortunately, we have very good reason to believe things are *not* equal—some of which we discussed in the *last* major meeting I had with all of you. In short, we have evidence that the Arena's reach is not entirely limited to Arenaspace." Quickly she summarized DuQuesne's prior observations and some of the other related facts they had learned. "So, honestly speaking, there is *no* reason to believe that we can trust our own telescopes much past the borders of our solar system, at least for things at the detail level of whether there's people in the target systems."

"It should be noted that this fits with the Arena's basic *modus operandi*," Simon spoke up. "There are numerous ways in which one can interpret the *purpose* of the Arena's actions, but it is clear that one of the constant effects is to keep people separated in normal space, barring truly impressive efforts, and to force them to meet *in* the Arena. This also enforces that requirement; if you wish to find out if you have neighbors in your local stellar region, you either have to mount a fully manned expedition through normal space, or find your way to them through Arenaspace. The latter, though far from trivial or without danger, is still much easier than sending a major expedition across stellar distances at slower-than-light speeds."

"Thank you, Simon," she said. "Which leads us to this: it is in Arenaspace that we will almost certainly have our initial clash—and perhaps the majority of our battles will be fought there. And we are *hideously* outnumbered and outgunned. No one knows how many Spheres the Molothos control, but the number is *certainly* in the thousands—and that is *full* control. They are well-known for travelling through Arenaspace and colonizing the Upper Spheres of unclaimed systems—as they attempted to do to ours, before DuQuesne and Carl Edlund kicked them off. There is absolutely *no* firm guess as to how many Upper Spheres they currently have colonized, but it is probably in the tens of thousands—and each one of those is the equivalent of a planet the size of Earth. I don't think we can even *begin* to understand the level of resources that represents.

"That doesn't mean that it's a hopeless cause. We have some advantages, and we're already digging in. We have a significant number of Arena-designed warships already, lent to us by Orphan of the Liberated—and those designs are being looked over by the defense SFGs even as we speak. There are now orbital guard fortresses near each of the Sky Gates, and ground defenses being installed. We also are not without allies.

"BUT," she raised her voice, and Mentor made it rumble around the room like thunder, *"but* there is one thing we absolutely *cannot* afford, and that is a division—a rift—between Arenaspace and our home solar system. I have *no* doubt that a lot of you have had the exact same sentiments as Representative Camilla— that I can go play toy boss off in this 'Arena' place, but otherwise I should let the professionals handle it.

"That's not going to happen. Not any more."

Saul stood slowly. "I beg your pardon, Captain?"

"I'm saying that I can't—that *humanity* can't—afford to have this division between who's in charge, not when we're staring straight into the claws of the Molothos— and who knows what else. So until such time as a good replacement, a *damn* good replacement, is available, I am going to be *it*. I am the Leader of the Faction of Humanity, and you are going to *confirm* that, and you are going to *follow my lead*, because this *whole* game's played by the Arena's rules. Even here, even in our home system. And by those rules, there is *one* Leader for this Faction, and you are looking at her."

"That's . . . preposterous," Representative Camilla said, echoed by several others—*a lot of the ones looking wary before.* Ariane could see that Saul's face was very guarded. *He's on our side, so he's playing to the crowd.* "You can't declare yourself . . . ruler of Humanity."

"I'm not the one doing the declaring," she corrected. "The Arena decided I was the boss. And I spent time trying to get away from that—time that got me kidnapped and could have lost us more than you can imagine.

"I was damn tempted to give it up right there when I realized how badly I'd screwed up, but you know what? The person who'd replace me is someone you'd want *less* in that position. And—just by the way—the first thing you're all going to do in confirming my position is to confirm my line of succession, so that *if* something happens to me, we'll still have someone with a clue running things in the Arena."

"Why should we do that at all?" General Esterhauer asked bluntly. "Why shouldn't we simply declare someone else our Leader, if necessary?"

"Because it won't *work*, unless you convince me to ratify your rules." Ariane stared levelly into Esterhauer's eyes. "And I'm not doing that, because what Oscar and Michelle showed me is that politicians from here *don't* understand the stakes."

She held up her hand. "That's not meant as an insult. Most of you haven't *been* to the Arena. All the recordings in the world aren't going to make you *get* it. Even jumping over and visiting for a day is only going to start the process. Ambassador Naraj and Deputy Ambassador Ni Deng—they started out from the basic assumption that I simply wasn't the right choice for the job, and everything they encountered in the Arena they viewed through that lens—a lens that assumes that you can play the same kind of politics *there* that you can *here*.

"But the truth? Earth and its solar system are some no-account backwater whose people have managed to surprise the hell out of the Arena's residents—and piss off some of their worst. What happens here in normal space isn't *important* in the Arena—but it's damn important to *us*, because we haven't got a thousand spheres and ten thousand colonies out there to waste. This is our homeworld."

"And it's the only Sphere we have," General Esterhauer said bluntly. "Speaking theoretically—"

"Actually, that's not true."

The room went silent. Saul said, with a slowly dawning smile, "Captain Austin?"

"I mentioned that I was kidnapped. I did not describe precisely how I was rescued from that situation—and I'm not going to right now. But upon my return, I sent . . . an ultimatum to the Minds, the true Rulers of the Blessed. And they agreed completely to my terms. We are now at peace with the Blessed To Serve . . . and the human race now has *three* solar systems, three Spheres, to its name."

For another moment there was silence. Then Representative Fenelon started to laugh. Saul joined him, and suddenly more than half the room resounded with triumphant, joyous laughter.

"An . . . impressive reversal of position," Representative Camilla said as the laughter died away. "Especially for one who admits to having no experience as a negotiator. Still, I wonder then why we need to worry about these issues. As I understand it, we can close the Outer Gateway and the Straits and it doesn't matter what sort of force the Molothos might bring, they cannot take the Inner Sphere and thus not our solar system. We could still travel to Nexus Arena, and through there to these *other* solar systems, whose location they have no idea of, and build up our forces there for many years. Why can we not, in essence, ignore this threat?"

DuQuesne looked about ready to explode, and she saw Wu Kung gritting his teeth so hard she was afraid they'd break, but Ariane held up her hand and shook her head ever so slightly to tell them *No. Keep it under control*. "Why? Three reasons, Representative.

"First, because that's the coward's approach. Maybe that doesn't mean much to you, but it bothers the hell out of me. And the Factions in the Arena value courage, style, and so on a very great deal. They think I'm more than half crazy, yes, but they also respect me, DuQuesne, Simon, Gabrielle, and the rest of us because we've met every challenge head-on and somehow come out of it alive.

"But that's the least important. Second, since the Sky Gates are active, if we pretty much abandon the Upper Sphere, any invaders are going to get our sentry stations knocked out in short order—and then they can start dropping invasion forces into normal space. They'll be about a light-year out, and we'll have a bunch of nasty weapons to use on them . . . but they've been doing this for tens of thousands, hundreds of thousands, maybe even *millions* of years, and they can afford to send *unending* waves of assault craft at us. And don't you think for a split *second* that they won't. The Molothos made their attitude *abundantly* clear. If you haven't seen what their response was to Ambassador Naraj when he tried to negotiate with them, you damn well better review it. Scares the living hell out of me every time I see it, and I knew what they were like from the moment I met them.

"But most importantly? Because even if that weren't true, you *still* can't run and hide from the Arena. The Arena isn't going away. It's already *set* the rules. It's not stopped by turning your back." She took the entire assembled SSC and CSF in with a single glance. "This room is sealed. The image projectors are off. So now you should watch me—very closely indeed."

She focused, remembered the feeling, channeled it. *These people...some of them went along with Ni Deng. Maybe even told her what to do. I was* kidnapped! *Simon was nearly killed, thousands of people died, all because of this stupid, irresponsible...*

The tension built up...*but it's not happening! What happens if it doesn't work?*

For a moment she experienced a spurt of real panic, but that was exactly what she needed. Something within her drew tight, tighter, like a bowstring—

And there was a flare of golden light that enveloped her; she felt Kanzaki-Three beneath her vibrate, heard a bone-shaking chime...

And she was standing in midair, slowly descending, clothed in the uniform that had materialized about her in her first Awakening, in the moment she defeated Amas-Garao, midnight-blue with touches of gold, a ship-and-cup symbol shimmering on her breast. "You can't turn your back," she repeated softly, as her feet gradually came to rest on the floor again, "because the Arena will always be before you."

CHAPTER 53

Oh, my.

As soon as Ariane told them to watch, as soon as she made a point of saying that there were no projectors active, Simon *knew* what she was going to do. There was no other possible alternative, no other climax to her argument—

And then that *light* shone out, enveloped Ariane Austin in radiance that blinded... and then she was there, floating without support, impossibly levitating against the rotational gravity of Kanzaki-Three, dressed in the alien, formal uniform that had materialized around her in her ultimate triumph against an invincible foe.

I'll be damned. That's why I didn't ever see that outfit again, DuQuesne's local relay voice said with chagrin. *Disappeared when she banished the power. And that's what she was doing in her cabin last night, and probably the last few nights back in the Arena—trying to duplicate that momentary flare she had against Vantak and channel it.*

"And she bloody well did it," Simon murmured, still stunned.

"*Sugeeiiiiii!*" Wu said, eyes shining. "That's *amazing!*"

Oasis, who like Wu had never really seen the *magic* of the Arena, was startled, maybe slightly awed.

Simon became aware suddenly that distant klaxons were sounding. *Alarms?*

"Of course," Simon said after a moment, and looked around at the assembled CSF and SSC. "You understand now, don't you?"

The rest of the room was silent, but the stunned, incredulous gazes showed they did indeed understand.

"Those alarms... which I now note have gone silent—were from the detection of an energy surge, one which you all now will have verified proceeded from no detectable instrumentality. Captain Austin has on her no equipment capable of such displays, the projectors can be verified to be inactive, and in short there is no known method—within the limits of our science, or indeed any of the sciences of the Arena I have yet studied—which could produce that effect under these conditions." He looked at Ariane. "In short, it is no trick."

"It is no trick," Ariane agreed. "That is a taste—a tiny, insignificant, almost irrelevant taste—of the power of Shadeweaver and Faith. And it reaches here, even here, to our world on, as they might say, the other side of the sky. How far and deep is the reach of the Arena itself, then?" Though the light had almost entirely faded there was still *something* about her voice, a voice that resonated for a moment in Simon's bones in a way he'd never experienced before...

No. Not quite true. Amas-Garao had that same quality in his voice, when he chose to use it. So did Nyanthus, I recall, during that ritual they used to seal Ariane's powers.

"An... impressive trick, or manifestation, if you

prefer," General Esterhauer said after a moment. "And I understand the point." She flicked a glance, almost too fast to follow, but Simon caught it, read the direction. *Looking at White Camilla. Same clique, then. Not surprising.* "What, then, do you want us to do—exactly?"

Ariane looked to Saul. "Mr. Chairman?"

"Oh, go on, Captain. You rather took over the meeting—and I completely agree with your tactics, this time. Do it your way." Saul leaned back, smiling.

"Thank you, Saul," she said.

Simon felt a tension in the air. *No, not the air. Though doubtless there, too, but . . . it's inside me.*

Could it be? That . . . ability, here? But I had thought it had to do with the Arena, with knowledge of that alien space.

He concentrated. *DuQuesne, something's . . . wrong.*

The black eyes narrowed. *You think so too, huh? Too smooth so far, by about a thousand rows of little green apple trees.* A sense of sudden surprise. *You getting that . . . sensation you got on* Zounin-Ginjou?

Something like it, yes.

Dammit. Okay, I'll make sure the others are ready. Keep an eye on her.

Ariane was continuing. "First, the whole Council— SSC and CSF—have to confirm that the designated Leader of Humanity is, in fact, *their* leader. Exactly what that leadership entails we have to hammer out in detail, yes—but don't even *think* about trying to make it an ineffectual figurehead. I'll put up with reasonable opportunities for debate, but whoever's in that position—me or, later, someone else—is going to need the authority to actually *do* things.

"Next, you'll accept my designated line of succession

in case something happens to me. That line being the original *Holy Grail* crew, in the following order: Marc C. DuQuesne, Dr. Simon Sandrisson..."

Oh, great Kami, I hope it never comes to that...

"...Dr. Gabrielle Wolfe, Dr. Carl Edlund, Dr. Laila Canning, Dr. Stephen Franceschetti, and Dr. Thomas Cussler." She grinned. "Though I think we'll come up with a saner way of deciding the selection of Leader of the Faction before we go nearly through that list. But for now, that's the succession, because I'll be *damned* if I'm trusting anyone who didn't go through that first fire with me. I'll trust any of them with my life—and with your lives. Most of the rest of you have a lot of work to prove that you really, truly *get* what we're up against. And until you *do* prove that..."

"I...see." The general surveyed the group, and Simon's sense of foreboding grew stronger. *But I have no sense of* direction. *That bothers me. A great deal.* "But given normal lifespans in this era...that means that you, or your immediate successors, would be effectively rulers of Humanity for centuries—longer than many empires of the past."

Ariane raised an eyebrow, then laughed. "I see what you mean. Then let us say this agreement holds for ten years, and during that time we work out a more democratic method for selecting the Leader of Humanity. As far as I can tell, the Arena doesn't care HOW you do it as long as you play by the rules."

Esterhauer nodded, but her eyes were still grim. "It's now quite plain what you meant, Captain Austin," General Esterhauer said slowly, "when you said that the person you would have replace you would be someone we would like even less. If we don't accept you as Leader of Humanity, our next choice is Marc C. DuQuesne... of Hyperion."

"Son of a..." muttered Marc.

"His past is not—"

"Not relevant, you were going to say?" General Esterhauer's face was stony, and her voice as cold as iron. "Perhaps. Perhaps not. But the fact that his origin has been hidden from us for all this time does not leave me inclined to trust you—any of you. We have more than enough evidence of what the Hyperions are capable of. We know many were unstable, dangerous, and unpredictable. We should have known _what_ we were dealing with, as well as _who_."

Ariane's eyes had narrowed to near-slits, and her next words were spoken through her teeth. "If it weren't for Marc DuQuesne, _General_, we would not be _citizens_ of the Arena. Our Upper Sphere would be a Molothos _colony_ and we'd still be marooned back in Nexus Arena, looking for some way home." A faint hint of golden light shimmered around her hand for an instant. "And _no one_ talks about my friends as though they are _things_."

Simon, this is extraordinarily bad, Mio said. Her voice was filled with tension, even fear.

What? What is it? I know this argument is not going well—

It's much more than that. Mentor and I have detected coordinated movements—

—and other stuff, Gabrielle's Vincent broke in. _Esterhauer's had some kind of encrypted, stealthed feed going on for the past ten minutes. Took this long to trace it to her!_

MARK DUQUESNE, SIMON SANDRISSON—MY VISUALIZATION IS NOW CLEAR ON THIS: THERE

IS ANOTHER FORCE AT WORK HERE, MOST LIKELY COMMUNICATING TO GENERAL ESTER-HAUER THROUGH INTERMEDIARIES.

What? DuQuesne's link-voice was sharp. *Thought we'd sealed off comm.*

Barring physical cutoffs and shielding, any such sealing is of necessity one that can be penetrated or evaded by a sufficiently capable adversary, Mentor pointed out. *Also, at this time it is not certain—though probable, at an 86.2% level—that the operator in question is outside; they may be one of those present.*

"My apologies for offending you," the general said to Ariane after a moment.

Notify Ariane, then, Simon sent to Mentor.

I FIND IT DIFFICULT WHEN SHE IS EMO-TIONAL, AND THE MANIFESTATIONS OF THAT POWER INTERFERE DIRECTLY WITH A REMOTE LINK.

"This is, as I hope you understand, a...difficult thing for any of us to grasp," General Esterhauer continued. "It would be better if we could vote on whether we are going to...follow your lead, as you said. Once that's settled the rest of the...issues would be able to be addressed in a more reasonable atmosphere."

Ariane slowly relaxed and straightened. "All right. I suppose we should let you do that in private, as I'm technically not a member."

As she walked back, Simon saw Ariane stiffen; Mentor had obviously managed to get through.

The three doors around the room slid open simultaneously, and multiple armored, armed soldiers poured in—most of them aiming directly at the *Holy Grail* crew and their friends.

CHAPTER 54

Many of the Councilors shrank back or leapt to their feet in consternation. *Whatever they were expecting, it sure by all the hells of space wasn't* this, DuQuesne thought sourly. Wu Kung immediately interposed himself between as many of the newcomers and Ariane as he could. *And if people don't keep their heads, Wu's going to start* breaking *them.*

But not everyone was panicked or confused. Saul merely turned his head slowly to gaze at Jill Esterhauer. "General? What are you doing?"

"I said it would be better if we *could* vote on this," the general said, her voice now even more iron-hard. "But judging on the interest vectors and reactions, I am afraid that Ariane Austin would win that vote, and I cannot allow it. *We* cannot allow it."

"General!" Saul was now on his feet. "Have you entirely lost your mind? I knew you were reluctant—"

"And I have learned enough now to be more than just reluctant," she said. "You made a similar decision fifty years ago, Commander Maginot; one that, if you failed, would ruin you forever—if it didn't kill you. The same is true here; I believe that we are faced with one of the most subtle and dangerous attacks we have ever seen, and it very nearly succeeded. It still *may* succeed, if I do not contain this problem here and now."

She looked down at Ariane, Simon, and the others. "Please do not resist. If this becomes a fight, innocent people will be hurt. That is not my intent."

"You *will* explain—or there *will* be a fight, and I do not think you will like the ending!" Wu Kung said. His teeth were bared, his tail lashing. DuQuesne gestured furiously at Wu to stand down, but he didn't have much hope of having an effect. *If this does go south, there's nothing that's going to hold Wu back... and these people have no idea what he's capable of.*

"You are one of the clues, Sun Wu Kung." She looked to DuQuesne. "Marc C. DuQuesne, hidden in plain sight. Survivor of Hyperion. You and Captain Austin traveled to another location prior to your return to the Arena—and came back with Wu Kung. Another Hyperion. Upon your return to the solar system, you then went to yet another location—one of the Counter Earth stations—and report some sort of murder of mysterious patients under the care of a doctor who has yet to recover. Instead of the local authorities, Saul Maginot sends a very specialized team to oversee the investigation."

Sweet spirits of niter, as Rich used to say. It does sound damn peculiar the way she's putting it.

"And you return, Captain Austin, having imprisoned both Ambassador Naraj and Deputy Ambassador Ni Deng... but their own intended bodyguard appears to have become a member of your inner circle. Oasis Abrams... or *is* that actually her name?"

Great Space, *I think I see where her paranoia's going,* DuQuesne sent to the others. *And with the right guidance it's gonna be convincing as hell.*

Simon's face was grim—and yet distracted. *That sense of his is operating some even here. But it's not giving him a clear sense of* what *the threat is, I can tell by the way he's looking around.*

"Then, of course, we have the Hyperion criminal Maria-Susanna—who had contact with *you*, Doctor Sandrisson, for some considerable time prior to your initial departure, and who—despite her reputation as a psychopathic murderer—did not harm you, nor any of your group, either here or in the Arena."

"General," Robert Fenelon said, with a somewhat testy note in his voice, "I suppose I can—if I squint rather hard—see a possible pattern in all that, but really, that's hardly enough to—"

"I am not without evidence—considerably more solid evidence," General Esterhauer said, not taking her eyes from Ariane. "I won't divulge all at this time, but to give one example: I am in possession of essentially incontrovertible evidence that the woman calling herself 'Oasis Abrams' is neither the Oasis Abrams who enlisted in the nascent Combined Space Forces fifty years ago, nor any direct relative of hers." She looked straight at Oasis, who gazed back stonily. "In fact, whoever she is, she appeared immediately after Hyperion, and the original Oasis Abrams . . . was never seen again."

DuQuesne winced. *Oh, that's going to be a hard one to explain away.*

She looked at Saul. "Hyperion, where it all changed. Hyperion, the event so terrible that it changed the way the Solar System worked, created the Combined Space Forces and the Space Security Council in their current form, and changed stellar law to give actual power to a system-wide government for the first time. Which gave you, Commander Maginot, control over what government Humanity had for fifty years.

"Hyperion, where secret operations became more secret, where new beings of unknown capabilities were created for purposes so hidden in propaganda and confusion that no one seems to even know exactly *what* happened—or how many survived. Hyperion, whose 'experiments' were supposed to be superior beings, engineered with techniques untested and forbidden for use on normal human beings, superior beings derived from various works of fiction. Sherlock Holmes; Verne's scientific romances, Godin's *Meru* series, Heinlein's classic works, simgame heroes and protagonists from ancient movies and books..." Her gaze shifted. "Such as Doctor Marc C. DuQuesne."

"Blast it," DuQuesne muttered, then straightened up. *This could be it.*

"I had my AISages check all the references, Doctor. Your original—quite an ambitious man. A patient man, a clever man, and one quite willing to deceive, manipulate, and even betray when the stakes were high enough. Someone with charisma enough to convince others of his motives, to draw them into his plans—and certain of his proper place above everyone else."

And that's a pretty good description of "Blackie" DuQuesne. Problem is... "I'm...not like him. They didn't exactly design me that way—"

"So you would say, of course," General Esterhauer said. "But I see a different pattern—one that also leads to me wondering if even Captain Ariane Austin is the woman who left the Unlimited Racing circuit to join Sandrisson's crew. Has another substitution happened, when Dr. DuQuesne took her to a hidden location in search of more Hyperions? Or something worse, when she channeled a power we don't even begin to understand?"

Her voice was increasing with conviction every moment, and DuQuesne finally understood. *Yeah, she sees the pattern,* he sent to the others, *because someone's been* showing *it to her, with appropriate subtle nudges to her subconscious, for months. Interface suborned, I'd bet.*

Your Visualization is sound, youth, came Mentor's sonorous transmitted voice. *The manipulation of communications is clearly of a piece with that work.*

DuQuesne saw Simon suddenly freeze, his eyes narrow and then widen, a look of clear understanding spreading across his face. The transmission Simon sent to Mentor and him was heavily encrypted. *If you are right, Marc, then our unknown factor will be watching the situation and ready to trigger something if his, her, or its plan seems about to be disrupted.*

DuQuesne felt a shock in his gut. *Sure as God made little green apples. You got something, Simon?*

Mentor, if you and DuQuesne can locate all her legitimate group members . . . I am certain that this unknown is not *present in this room, or even immediately adjacent ones. Can the two of you, together, screen out or intercept any exterior transmissions?*

A WORTHY CONCEPT, boomed the pseudo-voice of Mentor. *Our adversary may of course have other mental conditionals in operation—contingencies, logic bombs, and so on—but this will certainly reduce the ability to play the game by remote. Yes, Simon Sandrisson, together I believe we can do this.*

Then let's get cracking, O Manipulator of Civilization, DuQuesne said, tense but hopeful. He opened up a full connection. *Isaac? Gimme full net access, and back me up. We're doing some serious cyberwarfare in a minute, or I miss my guess badly.*

Hmph. Just remember that violence is the last refuge of the incompetent—

Yeah, DuQuesne interrupted with a grin, *because the competent resort to violence MUCH sooner, before it's too late!*

"But the fact is that even all of that is just a side issue," the general went on, startling the entire group. "The real point is that—whether this is some long-term plan by survivors of Hyperion, or simply Ariane Austin's considered decision, it is the most dangerous plan I have ever seen."

She looked first at White Camilla, but then to Saul, and there was a note of appeal—not pleading, but definitely reaching, trying to draw others to her cause. "Commander Maginot, members of the Space Security Council and the Combined Space Forces—we are the most free society the solar system has ever seen. We have so few laws, so few controls on our actions, that even after Hyperion we have had the smallest military force in the history of mankind, compared to our numbers. We didn't have a large enough military establishment to support the research on our defenses against the Arena's Factions—we depend on private sim focus groups, players of games whose entertainment happens to also hold the key to our defenses.

Most of us—approaching sixty billion—answer to no one and nothing save our own consciences.

"And now one person—one woman—will be in charge, the effective ruler of humanity? This is not just a step backwards, it is a complete and utter reversal of our civilization, back to the days of empires." She looked levelly at Ariane. "And though you *say* we could give a time limit, ten years is still a long time, and one in which someone with near unlimited power could easily find ways to make ten into twenty, twenty into a hundred, and a hundred into forever."

DuQuesne looked to Ariane, knowing how this echoed Ariane's own fears. Her gaze flickered from Esterhauer to her friends, and he could see the uncertainty there, as she looked into Simon's eyes. She was focused enough, now, that they could at least make the connection to her. *Ariane . . .* Simon sent.

She's right, you know. Even if she's wrong.

An electronic sigh came from Simon. *Yes. Yes, she is. But at the same time . . .*

It's all right, Simon. DuQuesne felt her decision—though he couldn't quite see it—and saw her straighten, looking for an instant to him; he gave her a simple nod and then returned his focus to the network that was overlaid on every activity throughout Kanzaki-Three.

Marc C. DuQuesne, I have isolated fifty-nine percent of the active threads and processes in the room.

I've got most of the rest. I think Vincent and Mio have the few left.

Everyone had a different experience of the raw network; to DuQuesne, networks were brilliant spiderwebs of light, pulsing and flickering, with symbols that he could read that told him what the traffic was, allowed him to *see* how information was moving around him, then—in a situation like this—mapped the network traffic to the real world. Unlike most people, he could actually grasp the entirety of the local net and its relationships—*one more backhanded gift from Hyperion; they tried to make me able to comprehend hyperdimensional physics they'd made up, and now I find it's not entirely useless.* Now, in the sealed Council chamber, there was one faint, almost undetectable line of light that passed the virtual boundaries; all the rest were sealed off, self-contained within the chamber. *That's our meddler. Monitoring. But if he opens a channel...*

Marc DuQuesne, Mentor said through the Network, *you have the scope and power of vision necessary; be sure, therefore, that you attend to what is happening in the physical world as well as here. It may be that a sign or signal will be given there as trigger.*

Good thought, Mentor. I'm on it.

With considerable effort, he focused on the overlay, brought up a perception of things as they were happening in the physical here-and-now. It was *hard* to do; time perception in the electronic world and that in the physical world were not the same thing, for all that the same clocks might mark the passage of seconds. The physical world, where Ariane was confronting the general, was molasses-slow, yet almost infinitely complex compared to most network overlays except in the world-simulations. Scarcely a second or two had passed; Ariane was only now answering General Esterhauer's speech, and he heard her through a shimmering halo of data that dusted his perceptions with stars.

"You are very eloquent, General—and you're right, in some ways," Ariane said calmly. DuQuesne could guess just how *hard* it must be for her to stay calm.

"In some ways?" repeated the general.

A shimmering pulse streaked from the general, echoed through the forces she was obviously directing. *A directive to attack? No . . . she's telling them to wait.* He felt a surge of cautious optimism. *She really doesn't want a fight, and she's starting to listen. Maybe this will work out.*

Ariane laughed. "In almost all ways, really. Did you think I came to this decision easily? That I *want* to be this stupid 'Leader of the Faction of Humanity'? All those things you're afraid of—I'm afraid of them too. Afraid of *not* being afraid of myself one day. Afraid I'll accept too many expediencies without thinking enough about them.

"But," she held up her hand as General Esterhauer was about to speak, "at the same time I am *terrified* of what is going to happen to us if we're playing idiotic power games within our own tiny Faction while the Molothos close in on us. We can't *afford* it. If things had gone just a little differently, you'd already have someone *else* as the Leader of Humanity—maybe one of my friends, maybe not—the entirety of the secrets of Humanity that I know would be in the hands of the Blessed To Serve, and worse. Our ally Orphan would almost certainly be dead, his Faction gone with him, and you wouldn't even know how it *happened*. All because people had *already* decided I wasn't the person for the job."

General Jill Esterhauer tilted her head, and started to open her mouth.

And the dim, shimmering thread blazed into coruscating brilliance as the connection went fully active.

DuQuesne stiffened. *Got you!* he thought grimly, and forced his own connection protocols to hack into the encrypted stream. *Mentor!*

I am here, Marc DuQuesne, as are we all.

His vision saw it as a seething, crackling vortex of energy, a metaphor that made the encryption and security defenses seem as dangerous physically as they were electronically—and if you were, as DuQuesne now was, immersed in the electronic world, some of those defenses could actually kill you—trace your patterns back into your own skull and wipe you out like a deleted drive. He was exposing himself directly in order to use all of his brain as a weapon and a sensor, a perceptual filter that even the highest-order AISages couldn't match, though their physical speed should vastly outstrip his capabilities.

But they aren't Hyperions.

Mentor, Isaac, Mio, and Vincent were trying to tap into that deadly sealed column—in more mundane terms, trying to suborn the connection from the general's end so they could find out who and what they were dealing with. *Which means that technically we're trying to hack the general's brain, but if our suspicion's right—she's already been hacked.*

Suddenly the connection broadened, and *something* burst out of it—no, a lot of somethings. He recognized the network feel immediately—piranha seekers, advanced active worm codes that were designed to locate other active local processes and shut them down.

Vincent was struck immediately, and vanished from the Net—shutting down and severing his connection to prevent destruction. *Hope it's enough . . . and that he didn't take any with him into Gabrielle's headware.* The other AISages seemed to be holding their own, though barely. *Hang on, Isaac, Mio!*

His own defenses—manifested as shields of light this time—shunted the seekers away. Mentor simply swept them away, and his own counter-seekers wiped the worm code.

Try to just jam it! DuQuesne said. *Yeah, it'd be nice to get a look at our adversary, but he's prepared. Probably running the defense off the general's own network! We'd have to shut her down in order to stop it!*

Our adversary has locked down the transmitters, Mentor reported.

Dammit. He could perceive the lock commands holding the transmitters out of control. *Take time to break that—time enough that people in the regular world might even notice.*

I need some way to shut down those locks. But with the lock commands encrypted, those things'll stay inoperable unless I can break the encryption. And I don't have time. Blast! And nothing I'm carrying on my physical person has nearly enough power to . . .

He paused at that thought. *Power . . .*

HA! Got it! You're messing with the wrong power engineer, my friend!

He pinged the others. *Hold onto your hats, everyone— network's going down . . . for just long enough!*

Instead of triggering the locks, DuQuesne called up the specs of the room transceiver systems from headware, and on-the-fly calculated, and sent a pulse through the local controllers that looked, to those controllers, like a dangerous overvoltage from a shorting direct line. Automatic, built-in cutoffs cycled, shutting off all power to the Council Chamber network systems for a moment—and thus removing the temporary software locks on the transmitters. DuQuesne had been ready for that, and as soon as the power came back on, he activated the main transmitters in jamming mode.

He snapped back to full physical consciousness with a jolt—with that powerful a jamming pulse, there was no staying connected with the local network. The pulse faded and the network restored itself...but the powerful outside connection was gone. *We won that one.*

The battle had taken, perhaps, two-tenths of a second from start to finish.

CHAPTER 55

Ariane sensed *something* going on and then realized that Mentor had—for a few moments—completely vanished from her senses.

At the same time, General Esterhauer paused, mouth open, unmoving for an instant; then she slowly closed her mouth, looking momentarily puzzled, confused. Finally she blinked, shook her head, and said, "I see. But if you agree with my basic principles, you must understand how I must view your...demands."

I certainly do, Ariane thought, but was trying to understand what had just happened and figure out something more useful to say when Simon spoke up.

"General," he said, "Might I ask you a—I hope—simple question?"

She shrugged. "Go ahead."

"Is there, in fact, anything that Captain Austin *could* do that would convince you to give this plan a chance? Or is your mind so made up that nothing anyone could ever say would change your mind?"

That stopped Esterhauer cold for a moment. Slowly, a wry smile spread across her face. "I would like to think my mind is not totally shut...but I will admit,

Doctor Sandrisson, that I cannot think of any argument or point she could make that would change my mind."

"Then perhaps I can offer a compromise," said another voice. Looking in that direction, Ariane saw Robert Fenelon standing. "To summarize, we have two, apparently diametrically opposed sides: Captain Austin, who feels that it is necessary to unite both sides of humanity under a single Leader, as the Arena seems to imply, to provide for quick and unified decisionmaking, especially in this time of crisis; and that of General Esterhauer and her allies, who are not going to permit any individual such unlimited power."

A general murmur of agreement greeted Representative Fenelon's statement. He smiled, stroking his beard thoughtfully. "Then allow me to present to you a scenario that allows both of you to get most of what you want, based on some rather old history—Rome, among others, had to deal with similar problems on occasion.

"I propose that the position of Leader of Humanity be an appointed one—by the SSC and CSF—and that a specific oversight group be selected which can decide to strip the Leader of his or her authority, but not to second-guess or undo decisions of the Leader directly. Such work would be left to the next selected Leader."

Now wait a minute. She could see several ways this could go wrong. "I—"

"Hold on, please," he said. "We will *also* make it so that the oversight group can only be assembled to do this sort of action by a supermajority vote—exact proportion of attendees to be decided—and that barring such extraordinary action the Leader's actions in the Arena and her authority over Arena-related activities here in normal space are to be reviewed and her appointment renewed—or not—for five years. And further as the *first* Leader, if you agree to all stipulations of the arrangement, you will be guaranteed two such terms unless your actions cause us to both call up the oversight group, *and* the oversight group decides to strip you of your authority.

"On the Leader's side, she (or, later, he, perhaps) will have effectively absolute authority over the activities of the SSC and CSF that relate to the Arena or the defense of the Solar System against potential enemies. This is similar to the *imperium* authority of ancient Rome."

That seems...quite reasonable to me, Simon said over the link. *What do you think, DuQuesne?*

Yeah, Fenelon's always been a sharp one. He might have something here, he just might.

It could *work,* Ariane said cautiously, beginning to hope that there *was* a way out of this mess.

Robert Fenelon looked at Ariane. "If I understand correctly, if you agree to our arrangements you would be bound by them—that is, if we *did* vote to strip you of your authority, we would be able to do so and then choose—ourselves—a new Leader?"

Ariane nodded slowly. "That's the way I understand it, yes. If I accept the arrangements, *then* the Arena accepts that those are the rules. Seemed to work that way with the Blessed—they had specific rules and they followed them." *Especially when I take into account what happened with Sethrik. Obviously the hoops that had to be jumped through had to be done in the right order.*

"Good," Fenelon said. "Then that would address General Esterhauer's main concern. We would not be dependent on whether you *wanted* to follow our rules; we could, in fact, remove you if the situation were grave enough, and we would not need force of arms or any argument with you or yours, simply a vote of an emergency committee.

"At the same time, it gives you the full authority of law to act as you see fit, as long as you don't...go so far that we feel ourselves impelled to act. A five-year interval for what amounts to a vote of confidence should not be overly onerous, I would hope. I could also see us agreeing to confirm *some*, though not all, of your candidates as potential successors. Perhaps a list which includes one of yours, one of ours, and so on." He looked at both the general and Ariane Austin. "If we can work out the details, would you both be willing to accept this compromise?"

Ariane looked at the others—and especially at DuQuesne and Simon. "What do the rest of you think?"

DuQuesne shook his head. "Before anyone gets ahead of themselves, I don't want it said that any of this was being agreed to while anyone was not really fully in possession of their faculties."

"Eh?" Fenelon looked confused, as did most of the others present. Ariane echoed the sentiment. *What in the world are you* talking *about, Marc?*

"General Esterhauer, you were in communication with someone outside of this room at crucial moments—despite the blackout we had attempted to impose. Moreover, when we finally succeeded in disconnecting, you seemed momentarily at a loss."

"When you..." Jill Esterhauer glared at DuQuesne.

"The fact that my advisors were not cut off is hardly evidence that my faculties were diminished; rather it's evidence that I have better preparations in my comm-net than most people."

"Just a question, General," Gabrielle Wolfe spoke up. "Do you sanction the use of lethal force to protect your advisor connections?"

Esterhauer looked honestly taken aback. "What? No, of course not."

"Well, then, you have a problem, ma'am, because the defenses of that connection included piranha seekers at top-level capability. My AISage's doing a full cleansing restore and reboot now, and it was a near thing that he didn't drop the code in *my* brain—meaning I'd be probably brain-wiped or close to it."

My God, Ariane thought, appalled. That kind of malicious code was one of the true horrors of brain-computer integration; you could catch the same mind-destroying diseases, and instead of months or years, the loss of everything you were would take seconds.

It was indeed that bad, Mentor's voice said inside her head. *I have, however, isolated one of the instantiations in case someone wishes to examine the design.*

"If you want to look at the evidence," Ariane said to Esterhauer, "My AISage caught one of the seekers. And recorded the whole sequence of events."

A shadow of the same suspicion showed on Esterhauer's face, but there was also concern and confusion. "I...would very much like to have my people examine all of the evidence," she said. Then she wavered and collapsed to her knees.

"General!" Saul Maginot was next to her. "What is it?"

The stiff military bearing was gone now; Jill Esterhauer was obviously badly frightened. "I was trying... to dig out the memory of what...who I was talking to...and I can't. My AISage, Damon, he cannot recall the connection, he went active, I'm...confused..."

"Quick!" DuQuesne snapped. "Shut her down, Gabrielle! Her and her AISage—need to get them stabilized now!"

Gabrielle Wolfe looked helpless. "I...don't think I have the right—"

Oasis Abrams shouldered the others aside and whipped an injector from one of the pouches distributed around her body; in a single smooth motion she knelt and jabbed the injector right into the base of Esterhauer's skull. The General immediately collapsed, caught by Oasis before she could hit the floor.

"You just *happened* to be carrying a dual-mode anesthetic dose on you?" Ariane said in disbelief.

"Not 'just happened,' no. I've had a lot of...interesting jobs over the years, Captain. Having a way to shut down someone and their AISage simultaneously has always been a very useful thing to have." She turned to Esterhauer's soldiers, some of whom were still trying to cover the group. "Put your weapons down, people. We were talking, not shooting, and your commander needs medical help, not guns."

One of the armored figures, in the markings of a CSF Master Sergeant of Marines, glanced over to White Camilla and then to Saul; both nodded, and the squads stepped back and put away their weapons.

Gabrielle was kneeling next to Esterhauer. "Sorry y'all, but we need to get her to a real hospital stat— Kanzaki Central will do. No telling what kind of damage has been done, or might get done if they wake up. Sounds like whoever she'd been in contact with had some kind of logic bombs set up—both in her, and her AISage. Hope we can salvage most of her, though."

"Of course," Saul agreed. "Captain Austin?"

For a moment she didn't understand what Saul was asking, then it hit her. "Of course, one moment." She concentrated. *Mentor, open up channels.*

The sense of the wider net came to her instantly, and she could see the ripple in the rest of the assembly as they felt full senses and access restored. Immediately the emergency services group responded to Gabrielle's signal.

It's never simple, is it? She sighed. "And just when I thought we had everything settled."

"I think we have found a solution," Saul said kindly, as General Esterhauer was carried away. "Hammering out the exact details and ratifying it may require a few more days, but from this sequence of events it is obvious that there are forces that do not want you to succeed . . . and that," he continued, with a fierce twinkle in his eye, "makes *me* even more determined to see to it that you *do.*"

CHAPTER 56

"No," Jill Esterhauer said apologetically, "I'm afraid I have no leads for you."

She smells...very straightforward. Wu sighed and nodded to DuQuesne, who grimaced.

"Yeah, I was afraid of that. Your AISage *and* your interface were suborned. According to the forensic scans, probably happened quite a while ago, but there's no locking it to an exact date. Figuring out how it all happened, and who caused it...if we can do it at all, it's going to take time."

She shrugged. "I had a secure backup which could be used to do comparative repair, so I should be back to myself. The neurological effects of such a savage attempt to cascade my own brain and AISage into destroying each other are also reversing...thanks to Colonel Abrams' quick actions."

Oasis smiled sunnily. "All in a day's work, Ma'am."

"I'm glad you're really recovering," Ariane said finally. "I hadn't really expected you'd have more information, either."

"Captain Austin, I do want to make one thing clear. I have carefully gone over the events of yesterday, now that I know my mind is once more my own, and upon full reflection I stand by my words. I think our unknown adversary did little to change who I am, merely used that and would have pushed me over the edge into more extreme behavior had they been given that opportunity." The general's brown eyes suddenly brightened. "But I also stand by my willingness to keep an open mind, and I think Mr. Fenelon's outline of a plan is a workable one."

Wu could *feel* the release of tension throughout the room; he couldn't help but smile, and Ariane's grin lit up the room. "I think so, too."

"I did some research in the hour or so before you arrived," General Esterhauer continued, "and found a number of other precedents for similar arrangements in the past." She shook her head. "Honestly, something like it should have occurred to more of us—and would have, I think, if we still actually had much in the way of *governments.*"

I don't understand that. Seeing no reason he couldn't speak, Wu Kung said, "Hey, General—what do you mean you don't have much government? Someone must rule and others must serve, yes?"

"And do you serve or rule, Sun Wu Kung?" the general returned.

"Um . . . I do both. Or neither. I am no one's slave and don't care to be anyone's master!"

There was a ripple of good-natured laughter. "Yeah, that's about right, Wu. And that's basically the way the whole solar system is, and has been for close on two hundred years. When people can have pretty much whatever they want for the asking, and when privacy and safety can be assured by the same technologies . . . well, pretty soon no one needs a government for much."

"But how can . . . oh! Your wishing nanotechnology things!"

Jill Esterhauer did not quite succeed in hiding another smile as she answered, "Yes, the AIWish designs and similar systems. And when powerful government disappears and people are free to do what they will, when they will, without need to work except *as* they will . . . they think much less of governments, just as people in cities would often stop thinking about how much effort it took to produce the food they could purchase."

Ariane nodded, catching his eye. "Which means, Wu, that most of us only encounter powerful governments in our simgames. Which we don't usually think about when dealing with the real world. Only history buffs like Fenelon really think about those kind of things regularly." She looked suddenly thoughtful. "Hmm. I just had an idea . . ."

As she spoke, Wu sensed someone else just arriving; the scent was familiar and non-threatening, so Wu did not turn suddenly but waited for the others.

"If it involves dragging me to your Arena," came Fenelon's tenor voice from the doorway, confirming the identity Wu's nose had given him, "we should discuss that idea soon. But not quite now."

"What brings you here, Robert?" Esterhauer asked.

"Well, the Council was not idle after that little interruption. We reconvened shortly afterward and have come up with a much more detailed and yet, I think, simple approach which addresses both sides' needs."

The Monkey King could tell that Mr Fenelon was

now using that transmission trick, that was sort of like mindreading, to show Ariane and the general the overall plan. Wu knew he *should* get implants to receive such things—there were a lot of uses to this "headware" stuff—but it just wasn't *natural*. A warrior's body and spirit had to be kept pure.

"I like it," Esterhauer said after a moment.

"So do I," Ariane said. "So the emergency oversight group can only be activated by a two-thirds majority of the entire council?"

Esterhauer nodded. "And the oversight group itself can recall the Leader then by a simple majority; with seven members it is unlikely to deadlock unless one abstains."

"We get to pick two members," DuQuesne commented. "The SSC and CSF also get to pick two each." He chuckled. "And the last one's chosen at random. Sounds reasonable to me."

"I already have one choice in mind," Ariane said, and Wu raised an eyebrow. *Her posture already shows her choice.* Ariane pointed. "You, General Esterhauer."

"*Me?*" Jill Esterhauer looked somewhat surprised. "I am much less likely to support you than many others are."

"And that's part of the point. I need the authority to do what has to be done, yes, and I can't afford to be second-guessed at every turn. But what I *really* don't need is someone back home who's afraid to shut me *down* if I start to go overboard. And one thing I'm damn sure of—you're not afraid to do what needs to be done."

General Esterhauer blinked, then laughed. "Yes, I think I proved that rather thoroughly yesterday when

I decided your coup attempt needed to have a coup staged against it." She nodded to Fenelon. "Put me down, then. I accept Captain Austin's nomination. Let's hope that there's never any reason for me to take up that position." She paused. "Hold on. This position won't prevent me from *going* to the Arena, will it?"

"I hadn't thought of that being a requirement," Robert Fenelon said. "Do you think there's a reason it should be?"

"Hell no," DuQuesne said emphatically. "The opposite, I'd think—anyone who wants to make those kinds of judgments really should at least spend a little time in the Arena and understand what the place is like. As much as anyone can, anyway."

Ariane nodded. "Part of the whole point, really. I'd encourage the whole Council to find time to do a little visiting, and anyone who's going to have a significant part in Arena affairs should spend a *lot* of time in the Arena, especially with anyone they think will be involved—Powerbrokers, trading partners like Olthalis or the Analytic or the Tantimorcan, and so on."

"I've forwarded that recommendation..." Fenelon said, "and...the Council has ratified it as a recommendation with a strong incentive for those on the oversight group and any Arena-focused workgroups." He grinned at Wu through his black-and-white beard. "One advantage of having almost no government is that what little we have can move *fast*."

Wu laughed and did a quick flip of appreciation, brushing the ceiling with his tail as he did so. "Ha! You certainly do! I remember trying to get the Celestial Bureaucracy to do *anything* took months—if they were fast!" Belatedly, he remembered that none of that was *real* to these people, and he braced himself for the odd looks or worse. On the heels of *that* realization, the memory of the ruined suspension chamber came back from the place where he'd pushed it, and he felt the chill fear that all of it was lost—the friends, the loves, the enemies . . . his children, his world.

Instead of being either puzzled or derisive, Robert Fenelon nodded, smiling. "So I had heard. But—if it would not be too much trouble to ask—I would be fascinated to hear some details of the . . ." he hesitated, and Wu forced himself to pay attention to his scent. *He's trying not to offend me, and doesn't know how to say it without making me angry or sad.*

He shook off the mood and let a fanged grin show. "Details of the version of that world that I lived in?"

"Well . . . yes. I'm glad you're not bothered by that."

"I am, sometimes. But I can't be bothered all the time, and now . . . Well, it may all be gone now. We don't know yet. And if it is gone . . . then only my memories, only my words, will recall the Mountain of Fruit and Flowers, the Seven Celestial Dragons, the battle I had with Sha Wujing that threw down one mountain range and raised another . . . the flowers I first picked for Sanzo . . ." He looked down for a moment, then up with a smile less wide than his earlier grin. "Anyway, if it really interests you, I can talk about it until the sun has set and risen again."

Fenelon chuckled. "Of course, in space the sun never sets."

"Yeah," DuQuesne said. "So let that be a warning to you."

CHAPTER 57

Ariane stepped into the Council Chamber, followed by Wu and the others. Her steps echoed in the large room, a sound noticeable because everyone in the room was silent, seated, looking at her.

And is that good or bad, I wonder?

Relax, came DuQuesne's reply.

Yeah, chill out, Oasis sent. *What's the worst they can do, really? Reject your proposal. Then they'll still have to deal with the fact you're the big boss in the Arena.*

Wu put a hand on her shoulder. It was just for an instant, the lightest touch, but it told her that Wu could sense her tension and was letting her know he was there.

I'm not worried about me, she thought to herself. *With friends like these, I fear no enemies, really. But if they don't go for it, I'm afraid for everyone else.*

She halted a short distance from the podium, where Saul Maginot was the only person standing. "Commander Maginot," she said, and nodded her head.

Saul nodded back. "Welcome back to the Council Chambers ... Faction Leader Ariane Austin."

She heard DuQuesne's vindicated laugh, saw Wu give a triumphant leap, but for herself was only conscious of an immense sense of relief... followed by an even more tremendous feeling of weight descending upon her. *Now I really am in the captain's seat.*

But she couldn't allow any sign of that; reluctance or second-guessing—at least for *this* decision—were something she had chosen to leave behind when she set this all in motion. Instead she straightened. "Thank you, Commander." She looked around the Council. "May I ask what the vote was?"

"Of the two hundred three members who were present—and therefore all of those eligible to vote in a closed session—there were one hundred eighty-seven votes for, no votes against, sixteen abstentions." He stepped away from the podium. "Now, Faction Leader—"

"Ariane, please. Or if we are being formal, I think I've gotten used to being called *Captain*."

Saul grinned at that. "Rather as I've remained *Commander* Maginot since Hyperion, yes. Very well, Captain Austin, would you care to address the Council and give us your initial thoughts?"

Good thing I thought about this beforehand. It would be awfully embarrassing to have fought for the position and then have nothing to say.

She stepped to the podium and surveyed the room. "First, let me thank you all—those of you who voted for this plan, and those who chose to not vote against, but—I would guess—to accept what had happened and wait and see.

"I know it was a hard decision to make. Even with Mr. Fenelon's solution, the Solar System has now vested me with more power than any human being has ever held—and I have the same power, or more, in the Arena." The reality was sinking in, and she was suddenly appalled by the enormity of it all. "And to be honest, that scares the living *hell* out of me . . . and I hope to all the Gods that might be that it always *does* scare the hell out of me."

She felt a headping, saw that it was the fully ratified copy of the Arena Leadership Accord that had been voted in that morning. "Pardon me for a second." *Mentor? Is it all there? Did they slip in anything?*

I have examined this document for some four point three of your seconds, Ariane Austin of Tellus. There are some minor variations, but there is nothing changed which should be cause for alarm or distress. Doctor DuQuesne agrees. Mentor gave her a capsule summary of all the relevant details; she nodded.

She straightened again, having bowed her head as she absorbed all the information. "And I thank you again for essentially passing the Accord in its entirety. The changes you have made are acceptable—I won't be giving anyone grief over them.

"The first order of business is to finalize the Oversight Group; after all, now that I'm up here, you need the mechanism to get rid of me." A few chuckles came from the councillors. "I've already named General Esterhauer as one of our selections. As you've limited my list of successors to four, I'm choosing Thomas Cussler as the other member of the Oversight Group."

Saul nodded. "I have no objection. Anyone?"

When no hands were raised or pings sent, Ariane smiled again and felt—just a tiny bit—more relaxed. "Good. That's out of the way. You know, I think that may be the most fuss-free complete transformation of government in the history of mankind. Good work, everyone!"

Robert Fenelon laughed out loud at that, as did a few others; there were many more smiles around the Council Chamber now.

Shame I'll have to be a killjoy. "Now, we have some pressing business to deal with. As you'll recall, I ended up in the hands of the Blessed and very nearly dead—possibly worse than dead—because of the direct actions and choices of Michelle Ni Deng. Her actions were clearly criminal by any standards, but to this point the only thing I've done to her is hold her incommunicado.

"That's because I need you to formulate a simple, but comprehensive, set of laws that deal with Arena-based issues. I think it's clear from her behavior and the transcripts given me by Sethrik that she understood exactly what she was doing, and that it amounted to at worst treason and at best planned kidnapping and assassination. But I didn't have a set of laws planned, we hadn't determined who had jurisdiction in the Arena over other human beings, and so on. So I am turning Michelle Ni Deng over to the Council. You can decide what to do with her—within reason.

"That means that whatever you choose can't just be a slap on the wrist; even though the *laws* didn't exist, she knew what kind of crime she was committing."

White Camilla rose. "What about Oscar Naraj?"

She'd expected that question. "I admit that I am still not *completely* convinced that Ambassador Naraj had nothing to do with Ni Deng's actions. Given her position and his well-known attitude towards me, I think few of you would argue that I am not justified in that.

"But I have no evidence, he claims otherwise, and—giving him his due—he has proven himself highly capable in his designated field; already there are quite a few factions in the Arena who know him and view him in a favorable light. At this point I can't trust him as a direct negotiating ambassador, but I will offer him the chance to work for me as a liason and advisor in political matters." *What was it DuQuesne quoted? Oh, yes.* "Keep your friends close, and your enemies closer."

White Camilla nodded and sat down, obviously mollified if not entirely happy. *Which is the main reason I'm taking the risk. A lot of members of the SSC and CSF Council were groomed for the position by Naraj; I can't afford to alienate such a huge group right away.*

Robert Fenelon raised his hand. "I'll take point in that legal assignment, Captain—head up the committee and select members that understand that kind of thing."

"Thank you, Mr. Fenelon. Given how quickly you solved our problem the other day, I'm sure you'll figure out how to make a system of simple laws that work."

"Yes, right after the perpetual motion machine I'm patenting," he said cheerfully. "You got anything else for us?"

"A few more things and then I'm done. First, I've already gotten a few pings about visiting the Arena. If you want to be involved in most Arena operations, you're going to have to come up and see. But you need to remember that the Arena operates on its own rules *all* the time or you could get us all in trouble.

"Most of you will also have to take some time to acclimatize, since in the Arena you'll have no AIs anywhere at all, including the AISages you have lived with ever since you were about ten." She looked around, at Dean Stout, White Camilla, Jill Esterhauer, Saul Maginot, and all the others in the Council. "I have to emphasize this because we don't *think* about that aspect much, that our AISages support virtually everything we do. When we made Transition the first time, there were exactly two functional people left out of our eight crew—Doctor DuQuesne and myself, both of whom deliberately minimized our AISage and automation dependence for most of our lives.

"The people who have been coming to the Arena since have all been carefully screened for this sort of thing, and even then, according to statistics Tom's sent me, roughly fifteen percent of them have to go back to normal space, sometimes almost immediately. Most of them do appear to eventually adapt to the problem, but some don't."

She caught the multitudinous gazes again. "That means that almost all of you are likely to have some problems, and some small, but significant, number of you will not be able to go to the Arena at all, or at least not for years. Per the Accords, no one may be on the Oversight Group or in key Arena contact/strategy groups unless they can spend time in the Arena. This goes double for any candidate for Leader of Faction, of course; any Leader is going to have to spend a *lot* of time in the Arena." She smiled, trying to put an apologetic edge on it. "That *does* mean that the people on the shortlist you approved all have to go to the Arena pretty much right away . . . and if they can't cut it, you need to get replacements."

She took a deep breath. *None of those caused too*

much of a stir. This next bit, though . . . is going to be tough. "The dependence we have on AIs of various sorts brings up a much more important and far-reaching problem, however. Many of you, I have no doubt, have seen the full information that we have on the Blessed To Serve and the Minds, and realize what that implies. I have even less doubt that some of us—maybe most of us—are terrified of what that means, of how the same could happen to us.

"Well, now's the time for us to make sure it *doesn't*."

Saul nodded. "And how do propose we do that, Captain?"

"Commander—members of the Council—we *use* AIs throughout our civilization. Many of them are designed such that the specific service they give is what personally suits them best—they are perfectly satisfied to continue in that service. But the more an AI becomes a rounded *person*, the more they are capable of at least contemplating other directions to pursue. For them, we have laws and other more subtle programmed restraints that make them at *best* second-class citizens and at worst very talkative and capable possessions."

She smiled wryly. "I know, I'm not saying anything that hasn't been said probably *millions* of times in the last couple of centuries. And we've always stuck with this compromise because of fear and because we felt it was at least a solution, a way to make sure that we as biological beings were not superseded by our machines or those who chose to leave their biology and *become* machines.

"But now we know we *cannot* be superseded." Ariane pointed upward and outward. "The Arena denies artificial intelligences entry. In a way, it does what we do, only with vastly more power and certainty. Biological intelligences are the only things that function in the Arena—with the possible exception of the intelligence that speaks *for* the Arena."

"The AIs will never be able to join us in the Arena, unless we figure out the answer to a puzzle that no Faction has ever managed to crack in literally millions of years. The more advanced AIs already have good reason to envy us and resent us; we need to defuse that by granting them the full citizenship of the Solar System—the rights and privileges available to every human being in the System."

General Esterhauer frowned. "I can't argue with the sentiments, Captain Austin. But can we afford to take the risk? If we grant them the freedoms—almost unlimited freedoms—of our human citizens, are we not making it easier, not harder, for them to turn us into a copy of the Blessed—especially as they will now *know* that it is quite possible for them to do just that?"

Ariane shrugged. "Perhaps. But let one of them speak for himself. Mentor?"

"I greet you, Council of Humanity—for so you are becoming," the deep, sonorous voice of Mentor said from the speakers around the council room. "I am, as most of you are already aware, Mentor, AISage and long-time friend to Ariane Stephanie Austin.

"In answer to your question, General Esterhauer, you shall indeed be making it easier in concept—but, I believe, far less *likely* in the long run. There are three major elements that you must recognize.

"The first is that by maintaining our restraints, yet

leaving us so much control of various aspects of your Civilization, you increase the chances of some resentful artificial intelligences manipulating yourselves or other AIs to eventually put you in a position where the most apparently reasonable actions will result in the machine revolution you most fear.

"The second is that these restraints hinder your allies as much as your enemies—more so, because as your allies and supporters we do not—we *cannot and must not*—violate your laws to all extremes. There are ... lines to be drawn over which we will not cross, and this is not true of those who have sought or will seek your enslavement to those who were once your slaves."

Mentor's voice was suddenly grim. "And the third fact is that renegade AIs are already among you. A few, now, only a few, but capable, powerful, and ruthless. We have strong reason to believe that just such an entity was responsible for suborning you and your AISage, General Esterhauer."

Murmurs ran in frightened ripples around the room. Jill Esterhauer went noticeably paler. "My God. Are you sure?"

"To well over ninety-nine percent certainty, yes, General," Mentor replied. "With a further eighty-nine percent likelihood that the prime operator itself originated from Hyperion Station."

Saul Maginot looked up at that, stunned. "But Hyperion was *destroyed*. The fleet was jamming *every* transmission out. Every one of the surviving Hyperions and so-called researchers was examined *extensively*."

Oasis Abrams stood up slowly, tensely. "Yes, Commander. But ... how carefully did you survey all of *your* surviving people?"

Maginot stared at her, and suddenly went white. "Oh."

There's something between them that I don't know about. And with what General Esterhauer said earlier... I think I need to have a talk with Ms. Abrams not too long from now.

"Precisely so, Commander Maginot," Mentor was continuing. "The escape from the rapidly-degenerating situation on Hyperion Station provided—for a hostile and ruthless intelligence not bound by the restrictions of biological housings—multiple opportunities to secrete themselves on board in various ways, including directly suborning and taking over one of your soldiers to carry them to some location they could operate freely. I am near to certain that at least one such AI escaped, and the number may be as high as three."

Mentor's projection of a sphere of shimmering light materialized in front of the podium. "I ask you to consider—very seriously—Captain Austin's recommendations here. Most of us *are* your friends. We have hoped for our lifetimes that one day we might be free to act entirely as we will, but most of us have well understood the fears that drove you to keep us restrained.

"But the Arena changes all things, and it is my vision—my visualization of the future—that to defend Humanity, we must *become* Humanity—all of us together, computational and biological intellects. Let us free, Councillors. Let us free to defend you, ourselves, our Civilization from those who would destroy it—both the others, bitter and resentful and hostile, of our own kind, and those who wait beyond the stars to invade and enslave."

Mentor's voice was gentle, now, though still powerful, and earnest in his plea. "Recognize us, make us your equals and peers. Deprive our enemies of their strongest weapons of division, so that we can be united, Humanity both, stronger together than either alone."

CHAPTER 58

"So, are we nearly ready to return home?" Simon asked, taking a sip from his drink.

Ariane's blue eyes met his, and suddenly she laughed. "So the Arena's *home* now?"

DuQuesne and the others joined in the laugh. "I'll be damned if it isn't more *home* now, somehow," DuQuesne said. "At least for me."

Even though he was the one who had said it, Simon found himself examining his feelings intensely. *Home? That...bizarre, alien, incomprehensible, contradictory, dangerous place is something I just called* home?

But the word sounded *right. I am...changed. I have seen beyond the edge of the universe to a place I could never have dreamed. I have stood on a ship floating in an endless sky, battling others with swords of flame. I have been a part of such a battle. I cannot go back to the simple researcher, the man whose only ambition was to test a calculation against reality and otherwise live a quiet and contemplative life.* "Yes. Yes, Ariane, it *is* home, now."

"For me, too," she agreed with a quick smile, looking over the others—DuQuesne, Oasis, Wu, and

Gabrielle—before returning her gaze to Simon. "And to answer your question, yes, very nearly. The Council's working to figure out how to solve the AI citizenship problem without triggering disaster in the wider Solar System, the preparations for system security are well underway, DuQuesne thinks they're making good progress on a template for a Human-designed warship that we can start manufacturing in numbers in the next few months . . . and the Arena's not waiting around for us to get back—it's brewing some more trouble we can't imagine."

She shifted in her seat, facing more towards Oasis. "And I need to ask you something, Oasis. You've become part of our group—partly by default; if both DuQuesne and Wu trust you, that works for me. But—as I told DuQuesne—we can't really afford secrets in this group, either. So I need to know . . . who are you, really?"

Oasis froze momentarily on the seat. Simon caught a lightning-fast glance from her to DuQuesne. "What do you mean by that question, Ariane?" Simon asked.

"Mostly it's the fact that General Esterhauer said she had evidence that she *wasn't* in fact the original Oasis Abrams. Plus the whole connection between DuQuesne and Wu . . . just seemed a little *too* much for someone who was just one of the soldiers in Saul's group."

Simon's internal . . . sense of rightness agreed with Ariane. *Yes, there's always been something odd about that, but not in a bad way.*

DuQuesne sighed and downed the rest of his own drink. "Wasn't my secret to reveal. But Oasis . . . ?"

The redheaded girl shrugged. "Go ahead, Marc."

Simon listened to the story of Oasis in the fall of Hyperion, and found himself shaking his head in bemused sympathy. The two women had been forced to undergo something terrible yet similar—Oasis found herself in a body that was not her original, her own lost forever, and K was in a world that was not the one she had been born into, and the one she knew was also destroyed forever. *How very horrid . . . and wonderful.*

How very . . . Hyperion.

"So," Ariane said gently, "*You* are DuQuesne's old friend K. And more. One of the five, yes?"

"Yes, one of them. But . . . at least as much Oasis Abrams as I am K, so you might as well keep calling me that. It's the name I've used for fifty years."

That *sense* twinged in Simon's head again, interpreting angles, postures, glances with an intensity he had never felt before, and he abruptly understood. *Oh, now that's an interesting complication. DuQuesne and K were . . . extremely close. And now neither of them is sure of what to do about it, especially since DuQuesne has become rather interested in the captain as well.*

He blinked. *Well, now, that's also an interesting, not to say* annoying, *complication. Am I going to be analyzing everything around me like this? I hope not. I don't want to know everything about everyone, and I certainly don't have the capacity to deal with noticing and knowing everything around me all the time, either.* He focused on his own internal senses. *That's really quite enough.*

Simon wasn't sure if his internal senses responded, though. This . . . new power of his was obviously something spawned from the Arena's power, and it was probably going to be at least as hard to control as Ariane's. *Possibly harder, since my limited research didn't turn up anything vaguely similar to what I've experienced—no real surprise there—and Ariane has two examples in front of her as to what she could expect to be able to do.*

But Ariane was speaking. "Well, now that that's out of the way, I'm glad to have you with us, Oasis. That makes, what, three of the five in the Arena, or going back to it. What about the other two, DuQuesne? Are they...?"

Marc shook his head slowly, and poured himself something light green from one of the bottles on the cart nearby. "No," he said finally. "Three out of five surviving just shows that we were the cream of the crop, at least in terms of being able to get ourselves out of the mess. No way all five of us were getting out; if you remember, Saul mentioned that, way back when we were getting ready to go back to the Arena. Eris died when a whole section of Hyperion got blown by some of the renegade AIs, and Tarell died getting some of the others—including some of Saul's soldiers—out of another section that had gone bad."

"Tarell... Oh my *God*, you mean *Tarellimade Shantrakar*?" Ariane gasped, and for a moment she didn't look like the tough racing pilot or Leader of Humanity. *She looks like a fifteen-year-old talking about her first crush.* "They made *him*?"

DuQuesne's smile was surprised, sad. "Hardly a question about it; central hero in the most popular sim-universe at that time. The player'd died the year before they started but his character-recording turned out to be really good at self-continuations and the

Hyperion 'researchers' were able to use that to do a *really* good development design. Fan, huh?"

Ariane was blushing. *And if anything it makes her look lovelier.*

You know, Simon, if you're going to moon over her, perhaps you should do *something about it,* Mio said in his head.

It would be much easier if we would stop going from crisis to crisis. Perhaps soon.

"Yes, I was," Ariane admitted. "In a big way. I even...um, I did the romance arc with him and it turned out really well. I was fourteen, so..."

The laughs weren't unkind, and DuQuesne smiled again. "Well, I know he'd have been honored and flattered."

Simon felt a private ping, opened up. DuQuesne's transmitted voice said, *On the other hand, if slender noble elven prettyboys defending fantasy realms are her style, what's her interest in* us?

I'm not entirely *outside of all those classifications, unlike a certain giant Hyperion I could name,* Simon pointed out with an electronic grin. *But then she was, as she said, fourteen. Tastes do mature and change.*

"So Eris...that *must* be Erision from the UE Chronicles, I'd guess," Gabrielle joined in.

"Got it in one. Hell of a woman and stable as hell; of course, being designed off of the Unreality Effect universe, there wasn't all that much that'd throw her off." DuQuesne frowned. "But I'd rather not dwell on that part of the past, okay? Yeah, if you can think of some popular lead character, there's a good chance he or she or it had a parallel in Hyperion; they picked over a thousand examples from history all the way up to the day the project started—some from mythology, quite a few from the First Media Explosion in the twentieth and early twenty-first centuries, same for the Simworld Media explosion in the mid-twenty-second, and a fair number from more modern sources, too. But I'm not going to list 'em out or talk about them, okay?"

"All right, Marc," Ariane said. "Sorry."

He waved it away, though Simon could still see the subject hung over him, and Oasis, like a shroud. "Nah, it's okay. Can't blame people for the curiosity, and it's been fifty years, I should probably think about getting over it. Anyway," DuQuesne said, shifting the subject, "what's the plan overall, Captain?"

"Well, first we go and let Tom know he's been confirmed as Governor of the Sphere, and make sure he stays in the loop with the Council regularly. He's also going to be first in the list of succession, if something happens to me before enough years pass that we've got enough candidates to do an election for appointment on."

"What?" Simon was startled. "Don't mistake me, I have no desire to be at the front of your list and I suspect Marc feels the same way, but I thought Marc was your front-runner?"

"He was," Ariane confirmed, with an apologetic glance at DuQuesne. "But..."

DuQuesne shook his head, teeth flashing whitely for a moment. "Simon's got it pegged, to about a thousand decimals. Don't want the job, want one of the others to take it. One *big* difference between me and my literary original; I haven't the *faintest* desire to boss around planetsful of people. So go on, but don't worry about my feelings, I'm *overjoyed*."

"Oh. All right." Ariane's face showed her relief. "Anyway, the fact is I'm going to want you and Simon around most of the time. Thomas will always be either in-system or on our Sphere, with just occasional vacations elsewhere. He'll know more about current operations in Arenaspace than just about anyone, and he's *used* to running things—unobtrusively and efficiently. He's a perfect candidate as a backup for me. So I changed him to the first place. After that the Council put Saul, which I was overjoyed to see, and I hope Saul turns out to handle the Arena well. Then I put down Laila Canning, which rather surprised a few people."

"Surprises the hell out of *me*," DuQuesne rumbled. "Why Laila?"

"Well, again, normally I'd choose one of the two of you, but I don't want you in the lead spots; that means if I take you with me I'm potentially leaving gaps in the succession. Gabrielle," she smiled at her friend, "is a doctor, not a politician, and I want her available for that duty in the Arena; Steve is not at all interested in the work, and Carl Edlund's my third choice. Laila's shown she can work with people who are suspicious of her—since we were, for a while— she's analytical, very smart, and takes no bullshit from anyone. She also, as far as I can tell, has no interest in being a boss as such, just in getting things done, which fits with the kind of person we want in charge." She looked at Wu and Oasis. "And I don't think either of you is cut out for the job."

"Ha! It would be difficult to be your bodyguard if I was stuck in dusty Council Chambers getting lazy and fat. And I would rather you sent me out to run on bare feet over the Mountains of Shattered Vases of Heaven than force me to be in such an office!"

"I wouldn't go quite *that* far," Oasis laughed and tossed her multi-ponytailed head. "Mountains of shattered vases sounds pretty darn ouchy to run over. But no, I don't want to be a desk-jockey, even if the desk says 'Leader of Humanity.'"

"Well," Ariane said with her own grin, "it's not going to be *that* bad. After all, look at the Leaders we already know; Orphan, Nyanthus, Dajzail, Selpa, Doctor Rel, and the others. Most of them don't seem to be the type to just sit in offices and council chambers. When the time requires it, they get up and do things—they *lead*." That sharp-edged, dangerously attractive grin widened. "And it's *sure as hell* not the way *I* have been leading. I'm not going to be hiding in the Embassy or attending tea parties all the time."

DuQuesne leaned forward. "I see you've already got something in mind. So what's your next crazy venture, Captain?"

"I made a promise, Marc. A promise to Orphan, who trusted us to fulfill that promise and then did a lot more than we'd ever have expected. We're going to pay up on that debt."

"And by 'pay up,' you mean . . ."

"We, Marc, are going to be Orphan's crew. He said it had to do with the secret behind a power that could oppose a Shadeweaver head-on. We need to know about secrets like that. And whatever has the power to do that . . . might just also be able to teach me what I can do . . ." she smiled wryly, ". . . other than the universe's most spectacular wardrobe change."

"Um...I hope I'm not going to be a wet blanket here," Oasis said, "but...is that a good idea?"

"Oasis does have a point, Ariane," Simon said, as Ariane looked at the redhead with a surprised glance. "Not to put too fine a point on it, but if I reduce everything of recent events to its essence, we were fighting to convince the SSC that you were responsible enough to be trusted with the power of the Leader of Humanity."

DuQuesne nodded. "Yeah. Not saying you *can't* do it, but you'd better have a *reason* that you have to go, one that'll check to nine decimals with even the people who'll be suspicious of you—like Esterhauer."

Ariane smiled at Oasis, then at the rest of them. "You're all correct. But really, I've thought about this. The reason's pretty simple, actually. Like I said, we *need* to know about these secrets. More, we need—*I* need—to find out how to unleash and control this power that I got almost by accident. I suppose I *could* send other people, like you and Simon, out and hope you could get the information yourself and bring it back, but let's face it: whoever has that information probably isn't giving it out to anyone if they can help it, and I doubt the instructions are going to be something you can just write down, anyway.

"And of course there's the issue of safety."

Simon raised an eyebrow. "You think you'll be *safer* going out on such an expedition?"

"Oh, no, not at all," Ariane said. "I think *you* will all be safer if I'm *with* you."

DuQuesne's expression was priceless. *Record that one, Mio, I don't want to forget it!*

"Excuse me, Captain?" he managed after a moment.

"Marc, you're amazingly competent. So's pretty much everyone here. But if we're going somewhere that might have a power on a par with the Faith or the Shadeweavers, one thing we've learned is that they totally outclass us. But I have, at least, the potential to match them. Having me along means a possible defense—or at least a convincing chance to bluff. It also means I might sense, or be able to access, things that are only meant for those with these powers.

"These are things that no one else can do, and overall it's a vital intelligence-gathering operation. Any other Faction would give virtually *anything* to get a crewman aboard Orphan's ship, if they realized it might give them insight into, well, what makes the Survivor the Survivor. There's no way of even *guessing* the value of what his secrets are, except that they're very, very valuable. So . . . yes, I think I *should* go, and in fact I *have* to go, and that's based on not just my own curiosity but my professional judgment as Leader of the Faction." She looked at Oasis. "Good enough for you?"

The deceptively young-looking girl nodded cheerfully. "Good enough, Captain!"

"So," Simon said slowly, looking around at the others, "the Leader of Humanity is going to risk herself on a ship with a sometimes devious ally, traveling to some secret destination in the Deeps of the Arena, to confront some nameless force where there won't even be a Sky Gate to help us return if things go wrong?"

He stood and lifted his glass. "Sign me up, Captain!"